Praise for *Gu*

'*A belated hallelujah for the latest from Mark Timlin,*
an audaciously plotted story of South London crime
that is epic in scope – and written with both heart and soul.
Don't miss.'
TANGLED WEB UK

'*Best known for his roisterous Nick Sharman Sarf London PI series, Timlin has finally*
written the book he's owed us for many years, and matures from his bad boy of Brit crime
fiction cherished status to a level of surprising wisdom and acute social observation.
Spanning several decades, this is a splendid evocation of crime south of the river, with a
wide cast of villains, cops, drug traffickers and not so innocent victims that often brings
to mind Coppola's Godfather movies. At twice the length of his previous novels, this is a
rewarding saga in which every character has a place and a purpose, however crooked the
path and every sudden, violent death feels like a
blow to your sympathies. […] A writer has come of age.'
GUARDIAN

'*The most impressive aspect of Timlin's compressed style is the*
constant juxtaposition of the witty and the tense'
SUNDAY TIMES

GUNS OF BRIXTON

GUNS OF BRIXTON

MARK TIMLIN

Published by
MAXCRIME

an imprint of John Blake Publishing Ltd,
3 Bramber Court, 2 Bramber Road,
London W14 9PB, England

www.johnblakepublishing.co.uk

First published as *Answers from the Grave*
by The Do-Not-Press Ltd, 2004
This edition published 2010

ISBN: 978 1 84454 924 5

British Library Cataloguing-in-Publication Data:

A catalogue record for this book is available from the British Library.

Design by www.envydesign.co.uk

Printed in Great Britain by CPI Bookmarque, Croydon CRO 4TD

1 3 5 7 9 10 8 6 4 2

Papers used by John Blake Publishing are natural, recyclable products made from wood
grown in sustainable forests. The manufacturing processes conform to the environmental
regulations of the country of origin.

MAXCRIME series commissioning editor: Maxim Jakubowski

This book is for Geoff Thorn
(1950–2004)
A good friend

PROLOGUE

In days gone by, what is now the Brixton McDonald's – at the multi-corner junction overlooked by Lambeth Town Hall – used to be a branch of one of the 'big five' banks. A clearing house for money from all over south London, it sat packed with cash, a peach ready to be plucked by anyone with enough brains and bottle to try it.

In those days there were criminals whose sole object in life was to hunt out such targets, research them thoroughly, then get together a team of likeminded individuals and take them down. One such criminal was Daniel Butler – Danny to his friends, of whom there were few. One Thursday morning in June 1982, when the rush hour was at its height and the bank was stuffed with notes awaiting collection by armoured car, he put his plan into action.

Danny had been a mod in the 1960s. An 'ace face', as he liked to be called. He'd cruised the streets of London like a king in his souped-up Ford Anglia, making acquaintances as he went: little gangsters who wanted money for clothes, records and cars without doing too much work. And from these young men he recruited a fine collection of villains who would make their mark on the underworld of the capital in the latter half of the twentieth century.

Now in his early thirties, Jimmy Hunter was one of those young men. When Danny had called him up, a month or so earlier, Jimmy had been only too pleased to come in as top man on the bank raid.

It was a simple plan: straightforward blagging with little subtlety. A straight in-and-outer. Danny lined up the job, brought in the personnel, supplied transport and ordnance, a getaway route, took his cut off the top and dropped back into the shadows. When it worked, it was financially rewarding all round. When it didn't... well, when it didn't he wouldn't be around to see it go bad. Danny made it his business to be in another country, if not another continent, when that happened. And on this job, the getaway was the problem. Danny didn't like it, but there was little choice. He'd explained as much to the little firm when he'd first outlined the plan to them. Do it, or don't do it, it was up to them. They'd all agreed to do it. On such decisions lives are changed – and lost.

The night before the job was due to go off, the summer warmth kept the streets of Brixton and the surrounding area busy until late in the evening. Stevie Little, known to his mates and most of the Metropolitan Police as Little Stevie Wonder, broke into Stockwell bus garage and had it away with a double-decker red Routemaster bus which he drove to a scrap yard in Clapham and parked up behind a pile of 60s and 70s motors waiting to be crushed into yard-square blocks of metal and rubber. He spent the rest of the night in the office drinking tea, reading ancient copies of *Penthouse* and *Playboy*, and listening to his portable radio.

The next morning at nine sharp, four men roughly the same age as Jimmy Hunter met at a coffee stall next to Clapham South tube station. Two drove to the rendezvous in a stolen Ford Granada Ghia, the other two went by public transport. In the boot of the Ford were two pump action shotguns, sawn off fore and aft and loaded with five double-ought shells, plus two six-shot .38 revolvers, along with four large nylon sports bags with webbing straps. Enough, Danny figured, to carry away all the notes in the bank's safe. Jimmy Hunter drove the car to the meet, the number two man, Dave Nicholls, in the passenger seat beside him. Jack Dewhurst caught a bus from Balham and Paul Walker took the Northern Line from Stockwell. By eight-thirty they were all drinking tea and smoking. No one ate. This was the biggie and none of them were hungry.

'How much do you reckon?' said Paul to Jimmy as he sipped his strong, sweet brew.

'Half a million,' said Jimmy, for the hundredth time since the gang had been recruited. 'Minimum. Maybe more, Danny said.'

'Jesus,' said Jack. 'Holiday in Spain.'

'A long one,' said Dave.

The men stood talking and smoking for fifteen minutes until Jimmy looked at his watch and said, 'Time'.

The men went to the car which was parked up in a side road a few hundred yards from the stall. They gathered around the boot and selected their weapons. Jack was to drive the car to the job and wait with the engine running as the other three went into the bank. Jack took a .38, as did Paul, the other two picked up the shotguns, wrapped in brown paper and slid them under their jackets before all four climbed aboard. As they settled in their seats, Paul, Jimmy and Dave each took a woollen cap from a pocket and pulled it on. Paul found the stopwatch that Danny had given him to time the raid, hanging it around his neck by its strap.

'Two minutes.'

Danny had told them so many times it was engraved in their minds. 'Two minutes from the off and you go, no more. Don't piss about, just leave.'

Jimmy knew that the getaway was the big risk. But then, everything in his life had been a risk for as long as he could remember. That was why he and Danny had impressed upon the rest of them that two minutes from the moment they arrived was all the time they could afford in the bank. He knew that, no matter how heavily armed they were or how ready they were to use their guns, some jobsworth would press the panic button. And Brixton nick was less than half a mile down the road in the direction they had to go; and, at that time of day, the traffic would be heavy down the Brixton Road. But there was a turning next to the old Bon Marché building where Jimmy's mum had taken him shopping so many times when he'd been a boy. And once in that turning, the narrow streets of Brixton twisted and turned away back to Clapham, where another stolen car was waiting.

If they could only get there, then they could vanish into south London without a trace. The cash would be delivered to Danny Butler's accountant to be counted and neatly laundered. Only then would they be paid in clean money. It took a little longer than doling out the loot in the back of the motor like they were used to, but Danny was careful, and being careful had kept him out of jail. If any of the blaggers didn't like the deal, then they could find employment elsewhere. Danny didn't care. There were plenty more likely lads out there looking for work.

Jack started the Ford's engine, and right on time, Stevie Little drove the Routemaster along Clapham High Street with the destination board showing: OUT OF SERVICE and a canvas strap looped across the rear entrance. At the sight of the bus, Jimmy turned to Jack and said, 'Do it.'

Jack put the gear lever into 'drive' and slid the powerful car into the traffic, taking up a position directly in front of the empty Routemaster.

The bank opened at nine-thirty am. At nine twenty-five precisely, the convoy moved slowly down Acre Lane until they came to the traffic lights outside, the Ford third in the queue of traffic. The men sat quietly, but the tension in the car was palpable.

When the lights changed to green, Jack let the cars in front go, then turned sharp left and stopped just past the pedestrian crossing. Stevie pulled the bus across three lanes of traffic, stalled the engine, hopped out of the cab wearing a busman's cap pulled low over his eyes, turned off the fuel cutout lever by the driver's door, and vanished into the crowd of pedestrians waiting to cross at the intersection towards the tube station. Immediately, a cacophony of horns began, and a young woman named Mavis Hampton opened the front doors of the bank ready for business.

Danny and Jimmy had been watching the doors for weeks from various points around the crossroads, individually or together, sometimes up close and sometimes on the far side of the street. They knew exactly what would happen next: Mavis would unlock the massive wooden doors with huge, round, brass handles – relics of the days when banks were strong and secure, the bastions of the establishment – fasten them back, greet any waiting customers and hold open one of the half glass doors for them, turn, stroll back to the security door at the side of the counter which led into the bank's inner sanctum, turn her key, go behind the bulletproof screen to do whatever she did to earn her crust, letting that door swing closed behind her.

That morning there were two early punters: a young Rastafarian in a woolly hat and a long overcoat, too warm for the weather, and an elderly woman with a shopping trolley. Mavis locked back the big, thick doors, smiled at the waiting pair and opened one of the inner doors for them to enter and do their financial business. But today something was different. Today, Mavis's worst nightmares were about to come true. As the civilians stepped inside, the three robbers pulled their caps down over their faces leaving only gaps for eyes and mouth, and sprung from the car as one, Jimmy carrying the four nylon bags over his shoulder. Almost unnoticed by the commuters rushing to work, they freed their weapons and burst through the bank's front entrance just as Mavis opened the security door. Jimmy leapt the few yards between them, pushed her through the doorway on to the floor, stuck the barrel of his shotgun into the back of her neck and screamed: 'No one move or she's dead!'

His two companions took up positions inside the foyer, Paul at the door with stopwatch and pistol, Dave inside, covering Jimmy and forcing the two customers to lie prone on the floor.

'The safe!' yelled Jimmy.

Barry Boswick, twenty-eight, undermanager of the bank, was just – as Jimmy knew he would be – opening the time-controlled lock of the main vault. He stood open mouthed at the sight of the three bank robbers who, it seemed, had arrived from nowhere.

'Keep going,' ordered Jimmy.

Barry considered for one second slamming the vault shut. When he saw Mavis, who he'd always secretly fancied but had never plucked up enough courage to ask out, flat on her face with a vicious-looking weapon drilling into the back of her pretty neck, he decided that discretion was the better part of valour, and did as he was told. He swung the huge, counter-balanced door open.

Jimmy saw the piles of cash inside and smiled as he sweated behind his mask. 'Now!' he yelled, tossing the four bags to Barry. 'Fill 'em up.'

Barry did as he was told.

Paul remained at his position by the door, stopwatch in one hand, pistol in the other. 'Come on, come on!' he screamed. 'One minute thirty

5

left.' He turned his attention to the customers on the floor for a moment and saw the young black man peering up at him. 'Face to the floor, you nigger bastard,' he spat. 'Don't look at me, or I'll fucking kill you.'

The black man showed his teeth at the insult, but did as he was told.

Outside was chaos. Cars piled up on all three approach roads behind the abandoned bus, just as Jimmy knew they would, preventing the coppers from arriving from any but one point of the compass. The road away towards London was empty, except for the idling Ford.

Money crashed into the bags as Jimmy oversaw the loading and Dave covered the staff and the two customers.

'Hang on,' shouted Paul as another customer entered the bank. Paul grabbed him by the shoulder and forced him to join those on the floor.

There was more money in the vault than any of the men had ever seen and it seemed to be taking forever for Barry Boswick, shaking with fear, to load it into the bags.

'Thirty seconds,' screamed Paul. 'Come on, quick.'

Finally, the job was done, the bags were full to overloading and the shelves of the vault were empty of everything except bagged change.

'Time!' Paul called out.

'Go!' shouted Jimmy who picked up the bags and threw one at Paul who caught it one handed, surprised at the weight. Dave hefted the other three and staggered into the foyer behind him.

Jimmy grabbed a bag, and all three ran from the bank out to the car, scattering pedestrians in their wake. Then it was inside the motor and away.

At least, that was the plan.

What three of the robbers in the car didn't know was that some days previously the fourth had been pulled in by the police over another matter entirely. A very serious matter, which might have cost him his freedom for a lot of years. As he sat facing Detective Constable Billy Farrow in an interview room in Brixton Police Station, the criminal in question told the DC every detail of the bank raid.

So, unknown to his companions, a police operation was laid on for that day, and as the robbery took place they were being watched from vantage points all around the bank by heavily armed members of the Flying Squad, Special Patrol Group and local CID.

As the gang headed for the car, the young Rastafarian reached inside his overcoat for the radio concealed there. 'Go, go, go!' said Detective Sergeant Winston Martin before helping the terrified customers to their feet and going to check on Mavis Hampton and the rest of the bank staff.

First to be picked up was Stevie Little as he ran down the stairs into Brixton Underground station. Two young constables, dressed in street clothes were waiting at the bottom and grabbed an arm each as he went to the ticket machine. 'Hello Stevie,' said the first one as he produced his handcuffs and cautioned the man. 'You should've stayed on the bus.'

'Shit,' said Stevie under his breath as he allowed himself to be taken without a fight.

Out on the street, the four other gang members were all now in the car and Jack stuck it into gear, let off the footbrake, swung out into the empty road and took off. But as he did so, cars converged from the side streets off Brixton Road and suddenly his escape route was blocked. Heavy steel barriers running down the middle of the street prevented him from doing a U-turn, so he shot up on to the pavement, sending startled pedestrians diving for cover, but even that route was blocked when a police van emerged from a pedestrian alleyway and slid in front of them.

'Bloody hell,' yelled Jimmy from his seat. 'Out! Take the money.'

Jack skidded the Ford to a halt on the wide pavement outside Morleys department store and the four men did as Jimmy had ordered, guns at the ready. Suddenly the streets of Brixton were a free fire zone.

Each man took a different route away from the stalled Ford. Paul ran back in the direction of the bank, saw an armed SPG officer, and grabbed a middle-aged woman on her way to do some shopping in the market as a shield. He held his pistol to her head, but two more blue-clad police carrying automatic weapons moved from the doorway of an office where they had been observing the scene, and he realised that he was outgunned. On the orders of the first officer, he released his hostage, dropped his gun and bag of loot and assumed a prone position on the dirty pavement.

Jack ran towards the open door of Morleys, but two coppers were waiting for him. When he saw his escape route blocked, he fired his gun twice at one of the huge plate glass windows of the store. It imploded in a cascade of broken glass. He jumped into the gap, kicking aside mannequins in scanty lingerie and, knocking aside anyone in his way, made for the back doors pursued by the two uniformed police officers. When he crashed out of the back entrance he was met by two more PCs, who had been alerted by radio. He raised his .38 and fired, hitting one of the uniforms in the side. Looking more surprised than hurt, the policeman leant up against a lamppost before sliding down into a sitting position. His oppo, who had expected to be well away from any shooting, drew and hurled his truncheon at the armed man, but missed. Jack turned on his heel and headed up a narrow alley between two high, brick walls. The two coppers from Morleys gave chase, whilst the officer who'd thrown his baton tried to staunch the blood from his mate's wound and call an ambulance on his personal radio through transmissions that were threatening to overload the frequency. Jack kept running, the two coppers sweating in pursuit. He turned another corner only to come face to face with a handsome young plainclothes detective pointing an automatic pistol straight into his face. 'Go on, son,' said the officer, the line of his immaculate suit only spoiled by the radio in his jacket pocket that was quietly spewing out commands and counter-commands. 'You like shooting at coppers, don't you? Try me.'

Jack thought for a second, then smiled and carefully placed his gun on the pavement as the two uniforms came round the corner behind him and pushed him head first into the wall, using their elbows and fists to constrain him as they cuffed him up and read him his rights. 'You should've waited a minute,' said the plainclothes policeman holstering his gun. 'And I could've shot him in self defence.'

Jack looked at the man over his shoulder and saw that he was deadly serious and that he had come closer to being killed than he liked. 'Bastard,' he said.

'Mr Bastard Sir, to you,' said the detective, and he hit Jack in the face.

Not with his fist. He didn't want to break his delicate knuckles. So he used the heel of his hand as some grizzled old copper had taught him when he first joined the force. Jack's nose broke, and blood poured from his nostrils.

'I'll remember you,' Jack said through teeth gritted with pain, shaking claret from his face.

'That's nice,' said the young copper. 'Do that. My name's Nick. What's yours?'

When Jack said nothing in reply, the detective just grinned. 'Take him away,' he said.

Dave, meanwhile, made a run for it across Brixton Road. He jumped over the barrier, dodged between cars heading out of town and headed towards Electric Avenue, where he hoped to lose himself in Brixton Market. But luck wasn't running his way that morning. From the direction of central London, his nemesis in the shape of an ancient white Ford Transit full of plumbing supplies and tools, was heading his way. At the wheel was a plumber named Phil Hardy. Not that his name matters. Phil was late for a job on Streatham Hill. And when he saw the lights at the junction start to change he put his foot down. The old Tranny wasn't in the best of condition and slightly overloaded, with rather less meat on the tyres than the law demanded. So when Dave ran out in front of him, and Phil Hardy slammed on the brakes, instead of a gentle deceleration, the truck broadsided, hitting Dave hard enough to leave a body-shaped dent in the dirty metal of the van. And also hard enough to split open the bag he was carrying over his shoulder and send the cash inside flying into the air, where it gently floated to the ground in a flurry of five, ten and twenty-pound notes. This naturally caused the good citizens of Brixton – who knew a result when they saw one – to stampede in a rush for the money.

Dave Nicholls's neck was broken by the impact, and he was dead before his body bounced on the tarmac. Jimmy Hunter had only been a few steps behind him, but he managed to avoid joining Dave as a Lambeth vehicle fatality statistic, as he body-swerved through the gentle rain of bank notes, dodging the vultures scrabbling for the money, and he was away. Jimmy hardly spared a glance at Dave's body. He was out of the game. One down, three to go. No time for recriminations. Once the job was blown it was every man for himself. That was the code.

DC Farrow, who, despite his junior rank, had instigated the obbo on the bank, followed Jimmy closely across the empty northbound lane, over the barrier and through the traffic. He also avoided obstacles and injury. 'James Hunter,' he called to Jimmy's retreating back. 'Armed police! Stop or I'll shoot.' But, as so many folks were fighting for the cash in front of him, it was a vain threat.

Jimmy ignored him and ran down the pavement between the buildings and the stalls on the edge of the road. He shoved early shoppers and traders out of his way, jumping over sacks of fruit and vegetables and boxes of cheap cosmetics and clothes, the bag of money weighing him down on one side, his shotgun on the other, clasped in his fist like an overgrown handgun.

Billy Farrow followed closely, feeling the sweat beginning to form on him, half from the exertion of the chase, half from fear of what the desperate, armed man in front of him might do if he was cornered. He knew Jimmy, probably better than he should, and he was aware of what he was capable of.

Then Jimmy Hunter was trapped.

As he came out in Atlantic Road, a squad car skidded to a halt opposite the entrance to Brixton rail station, blocking his escape. Jimmy swore and turned back just as Billy Farrow came round the corner behind him. Jimmy lobbed the bag of money at Farrow which caught him on the chest and sent him tumbling into the gutter, dropping his weapon. Jimmy Hunter laughed and raised his shotgun to his shoulder. Suddenly he recognised the policeman and hesitated. 'Christ. Billy Farrow, is that you?'

'Yeah Jimmy, it's me,' replied Farrow.

'Blue eyes, you fucking traitor. We trusted you.'

'Give it up, Jimmy,' shouted Farrow from the ground. 'We know everything. We've got the other car. There's no way out.'

'Like hell, copper,' said Jimmy, feeling his finger on the trigger. He knew it was all up, but he was determined that he was never going to go back to prison, where he'd spent so much of his life. 'Like hell I say.' He thought of his wife and two children back at home and what they were doing at that moment and what they'd be doing for the rest of their lives. Lives he would never see. So many birthdays and Christmases and anniversaries and good and bad times that he almost smiled as he tightened his finger further.

He saw Farrow put up one hand as if by doing so he could prevent the inevitable, and as he looked down into the deep blue eyes that had got Billy Farrow his nickname, almost without meaning to, Jimmy pulled the trigger and the hammer on the gun started the short journey towards the rim of the cartridge. Just a centimetre or two in distance, and a split second in time, but a split second that would stretch for more than twenty years before its echoes and reverberations would finally end.

ONE

The wind blows cold off the Thames at Gallions Reach in January. Straight from Russia in the east, across Europe, the North Sea and the lowlands of Norfolk, Suffolk and Essex. That particular January morning the river was running high and fast, reflecting the leaden sky over Docklands, and the breeze whipped little white horses on its surface.

The meeting was set for eleven. Sharp on the hour, a black left-hand-drive Range Rover Vogue with French plates slid on to Barge House Road next to Royal Victoria Gardens. The car sat, its motor idling to keep the heat going inside, until it was joined a few minutes later by a navy blue Bentley Continental that drew up to it, closely followed by a black Mercedes saloon. The Range Rover was grimy from the road; the Bentley and the Mercedes were both highly polished, with tinted windows that kept the identity of their occupants secret. The cars sat together, faint white exhaust pumping from their tailpipes, until the front passenger door of the Bentley swung wide, and a tall, balding man of about sixty emerged. What remained of his white hair was cropped close to the skull. He wore a navy blue overcoat with the dull sheen of cashmere, a navy scarf loosely tied that showed a white shirt and dark tie, navy suit trousers and highly polished black shoes. He closed the Bentley's door with a discreet clunk, raised his hand to the Mercedes, indicating to whoever was inside that they should remain there, and walked towards the Range Rover. As he did so, its driver switched off his engine, opened his door and got out. He too wore an overcoat, but of a cheaper material, black this time with a velvet collar turned up against the cold, a long muffler, jeans and Chelsea boots with a slight heel. His hair was thick, dark as the sky, although slightly peppered with premature grey, and long over the ears. When he turned to look at the limousine, his eyes were almost as dark blue as its paintwork. No one ever forgot those eyes. As he approached he half raised his hand in greeting to the Bentley's passenger, who reciprocated with a slight wave of his own.

When they were close, the balding man took off the black leather glove from his right hand and they touched palms, then hugged each other without embarrassment.

'Uncle John,' said the man in the black coat when they separated. He was in his early thirties, but his face was lined, the skin tanned, a dusting of a day's worth of dark beard covering his cheeks.

'Mark. It's been a long time. Too long. How've you been?'

'Not too bad. You?'

'Not great, I'm getting old, son.'

'Aren't we all.'

'You, you're just a baby,' said John Jenner. 'You still look like a bleedin' kid.'

'Don't you believe it,' said Mark and took a packet of cigarettes from his pocket. He extracted a cigarette from the packet and lit it with difficulty in the wind with a brass Zippo. Before he put the cigarettes away John Jenner took the packet from his hand and examined it. 'German?' he said.

'Last of the duty frees,' Mark explained.

Jenner looked at the Range Rover. 'French plates. You get around.'

'I do. But I'm back now.'

'Where you living?'

'Here and there. Nothing grand.'

'Nice car.'

'Belonged to someone I met,' said Mark.

'And he gave it to you.'

'Didn't have much choice.'

'Like that was it?'

'You know how it goes.'

The older man nodded. 'Let's walk,' he said.

The pair went down to the river's edge where the wind lifted the skirts of their coats and flapped them around their legs. Jenner put his glove back on and Mark sunk his bare hands deep into his overcoat pockets, cigarette in his mouth, and turned his back to the water.

'Who's in the Mercedes?' asked Mark.

'Some blokes.'

'What kind of blokes?'

'Just a bit of security.'

'And you have to hire security now. What happened to the rest of your firm?'

'Dead, dying, retired, lost their bottle. Times change.'

'They do that.'

'I'm glad you called,' said Jenner.

'I heard you wanted to see me.'

'Who from?'

Mark shrugged. 'Word gets around, you know how it is. I try and keep up with things. Lay a little money out and people keep me advised on what's happening.'

'I've got some problems.'

'I heard that too.'

'You hear a lot.'

'Like I say, I try and keep up with things.'

'You didn't keep up with us.'

'Dev always knew where I was if I was needed.'

Jenner shook his head more in sorrow than in anger. 'Bloody Dev. He would. You two always were as thick as thieves. He never said.'

'I asked him not to.'

'He's a law unto himself.'

'That's why I chose him to keep in touch with him. I knew he'd never let on.'

'Bastard.'

'You know you don't mean that. He's a good bloke. Taught me a lot.'

'Like how to get hold of nice motors like that one,' said Jenner, indicating the Range Rover with a nod.

'No danger.'

'Bloody Dev,' said Jenner. 'I never knew.'

'I thought it was for the best, John,' said Mark. 'After all that happened.'

Over to the south towards Kent, black clouds gathered like an angry mob waiting to do mischief and Jenner sunk his neck into his collar. 'Might get some snow later,' he said.

'Maybe.'

'It's bloody cold whatever. Dunno why I stay in this rotten country,' said Jenner.

'So go. What's stopping you? Spain's nice at this time of year, so they say.'

'And you'd know.'

'You said it. I get around.'

'So what brought you back, if not us?'

'You know. He'll be out soon won't he?'

Jenner nodded.

'And I'll be waiting, like I always said I would,' said Mark Farrow as he flipped his cigarette end into the freezing water.

They were silent for a minute, and only the sound of the river washing up against the pylons of the dock beneath their feet, and a distant police siren touched their thoughts. 'So, Uncle John,' said Mark. 'What's it all about?'

Jenner reached inside his coat and fished out a long cigar, found a windproof gas lighter in his pocket and took his time getting it lit to his satisfaction.

'I thought you gave up smoking years ago,' said Mark.

Jenner grinned through a mouthful of smoke that was whipped from his open mouth as he spoke. 'I started again,' he said. 'What's the point of prolonging the agony? You see, that's one of the problems I mentioned.'

'Whaddya mean?' asked Mark, and he frowned.

'I'm fucked, mate.'

'Uncle John?'

'The big C.'

'You're joking.'

'Wish I was. I'm rotten with it. Dev never told you that, did he?'

'No.'

''Cos he doesn't know. Only me, Martine and Chas do. Apart from you now, and half the bloody consultants in London by my reckoning.'

'How long have you known?' asked Mark.

'A while. Long enough.'

Mark touched his hand to his forehead, as if by doing so he could replay the conversation a different way. 'But these days…'

'No,' said Jenner, cutting him off. 'The quack says it's inoperable.'

'Second opinion?'

'This is the fourth opinion as it goes. And I'm fed up with geezers I don't know fiddling about with my private bits. And that fucking chemo screws you up, so I knocked it on the head.'

'Christ, I'm sorry, John,' said Mark, and he touched the older man on his arm.

The clouds were getting closer and the first flurry of snow as Jenner had prophesied hit the water and vanished as if it had never existed. 'Really sorry.'

'Don't worry about it, Mark.'

'How can I not worry?'

'There's no point.'

'But still…'

'Instead of worrying about something you can't do anything about, do something for me.'

'What?'

'Later. I'll tell you later.'

'So what's the prognosis, Uncle John?'

'How long have I got, you mean?'

'Well, I wouldn't exactly have put it like that.'

'You don't have to be squeamish, or dance around the subject Mark. A year maybe. Maybe a bit longer. I'll never get my bus pass now.'

'Christ.'

'It's all right, Mark. I've come to terms with it. Even joke about it. It's

17

the breaks. I've had longer than a lot of people I know. Better people too. Life's not fair, but then no one ever said it was.'

Mark hugged Jenner again, and there were tears in his eyes.

'You keep doing that and people will think we're a pair of poofs,' said Jenner, but Mark knew he didn't mean it, and besides, there were no hostile witnesses on that bitterly cold day on the side of the freezing waterway.

'I dreamt about Hazel last night,' said Jenner, changing the subject suddenly. Hazel had been his wife who had died ten years before of heart disease. 'I dream about her a lot these days. Cor, she was just the same.'

He brushed at his eyes with his glove. His eyes were wet too. 'Bloody wind,' he said. 'Making my eyes water.' Mark nodded, but they both knew the truth.

'I could actually touch her,' said Jenner, his gaze looking miles beyond the far river bank where the Millennium Dome loomed, large and empty. 'She was all warm, just like she used to be.'

'She was a great woman,' said Mark. 'She was like a mother to me. We had some laughs, didn't we?'

'Laughs. You remember that bloody laugh of hers? It was like a bloody corncrake.'

Mark smiled. 'And could she drink.'

'You and me both under the table,' said Jenner. 'But that's not why we're here.'

'Why?' asked Mark.

'Things are going mental over there,' said Jenner, taking in southeast London again with a sweep of the cigar in his hand. 'Something's going to give, and I'm too old and fucked up to sort it.'

'Like what? What's going to happen? Tell me.'

'It's all going to go off soon, I know it. Come back with me. It's been too long since you visited. Sort things out. There'll be blood on the streets if you don't. My blood. And I want what little time I've got left.'

'Jesus. But will I be welcome?'

'You're always welcome, you know that. Except you never come.'

'You know why.'

'But that's all in the past now.'

'Is it?' Jenner nodded. 'I'll take your word for it,' said Mark.

'You do that.'

'Fine.'

'Just tell me why you never got in touch before.'

'Oh come on, Uncle. You know. Christ, you better than anyone.'

'But me, Mark. I can understand anyone else. But why blank me?'

'I blanked everyone. It wasn't easy. Jesus, I left my whole life behind.'

'Not even a call until yesterday. Not one call in how many years?'

'Eight.'

'Yeah, eight.'

'I've been busy.'

'Too busy for me?' It was more of a challenge than a question. A recollection of favours done and favours owed that could never be repaid even if both men lived far beyond their allotted spans, which was unlikely for one of them at least. But most of all it was a simple reminder of a relationship that had lasted since the younger man had been a boy.

Mark Farrow smiled at the memories. 'All right, Uncle John,' he said. 'Tell me all about it.'

TWO

'I will. All in good time,' said John Jenner. 'But first, let's go for a drive.'

'Do what?'

'A drive.'

'Why?'

'Why not?'

'Where?'

'Some old haunts I want to show you. Remind you of things. We can have lunch.'

'Where?'

'Brixton.'

'Brixton. For lunch? What, bad pizza in the market? Or ackee and peas? Pie and mash? What?'

'You have been away too long. It's a hot spot now, Brixton. And as it goes there is a terrific new Caribbean restaurant I go to. Don't look like that. They've got tablecloths. It ain't like the old days with formica tables and kitchen chairs. They've even got a wine list.'

Mark Farrow grinned. 'All right, you're on.'

'We'll go in your motor. Come on, I'm freezing. I'll let that lot in the Merc know what I'm doing. They'll keep us company.'

The pair walked back to the cars and John Jenner keyed a number into his mobile and whispered some instructions. 'Who's driving you about these days?' asked Mark when he was finished, nodding at the Bentley, its engine still running.

'Chas of course. Always Chas. Wouldn't trust anyone else, apart from you.'

Mark laughed. 'Chas. Fuck me, I would've thought he'd've got his bus pass years ago.'

'Don't let him hear you say that.'

'Don't worry, I won't.'

They went together to the Bentley and the driver's window rolled smoothly down.

'Chas,' said Mark, squatting down on his haunches by the driver's window. 'How've you been?'

'Can't complain, Mark,' the massive man in the driver's seat replied with a voice that rumbled like an old volcano about to blow.

'We're going for a ride together, Chas,' said Jenner. 'Then on for lunch. Mark'll drop me back home later. I'm on my mobile if you need me for anything.'

'OK, Boss,' said Chas. 'I'll be there. You be careful. Hear?'

'You worry too much, Chas. I'm in safe hands with Mark and our friends back there.' He pointed with his thumb to the Mercedes Benz.

'And you don't worry enough,' said Chas. With that he let the window glide up, put the car into gear and pulled away from the kerb, did a three-point turn and headed back the way'd he'd come.

Mark Farrow and John Jenner went together to the Range Rover, Mark pressed the button on his key fob and the car's lights flashed once, the horn beeped and the locks opened. Jenner went to open the front left-hand-side door, then realised his mistake and walked around to the passenger side with a shake of his head. They climbed in, Farrow behind the wheel, where he keyed the ignition and pushed the heater control to full.

'Still at the old place then,' said Mark as they waited for the car to warm up.

'That's right. Just like always.'

'I'd've thought you'd've moved years ago. I was amazed when Dev told me you were still there. You must rattle around like a pea in a pod.'

'No. Chas lives there permanent now. And Martine's back.'

Mark looked surprised. 'Get away. Dev never told me that either. What happened to that husband of hers?'

'She caught him over the side with some bird. It's a long story. I'll tell you while we're eating. And don't take the piss out of that old house. We had good times there, didn't we?'

Mark nodded.

'Anyway, it's worth a fortune now. I had an offer of half a million a few months back.'

'Half a bloody million. You couldn't give those mausoleums away a few years back.'

'Like I told you, it's a hot spot. Now come on, time's wasting. Drive.'

'Where to exactly?' Mark asked.

'Just head south. Don't tell me you've forgotten the way.'

Farrow shrugged, started up and did as he was told. They motored down to the East India Dock Road closely followed by the Mercedes, took the Rotherhithe Tunnel south, then through the Elephant, Denmark Hill, Herne Hill, along the Norwood Road, and as Jenner directed, took a right at Tulse Hill station and drove up Leigham Vale until they stopped outside an old Victorian heap of a school.

'Hitherfield Road Junior School,' he said when the Vogue came to a halt.

'Yeah. This is my old school,' said Mark.

'And mine. This is where we met, your dad and me,' Jenner said to Mark. 'Year one, seven years old.'

'When was that again, Uncle John?'

'Don't,' said Jenner. 'You're making me feel old again. Billy was crying those blue eyes of his out after his mum left him that first morning,' Jenner went on. 'Couldn't even tie his own shoelaces. I had to teach him.'

'And you gave him a bloody nose,' said Mark with a laugh.

'Just showing him who was boss,' said Jenner, laughing himself.

'And then he knocked your tooth out.'

'It was loose,' said Jenner. 'I put it under my pillow and got half a dollar the next morning. That's twelve and a half pence to you.'

23

'The tooth fairy,' said Mark Farrow. 'I never did see that little bugger, much as I tried to stay awake.'

'Nor me, I think it was a conspiracy.'

'Good times,' said Farrow.

'But don't it look small? The school.'

'Yeah. We grew up,' said Mark. 'Where to now?' Under Jenner's instructions Mark rolled the car through back streets towards Brixton and this time Mark recognised the route and shook his head in disbelief. 'Christ, not the Strand.'

'The very place,' said Jenner. 'Our next school. Strand Grammar. Always bloody together. I couldn't get rid of the silly sod. He never thought I'd pass my eleven plus. Mind you, nor did I. I always reckoned I'd end up at the Brixton School of Building with the no-hopers. But I couldn't let my boy go to the big school all on his own. He'd have no one to protect him.'

'No one to get him into trouble more like,' said Farrow.

'You should've seen us, Mark,' said Jenner. 'That first day. All spiffed up like toffs. Caps, blazers, white shirts, grey shorts. Can you imagine it now? We weren't allowed to wear long trousers until we were in the second year. Reckoned we wouldn't get into so much trouble in shorts. Boy, were they wrong. The whole year our knees were skinned raw.' He laughed out loud at the memory and Mark joined in. 'Weeds, they called us new kids,' Jenner went on, 'and the older boys tried to put us head first down the toilets. We soon changed their minds though. Fuckers. They'd never seen a pair like us. Yeah, we showed 'em. Couple of them got bloody noses too, and they didn't try again. And we got threatened with six of the best by the head. We were shitting ourselves.'

'Did he do it?' asked Mark, intrigued at this insight into the childhood of the toughest man he'd ever known.

'No. We both cried our eyes out and he let us off. Crying with laughter more like. But he was always easy. Not like the bloke who took over from him later. He caned me so often I think I should have a permanent groove in my arse. I can't believe I let it happen, but things were so different then.

And I knew if my old man found out he'd give it to me double. Now I reckon the bastard was coming in his undies when he gave me six of the best. But he's dead long ago, and I danced with joy when I heard about it.'

The Vogue stopped in Elm Park, Brixton Hill, the Mercedes still close behind. They were outside another Victorian old school building, this with a statue of some old philosopher with an open book on his knee and a young boy beside him, mounted high on one wall. They both got out.

'He always hated that bloody statue, your dad.' said John Jenner. 'Scared the life out of him. He was always scared without me around.'

'You were his best friend,' said Mark Farrow.

'This place looks small too,' said Jenner. 'Dump. Good job it closed years ago.'

'What is it now?'

'Adult education centre,' replied Jenner.

Mark looked up the road, a puzzled look on his face. 'Where's my old school then?' he asked. Tulse Hill Comprehensive, the massive building that once dominated the sky line of that part of south London, was gone.

'Knocked it down years ago. It was rotten with asbestos and everyone round here hated it from day one.'

'Me included,' said Mark.

'Yeah, I know.' said Jenner. 'Come on then, let's go and have something to munch.'

THREE

The Range Rover and escort pulled away from the kerb again, drove down Elm Park, turned right on Brixton Hill and headed towards the centre of Brixton. 'It's called Tootsies,' said Jenner. 'The place we're going.'

'Sounds great,' said Mark.

'Don't take the piss. You'll love it, I promise,' said John Jenner as the car eased its way through the heavy lunchtime traffic, past Brixton prison, which he didn't give a second glance, although he felt the small hairs on the back of his neck rise at the sight of it.

'That fucker's in there, isn't he?' said Mark Farrow as if reading Jenner's mind.

'Yes.'

'Told you I kept in touch. Nice to know he's banged up and we're going out for a meal.'

'If you say so.'

'I say so, Uncle. It's a been a long time, but soon I'll get to meet him one way or another. Then it'll be all over.'

'Are you sure you want that?'

'Sometimes it's been the only thing keeping me going.'

'Fair enough.'

'Fair enough it is, but I'm not going to let him spoil you buying me lunch.'

Being stuck in a queue of cars, trucks and buses, Mark Farrow had plenty of time to look around as they inched along. 'You're right, it bloody well has changed round here,' he said. 'What happened? Where's all the dumpy old shops that looked like they hadn't made a sale in twenty years? The ones with a cat asleep in the window on top of a pile of dead flies?'

27

'The trendies moved in. Turned the place upside down.'

'I never would've believed it.'

Jenner told Mark to turn the car off the main road towards Clapham, where they took a right and spotted a smart-looking restaurant with a neon sign over the door that read *Tootsies* in blue and orange script.

There was an empty parking meter a couple of doors up and Mark slid the Vogue on to it. The two men exited the car and Farrow put coins in the meter. The Mercedes pulled up behind it, and, as Mark looked around, John Jenner went and had a word. When he got back, he said: 'They'll be here, and I've told them to feed your meter if it runs out.'

'It's not a problem, the car isn't registered to me.'

'Never thought it was, but they tow them away these days.'

'Bastards.'

'You said it.'

The pair went through the glass door of the restaurant to be met by a short black man in a tight, shiny, black single-breasted suit and a snowy white button-down shirt open at the neck without a tie. 'Mr Jenner,' he greeted them. 'What a pleasant surprise.'

'Got a table for us, Delroy?' asked John.

'Always for you, sir,' replied the black man. 'Your usual?'

'If it's free.'

'Of course.'

They were led through the warm, spicily scented room to the back, where a table for four was set on a cloth as white as his shirt.

'Delroy, I'd like you to meet Mark Farrow,' said Jenner before they sat.

'A pleasure,' said Delroy, shaking Mark's hand.

'Nice to meetcha,' said Mark.

'He's been away for a while,' said Jenner as Delroy cleared away two of the place settings before taking their coats, gloves and scarves. 'Just showing him the changes round here.'

'A miracle of regeneration,' said Delroy in reply.

'I hardly recognised the old place,' said Mark.

Delroy swiftly offloaded their outer garments to the cloakroom, then took their order for drinks. Gin and tonics for both.

'You all right to drink, Uncle?' asked Mark when the black man was at the tiny bar.

'No. But who cares?'

In a moment Delroy was back at the table. 'Any water, gentlemen?' he asked. 'Not for me,' said Mark. 'Uncle John?'

'Uncle John,' echoed Delroy. 'You two are related?'

'Not really,' explained Mark Farrow. "It's just what I call him. Always have. But we're more family than most families, if you know what I mean, Delroy.' Delroy nodded.

'And no water for me either,' said Jenner. 'I know what fishes do in it.' A joke which Mark had heard a thousand times before, but which still brought a smile to his face. John Jenner never changed much. 'So what's good today, Del?' Jenner asked.

'My mother's pumpkin soup, special today.'

'The pumpkin soup,' echoed Jenner. 'Got to have some of that. Bloody marvellous. Where is Tootsie, by the way?'

'In the kitchen as always, Mr Jenner,' replied Delroy, and as he noticed Mark's puzzled look, he explained. 'Tootsie's my mum, Mr Farrow. The finest Caribbean chef in London bar none.'

'I'll second that, Mark,' said Jenner. 'Is she coming to see me, Del?'

'She'll be out later as usual, Mr Jenner. I'll tell her you're here.'

'Send her in a rum and tonic on me.'

Delroy smiled, showing a mouthful of teeth as white as his shirt. 'No problem. She'll appreciate that.'

'So what else is on the menu?' asked Jenner.

'The usual. Jerk chicken, goat curry. All very good.'

'We'll take some of each,' said Jenner, looking over at Mark.

'Fine by me. You order for both of us. Seems like you know the place.'

'Mr Jenner is one of my favourite regulars,' said Delroy. 'And his lovely daughter. How is she today, sir?'

'Just dandy,' replied Jenner. 'And bring us some dirty rice and peas, okra and maybe a little something with chilli. And Delroy, take something out to the boys in the Mercedes outside if you don't mind. The black one. They'll be hungry I expect. Put it on my bill, of course.'

Delroy smiled. 'All in order, Mr Jenner. Wine for you both?'

'Something white and light and cold if the chilli's hot.'

Delroy smiled again. 'I know just the thing,' he said and left for the kitchen as a beautiful black woman brought their drinks.

'Got this place sussed, Uncle John,' said Mark when she had gone.

'Put a bit of dough in as well,' said Jenner. 'Del was having a rough time with some ragamuffin boys. I sorted it all out.'

'Where are they buried?'

Jenner laughed out loud. 'That's not the way we do it around here, these days.'

'What then?'

'Just a few words.'

'I can imagine. And, talking of the lovely Martine, what happened between her and her old man? He wasn't knocking her about, was he?'

'Knocking Martine about? I don't think so. About as much chance of her taking that as her mum. No. Like I said, he was playing away and he got captured. She moved out of the house in Guildford and back in with me. He got a bit lairy, but I sent Chas down with her when she cleared her stuff out.'

'I'd like to have seen that.'

'Me too. Anyway she left him a few memories.'

'Like?'

'She cut up all his flash suits and poured the contents of his wine cellar into the swimming pool.'

'And he didn't object?'

'No. Chas made sure of that.'

'How old is she now?'

'Still six years younger than you, and looks like a dream.'

'I'm sorry I missed the wedding. How long ago was that again?'

'Five years.'

'So long... Does she still hate me?'

'She never hated you, Mark. She bloody worshipped the ground you walked on. Trouble was, you always ignored her.'

'She was a bloody nuisance though, Uncle John, wasn't she? Always bloody hanging round putting in her two penn'oth. Always nicking my things and hiding them.' He laughed at the memory. 'Christ, but I had to lock my bedroom door every time I went out.'

'I remember.'

'Is she at home now?'

'No. She got herself a job up west. I told her not to bother, I'd take care of things. But she's independent, just like Hazel was at her age.'

'Hazel,' said Mark raising his glass. 'Here's to her.'

Jenner touched his glass to Mark's and they drank. 'I'm looking forward to being with her soon,' said Jenner.

'Don't say that, Uncle John.'

'It's true.'

'I'm sorry, really sorry. I can hardly take it in.'

'Now don't get maudlin on me, Mark,' said Jenner as a waiter appeared with two steaming bowls of soup and the bread basket, then went off for the wine which Jenner tasted and approved of. The waiter filled their glasses, wished them bon appétit and left them alone. 'Get into this soup. Just the thing for a day like this,' said Jenner, smacking his lips in appreciation as he took a mouthful.

Mark tasted some too and raised his eyebrows. 'Bloody hell,' he said. 'You're right. This is fantastic.'

'Old St Lucian recipe, handed down from mother to daughter. Or son in this case.'

When the edge of their appetites was sated, Mark put down his soup spoon and said. 'OK, Uncle John, we've had the sentimental journey, and you're spoiling me with good food and booze. So tell me, what exactly is going on?'

Jenner blew though his teeth, put down his spoon also and said: 'Well, Mark, it's a long bloody story.'

'I've got no pressing appointments.'

'OK, son, I'll tell you.'

He gathered his thoughts as the waiter reappeared, cleared away their soup dishes, and poured more wine, before Delroy himself bought out the main courses, covering their table with steaming dishes of delicious-smelling food. 'Enjoy,' he said when everything was set to his satisfaction. 'Your men have food, and Mother will be out to see you when you're finished.'

'Fine, Delroy,' said Jenner. 'We'll look forward to that.'

'Come on, Uncle John,' said Mark Farrow when they were alone again. 'I'm trembling with anticipation.'

'It's all going to hell, Mark,' said Jenner, tinkering with the food on his plate. 'To hell in a hand basket. You know what I do. How I earn a crust. It used to be easy, but things are changing. Changing fast. I mean, just look around you. No one ever expected this part of the world to end up like this. Half a million pound houses and carrot cake for sale at the local flea pit. But underneath the surface it actually hasn't changed that much. Just take a walk through the council estates. Burnt out flats and cars, syringes in the stairwells. What you see on top is cosmetic. What's really changed is the gap between the rich and the poor. And there's some seriously rich people round here now. Biggest growth industry apart from organic food is security systems. Those rich folk aren't fools. They want to protect what they've got. And at the other end of the scale, the conmen and thieves know there's a lot more to score.'

'Sorry, Uncle, I still don't get your point,' said Mark.

'Listen, son,' said Jenner. 'Society came off the rails in the Eighties. If you can't handle that you're a fool. And I ain't one. I got O levels. Christ knows how. Few enough I'll admit. But in hindsight I know that with a bit of graft I could've got a lot more. Maybe even gone to university. But boys like me didn't go to university in those days. Or precious few. But I read books. I studied politics. That's how I got to be boss. Now I'm dying. There's no oddsing that, and to be honest it's all slipping away. There's all sorts of chancers coming up. All sorts of gangs trying to muscle in on my territory. Portuguese, Chinese, Asians, and blacks. The blacks are the worst with their crack and guns.'

Mark looked round the restaurant and was aware of the irony of John Jenner's last remark but let it go.

'We've been getting soft over the last few years. I need someone to come in and sort things out. Someone who knows what they're doing.'

'You mean me, Uncle?' said Mark. 'No. No chance.'

'Think about it for a minute.'

Mark shook his head.

'And Jimmy Hunter's due out soon. A few months. And he's going to be looking for trouble.'

'So?'

'He killed your father, Mark. My best friend.'

'And I'll be waiting.'

'So wait at the old place. Wait with us.'

'I dunno, Uncle. It's so close now, I don't want anything to get in the way.'

'Nothing will. What are you doing right now that's so important?'

'Nothing. Just hanging around.'

'So do what I ask. Come back, son.'

'Uncle John…'

'Come back home with me this afternoon,' said Jenner. 'We'll talk. You can stay over. Your old room's still there.'

'Really?'

'Really. Just as it was. I get the cleaners to change the sheets every couple of weeks. They think I'm mad of course, but they get well paid for what they do. We'll talk more. About your dad.'

'You never did talk much about him.'

'No. And that was probably a mistake. Come on, what do you say?'

'I say that this is excellent goat curry,' said Mark. 'Now come on, dig in or your mate and his mum aren't going to be best pleased.'

'You can say that again,' said Jenner. 'And believe me, Tootsie's someone you don't want to upset.'

So they ate their food, the previous subject left untouched, merely talking about old times and people, many that Mark hadn't seen or thought of for years.

The food was good, and when the dishes were all but empty, and their stomachs all but stuffed, a short, plump black woman in chef's whites with a bandanna over her hair came out of the kitchen and waddled over to their table. Both men went as if to stand but she waved them back, grabbed an empty chair from the next table and joined them. She pulled the bandanna off kinky black hair laid out in corn rows, wiped the sweat from her face, leaned over and kissed Jenner on the cheek.

'How are you doing, John?' she asked.

'Fine, Tootsie, just fine.'

'Truth.'

'Not so good.'

'I'm sorry. But you enjoyed the meal?"

'Fabulous as ever.'

'So why you left so much?'

'A morsel.'

'That morsel could feed a family back home,' she said with a stern look in his direction.

'I apologise, Tootsie,' said Jenner.

Mark could hardly believe his ears. It wasn't like his uncle to apologise to anyone, let alone a woman. Especially a black woman. Things had certainly changed in his absence.

'I'll have it put into a doggie bag,' she said. "Snack it up later with a cold drink.'

'We'll do that.'

'And who is this fine young man? Delroy informs me he's your nephew. Why have we never seen him in here before?'

'This is Mark,' said Jenner. 'A nephew by adoption. His father died a long time ago, and his mother...' He didn't finish the sentence. 'He needed a good home.'

'And you gave him what he needed,' Tootsie finished for him.

'That's right,' said Mark, looking up and extending his hand to the woman. When she looked into his eyes, her own widened, and for one moment he thought she was going to cross herself. My bloody eyes, he thought. Things like that often happened to him.

She recovered quickly and took his hand in both of hers and looked at his palm. 'You have had troubles, young man,' she said. 'Bad troubles.'

'Tootsie's a bit of a soothsayer,' explained Jenner.

'You're right there,' said Mark, replying to the woman and making no effort to remove his hand. 'And something tells me they might just be starting again soon.'

'A boy needs a mother,' Tootsie went on, ignoring his last remark. 'I know. The Lord only knows where Delroy would be without me to keep him on the path of righteousness.'

'I had a mother,' said Mark. 'Two in fact. One wasn't quite up to the job I'm afraid.' What am I saying? he thought. Why am I telling this woman anything? Then it occurred to him that it was for the same reason that his uncle had apologised to her. There was something about her that demanded truth and respect. 'I left her, abandoned her,' he went on. 'It was the worst thing I ever did. Almost.'

'You couldn't have stayed, son,' said Jenner.

'Let him speak,' said Tootsie. 'Let the boy speak for himself.'

'But I had another mother,' Mark continued. 'A beautiful woman. John's wife.' But she left us, he thought. Abandoned us, before her time. Although it wasn't her fault. And we had to watch her die, day by day, bit by bit. Getting old in front of our eyes. Fading away until she finally left. He didn't speak his thoughts, but he saw that Tootsie understood.

'I know about Hazel,' said Tootsie. 'Many a night your uncle and me have sat up late with the rum bottle setting the world to rights, and telling stories of our youth.'

'We'll do it again soon, I promise,' said Jenner.

'Did that stuff I gave you help with the pain?' she asked.

Jenner smiled. 'Yes. At night it helps a great deal.'

'Good. And thanks for the drink, John. It cooled me down plenty.'

'A pleasure.'

'Well, I'll leave you boys now,' she said. 'I can see you have much to talk about. But don't be strangers. Come again soon. And bring Martine. She lights up this place like a lantern.'

'Just like her mother would've done,' said Jenner, and smiled again at the memory of his wife.

Tootsie stood, collected the dishes and headed back to the kitchen. Delroy came and took their orders for sweets and coffee. When he'd gone Jenner said, 'So. You going to stay tonight or what?'

'If you tell me about my dad.'

'Not all of it.'

'Some.'

'All right.'

'Then it's a deal.'

FOUR

It took his uncle what seemed to Mark like an age to settle the bill, and included a trip to the kitchen to shake hands with the other staff and collect the leftovers, all neatly parcelled up in foil containers. When they finally got outside, it had been snowing again, the pavements were dusted with white and the black clouds were in a holding pattern over south London.

Once inside the Vogue, Jenner said, 'You know the way,' and the car took off towards Tulse Hill and the house where Mark Farrow had spent so much of his youth, still tailed by the Merc. When they got close, Jenner hauled out his mobile and phoned Chas. 'We're outside, open up,' and as they approached the detached house, which sat behind high walls with twin automatic gates allowing access to the short U-shaped drive, the gates opened and Mark parked the Range Rover next to the Bentley. The Mercedes took up a position half straddling the pavement opposite.

'Come on in and have a drink,' said John Jenner.

The inside of the house was warm and comfortable with lights glowing against the late afternoon London gloom.

'You haven't changed it much, have you?' said Mark, taking off his coat and muffler and throwing them over the back of a chair.

'What's the point?' said Jenner. 'Hazel had it done up nice. It always suited us, didn't it?'

'It certainly did,' said Mark, sitting on a long, plush sofa and accepting the brandy that Jenner gave him. 'So where's Chas live?'

'In the granny flat,' said Jenner. 'But don't call it that, he gets a bit peeved.'

Mark laughed and took a sip of his drink.

Jenner sat in an armchair opposite, winced, and took a hand-rolled cigarette from a silver box and lit it.

'You smoking spliff?' said Mark when he smelt the smoke.

'Medicinal purposes only. I get a bit of pain about this time of day. It helps. This is the stuff Tootsie got me. Best St Lucian weed. Want one?'

'No. I'll stick to these,' said Mark, taking out his cigarettes and lighting up.

'Did you hear they made it semi-legal round here?' asked Jenner.

'I heard something like that on TV.'

'I'm glad you've heard something at least. Who'd ever have thought it? After all the bloody fuss and bother they used to make over it. Once upon a time this spliff alone would've got me a couple of years inside.'

'Hard to believe,' said Mark.

Jenner took a long drag of weed. 'But we had some fun. Happy days.'

'Tell me about them. You never have.'

'Later. First of all I want to know if you're going to come down and give me a hand.'

'It could get heavy, couldn't it?'

'Very. I don't like to ask, but with me being the way I am I'm not up to it any more.'

'I can't very well refuse, can I?'

'You could've just not bothered to get in touch.'

'I knew it had to be important. You haven't tried to get me before.'

'Not because I didn't want to. I just thought it was better to let you have your head.'

'And I'm grateful for that. Grateful for a lot of things. You know that. The way you took me in...'

'I always wanted a son,' interrupted Jenner.

'You've got one.'

'Good. So? You up for it?'

'I suppose so.'

'Good. It's good to have you back home, Mark.'

'Home. Now that's not a word I've used much lately.'

'You can now.' And so they sat together recalling good times as the afternoon turned to evening, the sky grew darker and the snow fell fitfully on the just and the unjust alike.

Around seven they heard the front gates open and the rumble and grumble of an engine. 'Martine's home,' said Jenner.

'What's she driving?' asked Mark. 'Sounds interesting.'

'One of those new Mini Cooper S models,' said Jenner. 'Dev got hold of it and tweaked it up a bit. Goes like shit off a shovel.'

'Dev,' said Mark. 'I can't wait to see him.'

'You will, soon enough.'

'Sounds ominous.'

The sound of voices came from the hall, Chas's deep vocals and a woman's surprised response, the living room door burst open and in she came. Martine Jenner was dressed in a long camel hair coat. Her red hair was damp from the snow, and its curls corkscrewed halfway down her back. Her skin was very white and her dark eyes sparkled as she spotted Mark.

'Hey, blue eyes,' she said. 'Long time. I thought you were dead.'

Mark looked at the young woman standing in the doorway and laughed out loud. 'Christ,' he said 'The brat has grown up.' He could hardly believe it. The last time he'd seen her she'd been attractive. But now she had matured into a beauty, the spitting image of her mother as he remembered her. It was uncanny. He looked at John Jenner and knew that he saw the same.

'You'd better believe it,' she replied. 'And you've grown old.'

''Tine,' warned Jenner.

'Leave her, it's all right,' said Mark.

'Why didn't you come to my wedding?' she asked. 'You could've got off with one of the bridesmaids. Or their mums.'

'I didn't miss much by all accounts.'

'You cheeky sod. Dad, tell him.'

'You started it,' said Jenner, memories of so many times when he'd been called in to referee between them in the past.

'You always did take his side,' said Martine.

39

'That's not true.'

'Sorry, Martine,' said Mark, seeing the hurt in her expression. 'I was out of order.'

'So was I. Now come here so's I can give you a cuddle.'

Mark stood up and she gave him a quick hug before going over to her father and kissing him on the cheek. 'How many of those have you smoked today, Daddy?' she asked, looking at the roach in the ashtray.

'Enough.'

'You had your morphine?'

He shook his head. 'Me and Mark have been talking.'

'I just bet you have.' She turned on the younger man. 'He should be resting, not sitting up here talking to you.'

'I'll be all right, 'Tine,' said Jenner. 'There's things we have to talk about.'

'You'll kill yourself,' she said, her expression softening.

'It's not me that's killing myself, it's this damn cancer. Mark's staying over. I'll rest later. What are you doing? You eating with us?'

'No. I just came back to change. Girl's night out.'

'Up west?'

'No. There's a new bar in Clapham. Lots of lovely men.' And she looked at Mark with a challenging expression.

He'd sat back down again and pretended to pay her no attention.

'Right,' she said. 'I can tell you're going to ignore me. I'll go and have a shower and put on my gladrags. I don't want to take the car in this weather. Can Chas drive me? It'll only take him twenty minutes.'

'Course he will,' said Jenner. 'How're you going to get home?'

'I'll get a cab.'

'Is the snow getting worse?'

'It comes and goes.'

'Well, take your mobile and call us if you need a lift home.'

'Have you ever known me to go out without my mobile?' she said back.

'No, love. I know it's welded to your ear. I have to pay the bills.'

'Don't be a meanie.'

'Have I ever been?'

She went over to him again and gave him another kiss and a long hug. 'Never. Not my dad.'

'Go on then, 'Tine,' said the older man. 'Go and make yourself beautiful.'

'More beautiful, you mean.' She danced out of the room and up the stairs.

'Tootsie was right,' said Mark. 'She does light up the room. I'd forgotten.'

'She's still hurting though,' said Jenner. 'Don't you believe all that.'

'I could tell. What was he like? The husband.'

'Not good enough for her.'

'You'd say that if it was Prince Charles she'd married.'

'Especially if it was Prince Charles.'

'Bad example. But you know what I mean.'

'Course I do.'

They sat talking for another few minutes before there were foot steps on the stairs again and Martine burst back into the room like a small tornado. She'd changed into a short black dress, black nylons and high heeled strappy shoes.

'Just the thing for the weather,' said Mark dryly.

'But I've got a Bentley,' said Martine, and stuck out her tongue. Her face was newly made up and she did indeed look beautiful as she shrugged back into her coat. 'Coming, Chas,' she shouted over her shoulder. 'Won't be late, Dad,' she said. 'Work tomorrow. You'll be here for breakfast, Mark?' And when he nodded, she said. 'It'll be just like old times.'

'What, you in your Rupert The Bear jammies?' said Mark.

'I don't wear jammies to bed anymore,' she said. 'You'd be surprised what I do wear.' Mark laughed.

'You take care,' said her father as she kissed him farewell.

'Always do,' she said and vanished, slamming the door behind her.

'Except when it comes to husbands,' he said with a trace of bitterness. 'Now where were we?'

'You were going to tell me about you and Dad,' said Mark.

'What, when we were at school?'

'No, later than that. When you started all this. Before he became a copper.'

'All right, son,' said Jenner. 'But you've got to remember, it was a different world in those days.'

FIVE

It had been summer then. The late summer of 1965, and John Jenner was nineteen years old. He remembered the morning as easily as if it had been yesterday. Sitting in that elegant room talking to his late best friend's son, the memory was so clear he could almost smell it. The excitement. The possibilities.

The mid 60s, and, like the song says, England swings like a pendulum do. But it hadn't swung soon or hard enough for John Jenner and his best friend Billy Farrow, so they decided to do something about it. They'd talked about it often. There they were in their late teens, going nowhere, whilst other boys of their own age were killing and being killed in southeast Asia, and others were jetting about the world making fortunes with their music. Something seemed to have gone wrong with their lives.

Pills were the answer. Little blue, yellow and purple pills chock full of amphetamines that fuelled the lifestyle of mods and rockers alike. John knew how to get hold of thousands of them. And at a tanner each – forty for a pound in the pubs and clubs of London – and an investment of precisely nothing to get them, he and Billy would be rich within weeks if not days. John worked in a print works in Stockwell. He earned the princely sum of fifteen pounds a week before deductions. He made up his wages with petty theft and shoplifting. He knew that couldn't last. Eventually he'd get his collar felt and go away. So be it, he thought. But if he was going to do bird it would be for something worthwhile. Hence the burglary he was planning. He knew about the pills because the firm he worked for did some printing for a pharmaceutical import/export company, and he'd been sent down with proofs enough times that he almost had free run of the place.

Simple.

That summery Saturday morning, John woke up in a strange bed in Edith Grove, Chelsea, just a few hundred yards from the big river.

In those days, John was a handsome young man, everyone said so. A shade over six feet tall in his socks, his Anello & Davide elastic-sided boots adding two inches with their Cuban heels. His hair, which was thick and curly just like his daughter's would be in thirty-five years time, had been allowed to grow into a full *Beatles For Sale* LP cover style, and his dress was on the cusp of mod and rock star. That Saturday morning he was wearing black drainpipe trousers, a pale blue tab-collared shirt without a tie, and a blue and white striped single breasted seersucker jacket with narrow lapels and three buttons. The previous night he had dropped into a club in Fulham to see a new band, and had met the girl who was fast asleep in the narrow bed on which he sat to tug on his boots.

John hated putting on soiled clothing. He hated not having shaved and being forced to clean his teeth with a stranger's brush. But he'd enjoyed fucking the girl he'd met at the club. She was what the boys he ran with called 'a posh sort', and he couldn't wait to tell them what contortions he'd put her through that'd left her still snoring under the tangled sheets as the sun rose high over London town.

The house was crammed with bedsits and somewhere he heard a toilet flush and someone had a radio playing, tuned to one of the pirate stations. The song was 'Satisfaction' by the Stones, and he sat for a moment and listened to it, strained through the tiny speakers of the transistor.

He smiled to himself and shook the girl's shoulder as he remembered the satisfaction they had both enjoyed all night long.

'Whassamatter,' she mumbled after a minute.

Now what the fuck was her name? he thought, and then it came to him. 'Matilda,' he said.

'Wha'?'

'I gotta go.'

'What time is it?'

He looked at his cheap watch. 'Ten.'

'Shit. Middle of the night.'

'Sure. But I got things to do.'

She opened her puffy, mascara-smeared eyes. 'Don't go,' she said. 'We can screw again.'

'Did you like it?' he asked.

'Lovely. I'm all sticky and sore.'

'Me too. But I've got to meet someone. Business.'

'Sure?'

'Sure.'

'You cockneys are all the same. Love 'em and leave em.'

He grinned, leant down and kissed her, and her sweetsour bed smell almost made him relent and get back in for another go. 'I'll call you,' he said.

'No you won't.'

'Course I will.'

'Promise.'

'Promise.'

She sat up and the sheets slid off her breasts and the sight of her baby pink nipples reinforced his urge to stay, but he knew that Billy would be calling for him soon, and if he didn't show he'd never hear the end of it.

'Give us that pen,' she said. He passed her the Bic and she wrote a Chelsea number on the back of his hand.

'The Yardbirds are on at the Marquee on Monday. Will you take me?' she asked.

'Sure.'

'Then call me.'

He kissed her once more and checked his hair in the mirror before he left. He never saw her again.

Outside the sun was shining and the birds were singing, and the red buses running down the King's Road sparkled like new. John smiled and strolled down to the river and looked down at the mud exposed by the low tide and decided that there was no greater city in which to live. And Saturday morning was the best time of the week. Especially when it was the one Saturday in four he didn't have to turn up to work. Not long now,

45

he thought, and I'll have every Saturday off. Every day of the week for that matter.

He hopped on a 137 bus to Streatham Hill, then walked to his parents' house in a narrow, mean street between Brixton and Tulse Hill.

It took him well over an hour to make the journey. Christ, he thought, I've got to get a car. He'd had his licence for six months already, but the deposit for a motor was still well out of reach. Not for much longer, he thought, as he trudged the last half mile. The midday sun was hot and he was sweating through his creased clothing, and the cheap leather of his boots. One day soon I'll have a hundred pairs, he thought. If they get dirty I'll just chuck them away. The thought cheered him up and he straightened his shoulders and lengthened his stride as he entered the street he knew so well.

His mum and dad were sitting in the kitchen when he arrived home, listening to the same station that had been playing at Matilda's. His father, Arthur Jenner, detested modern pop but the boy and his mother persisted, and during the day when there was nothing on the TV, he relented, even if he still moaned and groaned that he couldn't understand the words of the jungle music. He worked as a market porter at Covent Garden Market and had only arrived home from work a few minutes before John rolled in. As usual, he'd been to one of the market pubs on his way and smelled strongly of mild and bitter.

'What time do you call this?' he said when his only son walked into the room.

It was par for the course, the sort of family exchange that had become ritual as John had got older. Almost a game. John made a big deal of examining his watch face. 'Eleven thirty precisely, and all's well.'

'Don't be funny with me, boy. Out all night with some loose tart I suppose.'

'Arthur,' said Margaret Jenner. 'Really.'

Then his father turned on her. 'And turn that sodding racket off.'

'It's the new Hollies single,' John protested. 'It's the business.'

'I don't care if it's the new pansy's single. That's what they are and you as well,' said his father.

46

Before Arthur could get into his stride, they heard a ring at the front door. 'That'll be Billy,' said John, relieved at the interruption.

'It might be the man from the Pru,' said Margaret. 'Or the milkman. He wants paying.'

'I'll go and see,' said John, leaving the kitchen and walking the length of the short hall to open the front door. It was Billy. 'Thank Christ,' said John. 'The old man's doing his nut as usual.'

Billy was still strictly mod. That morning he was dressed in pristine brown suede Hush Puppies, white socks, checked hipsters with a slight flare, held up by a wide, white leather belt, a navy blue button down shirt with a massive collar and a scarlet jacket in the same style as his friend's. 'Come on in, blue eyes,' said John. 'I've just got home.'

'Where you been?'

'I went to that new place in Fulham. Met a bird. Had it off. You should've seen her. Well tasty.'

'You lucky sod.'

'I told you to come.'

'I've got no dough.'

'You will have.' And he led his friend back to the kitchen.

'Hello, Billy,' said Margaret. 'Cup of tea? Something to eat?'

'Are you feeding the whole world now?' said Arthur. 'You'd think we were made of money.'

'Don't pay any attention, love,' said Margaret, busying herself with the kettle.

'Just a cuppa please, Mrs J,' said Billy.

'And I'd better get changed,' said John. 'I fancy a trip up west, have a gander at what's new round the shops.'

'Poofs,' said Arthur. 'The pair of you.' And the boys laughed out loud.

Billy's hair was strictly mod, too. Lighter than his friend, it was razor-cut with a one-inch part at the front and a slight bouffant backcombed over the crown. That was poofy too, according to Arthur. Almost everything the boys did was poofy according to him. Arthur still sported the short-back-and-sides he'd kept since his army days, when his drill sergeant had assured him that only homosexuals grew their hair long. The fact that the neighbourhood girls flocked around his son and his friend was still a source of amazement to the older man.

'A spell in the army would do you both good,' Arthur said. 'Why they ever stopped National Service I don't know.'

It was an old song the boys had heard a million times before and they pulled faces behind Arthur's back. 'Leave them, Art,' protested his wife. 'They look lovely.'

'Lovely,' said Arthur getting into his stride, but knowing he couldn't win and deep down not really wanting to. 'I'll give 'em lovely. Got a job yet, Bill?' Billy had had several jobs since leaving school but hadn't been able to hold on to any of them, which was a source of constant irritation to his own father.

'Still looking Mr J,' he said. The conversation reminded him too much of what he got at home.

'You wouldn't last long in this house, I'm telling you. Now I'm going to the lav',' said Arthur, and he took his *Daily Mirror* and retired to the outside lavatory where the rest of his family knew he'd probably stay for at least an hour.

'Take no notice,' said John's mother. 'It's just his way.'

'Sure,' said John. 'Now I've got to have a bath and get changed. Give me half an hour.'

He went next door to the tiny scullery and shut the door firmly behind him. Christ, he thought. I can't wait 'til I get somewhere with a proper bathroom and a lavatory where you don't have to go out in the rain to have a piss and freeze your dick off when you're doing it, let alone anything else. He took the lid off the narrow, battered bath where it doubled as a seat or a shelf, and turned on the tap that set the Ascot water heater belching and farting as it sent a stream of boiling water into the bath tub.

When he was satisfied with the temperature, he hopped in and shaved whilst he was sitting in the water, peering into a tiny mirror surrounded by seashells and the slogan 'A Present From Scarborough', and using a plastic jug for a shaving mug. Once clean he let out the water and ran a rag round the tidemark. With a thin towel wrapped around his waist, he went back into the kitchen.

'Wow,' said his mother. 'Charlton Heston.'

'Yeah, Mum, sure. Got any clean shirts?'

'I'd never live it down if I hadn't. They're in your room.'

John's small bedroom was in the eaves of the house and there was scarcely room in it for a single bed and a chest of drawers. The house was really too small for the three of them, but Arthur refused to contemplate moving and he told John in no uncertain terms that if he wanted somewhere bigger to sleep he'd bloody well better get out and find one.

John went up the two flights of stairs into the tiny, hot, airless room and found half a dozen pristine shirts hanging up behind the door. He chose a pink, frilly-fronted item from the same shop that The Kinks bought their stage clothes. It had already almost caused several fights in that tough part of town. He teamed it with tight, narrow-legged jeans, desert boots and a black leather jacket.

He went back downstairs and pulled Billy out of the kitchen where he'd just finished his tea. 'See you later, Mum,' he said as they left.

'Are you back for tea?' she shouted behind them.

'No,' replied her son. 'There's an alldayer at the 'Mingo, then we're off down the Scene. We'll be back in the morning.'

'You boys,' she said exasperatedly. 'Just be careful. You hear.'

In fact they had no intention of visiting either of the clubs they'd mentioned. But they still made the long trip up to Soho. Soho was where John and Billy felt most at home, where they occasionally caught sight of their favourite group members. They felt that they fitted into the area, and they headed for their favourite café, the Blue Angel, to discuss their plans.

Once inside, at a quiet table, with a cup of frothy coffee each, they went over them for the last time.

'Right,' said John out of the corner of his mouth. 'The warehouse is underneath the arches at Vauxhall. It's a piece of cake getting in. Just a crappy old burglar alarm with wires sticking out everywhere. I had a good look last week. We cut those and jemmy the door. Wally's borrowed his brother's van. We need that to get the pills to the shed.'

Arthur had an allotment by the railway in Herne Hill that he never bothered with. Why bother growing your own when you worked at Covent Garden, where the fruit and veg just dropped off the shelves and into your voluminous pockets? he'd say. But he refused to give it up as it was the right of every Englishman to have a piece of land to work. That summer John and Billy had volunteered to tidy up the place, much to Arthur's amazement. That gave them access to the shed on the tiny patch of land. It was secured by a padlock to which John now had the only key. There was a narrow side street beside the allotments where they could park the van and so transfer the pills. Wally was an old mate. Another mod, he'd give them the use of his brother's old minivan in exchange for speed. Simple.

'What time we meeting him?' asked Billy.

'Ten. It won't get dark 'til then this time of year.'

'So what do we do now?'

'Go to the pictures. There's the new James Bond on at the Odeon. We can sit through it twice.'

Which they did.

At ten o'clock that night, John and Billy were waiting near the Oval tube station when Wally arrived in the van. Earlier that week John had dropped off a couple of pairs of gloves and two torches at Wally's place and they were waiting for them underneath the front seat. The two youths climbed into the tiny vehicle: John in the passenger seat, his friend in the back, moaning about the dirt that was getting on to his trousers. 'You'll be able to buy a dozen new pairs next week,' said John as the van drove off towards Vauxhall.

The job was as simple as John had said it would be. Once over the front fence, the alarm succumbed to the blades of the wirecutters, and the lock on the front door of the warehouse was almost laughably simple to break open. Once inside, John and Billy, with Wally at the door keeping watch for passing coppers, found the boxes full of jars of amphetamine tablets, one thousand per jar, one dozen jars per box. There were ten boxes in all. The two boys' heads swum at the thought. Then John found something else. By the light of his torch he saw a box marked 'Mandrax Tablets'. Mandies. The famed sleeping pill that was also reputed to be an aphrodisiac. 'A mandy makes 'em randy' was what he'd heard. And there were two boxes of them. One thousand to a box. The three of them swiftly transferred the twelve cartons to the little motor, then headed for Herne Hill.

There the transfer was quickly made and Wally took his payment of a thousand purple hearts. John thought it was a bit much, but a deal was a deal. At least it would keep Wally happy for long enough to give them a chance to move the swag again. An old mate or not, if Wally knew where the drugs were, the chances were he'd come back for more.

John and Billy watched as the tail lights of the minivan vanished up Denmark Hill and they shook hands. 'We've done it, mate,' said John. 'We're going to be rich.'

SIX

'And that was how it all started proper,' concluded John Jenner. 'I never really knew about all that.'

'You never asked.'

'I know. I was too full of myself. So what happened next?'

'Lots. I'll tell you another time. There will be another time, won't there?'

'Looks like it, don't it? Now I'm back in the bosom of hearth and home.'

'Yeah. You haven't seen your room yet. You hungry?'

'Not really. I'm still stuffed from that lunch.'

'Yeah, me too. But I've got to eat regular. Got to feed the cancer or else it gets angry and gives me grief.'

'I don't know how you can talk about it like that.'

'Because it's part of me. As much a part now as my eyes and ears.'

'But it's going to kill you.'

'Well something had to.'

'Does it scare you?'

'Terrifies me more like. Not the dying part, or the being dead. I don't think we go up in front of Saint Paul with his big book of what we did right or wrong. Mind you, if we do I'm destined for...' He held up his hand with the thumb down. '...I reckon you just go to sleep. Must be nice. I just hope you don't dream. Some of my dreams...' He didn't finish the sentence. 'No. What frightens me is the pain getting worse and not going away. Or even worse, dying alone. That's why I want you here. You and Martine and Chas. As much of my family as there is left.'

Mark felt tears sting his eyes again. 'You won't die alone, Uncle John.

53

Not whilst we're around.' But he felt he was getting in too deep and changed the subject. 'So who does the cooking these days? Not you, I bet.'

'Chas mostly.'

'Are you kidding me?'

'Not at all. When we're not out and about, which ain't often these days I'm afraid, he's in front of the cooking channel on cable. He loves it.'

'What about Martine?'

'Martine? You're having a laugh, aincha? She can cook all right, just like her mum. When she can be bothered, which ain't often. So all she does is wreck Chas's kitchen and leaves him to clear up. He curses her out.'

'I bet he does.'

'Anyway, I heard him come back just now. I'll get him to knock up something. Now come and see your room.'

They got up out of their chairs and went hunting for Chas. As promised he was watching a celebrity chef preparing a feast on a TV in the kitchen at the back of the house. Since Mark had last been around it had been extended and modified and looked like something out of a TV studio itself with a large central cooking range and shiny copper saucepans hanging from chrome rails. 'I'm impressed,' said Mark, looking round.

'So you should be,' remarked Jenner. 'Cost me an arm, a dick and a leg, this lot.'

'Worth it though, boss,' said Chas. 'Get you something?'

'Something light.'

'No worries,' and the huge man donned a stripy apron without sign of embarrassment and peered into the mighty fridge that dominated one corner of the room.

'Nothing for me thanks, Chas,' said Mark. 'I had so much at Tootsies, I don't think I'll ever eat again. There's leftovers in the hall by the way.'

'Just wait 'til you smell my cooking and you'll regret it,' said Chas.

'We'll be upstairs,' said Jenner and led the way back into the hall and up the main staircase that Mark remembered so well from his youth. When they got to the top, Mark hesitated outside the glossy white painted door.

'Go on then,' said Jenner. 'Take a look.'

'It's been a long time.'

'You keep saying that.'

'Because it's true.' Then he grasped the handle, opened the door and stepped back a dozen years.

The room inside was just as he remembered it. A single bed with a duvet cover decorated with the faces of Matt and Luke Goss, the twins in the teeny group Bros, dark red carpet, dark red curtains open overlooking the back garden that was salted with snow. Pop group posters on the walls, a small TV set, a record player, and all along one wall, thousands of records, a legacy from his uncle.

'Bros,' he said. 'What's all that about?'

'You liked them.'

'No I didn't. You bought me that to take the rise one Christmas and I wouldn't use it.'

'Yeah, OK. We stuck it on when you phoned.'

'You knew I'd come back.'

'Sooner or later.'

'You're a manipulative old sod, you know that.'

'So I've been told.'

Mark walked over to the shelves. 'And your records. I thought they'd all be gone.'

'Never. Some of them are worth fortunes.'

'I know.' Mark turned to the older man and hugged him tight. 'Christ, Uncle John. What happened to all those years?'

'They went, son. They just went. I had Martine clear her stuff out of the bathroom next door. She's got an en suite, but you know women. And we put all the necessaries in the cabinet. Razor and that.'

'I don't believe this.'

'I was just hoping, Mark. Just hoping.'

'Well, here I am.'

They stood together in the room for another minute, and then went back down to the living room. From the kitchen came the aromas of food cooking.

'Chas was right,' Mark said. 'That does smell good.'

'I told you. Chas has found his forté.'

'Didn't he ever find a woman?'

'I never knew he lost one.'

'You know what I mean.'

'I don't enquire too much about Chas's sex life. He comes and goes, but he's never got webbed up with anyone.'

'What'll happen to him?'

'When?'

'When something happens to you.'

'He'll be well looked after. So will Martine. So will you if you'll let me.'

'We'll see about that.'

They were interrupted when Chas came into the room, still wearing his apron and carrying a tray, the contents of which he used to set the table by the window. He went out again and returned with a plate of food. 'Omelette and salad,' he said. 'Nothing special.'

'Looks good,' said Jenner.

The big man looked down at him and smiled. 'The best,' he said, 'I'm going to have Tootsie's stuff for my supper.'

After he'd eaten, Jenner lit another joint and said. 'I'm going to turn in soon. I need my beauty sleep. You stay up as long as you like. Watch a film.' He pointed at a row of DVDs next to the widescreen TV in the corner. 'Got some good gangster ones there.'

'I bet you have.'

'American mostly, Brit ones are crap. That Guy Ritchie, what a wanker. Or listen to music. Just do what you like. It's liberty hall here.'

'Thanks, Uncle John.'

'Chas'll lock up. He'll wait for Martine. He don't sleep much these days. He'll make breakfast in the morning. Anytime you like. I sleep in.'

Mark was beginning to understand the seriousness of the illness that afflicted his old friend. In the silence that followed, Mark heard scratching at the door. 'What the hell's that?' he said.

'Get it will you, son,' said Jenner.

Mark went to the door and slowly opened it to reveal a scrawny old tabby standing outside. The cat opened its mouth and let out an almost silent yowl before limping in.

'It can't be,' said Mark. 'Is it? Lily?'

At the sound of her name, the cat raised its head, showing white, almost sightless eyes, and yowled again. 'Christ, it is,' said Mark. 'I thought she'd be dead and gone years ago. How old is she?'

'Twenty, twenty-one,' said Jenner. Those Burmese moggies live to a ripe old age.'

'Hazel's cat,' said Mark, closing the door and sitting again. 'That's amazing.'

Jenner's wife had loved Lily, who she'd saved from being destroyed by a neighbour with too many kittens, and she'd spoilt her rotten.

'I said I'd look after her, and I have,' said Jenner. 'She's almost blind, and a diabetic, but she still sleeps with me, and until her kidneys go and she starts pissing the bed, I won't have her put down. Though sometimes I think it would be kinder to do it.'

'She used to sleep with me sometimes,' said Mark.

'She's a bit of a tart is Lily. She'll sleep with anyone. If she tries it on again, kick her out. But don't kick her too hard, she's fragile.'

'Course not.'

The old cat made her slow way across the carpet and headbutted Jenner's leg. He picked her up and put her on his lap, relit his spliff, leant down and let out a mouthful of smoke. Lily lifted her head again, breathed it in, turned round and went straight to sleep. 'She loves a bit of draw,' said Jenner. 'Helps her kip. A bit like me.'

'I don't believe you, Uncle,' said Mark.

'Time for bed for us both,' said Jenner, and with that, he pushed himself to his feet, hoisting the cat over his shoulder. 'I'll see you tomorrow, son,' he said. 'It's been a good day. A hell of a good day.'

'I'm glad.'

'Too long coming though.'

Mark just nodded and looked up at his uncle. This once hard man. This

Jack the lad. Now old and racked with cancer, clutching his dead wife's cat as if it was a straw to save him from the freezing sea of his own fate.

'Goodnight then,' said Jenner.

'Goodnight, Uncle John.'

'You could just call me John, you know. That uncle business makes me feel ancient.'

'Force of habit.'

Jenner smiled and left the room.

After he'd gone, Mark mooched around the room that had changed little in the years he'd been gone. The DVDs were new, and the home cinema too, but otherwise things were much the same. He looked at the books on the shelves. Crime fiction mostly, and some autobiographies by London criminals. He smiled at himself, thinking that maybe John Jenner had fancied doing one of those himself. He opened the silver cigarette box and looked at the neatly rolled joints and was tempted for a moment, but he shook his head, closed the box and decided to go to bed himself.

He went back up to his old room. It was strange, more than strange to find himself there. But it was warm, the bed still fitted his contours when he laid on it and stared up at the familiar ceiling. After a few minutes he went to the bathroom next door which had always been his alone and found a new toothbrush and toothpaste, soap and flannel, laid out on the washbasin, razor and shaving cream in the mirrored cabinet. He looked at his reflection and smiled wryly. It had indeed, as John Jenner had said, been a hell of a day. He cleaned his teeth, relieved himself, washed his hands and went back to the bedroom where he undressed, slid under the Bros duvet and was soon asleep.

A noise awoke him sometime later. He had no idea what time it was. The door was open to allow light in from the hall and he saw that Martine was standing in the doorway. 'The prodigal returned,' she said, and he couldn't decide whether she was glad or sorry. Even from the other side of the room her perfume filled his head and he felt dizzy, although it might have been from the amount he'd had to drink during the day.

'Just for tonight,' he said. His throat was dry and his tongue felt huge in his mouth.

'No. You're back. I can tell.'

'Is that bad?'

'No. Dad needs someone.'

'What about you?'

'I'm a girl. It's not the same.'

'I'm sorry.'

'Don't be. It's not your fault. It's just the way it is.'

'Did you have a good time tonight?' he asked.

'Yeah. Not bad. Danced on the tables, that sort of thing.'

'What time is it?'

'What does it matter? You didn't wait up for me.'

'I didn't think you'd want me to.'

'You'd be surprised.'

'Maybe.'

'I used to do this years ago. Did you know that?'

'Do what?' He was confused.

'Creep into your room when you were asleep and watch you.'

'Did you?' Now he was genuinely surprised. 'Why?'

'Because you were beautiful. I don't think you knew how beautiful. That's what made it special. All my girlfriends at school had crushes on you.'

'Did they? I never knew.'

'You could be very thick sometimes.'

'I know.'

'So what happened, Mark? Did you take an ugly pill?' But there was no malice in her voice. He touched his face and felt the lines and the rasp of his beard.

'Life happened to me,' he said.

'It happened to all of us.'

'But it hasn't affected you the same.'

'Thank you, kind sir. Anyway, I'll let you get back to sleep. I didn't mean to wake you.'

'I'm glad you did.'

'Good. I loved you, you know.'

'What?'

'I was in love with you, just like all the other girls.'

'I never knew that either.'

'But then, things change don't they?' She wiggled her fingers and shut the door so that he was in darkness again, apart from the reflection from the snow outside. He slumped back on his pillow and blew out a breath. Jesus, he thought. What am I letting myself in for here?

SEVEN

Mark woke early. He rolled out of bed, checked the stairs for Martine and slipped quietly to the bathroom in his shorts. He didn't want to engage in another conversation with her and her sharp tongue without at least a cup of tea inside him, and preferably with his clothes on. He locked the bathroom door, made his ablutions, had a quick shower, shaved, and went back to get dressed. When he drew back the curtains he saw that it had snowed heavily in the night. The garden below looked beautiful with only a few bird and cat prints to spoil the pristine white.

He got dressed in yesterday's clothes, ignoring the fitted wardrobe which held God alone knows what fashion mistakes from the past and went downstairs to the kitchen. It was just before nine by his watch. Chas was *in situ*, watching the BBC news. The kitchen was warm and smelled of cooked bacon.

'Morning, Chas,' said Mark.

'Morning, Mark,' replied Chas. 'Sleep well?'

'Not bad. It was weird.'

'I expect it was. Tea or coffee?'

'Tea I think,' said Mark, unused to being waited on.

'Any breakfast?'

'Maybe later. Who's about?'

'Just you and me so far. Martine will be down soon and when she's gone to work I'll take the boss up a cuppa.'

'How is he, Chas?' asked Mark. 'How is he really?'

'He's dying.'

'So it's true.'

61

'Course it is. He wouldn't lie to you about a thing like that. It comes and goes. Remission, then bad times. Remission again. You ever known anyone with cancer?'

'No.'

'It's a filthy thing but he's coping with it. Seeing you's cheered him up.'

'Why didn't he get in touch before?'

'Scared you wouldn't come.'

'I'd walk over hot coals for that man.'

'You haven't seen him in years.'

'You know why.'

'You should've done.'

'I know,' said Mark. 'Don't you think I feel bad enough about it without you getting the cosh out?'

'OK, Mark. But I thought it should be said.'

'And now you've said it.'

'No hard feelings I hope.'

'What do you think?'

'I think it's good to see you back.'

'And I think it's good to be here.'

'Fair enough,' said Chas. And Mark knew that things were all right between them. Just like old times.

There were footsteps outside the kitchen and Martine entered, interrupting their conversation. Today she'd dressed warmly, with fur-lined boots.

'Will you look at the weather?' she said. 'I might get lost in a blizzard.'

'Not much chance of that with that nanny you're wearing,' remarked Chas. Martine's overcoat was bright scarlet with a fur collar. Red hair and red clothes often didn't work, but with Martine they did. In spades.

'Do you like it?' she asked, doing a spin. 'It's new.'

'Lovely,' said Mark.

'What about breakfast?' asked Chas.

'I'll get something at work.'

'No you won't. Take off the coat and sit. I'll get you some eggs.'

'Oh Chas, don't fuss. I was just leaving.'

'Don't "oh Chas" me. You're not going out on a day like this without something inside you.'

'I'll be late.'

'Blame the weather.'

'He's just like Mum used to be,' said Martine.

Mark laughed at the memory. She was right. Hazel had never let them out in the morning without something to eat, despite their protests. 'Breakfast is the most important meal of the day,' he said. Just like Hazel.

Martine squidged up her eyes at him. 'Don't you start,' she said. 'It's bad enough with Chas bossing me about.'

'I wouldn't dream of bossing you about, Martine,' said Mark.

'You'd better not.' But she did as she was told, took off her coat, hung it outside the kitchen door and came back for a plate of toast and scrambled eggs. When she was finished Chas said, 'Let me run you up to town.'

'No, Chas, you're all right. The roads'll be terrible. I'll get a bus to Brixton and go by tube.'

'You're quite the democrat these days, aren't you?' said Mark. 'Seems to me I remember you having to get driven everywhere when you were a kid.'

'I told you last night, times and people change. I work for my living and I enjoy every minute of it.'

'Selling cheap schmutter at inflated prices,' said Chas.

'The clothes at the shop are the best, Chas, and you know it. Stop ganging up on me, the pair of you.'

'OK, miss,' said Chas and gave her a hug as she got up to go. 'But call me if you need anything.'

'I will,' she said, kissed him hard on the cheek, wiggled her fingers at Mark just like she had done the previous night and left the room. A minute later they heard the front door slam and peace descended on the house.

'She's... er, quite a girl,' said Mark.

'They broke the mould. Only one like her was Hazel,' said Chas.

'Yeah.'

'You want some breakfast yourself now?'

'Yeah. Watching her eat's given me an appetite.'

'Full English?'

'Sounds good.'

Chas got out the frying pan and prepared eggs, bacon, mushrooms and fried bread which Mark wolfed down. When he was finished and the china and cutlery was in the dishwasher, Chas said, 'So what have you been up to all this time?'

'What a question,' said Mark. 'It's been eight years.'

'I know. I've been here all that time and watched the boss wishing you were too.'

'Come on, Chas. I had to go.'

'I know. But where?'

'Didn't Dev tell you?'

'I heard you kept in touch. Little Irish git never let on.'

'I told him not to. I'd've known.'

'I know you would've,' said Chas. 'We'd've been out for a visit.'

'I moved around.'

'Where to?'

'All over Europe.'

'How come?'

'I fell in with this bloke.'

'What bloke?'

Mark knew he'd have to tell at least some of the story, so he lit up a cigarette, took an ashtray from the stack on one of the units and began. 'When I left London I went down to the coast. Got on the ferry... You know, walk on, walk off, and went to France. I had my passport, but they hardly bothered with it. Then I caught a train to Paris. Hung out for a few days and got a job.'

'What kind of job?' asked Chas.

'In a bar. Started out cleaning up, washing up. You know the sort of thing. Casual. Then one night one of the barman didn't come in and I filled in for him.'

'You speak French now?'

'*Un peu.*'

'Do what?'

'A bit.' Mark held up his forefinger and thumb a half inch apart. 'It wasn't hard. Most of the people spoke English, though they don't let on until they get to know you. I made mistakes, but I learned. I was young and I think the bloke who owned the place fancied me.' He saw the old fashioned look on Chas's face. 'But don't worry, Chas, he didn't do anything about it. He had hot and cold running geezers up in his flat. He didn't need me.'

'Where did you live?'

'Got a room with one of the chefs. Mental. He was always out of his head on some designer drug or another. But when the tips started coming in I rented a room off of a customer who had a little house up in Montmartre. Fucking beautiful it was. High ceilings, roof terrace and just down the way from the bar. Life was good. Then I met someone.'

'A bird?'

'No. Another bloke. Old boy. Name of Cam. Mr Cam everyone called him. I never knew what his other name was, or if that was his first or last. He could've been sixty, could've been eighty. And he wasn't gay. He wasn't much of anything. Just a nice old bloke as far as I was concerned.'

'So what happened?'

'He used to come in the bar every night and sometimes lunchtime. Tiny bloke. Only about five foot tall. And… Well I never worked out what he was 'til he told me. I knew he was from the far east, but I had no idea where. Then one night we was rabbiting. He spoke English better than you and me, and he let on. Vietnamese he was. From the south. Pissed off when the Americans left. He'd been up to something dodgy, I found out later. Buying black market stuff from the Yanks. Petrol, weapons, anything. Anyway, he'd been to a French school when they were trying to occupy the country

65

before the Americans came, and was as good at French as he was at English, so he moved to Paris and set up in business.'

'What kind of business?'

'Monkey business. But at first he told me he was importing works of art. He looked the part too. White hair, smart suits, and spats would you believe. Anyway we got friendly. He loved the steak and chips in the bar and he was a good tipper. So one night I was locking up the place. Yeah, I got to be trusted enough to have the keys, and the old boy had been in, and when I came round into the alley at the back of the place to dump off some rubbish, there he was along with four other Asian blokes. But big blokes. And they're jabbering away at each other and I can see it's all about to go off. Now, I've been a good boy all the time I've been in Paris. Kept my nose clean. But I'm not going to have all this. I could've just pissed off but instead I get involved. The old boy tells me to leave it, but I don't. You know me.'

Chas nodded.

'And one of these other blokes gives me a shove and I shove back and away we go. Blimey, I've never seen anything like it. The old boy's like bloody Jackie Chan. Bish, bosh, he's off and we do for them.' Mark laughed at the memory. 'At least he does three and a half of them and I do half of one, and I'm on the floor covered in blood with my jacket all torn, and the old boy's standing there and his suit ain't even creased. So he picks me up and takes me round the corner to this little club I know nothing about, and he says, 'No cops,' and I say back that it would never occur to me to call them, and he gives me a funny little look but don't say nothing. And this club's full of Vietnamese too, and they start on at him because apparently they don't want any round eyes there. That's what they call us – round eyes. But he's as good as gold. He starts on at them in Vietnamese and must explain what happens, because after a minute they're all over me like a rash. Anyway the barman gives me a large brandy and then Mr Cam whizzes me upstairs to his flat.

'It turns out he owns the whole gaff, see. And there's this beautiful Vietnamese girl there. His granddaughter I find out later. Her name's

66

Lan. So she cleans me up and takes my jacket to mend where it's torn. Anyway, to cut a long story short, when I'm patched up, he calls me a cab and sends me home. The next day I'm as stiff as a board and call in sick. It's not a problem. But in the afternoon when I'm sitting in front of the telly trying to make head or tail of some old American film dubbed into French there's a knock at the door and it's him. He's bought me a big bag of fruit and a bottle of some Vietnamese rice wine and we sit down for chat.

'He tells me that the blokes who gave him a hard time are North Vietnamese gangsters trying to muscle in on his club which was why he wouldn't call the cops. And he's grateful for my intervention as he calls it. I tell him I'm sure he didn't need it the way he could handle himself, but he's still full of thanks and tells me if I need a doctor he'll cough for the bill. I tell him I'm fine, I've had worse, and end up telling him the story of why I left England. Not all of it mind. And suddenly he asks if I've ever killed anyone. Well, you can imagine that sort of puts the kibosh on the conversation there and then. Except I own up. I tell him yes I have, and he tells me he guessed. Can always tell. Which, as it goes, tells me a bit about him too. And he offers me a job there and then. He likes my bravery and loyalty he says. I just tell him I didn't like the odds, and he laughs. So he should've, as he could've sorted twice as many in my opinion without breaking a sweat. Import and export? I say and he laughs again. And that's when it all started.'

'Christ,' said Chas. 'Do you speak Vietnamese now and all?'

'*Di di mau,*' said Mark.

'What's that mean?'

'Piss off.' He laughed.

'And did you take the job?'

Mark nodded. 'Sure.'

'What was it?'

'He asked me to kill someone.'

Chas didn't speak for a moment, and when he did he said, 'And did you?'

Mark nodded. 'Sure. I'd had the practice and the money and hours were better than working in the bar.'

Chas nodded, then looked up at the kitchen clock. 'Blimey, is that the time? I'd better take the boss up his tea and see if he needs anything.'

'Times certainly have changed here, Chas,' said Mark as Chas boiled water and put tea in a pot.

'How so?'

'You used to be an enforcer. Now you're chief cook and bottle washer.'

'I do what needs to be done. But don't get the wrong idea. I can still do the business when necessary. I ain't gone soft because I've bought a cook book or two. No one should ever make that mistake. It could be fatal.' And with that he left the kitchen, tea cup on a tray, leaving Mark to think about what he'd said.

John Jenner came down later in his dressing gown, grey stubble on his cheeks.

'A good night?' asked Mark.

'Not too bad. Only about half a dozen trips to the pisser. That's good for me. What are you going to do today?'

'I'm going to shoot back to my place and pick up my stuff.'

'And then?'

'I'm going to have a think about what you said.'

'Good.'

'What about you?'

'I'm going to take the paper back to bed with me, do the crossword.'

'Still crosswords eh, Uncle?'

'It keeps my mind sharp. Will you call me later?'

'Course I will.'

And they left it at that.

In fact John Jenner had had a particularly bad night. Seeing Mark Farrow again had brought back a lot of memories. Some pleasant, some not so. And talking about Hazel had brought back the worst. She'd always been the lively one out of the two of them. The heart and soul of a party that lasted a lot of years. But then she'd started to slow down all of a sudden; the heart had gone out of her soul. But she refused to see a doctor, though Jenner nagged her rotten. It was only when she collapsed one day whilst out shopping in Oxford Street that she was forced to: an ambulance took her to Queen Mary's Hospital. When John Jenner arrived a couple of hours later, the cardiac consultant gave him the first of several bits of bad news. As far as they could tell at that early stage there was a problem with one of the valves in her heart and she needed immediate surgery. The valve was replaced with a mechanical one that ticked like a ten bob watch, but Hazel never really recovered. There was talk of a heart transplant, but even though John moved heaven and earth, the right match never turned up. And all the money in the world couldn't buy his wife's life back. Watching her die was the worst. Just as Mark had remembered the previous day in the restaurant. Watching the woman he loved fade to a shadow of her former self, her once lustrous red hair growing thin and dull and falling out in handfuls. And the light in her eyes slowly being extinguished.

John Jenner hated to admit it, but when the end came it was almost a relief. Hated to admit it, and hated himself for feeling that way. Feelings he'd never shared with anyone, but which came back to haunt him in the darkest hours of the night. And now, he was fading himself. 'Serves you right,' he said to himself as he slowly made his way back to his bed and the *Telegraph* crossword.

Mark Farrow drove to Canvey Island around noon. He'd rented a place there to lie low until Jimmy Hunter came out of prison. But the word that John Jenner needed to see him urgently had changed all that. Not that he was sorry. The place he'd rented was a dump, and he wouldn't miss it. By the time he left Tulse Hill, the snow had stopped and the roads had been salted.

The chip shop underneath his flat, if that wasn't too grand a title for the couple of rooms he inhabited, was doing a desultory lunchtime trade when he got there. He dragged open the warped old double doors in the alley at the back of the shop and parked the Range Rover next to an overflowing dumpster that stank of rotten fish even in the freezing cold. He sighed as he climbed the icy, metal flight of stairs to his door. The place might be rank, he thought, but at least I could get the car out of sight. It was probably the sharpest motor for miles, and although not strictly his property, he didn't want it stolen or damaged. Too much hassle.

He unlocked the door and slammed it behind him. The temperature in the flat was sub zero. There was no central heating, only a couple of ancient gas fires. He went into his living room and drew back the curtains, allowing the thin daylight into the room. He looked around in disgust as he shucked off his overcoat and muffler and threw them on to a chair. He struck a match and the fire came to life with a burp, as he dropped into his lumpy armchair and surveyed the room, contrasting the dirty, scored beige wood chip wallpaper, the thin carpet and mismatched furniture with the inside of his uncle's house. As the room warmed the window steamed and he went into the kitchen and put the kettle on. One mug, one plate, one knife, fork and spoon sat on the draining board by the sink. He found still fresh milk in the fridge, which he admitted was the one advantage of a freezing room. A teabag and sugar went into the mug and he brewed his tea, dropping the sodden bag into the Asda carrier that served as his dustbin and went back into the living room.

He looked through the few vinyl albums stacked against the wall, picked out an ancient copy of *Otis Blue*. It was an original American pressing on the yellow Volt label and would have been worth a fortune if not for the fact that the sleeve was torn and the grooves scratched, But Mark didn't care. He put it on the turntable of the ancient record player he'd picked up at a boot sale, side one, track one, and let the first few bars of *My Girl* fill the room, thinking as he did that there was probably a mint copy back at John Jenner's house.

He smiled to himself, sat back down and thought about what his uncle had told him. He knew it was time he got his life sorted out. He was just marking time there on Canvey. Hiding from his past, his parent's past, his surrogate uncle's past and everything that was happening in south London.

70

His time away had changed him. It would've changed anyone. He let his thoughts drift back.

When his father had been killed, Mark had been just a kid, his mother was in her early thirties and couldn't cope with what had happened. Suddenly losing the only man she'd ever loved, being at the centre of a notorious murder case, and being left to look after a child alone had been more than she could deal with. She'd never been strong. Billy had been the strong one in the family. And after all the fuss had died down, Jimmy Hunter given his life sentence and the case closed, she went from bad to worse. There was money. The Met made sure of that. Compensation and a full pension meant that Susie Farrow and her son wouldn't starve. In fact, if Susie had been forced by penury to look for a job, things might never have ended up the way they did. But a widow with a bit of money would always be the target for men. And men came and went until Bobby Thomas turned up and didn't go away again.

Bobby was a boozer who dabbled in drugs on the side. Nothing serious really. He liked a joint and maybe some coke at the weekend with the odd pill now and then. Nothing to get excited about. But when he was pissed up and speed ran through his veins he tended to get a bit violent. And Susie was no match for him. Nor was twelve-year-old Mark Farrow. He'd tried his best, but Thomas was a big man and loved to show just how big. Especially with women and children. Susie had been an orphan and never really got on with Billy's mum and dad, and Bobby Thomas didn't encourage any contact, until eventually they just faded out of Susie and Mark's life.

At Mark's father's funeral, John Jenner, just another big man in a dark suit and black tie who wouldn't go to the wake after the service because of the big police presence, had spoken briefly to him, and given him a plain white card with his name, address and telephone number printed on it. He'd told the boy he was an old friend of his dad, and if he ever needed anything, anything at all, he was to ring the number. Anytime, night or day. Just do it, the big man in the dark suit had said before he'd climbed into a green Jaguar driven by an even bigger man who wasn't introduced.

As Thomas's drug and alcohol consumption – financed mostly by Susie's money – increased, so the violence worsened. What had been just a few digs, the occasional slap and twisted arm, escalated. In the summer of 1985, Thomas and Susie got married. The beatings took on a new edge, and with them, Susie, encouraged by her husband, began to drink more, sometimes also joining him in his drug taking.

Mark was at his wit's end. His school-work, which had never been much cop, went from bad to worse. After one particularly bad weekend, he took the card that he had hidden on the evening of his father's funeral and called the number. A raspy voice, sounding like the creature from the black lagoon, answered after half a dozen rings and Mark almost hung up. Stutteringly he asked for the name on the card, and the voice demanded to know who was calling. Mark almost wet himself, and only the thought of his drunken mother, crying herself to sleep in the bedroom upstairs stiffened his resolve. He gave his name, the phone went down with a bang and after a minute, a softer, but still frightening voice took over.

Mark told the owner of the voice what was going on, and after a second's pause he was told to wait where he was. It didn't occur to him until years later that whoever he was talking to knew exactly where that was. Thomas was still snoring in front of the television when there was the sound of a powerful engine outside, a soft tap on the door and the two men from the cemetery, the driver, a man mountain who simply introduced himself as Chas, and the man in the dark suit now wearing a leather jacket and jeans were on the doorstep. With them was a redheaded woman wearing a black leather suit and high heels. Jenner called her Hazel and she was the most beautiful woman Mark had ever seen. For a second he felt disloyal to his mother for thinking that.

The next few minutes mapped out Mark's future. The woman went upstairs to the bedroom to see to Susie. John Jenner and Chas went and found Thomas. They dragged his comatose form out on to the back patio, Chas filled a vase with cold water from the sink and tossed it into Thomas's face. He came to with a start. When he saw the two men, with Mark in the background, he demanded to know what was going on.

Neither man spoke, just stared with disgust as he blustered about calling the police. Then Chas produced a sawn off baseball bat and proceeded to give Thomas a beating. His arms, legs, back and groin took the brunt of Chas's fury until Jenner stepped in to restrain him. Chas asked Mark if he wanted to give his stepfather a few licks, but he refused. They left Bobby Thomas groaning in agony on the floor and went into the kitchen where Mark stood trembling with a mixture of elation and fear whilst Chas and Jenner helped themselves to beers from the fridge. When Hazel came down she told them that the girl needed the hospital but wouldn't go.

She asked the boy if he wanted to get some things together and come with them, but Mark refused again, being terrified of what would happen when Thomas was alone with his mother. He was told not to worry, just to go and pack a bag. But he knew he couldn't leave her in pain, not even at the behest of the beautiful Hazel.

'John,' said Hazel.

'He's got to please himself,' said Jenner.

'We can't leave him here,' said Hazel.

'If that's what the boy wants.'

Before they left, Jenner went outside again and Mark saw him kneel beside Thomas and talk to him, his mouth close to Thomas's ear. He spoke for a long time. When Thomas nodded, Jenner rose and collected Hazel and Chas and they left. 'The offer's open,' he said before he closed the front door. 'Anytime. Nothing's going to happen to you now.'

'Thank you,' said Mark to their retreating backs before going upstairs to tend to his mother.

The atmosphere in the house was never the same again. Mark realised for the first time in his life that some things, once done, can never be undone.

The beatings ceased for a while, but as the bruises and the memory of that night faded from Thomas's body and mind, slowly and inevitably they started again. But he never touched Mark again.

One Sunday night a year later, Mark faced his mother and told her that he couldn't go on the way they were. 'He'll end up killing you, Mum,' he said. 'You know he will. Why do you let him do it?'

'No,' she replied, unsteady on her feet from two days of drinking, her once pretty face now ugly from the alcohol. 'He doesn't mean it. He loves me.'

Mark also learned that year that people saw and heard what they wanted to, and with the best intentions in the world, some people refused to be helped.

That night he did pack a bag, leaving most of his possessions behind. As midnight struck, he left the house for the last time and walked to all the way to John Jenner's, through a light rain that helped disguise the tears that were running down his face, the card he'd been given clutched tightly in his fist.

That night was one of the last times he ever saw his mother alive.

EIGHT

Not too far away from where Mark had eaten the breakfast that Chas had prepared for him, another man was also considering his past and future. But he hadn't enjoyed scrambled egg, bacon and mushrooms on a cheerful checked tablecloth in a warm kitchen. Instead he'd eaten porridge and toast courtesy of Her Majesty in a miserable dining room inside Brixton prison. The same grim set of buildings that John Jenner had checked from the Range Rover the previous day as Mark had driven him down Brixton Hill on their way to lunch. After breakfast, Jimmy Hunter sat in his chilly cell, looking out over a courtyard where the clean snow was already a filthy grey. Everything around the prison soon took on that colour whatever the weather, and Hunter had seen almost twenty years of the seasons changing from one cell or another the length and breadth of the country.

At first they'd moved him often, the authorities taking a grim pleasure in shifting him from prison to prison. The Isle of Wight, Birmingham, Manchester, Carlisle, Newcastle. The list was as long as the number of penal institutions in the United Kingdom. Always at short notice. Sometimes in the dead of night he'd be woken up by the screws, told to gather his few possessions, slung into the back of a barred van and driven to his new home. But eventually the moves had become less and less frequent. Times changed. Staff changed. And there were other, more recent villains to be sorted.

Not that Jimmy had been totally forgotten. He was a cop killer after all. A mad dog shooter who had nearly died himself after being shot three times just down the road from where he now sat.

He recognised a certain irony in that. The policemen who'd fired without challenging him that morning in 1982 had wanted him dead. He knew that. It stood to reason. He'd killed one of their own. One of his own if the truth be known. At least he had been one of his own when Jimmy had run with John Jenner and his mob. They'd never been nicked. That was how Billy Farrow could change horses in midstream. There was no record of his crimes and misdemeanours. Jimmy had thought that Jenner would use his knowledge of Billy against him, but Jenner stayed loyal to his old mate. Mug. But when it was just between the two of them that morning in Brixton market, Jimmy couldn't resist putting him away. He could still see Farrow's hand raised as if to ward off the shot, but you didn't ward off the contents of a shotgun cartridge loaded with double ought at point blank range. The force of the shot had chopped off Farrow's hand at the wrist before blowing a hole in his chest big enough for a cat to walk through. He hadn't stood a chance.

The copper who'd shot Jimmy had knelt over him as he lay, bleeding in the gutter next to the body of DC Billy Farrow and told him to die. He remembered the face looming over him saying. 'Jimmy, you bastard. We've called an ambulance, but it'll be too late. You're done for, you fucker.' Then he'd kicked him.

But that copper had been wrong. Even with three holes in him, Jimmy Hunter had refused to roll over and let his life slip away. One bullet had gone straight through his left thigh, exiting out of his leg without touching bone. Another had gone through his shoulder, smashing his collar bone as it went. That shoulder still ached on cold mornings like this. The third was the worst. The one that should have ended his life. A gutshot by a bullet that had run around inside him and had to be dug out by a stream of surgeons at King's College Hospital. He still had the scar. A second belly button about three inches to the right of the original.

Twenty years, he thought. Twenty years, and now his release date was in sight. By the spring he'd be out. Full sentence served. Jimmy had been up in front of several parole boards over the years, but his attitude and his behaviour inside had always resulted in a knock back. But now there was nothing they could do to prevent his freedom as long as he kept his nose clean. But then, a few months inside was still a long sentence. Prison time wasn't like time outside. An hour could seem like a day behind bars. A day like a year, as the second hand on his battered alarm clock slowed in front of his eyes and he could hardly see movement of it at all. Outside time could fly by unnoticed. Like those early days with Marje, when her dad had forbidden her to see her bad boy boyfriend. Those minutes they'd managed to snatch together when their love was new had flown by.

He still thought of Marje a lot, although she was two years dead. He'd been in Belmarsh then, down Woolwich way, and the funeral had been in Norwood cemetery. Jimmy Hunter wasn't a sentimental man. Never had been much, and what sentiment he'd held on to had been leeched by his time in jail. But Marje had been a good wife. It was him that had let her down. What woman could be expected to wait the twenty years the judge at the Bailey had given to Jimmy Hunter? She'd loved Jimmy and she'd loved the son and daughter he'd given her. In the early years of his sentence she'd followed his wagon from prison to prison, spending what little money he'd left her on train fares to see him. She brought their children with her. Dragging the bewildered boy and girl from town to town, from visiting room to soulless visiting room.

Then one day she'd come alone. She'd told him they wouldn't be coming any more. Told him she'd met someone else. A quiet man. An honest man who was prepared to give all three a new life. He received the divorce papers in prison and signed them in his own blood. At first he'd sworn vengeance, but as the years passed it had seemed less important, although he often wondered how the children had grown. He'd never even known the name that Marje had taken, and whether the children had taken it too, although nothing was ever mentioned about formal adoption. He imagined it was because, then, he'd have to know the identity of the man who'd stolen his family. But as his sentence shortened he became determined to find them upon his release. He didn't really know why. It had been a surprise when the governor at Belmarsh had summoned him for an interview and told him that his son had phoned with the information that his former wife was dead. There was no other message, and his request to attend the funeral was denied.

It was almost ten as he lay on his bunk thinking. Time for his coffee. Where was that fucking Terry the Poof? He'd been getting slack lately. Spent too much time on the landing whispering to his 'ginger' mates and comparing tattoos. If he was giving it out to anyone else there'd be trouble. Or if he was back on the smack.

That was the trouble with sex inside. Too many of these young kids who gave it up in exchange for being looked after by just one con were hooked on class A. And there weren't enough needles to go round. Or condoms, for that matter. Billy had long ago given up penetrative sex with his ladyboys. He'd seen too many hard cons gone skeletal with AIDS to risk that. And besides, he was no shirtlifter. But a man had needs, and twenty years without a woman was a hard thing to bear. He laughed to himself at his little joke. It had taken him a long time before he'd started using boys. Years. The first one had been a cellmate at Strangeways. Not that the boy should've been there anyway. It was a hard man's jail. That joke again. Jimmy had been in the fifth year of his sentence when he'd been moved there from Swansea. The kid had been pissing himself at the thought of sharing a cell with a lifer. Jimmy ignored him at first, even when the kid offered to slop out for him, make sure his clothes were cleaned and ironed at the prison laundry where he worked and even change his library books for him. But it was the night the boy everyone called Lucy let his long hair down and put on full make up and a pair of white cotton ladies knickers that changed Jimmy's life.

At first he laughed, then he got angry when he felt his penis harden at the sight of Lucy on the cell floor doing calisthenics until his white body shone with sweat. He grabbed the kid by the throat fully intending to beat the living daylights out of him, but instead allowed him to rub at the hardness in Jimmy's trousers, then release his cock and suck him off, all the time looking up at him with his soulful brown eyes until he came. Jimmy was furious with himself for allowing Lucy to smear his penis with lipstick and did give the boy a good hiding. The same sort of hiding he gave him every time their tryst was repeated, which was often.

But Lucy was long gone, as was Alphonse, a black boy from the Leeward Islands doing time for mugging old ladies, Poppy, a scouser, and so many others. Jimmy had all but forgotten their names. Terry the Poof was the latest, a car thief from Reading who was going to be in big trouble if he didn't show up soon with Jimmy's coffee in a china cup, not a thick mug. If he's out scoring, thought Jimmy, I'll do for the little bastard.

Not that he hadn't tried drugs himself. On the out he'd just had a bit of smoke and the occasional spot of speed. Who hadn't given that a go in the 60s and 70s? But inside, over the years, it had been just about everything. Acid, smack, coke and, recently, ecstasy. There were other more powerful drugs going the rounds too – names like Ketamine, angel dust and horse trancs. Everything under the sun and some that rarely saw the light of day. But Jimmy had packed it all in a few years back. Too many casualties.

And soon he'd be free. Not a young man admittedly. The next biggun was 6-0. But he was still fit. Still got some lead in his pencil, and when he got out, there were some scores to settle.

He smiled at the thought, then his smile dropped.

Where the hell was that bloody coffee?

NINE

U nder the muddy sky of that January day, there were a lot of people thinking about the past and the present. Maybe it was the time of year, or maybe it was a premonition of things to come. Up the road from Brixton prison, inside an office in Streatham Police Station, Detective Sergeant Sean Pierce was at it too. His computer was down, and he was kicking his heels waiting for it to reboot, passing the time doodling the stick figure of a hanged man on his pad and letting his mind wander. Twenty years, he thought. And now the bastard's going to come out. And what will we all do then? Everything's a lie, he thought. Even my sodding name. But he and his mother and sister had happily taken it when Tom Pierce had asked Marjorie Hunter to marry him. Not everyone would've done that. Not married a cop killer's wife and taken on his two brats. And brats they'd certainly been, him and Linda. But then, who could blame them? Years of being teased by their schoolmates for being the children of a murderer had made them what they were.

So when Tom Pierce had come along and courted Sean and Linda's mother, they'd almost bitten his hand off. Tom was steady, you see. Working for the gas board at their offices in Croydon. A decent house and a decent car. Regular money and even a Christmas bonus. A job for life he'd told them. He'd believed that and so had they. But that had been the old days. After Tom had been pensioned off at fifty-five as too old for the new technology, he'd barely lasted another couple of years before dropping off his perch.

And then Marjorie had died. As much from a broken heart as cancer, Sean believed. He hadn't thought she'd really loved Tom when they'd married, but sometimes love can grow on the stoniest of ground.

The brother and sister had survived. Sean had joined the police under the name of Pierce. Why not? It was his name. And he was honest, was Sean. Sometimes too honest for his own good. It wasn't his fault his father had been a thief and a murderer. This was his way of making up for James Hunter's bad deeds. And then Linda had married Andy Spiers, another good man with a regular job, a decent house and a decent wage. He'd worked for a multinational company on the sales and marketing side. Then, on his way to a big meeting up north, the driver of a highsided truck owned by another multinational had fallen asleep at the wheel of his vehicle, swerved over to the overtaking lane and swatted the car, in which Andy Spiers had been a passenger, then travelled through the central reservation and head on into a Rover 75 saloon speeding towards them. Only the driver of the truck survived the multi-vehicle pileup that followed. Sixteen dead all told. It had been headlines for a day, page five for two more, then more or less forgotten after that. Linda had a pension from Andy's firm, his life insurance, and mortgage protection had paid off the house. The truck driver's firm had paid big compensation out of court, not wanting their company name smeared all over the papers again. Financially she was secure. But emotionally? Sean didn't know.

After the accident, he'd temporarily moved out of the police section house and lodged with her and her kids, Luke and Daisy. A flat over the garage in the house in Purley. But what had started out on a day to day basis seemed to have become permanent. Sean didn't mind in the least. Lodged. Blimey, he thought. We've been lodged together as long as I can remember.

But what will happen when Jimmy Hunter gets out? wondered Sean. Will he just vanish into the world of social services and cheap bedsits, or will he come looking for us? And what will we do if he does?

Being a copper, Sean was well aware of his father's movements over the last few years. But, as no one on the force knew of his history, he'd had to be discreet. Even when his mother had died and he'd telephoned Belmarsh to let the governor know, he'd not given his new name. Christ, he went hot and cold at the thought of anyone finding out who he really was. It wouldn't look too good in his police personnel file. Not that he'd have one if the news did get out. Just a big RESIGNED written in thick black letters.

In truth he didn't know why he'd bothered to let his father know at all. Just a kind of closure, he supposed. And at the funeral he'd half expected Jimmy to turn up dressed all in black. Not that he could remember much about Jimmy Hunter, having been just a boy when he'd gone inside for the last time. His mother had often told him there was a close resemblance between them, and sometimes, when he shaved in the morning, he would wonder just how close. All he could recall was a big, rough man who smelled of tobacco who would lift him up in his muscular arms and swing him round the room whilst his mother begged him not to drop the boy. And Linda could remember even less when they spoke about him, which wasn't often.

Sean continued to doodle on his pad. The hanged man motif over and over again, until he noticed what he was doing and ripped the sheet off the pad and threw it in the wastepaper bin.

And finally there was John Jenner. Up in his bedroom in the house in Tulse Hill, stroking the sleeping cat beside him. He too thought back over forty years.

He wondered about the story he'd told Mark the night before, and laughed at the memory until he began to cough and he cursed the disease that was slowly but surely stealing his body away from him. But he wouldn't fight it. He'd learnt to live with it instead. Like he'd said to Mark, it was a part of him. Even though it was killing him, and itself with him. Ironic. He hated reading in the papers about people who had 'lost their battle with cancer' as the obits put it. Fuck 'em. Most of them wouldn't know a battle if it jumped up and bit their leg. Never fought a battle in their lives. Not like him and his crew. Jesus, but we were the lads, he said to himself, as he laid down the unfinished crossword and his pen. He'd only just started the story of the little firm he'd built up from scratch with Billy Farrow, before Billy made his life changing career move from one side of the law to the other.

It started in the old Marquee in Wardour Street. He and Billy were still punting the pills they'd stolen when someone decided to rip them off. John and Billy and an older man, still trying to be seriously mod but lacking both the hair and the style to get away with it, were crammed into the last stall in the malodorous toilets of the club and the older man, a geezer from Hackney called Maurice Wright, had a small handgun stuck into John's side. 'Fuck me,' said Billy. 'Is that real?'

'As real as can be,' said Maurice. 'Now, this is my turf, and if you come in here flogging cut-price pills again I'll kill both of you.'

John felt his stomach lurch and hoped that he didn't disgrace himself by soiling the seat of his brand new beige cotton flares from Lord John.

'Fuck off, Maurice,' he said. 'You ain't got the bottle.'

Maurice cocked the hammer of his pistol and asked. 'You want to find out? Now I want what you've got on you, then the pair of you will fuck off out of Soho for good.'

'No chance,' said John.

'Listen, cunty,' said Maurice. 'I'll use this if I have to. So why don't you just give them up, and the cash you've nicked off me, and we can all part friends.'

Grudgingly John took out an envelope containing about a hundred doobies and a wad of ten shilling and one pound notes and handed them over.

'Nice,' said Maurice. 'Very nice. Now, like I said, piss off out of here and don't come back.'

'See you later, Morry,' said John, apparently not scared at all of the gun stuck in his ribs.

'Not if I see you first.'

The two boys came out of the stall, through the club and into the warm air of Wardour Street that was still twenty degrees cooler than inside the packed club.

'Fucking terrific,' said Billy.

'Not to worry,' said John. 'Plenty more where they came from.'

'I nearly shit myself.'

'Me too, but it'll be his turn next,' said John.

'We ain't coming back here,' said Billy, who, although no coward, had not been happy to see a gun involved in their little business.

'Ain't we?' said John. 'Don't you believe it.'

'What do you mean?' asked Billy.

'You'll find out,' replied John. Billy didn't like the expression on his friend's face. In the orange light of the street lamps it looked like that of the Devil himself.

'Tell us.'

'Saturday. Dave Clark Five at the Tottenham Royal.'

'So?'

'So we go.'

'But Maurice'll be there.'

'Yeah.'

'With his mates.'

'Yeah.'

'And he's got a fucking gun.'

'So?'

Billy stopped and grabbed John's arm. 'So he's warned us off...'

'Fuck his luck. Are you with me?'

'Course I am. No question.'

'Then don't worry, son,' said John, pulling his friend close and looking him in the eyes. 'We're fucking minted.'

'Yeah, you're right,' said Billy. 'Bleedin' magical, that's us. Fuck Maurice's luck, he doesn't know who he's dealing with here.' And the pair lost themselves in the bright lights, almost dancing along the pavement as they went.

John bought his first gun that weekend. He got it from an old soldier who ran a pawnbroker's shop in Lewisham. He told John he had liberated it during the First World War from an officer he'd killed after he kept trying to send him and his mates over the top at Ypres. John knew it was that old but didn't believe the story. The man sat behind the counter of the dingy emporium dressed in a filthy, food-stained sweater and trousers that smelled of piss. He had half a dozen cats and they slunk around John's legs as the two men, one just a boy really, the same age as the pawnbroker would have been at the time of the story he told, talked. The rumours locally were that, if the women of the parish need to claim their belongings but didn't have the wherewithal, then they could take the old man's cock out of his trousers and suck him off. Then they got the goods and the cash too. John couldn't believe that any woman could be that hard up. But the story persisted until the shop burnt down one night in 1969, and the old man and several of his cats perished.

The revolver was a Webley & Scott .455 calibre Mark III Government Model with a seven and half inch barrel and hinged frame. It needed special ammunition made only by Webley themselves. The bullets looked as ancient as the seller, but he assured John they still worked. John didn't think to ask how he'd know. There were six in the gun and he had six spare. The whole deal was available for a bargain price of fifty quid, a fortune. John did the deal on the Saturday morning of the Dave Clark Five concert. He shuddered as the old man's hands touched his, and the cats rubbed up against his trousers. But a gun was a gun, and as soon as the transaction was done he fled back home.

He showed Billy the pistol in his bedroom when he arrived. It was massive, and fully loaded weighed almost three pounds. 'Fucking hell,' said Billy. 'Are you sure? If we get nicked with that we'll go down.'

'Then we won't get nicked then,' said John. 'This is groovy. It'll show that fucker Maurice.'

'Not 'alf. Are you going to use it, John?'

'Not much point not to,' replied John.

'But you ain't going to kill him?'

'No, you silly sod. Just hurt him bad.'

'Christ, mate, this is serious.'

'So's being scared to go up west,' said John.

'Yeah,' said Billy. 'That won't do at all.'

'We need a motor,' said John. 'How about Wally?'

'If he's about.'

'Go and give him a call, will ya mate?' The Jenner household, like so many at the time, not only had an outside lavatory, but it also did not have a private telephone. Wally's dad, being something in the city, did.

Billy went out to the nearest callbox and John unloaded the gun. Being something of an aficionado of crime books and films, he cleaned the gun as well as he could with what was available in the house. Just as well, he thought, as he pushed a lump of cotton wool on the end of one of his mother's knitting needles through the barrel and dug out what looked like an ounce of muck. The last thing I need is for this bloody thing to blow up in my hand.

Billy came back with good news. For a fiver, plus ten bob for petrol, Wally would chauffeur them to to Tottenham, wait and return.

'Terrific,' said John, tucking the Webley inside the waistband of his jeans and trying a fast draw which snagged the front sight of the gun in his belt. 'Billy. Tonight you and me are going to make history.'

And make it they did.

The shoot out in the Tottenham Royal made the front pages of Monday's papers, and John and Billy's reputation for ever.

Wally drove them up to north London in his Minivan. All three boys were flying on purple hearts and John had bought a bottle of vodka and some Cokes and doctored the soft drinks with the liquor, which was passed around the van until all three were drunk.

'Want me to come in?' asked Wally when they'd parked the vehicle at the back of the dance hall.

'No,' said John. 'This is our job. You just wait here.'

'How long?'

'As long as it takes.'

'Got any fags?'

John passed over a half empty packet of Bristol, today's cigarette, if the television adverts were to be believed.

'A light?'

'Don't you ever buy your own?'

'Not if I can help it.'

John felt around in his pockets and found a book of matches and tossed them into Wally's lap. 'Want me to smoke it for you too?' he asked.

'That's all right, mate,' replied Wally with a big grin as he lit up. 'I can manage.'

'Fine,' said John. 'Just be here.'

'I will. You owe me five quid, remember.'

John and Billy exited the car and joined the throng queuing to hear the last local performance of the 'Tottenham Sound'. The Dave Clark Five were due back in America where their popularity at that time, as one of the top three British invasion bands, was huge. The ratio of birds to blokes inside was about five to one and the smell of so many perfumes made the boys wink at each other as they squeezed through the crowd, rubbing up against as many girls as they could on their way to the ticket booth.

They paid their six and sixpence each and were soon inside the massive interior of the hall.

'Maurice always hangs out by the bar,' said John. 'Near the gents so he can do his business inside.'

'That's where I like to do my business too,' said Billy with a grin. 'Inside the gents.'

'Shut up, you prick,' said his friend. 'Be serious. I'm going to shoot that cunt tonight, and fuck knows what'll happen then.'

'Just don't kill the bastard, that's all,' said Billy.

'Fuck off. I already told you. I'll shoot him in the leg. I just want to frighten the cunt.'

'Don't forget he's got a gun himself.'

'I won't, stupid. But will he use it?'

Billy was suddenly terrified. He worshipped his friend and couldn't think what life would be like without him. 'You'll be careful won't you? This ain't a film.'

John winked at him, but didn't know if he'd seen it in the light from the massive mirrorball that hung from the ceiling. It turned slowly in the heat from the dance floor. 'Don't you worry about me, son,' he said. 'I'm just going to give the sod a fright. I'll teach him to nick our stuff.'

'And our money,' interjected Billy.

'And the dosh. Now go and get us something to drink while I take a wander. I'll meet you back here in ten minutes, all right?'

'All right,' said Billy and began to fight his way through the scrum in front of the bar.

The drinks of choice that night were gin and orange squash (no ice) for the females and light ale for the blokes. Billy caught the eye of a tasty looking barmaid dressed in a short skirt and a pink fluffy jumper that showed off her best assets to the max, and yelled for two lights over the hubbub of Billy Preston on the sound system. She produced them and he gave her a bunch of change and pushed his way backwards out of the crowd. There was no sign of John, so he put his bottle on the shelf that surrounded one of the doric columns that held up the Royal's roof and found his cigarettes. He lit one up and checked out the talent. John could look after himself.

Meanwhile, John Jenner had spotted Maurice in his usual spot, surrounded by his mates and their girls eager to get smashed on Maurice's stash. He too pushed himself through the throng and tapped Maurice on the shoulder. 'Blimey,' said the older man. 'Fancy seeing you here, Johnny.'

'Got a minute, Maurice?'

'For you, anytime. No hard feelings about the other night I hope.'

'Not one. I just want to talk business.'

'Spot on, son. Come into my office,' and they both made their way into the gents. 'So what's it to be?' asked Maurice when they were inside, alone except for a solitary mod emptying his bladder into the urinal.

'I was thinking about a partnership,' said John. 'I've got a lot of gear.'

'So I heard. That place in Vauxhall wasn't it?'

'Never mind,' said John as the mod did up the zipper of his purple jeans and with a grin to Maurice left the lavatory without washing his hands.

'So?' said Maurice.

'You done us up the other night,' said John.

'Yeah. Sorry about that. But you kids gotta learn.'

'Maurice, you're a cunt, and I don't like you,' said John pulling the pistol from under his jacket. 'In fact I've come up here to tell you that if you stick your nose in my business again I'm going to shoot it off.'

'You're kidding.'

'No. And you remember what I said about no hard feelings?'

'Yeah.'

'I lied.'

And John pulled the trigger.

The explosion was the loudest sound he'd ever heard. He'd not had a chance to try the pistol out and had just trusted the old man in the pawnshop. Trusted him that the gun would work. Trusted that the bullet would fly, and fly it did. Straight into Maurice's leg and out through the other side jetting a spout of blood across the white tiled walls of the toilet, and the recoil from the antique firearm almost took John's hand off at the wrist.

'You fucker!' screamed Maurice as his leg gave way and he fell to the floor. 'You dirty little fucker!'

'That's the difference between you and me, Mo,' said John, his ears ringing from the report. 'You just show your gun. I use mine. And if I ever, ever, see you again anywhere where I'm doing business, I'll finish the job.'

And without another word, he spun on the Cuban heel of his Beatle boot, left the toilet where outside Dave Clark and his band were just hitting their stride through *Glad All Over*, and the beat of the bass drum had drowned out the sound of the shot. He found Billy, and steered him through the crowd of dancing fans, outside into Tottenham High Street and to Wally's waiting Minivan.

'What happened?' Billy asked as the small van sped through the streets towards the river and south London beyond. 'What happened?'

'I shot the fucker, didn't I?' replied John proudly, although his hands were shaking so much he could hardly light the cigarette from the packet Wally had left on the dashboard. 'It was just like fucking *Shane*.'

'Fucking hell,' said Billy. 'You're fucking mad, John.'

'Not half as mad as him.'

'Did you kill him?'

'I only shot him in the leg.'

'That could still kill him,' said Wally, who was also something of a connoisseur of American crime films and pulp fiction.

'Do me a favour,' said John. Then laughed. 'Fucking too bad if it does.'

'Did you get our money back?' asked Billy.

Shit, thought John. I forgot all about that.

'No,' he said after a minute. 'I said you'd pop round and collect it.'

TEN

Mark stayed in his flat for the rest of the afternoon, surrounded by the smell of stale chip fat, his ancient record player and portable TV his only companions. In fact, they'd been his only companions since he'd moved there a few weeks previously. During those weeks no one but him had passed through the doorway. But that was nothing new. For the past few years his life had been lived in a succession of apartments of varying degrees of luxuriousness – or lack of it – alone with no friends or lovers. This was probably the worst, but he'd needed to conserve his financial resources as he waited for Jimmy Hunter's release. The last Christmas had been the most miserable that he could remember, with a frozen turkey dinner for one his only concession to the season. And on New Year's Eve he'd gone to bed at ten with a bottle of brandy, a pack of cigarettes and BBC Radio Essex for company.

Twilight came early that January day, and Mark thought back to the Christmases he'd spent with John, Hazel, Martine and Chas down in south London. He'd been happy then. Or at least as happy as he could ever remember being. Not that happiness had ever been a big part of his existence; it had always seemed just out of reach. Something that other people experienced, but which had always eluded him, like that pot of gold at the end of the rainbow.

The Jenners' house had always been warm and cosy, with a massive Christmas tree twinkling in the living room, under which mysterious boxes kept appearing. Hazel had loved wrapping parcels, making them bright and colourful with different papers and ribbons. Almost too good to open, John Jenner had always remarked. Not that it stopped Mark and Martine ripping them to shreds early on Christmas morning, before the grownups were fully awake. Then Hazel would make breakfast before getting down to the serious business of preparing the lunch. And what lunches they were. Always enough to feed the five thousand, with some to spare.

Mark wondered what Christmas was like there without her now. There'd only been a couple afterwards when he'd been around, and cheerless celebrations they had been. No doubt these days Chas cooked a feast, but there would always be memories and an empty chair at the dining table. Maybe two.

Mark found a bottle of cheap scotch in his cupboard and sat in the ratty armchair drinking until it was almost too dark to see. It was Make Your Mind Up Time and he knew it. He could go back to London and do what John wanted or he could vanish again, this time for good. There was no middle way now that he and John had made contact again. And John needed Mark's help, just as the older man had given him so much help in the past. He had money enough to go and get somewhere warm. But what would he do there?

'Bugger,' he said aloud at last. 'It's time to shit or get off the pot.' But he knew, as he'd known since he had spoken to John, that there was really only one answer he could give.

When the bottle was empty, and night completely covered Canvey Island, he pulled his phone from out of his overcoat pocket, switched it on, saw there were no messages, and selected John Jenner's number on the memory. The phone rang once, twice, three times, before he heard John's voice say, 'Jenner.'

'Uncle John,' he said.

'Hello, Mark. How's tricks?'

'Not so dusty.' It was an old routine they'd used for years. 'You in tonight?'

'Yeah.'

'Then tell Chas to break out the fatted calf, I'm coming home.'

There was a long silence.

'Uncle John, you there?'

'I'm here.'

'Well?'

'How long you going to be?'

'I've just got to pack up here. There's not much. Bugger all in fact. I think I'll leave most of it for the binmen.'

'You're sure?'

'Course I am. You knew you only had to ask.'

'People change. I wasn't sure at all.'

'Whatever. I'm on my way.'

'I'll leave a light in the window.'

'I'll call when I'm close. And one thing, Uncle John…'

'What?'

'Get rid of that bloody Bros duvet.'

'It's as good as gone.'

'I'll see you later then.'

'Look forward to it.' They broke the connection.

Mark shoved his few clothes into a battered leather bag, then looked round the flat. Like he'd said, there wasn't much. He flicked through his few albums, then shook his head. Fresh start, he thought, and abandoned the lot: records, record player, TV and the contents of the fridge and cupboards. He switched off the fire and lights and, without looking back, took the front door key down to the chippie and lodged it with the girl behind the counter. 'Tell the landlord I got an offer I couldn't refuse,' he said to her. 'I'm paid up 'til the end of the month and he can have what I've left for the inconvenience.'

She was a sweet thing, although not very bright, and she'd harboured certain feelings for the handsome, sad looking man with the brilliant eyes who now and then popped in for cod and chips and a pickled onion. 'Will we see you again?' she asked as she dished out a fish cake to a waiting customer.

''Fraid not, love,' replied Mark, and he winked at her. 'Be good.' And he walked out into the freezing night, opened the yard doors, aimed his remote at the Vogue, got in, started it up and drove off in the direction of London, leaving them open behind him.

Bloody hell, he thought. What am I getting into?

It was late by the time he got to London and the roads were slick with ice, making driving dangerous, even for a 4WD, but he was in no hurry. He knew that as soon as he walked through the door of the house in Tulse Hill, nothing would ever be the same again for him or for its occupants.

When he reached the top of Jenner's street, he stopped, selected the number on his mobile and the phone was answered in a second. 'Let down the drawbridge, Uncle John,' he said. 'I'm just up the road.'

'Flash your lights at the front,' came the reply, which Mark did and the gate swung open. The black Mercedes, or one similar, was still parked across the street, its windows misted by the occupants' breath, but they made no move. Mark parked his car, grabbed his bag and walked to the already open front door and went inside. The gate closed behind him with a clang of metal on metal. Could be the condemned cell, he thought briefly, but dismissed the thought as quickly as it came.

John Jenner was waiting in the hall and they embraced and Mark felt such a wave of nostalgia sweep over him that he had to swallow hard. 'Welcome home properly, Mark,' said Jenner with a catch in his voice. 'I knew you'd come.'

'You know me too well.'

'I don't really know you at all these days, Mark. But that'll change I hope. Come inside and get warm. Everyone else is in bed. I've been waiting up for you.'

Mark did as he was told, leaving his coat in the hall, and he sat on the couch in front of the fire as John Jenner poured two large brandies. He passed one to Mark, sat opposite him and they toasted each other. 'So where do we start, Uncle?' asked the younger man. 'What do you want me to do?'

'I've got an easy one for you first,' said Jenner. 'A little pickup job.'

'Fair enough. On my own, or with Chas?'

'All Chas wants to do is cook these days, whatever he says. He's getting old. He's all right as a driver, but anything else…'

'He sorted out Martine's old man, didn't he?'

'This is a bit different.'

'All right, Uncle, I know. A bit dodge, is it?'

'Could be.'

'Shit. Talk about throwing me in at the deep end. What is it I'm collecting?'

'Does it matter?'

'Course it does. I've got to know what's what.'

'The usual. Just a bit of gear.'

'Smack?'

'Coke.'

Mark nodded. 'Whereabouts?'

'Little Chef on the the A33 towards Basingstoke.'

'When?'

'Tomorrow afternoon. One o'clock.'

'Christ, that soon. You were pretty sure of yourself, weren't you?'

'No. Just hoping.'

'And what would've happened if I hadn't come back?'

Jenner shrugged. 'I'd've found somebody.'

'What, overnight?'

'Or I'd've gone myself. It don't matter, does it? You're here now. You'll go, won't you? We could use the readies. The old firm's a bit boracic. Those fucking minders outside are costing me a small fortune.'

'Yeah, I'll go, Uncle, but I'm not happy about it. Sounds like you know something I don't.'

'Everybody knows something other people don't.'

'How will I spot them?'

'Silver Mercedes van with a black stripe. German plates.'

'Fair enough. How'll they find me?'

'They know what motor you're using.'

'Which is?'

'Dev's got you a Ford Cosworth. Don't look like much apparently, but it drives just fine.'

95

Dev Murphy had been Jenner's mechanic for as long as Mark could remember, a bad-tempered Irishman who could charm any engine to do exactly what he wanted. He'd taught Mark early on how to steal cars, which had been priceless information in later life. And Dev had been Mark's only point of contact in London during his time away. They were friends, and Mark had discovered that friends were few and far between.

'Sounds all right. Where is it?'

'At his place in Herne Hill.'

'I can't believe he's still there after all this time.'

'He'll be buried there.'

'He's not the only one if what I've heard's true.'

Jenner smiled. 'Now you'll need something to keep you company in case there's any trouble. Can't be too careful,' he said.

'I thought everything was going to be cool.'

'It will be.'

'Are these people all right?'

'Always have been before.'

'Who are they?'

'Better not to ask.'

'I don't like this, Uncle…'

'You have to take some risks in life,' said Jenner.

'Yeah, sure.'

'So, you want something?'

'I'd better I suppose.' They both knew what they were talking about.

'Let's take a look then,' said Jenner.

'Still the same place?'

Jenner nodded. 'Come on,' he said.

They went down into the cellars that stretched underneath the house. It was cold down there, and damp, and smelled faintly of cats. Both men had to stoop to get under the beams that supported the floor above. At the far end there was an area that was going to be converted into a sort of den, but it had never been finished. Jenner had lost interest after Hazel had died. Part of it had been partitioned off, and the walls had been clad in dark pine.

Jenner pressed one section and it popped open to reveal the face of a large combination safe. He spun the dial and pulled open the door. Mark remembered the first time his adopted uncle had shown him the safe.

'What do you see?' he'd asked when he'd opened it.

The teenage Mark had peered inside. 'Some readies,' he replied. 'Some papers, and some jewel boxes. Are they Hazel's stuff?'

'Yes,' John Jenner had replied. 'Her best tom. A couple of rings and necklaces I've bought her over the years. Is that all?'

Mark had looked again and nodded.

'Check this,' John had said. He'd pressed something inside the safe and the back had opened inwards, a tiny light had come on and Mark had drawn in his breath sharply. Inside the hidden compartment had been several handguns hung up on pegs, plus boxes of ammunition and a couple of leather holsters.

'Cool,' Mark had said. 'Very cool.'

He felt much the same that winter's night as John did the business again. 'Open sesame,' he whispered.

Inside the front of the safe was a large canvas bag that John Jenner tugged out and dropped on to the floor. 'The dough,' he explained.

'How much?' asked Mark as he hefted the bag. It was heavy.

'Two hundred K. All old notes. Nothing consecutive.'

'I thought you were skint.'

'That's it, Mark,' said the older man. 'That's my net worth apart from the house and the car and all the toys. And I had trouble raising that. That's why I need someone I can trust to do this.'

'I hope your trust isn't misplaced.'

'It's not. I trained you too well.'

'Yeah,' said Mark, but it sounded hollow even to himself.

Jenner grinned, showing his teeth and opened the back of the safe. 'Now what do you fancy?' he asked. 'Revolver or semi?'

'Semi will do me,' said Mark.

'Prone to jamming.'

'But flatter. Less bulky.'

'You're the boss. Colt or Browning?'

'Got a Browning niner?'

'Of course. Weapon of choice on the mean streets of Brixton.'

'That'll do me then. Whatever the brothers go for is OK by me.' John Jenner withdrew a metallic blue Browning nine-millimetre semi-automatic and gave it to Mark. He checked that the magazine was out and the chamber was clear before dry firing the weapon. John passed him a clip and a handful of bullets. 'Got a cleaning kit?' asked Mark.

'It's clean,' said Jenner.

'I prefer to do it myself, Uncle,' said Mark. 'No offence, but if I've got to carry it…'

'Sure, son,' said Jenner. 'That's what I like to see, a man who respects his weapon.' He reached in again and came out with a boxed cleaning kit and a container of gun oil. 'Holster?' he asked.

'Why not? They always stick in my spine when I put them down the back of my pants. Especially when I'm driving. Now I'm tired. If I'm working tomorrow I'd better get some beauty sleep.'

'No worries.'

Jenner shut the hidden compartment, put the bag of money back into the safe, closed it and they went back to the living room, Mark carrying the gun and accessories. They swallowed the remains of their drinks and went to bed.

Once inside his room, Mark saw that the Bros duvet had been replaced by one of plain navy blue. He sat on the bed and laid out the cleaning kit on the beside table, cleaned and loaded the gun, stashed it under his pillow and went to bed. After he'd undressed he locked the door. He didn't want any visitors tonight.

Sweet dreams, he said to himself, before falling quickly asleep.

The next morning Mark lay in bed until he heard movement, then waited for the front door to slam and he assumed Martine had left for work. He got up then and went to the bathroom. Afterwards he went downstairs and found Chas in the kitchen. 'Morning,' he said.

'Morning, son. I hear you're back for good.'

'For good or evil, one of the two,' replied Mark, pouring himself a cup of coffee from the pot on the stove. 'Uncle John about yet?'

'I took him up a cuppa. He's awake.'

'Can I go see him?'

'Course. He's expecting you. Breakfast?'

'Not hungry, mate.' In fact Mark's stomach felt like his throat was full of cement and he had to force the coffee down.

'I'd come with you today,' said Chas. 'You know that.'

'I know. But Uncle John's got this earmarked for me.'

'Fair enough.'

'Right. I'll go and talk to him. See you in a bit.'

Mark left the kitchen and went up the four flights to his uncle's room which took up what had used to be the whole attic space. He knocked and his uncle called, 'Yeah?'

Mark went inside and John Jenner was sitting up with a cup of tea, the day's papers spread around him, and Lily asleep at the foot of the bed. 'Mornin', said Mark.

'Good morning,' replied Jenner.

'How you doing?'

'Not too bad. All the better for you being here.'

'Thanks. Can't say as I feel the same.'

'Butterflies?'

'Feels like bloomin' carrier pigeons as it goes.'

They both laughed. 'One o'clock, you say, the meet?' said Mark, peering through the curtains at the outside world. The sky was black towards the south, but the temperature had risen slightly overnight, and there were only scraps of snow left on the ground and the bare branches of the trees dripped icy water.

'S'right.'

'Silver Merc van with a black stripe.'

'Got it.'

'I reckon to allow a couple of hours for the trip, just to be on the safe side. I want plenty of time to look around.'

'Whatever.'

'And Dev's got the motor.'

'No danger. It's waiting for you.'

'OK. I'll shoot over to Herne Hill about ten. I'll walk there. Go across the park. Then I'll take a slow wander into the country. Have an all day breakfast maybe. I might be hungry by then.'

'Whatever you want, son. You're the boss.'

'No I'm not. Anyway, I'll leave you to get up.'

'See you in a minute.'

'You will.'

Mark went back to his room, checked the Browning again, put on a sweater over his shirt and the shoulder holster over that. He pulled his clothes straight as they'd go and holstered the gun, then slipped on his leather jacket and a pair of thin leather gloves and checked himself in the mirror in the bathroom. Even with the jacket unzipped, nothing showed. Fucking Dirty Harry, he thought as he drew the gun that came easily out of the oiled leather. When he went downstairs his uncle was in the kitchen with the bag of readies.

'You'll take care of this, won't you?' he asked.

'Course I will. I just look like I'm going away.'

'Let's hope not,' said Jenner.

'They'll have to catch me first.'

By ten he was ready to go. 'Dev's expecting you,' said Jenner. 'Good luck, son.'

'Later,' said Mark and left.

Outside the temperature was plummeting again and he took off at a brisk pace for Brockwell Park and Dev's garage beyond. The walk took about thirty minutes and Mark enjoyed seeing the old landmarks, and he almost forgot the trepidation he felt about what he was about to do. Suddenly the thought of the many places he'd stayed in over the past eight or so years didn't seem so bad compared with the prospect of a prison cell. The sky was still dark, but the snow was holding off. When he reached the garage under the railway arches next to Herne Hill station where he'd spent so many days being taught about car engines, the sliding door was slightly ajar and he squeezed through. A partitioned-off section at the back acted as an office and he pushed open the door to find Dev sitting at a paper-strewn desk next to a space heater that blasted out hot air.

'You want to be more careful,' said Mark. 'You never know who's going to sneak in here.'

'Jesus Christ,' said the white-haired man at the desk with a start. 'Mark. How the devil are you?' Dev spoke with an Irish accent that fifty years in London had hardly changed, though in other ways he had changed plenty. As he came round from behind the desk Mark closed the door and saw that Dev had a acquired a bad limp and that his hands shook slightly. His uncle's firm are all growing so old, he thought. No wonder he wants some new blood.

Dev hugged Mark hard. 'It's been too long, boy,' he said. 'We've all missed you.'

'I missed you too.'

'You know it was hard keeping our letters and phone calls secret. John gave me a right bollocking when he heard I'd known where you were.'

'That was the deal, Dev. I'm sorry I made you lie to him.'

'I never lied, Mark. I was just a wee bit economical with the truth, as the politicians say.'

'Whatever.'

'But I tell you, we're all glad to see you back where you belong.'

'I'm glad to be back.'

'Cuppa tea?' asked Dev.

'OK. But let's make it a quick one. Places to go, people to see, you know what I mean.'

'Indeed I do.'

Dev plugged in the kettle and put tea bags, milk and sugar into two shabby mugs before adding boiling water, passing one to Mark and taking the other back to his chair. Mark perched himself on the edge of the only other seat in the room, a stained and sagging armchair missing one leg and propped up by a pile of back copies of *Auto Trader*. 'I see you've got the customer service part of the business sorted, Dev,' he said,

'Ah fuck 'em. They come here to get their motors fixed cheap. That's all they care about.'

'So what you got for me?'

Dev gave him a sly smile. 'A right little goer. A Cosworth Sierra. One of the last ones made. Permanent four-wheel-drive, power brakes and steering. All in all a sweet little motor.'

'Nice. But you don't have to sell it to me, Dev.'

'Sorry. I get carried away.'

'I know, mate. I remember. Kosher, is it?'

'Well, not quite. You know they were they most nicked motor in the country once.'

'So I heard.'

'Well… this one might be a bit, you know, iffy.'

'Not a cut and shut, promise me that. It ain't going to split in two if I put my foot down.'

'As if. It's all one motor, but with a few bits of some others bolted on, if you know what I mean.'

'Great. But then, as I'll only need it for the day, I don't suppose it matters.'

'It looks a bit scruffy too, but it goes great. That I can guarantee.'

'As I remember, your guarantees last until the motor's off the premises and the cheque's cleared.'

'Never take cheques. That's for mugs. You're family. For you, it's only the best.'

'Let's see it then. Where is it?'

'Out back. I didn't want anyone getting too busy. I still get the occasional visit from Old Bill, believe it or not.'

'No, really? I can't imagine why.'

'Cos they're nosy bleeders, that's why.'

They finished their tea and Dev followed Mark out into the garage, then through a small door that he unlocked, and led into a yard at the back. Under a tarpaulin that cascaded water when Dev pulled it off was a white

Ford Sierra Sapphire Cosworth on an 'L' plate. The paintwork was dull and the leather interior needed some work, but it still looked like a ravenous shark about to chew up some hapless swimmer. Out of his pocket Dev pulled a set of keys big enough to choke a horse, flipped through them, selected one, pulled it off the ring and gave it to Mark, who unlocked the boot – which was empty apart from the spare wheel, a jack and a plastic petrol can – and dropped in the bag of money. He went to the driver's door and settled into the bucket seat behind the wheel, fired up the engine which rumbled into life on the first try and soon settled down to a powerful-sounding burble. 'Sounds all right,' he said.

'I've done the brakes,' said Dev, 'Checked the levels and filled the tank. You'll be all right with this one, I promise.'

'I'd better be,' Mark said.

Dev whacked Mark on the shoulder through the open window, before dragging the gates of the yard open. Mark reversed through, then engaged first gear and steered the car towards the main road. In the rear-view mirror, he saw Dev give him a wave before he pulled the gates shut again. Mark gave him a thumbs up through the open window, turned on to the Norwood Road and headed west. The car responded well and Mark set the heater to warm and switched on the radio. He found a music station and worked his way along the South Circular until he saw the familiar signs for the M4 and the west. The traffic was heavy heading out of town, not helped by the wet roads, and the clouds were the colour of old bruises as he finally crossed the river at Kew and took the shortcut through to the A4 under the Chiswick Flyover that dripped water down from its cracked concrete. He drove the Ford up the ramp and joined the traffic flow before the road became motorway, two lanes expanded to three and Mark could put his foot down. Not too much, as he didn't want to get stopped by a traffic patrol, but just enough to clear the Cosworth's throat and feel what it could do.

He listened carefully as the car's revs mounted and the needle on the speedo swung up to the ton. Everything seemed to be working OK as Dev had promised, and after a few miles Mark slipped the car into the slow lane, keeping an eye out for anyone with undue interest in him. He'd been watching the road in the rearview mirror since he'd left Dev's garage and didn't think he was being followed. But there was something about his uncle's attitude that worried him. He came off the motorway at junction five, went round the roundabout twice then rejoined and pushed on to the services just past the Basingstoke turnoff. He stopped for a coffee, taking the bag of cash with him. You can never be too careful, thought Mark, looking out for hardfaced men of one side of the law or other. All he saw were reps, truck drivers, mums, dads and kids at the fag end of their Christmas holidays, selling, working, shopping or just having fun. All the normal things he'd never really done in his life. Mark realised then how alienated he'd become from regular people.

As the hands of his watch moved slowly towards the time of the rendezvous, he went back to the car where he stuffed the money bag between the front and rear seats, then drove back on to the motorway, came off at the next junction, went round and headed back in the direction of London before taking the A33 exit and driving down towards Basingstoke itself, as he'd been told to do. Within a few minutes he spotted the Little Chef on the right hand side of the road and stopped just past it in a layby with a view of the car park. It contained half a dozen cars and vans, but so far no silver Mercedes truck. The building was single storied, the tarmac area outside a little too big for the job since the motorway services had opened just a few miles away, and the front was protected by a white picket fence. Beyond this were flower beds, probably vibrantly coloured during the summer, but now just muddy patches with a few bits of green poking through yesterday's snow.

At ten to one, Mark did a swift U-turn and slid the Ford into the restaurant's car park, drove to the end under a leafless, dripping tree, stopped the engine and sat. The radio burbled in the background and just as the one o'clock news came on, the truck he was waiting for came off the road, circled the car park and drew up next to Mark's car, all but hiding it from observation from the Little Chef's big picture window. There were two people in the cab who briefly spoke before the righthand door opened and a tall, thin man in a parka, jeans and baseball cap got out. Mark slid down the passenger window of the Cosworth and the chilly breeze ruffled his hair as it finally began to snow. The man stepped towards the Ford, hunkered down and said through the window: 'You got something for me?'

Mark nodded, and the man opened the door and got inside. He smelled strongly of foreign cigarettes and spearmint. 'Show,' he said. He had a faint trace of an accent that Mark couldn't place.

'Where's the stuff?' asked Mark.

'Don't worry about that.'

'But I do.'

Mark hated this sort of thing. Everyone involved trying to show how hard they were. How macho. It was always the same, nothing changed.

The man sensed his discomfort, got it confused with aggression and said: 'Be calm. It's in the back of the truck.'

Mark sighed. 'OK,' he said. 'I was told you could be trusted.'

'I should think so,' said the man, the incongruity of his hurt innocence not lost on Mark who leaned back and hauled out the money bag. 'Check it,' he said.

The man put the bag on his knee and opened it. He looked at the money all gathered up in thousand pound bundles and smiled. 'Your side is trustworthy too,' he said. 'No problems ever.'

'Good,' said Mark.

'I'll count this inside,' said the man.

'Fair enough.' Mark actually didn't care any more. If they were going to take him out, so be it. But he checked the gun inside its holster nevertheless as they got out of the car and walked towards the truck, just casually like he was scratching an itch. The foreign man was facing away from him, and between him and the driver, so Mark was sure neither of them noticed.

The man pulled open a sliding door on the side of the van and climbed inside. Mark followed. The interior was warm and luxuriously furnished, with two revolving leather captain's chairs, carpet, a sofa bed and built-in cabinets. Very nice, thought Mark, a real home from home. The man flicked on a light switch and indicated that Mark should sit. When he had, he slid the door shut and sat down himself.

'This is what you want,' he said, shoving a metal briefcase towards Mark, who hauled it on to his lap and slipped the locks. Inside were the usual kilo packets, neatly wrapped in clear film and sealed with tape.

'Check any one,' the man said, pulling bundles of cash out of the bag. 'Be my guest.'

Mark was no chemist but he knew dope. He picked a packet at random, split the film with his thumbnail and took a taste. His tongue and gums numbed up nicely and he shuddered as he tasted the metallic bite of good cocaine. 'Yeah,' he said, sucking the residue from his lips and swallowing again. 'Seems all right. But then I'm just the courier. Any problems and I daresay you'll hear from my principal.'

'We've never heard from him yet,' said the foreign man who was busy splitting the bricks of money and feeding them through a note-counting machine which he'd produced from one of the fitted cupboards. 'At least, only to order more.'

'That's OK then,' said Mark. 'Got any tape for this?'

The man pulled a roll from his jacket, tossed it over and Mark resealed the packet and put it back in the case which closed with a click. 'How long you going to be with that?' He indicated the money.

'A minute,' said the man as the machine finished counting and satisfied, he put the cash back in the bag and zipped it shut. 'All seems to be well.'

'Then I'll say ta ta,' said Mark, and when the man frowned, he added, 'Goodbye.'

'Oh yes, goodbye,' said the man, and they both stood and he stuck out his hand.

Mark shrugged and shook it.

The man turned and tugged the sliding door open again, and indicated Mark should lead the way. 'After you,' said Mark, and the foreign man pulled a face but didn't speak and jumped out in the snow which was starting to come down heavily. Whilst they'd been in the back of the van the sky had darkened considerably and the lights around the car park had switched themselves on. Mark followed the man out of the truck and headed straight for his motor.

'So far, so good,' Mark said to himself, but he spoke too soon.

He reached the Ford's driver's door and opened it, seeing that the man had swung open the front passenger door of the Mercedes. In the far corner of the parking area Mark noticed a car start and its lights came on full beam. Then, in a split second that slowed like a piece of film stuck in the gate of a projector, he saw that no one had recently walked across the tarmac, which was already lightly covered with snow, towards it.

Something's wrong, he thought.

Footprints. No footprints.

The car's motor revved and it headed straight towards the Cosworth and the van. 'Fuck,' he shouted to no one in particular, throwing the case into the passenger well, falling into the driver's seat, banging his knee painfully on something as he did so, and hitting the ignition key which was still in the lock. The engine caught at once and Mark slapped the gear lever into first and took off, the driver's door still open. Then another car, headlights flaring, pulled in across the entrance to the carpark and Mark aimed the Ford at the empty flower bed as the swinging door hit the back of a parked Transit and slammed shut.

Yet another car started and headed in pursuit of him, but Mark whipped the stick into second, slammed his foot on the accelerator and rocketed past it, just clashing bumpers as they went. The Cosworth flew over the black earth and ripped through the fence as Mark pulled the steering wheel hard left and swung out on to the road in the direction of the motorway, leaving a long black mark on the tarmac and several angry drivers in his wake. He went through the gears fast and kept his foot hard down as the speedo ran up to seventy, then eighty, as he overtook everything in his way, lights on full beam and hand hard on the horn. All the other cars on the road had their lights on too, because of the weather, so it was difficult to make out who was chasing him and who just going about their normal business. The motorway signs got more frequent, flipping past like playing cards. When Mark reached the junction, he shoved the Cosworth through the roundabout and on to the slip road, cutting up a big sixteen-wheeler who showed his anger with three blasts on his klaxon. Was it cops or was it bad guys? Mark kept wondering. Who the fuck were those people at the restaurant? Was it a bust or a stitchup?

By the time the car reached the end of the slip, Mark had pushed the speed up to one-twenty and still climbing. He blasted out on to the motorway, dodged between two slow-moving trucks and headed straight across to lane three. The rest of the traffic looked like it was standing still as he pulled back and forth into the middle lane to pass traffic travelling at the speed limit. The snow was getting heavier and the traffic, apart from the Cossie, was slowing. 'Come on you fuckers,' Mark yelled as he swerved through the cars. Then in his peripheral vision he saw blue lights flashing as a police jam sandwich joined in the fun just behind him. At this rate he was going to end up doing five miles per hour and getting jammed up as the traffic slowed before Chiswick again, and then the cops could box him in and it would be all over.

Mark bullied his way back into the fast lane again and slowed to a legal seventy, the cop car still following but unable or without the bottle, or maybe under orders not to force its way through the thickening traffic on Mark's left. He was looking for a way out and suddenly it presented itself. Up ahead, but getting closer by the second, the central barrier was broken for maybe three car lengths, and instead of a waist-high hard metal barrier, all that kept the opposing traffic apart was a line of red and white plastic bollards, maybe two foot high, screwed into the ground. Mark downshifted, the Cosworth's gears shrieking in protest, jammed the brakes on hard, saw the terrified face of the driver of the car following him as he braked too, probably sending a domino effect as far back as Swansea, and with a tug to the right and a clatter of plastic on the undercarriage, Mark was going the wrong way down the west-bound motorway.

Cars, trucks, cabs and lorries were heading his way and he left a skidding, brake-screaming carnage around him as he cut across the approaching traffic going up through the box again and found the hard shoulder, praying that no fucker had broken down and was being fixed by the AA or RAC, otherwise they were all going to be in for a big surprise.

He almost laughed out loud as he saw the effect he was having on the oncoming vehicles, and then like the answer to a prayer there in front of him was a slip road joining the motorway, which he took, bounced across the central reservation again, leaving what sounded like vital parts of the Ford clattering into the gutter as he joined the correct lane of traffic leaving the westbound M4.

Mark took the first turning, a road heading God knows where, the wipers slapping and the snow hitting the windscreen like chunks of paper tissue. And then, just ahead, he saw a bus pulling into a stop. Mark swerved round it and slowed slightly. Where's the next bloody bus stop? he wondered. And, a mile or so further, he saw one. And right next to it it was a turning. He swung the Ford into it and a few yards down on the left was the entrance to a narrow lane. Mark pulled in, bare twigs scratching the side of the Cosworth, and braked to halt. He got out, forcing the door hard against the hedge, taking the briefcase with him, his brain speeding from the hit of coke and the excitement of the chase. Despite the dropping temperature his body was slick with sweat that felt like it was freezing on his skin. Who the fuck touched this motor? he thought, almost hopping from foot to foot with excitement and fear. Dev had a record as long as the Blackwall Tunnel, his prints were on file, and Mark didn't want to leave any evidence of his involvement. He ran to the back of the car and opened the boot. Just like he remembered there was a can lying next to the spare wheel. Water or petrol? he wondered as he shook the can and opened it. He recoiled slightly from the fumes. Terrific, he thought, and splashed fuel on to the boot's carpet then took the can back to the front of the car and threw the rest over the driver's seat and into the front well of the Ford, heaving the can into the back.

Matches. Matches, he thought. Christ I'm not ready for this. He slammed open the glove compartment and inside was a half empty book from a restaurant in south London. 'Thank you, God,' he said aloud, lit a match, set fire to the rest and tossed the whole book on to the front seat. The last thing he saw as he closed the door was a blue flame dancing across the leather interior. He picked up the briefcase in his gloved hands and ran back to the main road just in time to hail the bus, an old green and white doubledecker that had seen better days. Its destination sign read ETON. Always wanted to go there, he thought as he asked the driver for the town centre, paid the fare and ran upstairs. There were just two passengers sitting in the front and he moved to the rear and collapsed into the back seat. He was still shaking as the bus gathered speed. He looked over his shoulder and over the tops of the hedges he saw an orange glow though the fast-gathering darkness and the falling snow. Then, above the noise of the ancient diesel he heard the sound of sirens and two police cars, blue lights flashing, breasted the hill behind them and gained fast on the bus.

'Oh shit,' he whispered and reached for the comfort of the butt of his pistol. But the two squad cars raced past and were soon lost to sight. Mark laughed out loud and as he took one last look behind he imagined he heard the explosion as the Ford's petrol tank caught and in the distance the orange glow grew brighter.

Once at the Eton town terminus Mark followed the signs to the railway station, caught the next train back to Paddington, which luckily arrived just a few minutes after he'd bought his ticket, as he didn't fancy sitting around in the waiting room. The train sluggishly wove its way through the outer, then inner suburbs, stopping at every station on the way and it was late afternoon before Mark caught a bus to south London.

When he got off at Tulse Hill he called the house on his mobile. 'Christ, I thought you were dead,' said John Jenner when he answered. 'You've been on TV. Local news.'

'Terrific,' said Mark.

'Where are you?'

'Just walking up the road.'

Jenner met him at the gate carrying an umbrella to protect him from the snow. They went indoors and Mark hung his jacket over a chair as Jenner checked the bag. 'Was it cops chasing me?' asked Mark after he poured himself a large brandy.

Jenner nodded.

'Did they get the other guys?'

'Looks like it.'

'Are they they gonna grass us up?'

'They wouldn't dare. Anyway they don't even know who we are, same as I don't know them. We just communicate by safe phone.'

'Thank Christ for that.'

'You did well. What happened to the motor?'

'Burnt it out. Wasn't that on the news too?'

'No.'

'You knew, didn't you, Uncle?'

'No.'

'Yes you did.'

'I thought something might happen, but I wasn't sure.'

'Well, thanks for sharing.'

'I thought if I did you wouldn't go.'

'Too bloody right.'

Jenner smiled. 'But you did it, Mark. You came good. I'm proud of you.'

'If you ever do anything like that again, I'm off.'

'I won't, I promise.'

'Jesus, Uncle, give us another drink will you. I'm spitting feathers here.'

ELEVEN

Sean Pierce heard about the aborted bust by the Thames Valley drug squad during his normal course of duties the next morning. It was just another war story as far as he was concerned. Some crazy crackhead in a souped up motor causing mayhem on the motorway. A burnt out Ford had been discovered, and the local force had captured a pair of foreign nationals carrying two hundred grand in used notes. The Ford's driver had got away. Nothing new there, and nothing for him to worry about. Just another crime report amongst hundreds. A little more exciting than the average domestic dispute, that was all. At least interesting enough to get a mention on *London Tonight*, and would probably make headlines in the *Eton Gazette* or whatever the local paper down there was called, but that was it. Or at least he thought so.

At the same time as Sean was reading about his exploits, Mark woke up with a slight hangover, a little way up the road. He, John and Chas had sat up into the small hours discussing what had gone wrong with the exchange and its possible ramifications, at the same time drinking John Jenner's bar dry.

'If I catch whoever grassed us up, I'll castrate the fucker,' were the last words Mark remembered as John Jenner had made his unsteady way to bed around four o'clock.

Mark wiped the sleep from his eyes and went to the bathroom. Once dressed he wandered down to the kitchen where Chas was sitting reading *The Sun*. 'A star,' he said.

'What?'

'You got a mention. You'll have to start a scrapbook.'

Mark leaned over his shoulder and read the short news item on page

113

six about the previous day's goings on. 'Bloody hell,' he said. 'I hope there's not many like that.'

'Feeling a bit rough, son?' asked Chas, looking into Mark's dull and bloodshot eyes.

'Just a bit.'

'Cuppa tea and a bacon sarnie'll set you right.'

Mark nodded weakly and took a seat at the kitchen table whilst Chas busied himself preparing the breakfast. 'Anyone about?' he asked.

'Martine's gone to work and the boss is having a lie in.'

'What bloody time is it then?' asked Mark, having left his watch somewhere in his room.

'About ten. I let you kip in.'

'Thanks,' said Mark as he accepted a mug of tea and felt better straight away at its hot sweetness. 'What now?'

'How do you mean?'

'Well, haven't we got to get the stuff out of the house?'

'No worries. It's all arranged.'

'Is it going to be picked up here?'

'No. You're going to drop it off.'

'Oh shit.'

'No worries. It's a piece of cake.'

'I seem to remember someone saying something similar about yesterday, and I ended up almost totalling myself on the sodding motorway.'

'But you didn't, son, did you?' said Chas, dealing rashers on to buttered wholemeal. 'That's the point.'

Upstairs, John Jenner was waking up himself. He lay in a marriage bed that now, without his wife and with only an old cat for company, seemed to him as big as an aircraft carrier. Although it had been over ten years since she'd died, John still thought of her every day, and often had conversations with her as if she were still there, lying next to him. He smiled at the thought of her, although it was a bitter smile edged with tears. He'd tried to find another woman after her death, but no one came close. No one knew their private language or their shared jokes, and no one could ever know what it had been like for John and Hazel, as together they'd built up a successful criminal empire.

His thoughts then turned to Mark. He was so much like his father, yet so different. Billy Farrow had let John down badly, leaving him to run the gang alone when he'd joined the police. But at least he'd been enough of a good friend to leave him alone once on the force. It must have given Billy sleepless nights to have known so much about south London's premier gangster and yet never to have nicked him. But then, John knew where the bodies were buried in Billy's past and, for his part, had never said a word to anyone about that. They'd maintained an uneasy truce until Billy had died.

Jenner reached for the syringe and amp of morphine on the bedside table and measured out his morning dose. It was later than usual and the pain had woken him. Shit, he thought, when will all this end? But of course he knew. It would end in the graveyard, where everybody ended up eventually.

Expertly, he slid the needle into a vein and pushed down the plunger so that the warmth of the drug replaced the cold of the cancer's bite and he lay back on his pillow and let his mind run away with itself.

* * *

Back in the summer of 1965, John Jenner hadn't sent Billy to talk to Maurice Wright in the hospital where he'd been admitted for his gunshot wound. He went himself. In fact he went twice, because the first time the nurse on duty told him that the police were still interviewing Mr Wright.

'Fine,' he said, giving her the bunch of flowers he was carrying. 'I'll call again.'

'Any message?' she asked.

'Just tell him a friend called,' he said with a grin and left.

The second time, Maurice was alone and John found the side ward where he was sequestered without help. 'Maurice,' he said as he entered and closed the door behind him. 'I see you got my flowers.'

Maurice Wright almost jumped out of bed at the sight of the man who'd shot him. 'For Christ's sake,' he said. 'What are you doing here?'

'Just visiting a friend,' said Jenner, drawing up a chair to the side of the bed and plucking a grape from the bowl of fruit on the locker next to it. 'Don't worry, I'm not armed. I come in peace.'

'Piss off.'

'What you going to do about it, Maurice? Is that a pistol in your jammies or are you just pleased to see me?'

'I'll call a nurse.'

'Blimey, you've got me right terrified. If you'll just listen…'

'You've got nothing to say that I want to hear.'

'On the contrary, Maurice,' said John, leaning closer. He was beginning to realise the power of words as well as the power of violence. 'You should listen to me now and listen good. Otherwise the next time I might be taking flowers to your funeral.'

Maurice visibly paled to the colour of his bed sheets. He'd learnt at least one thing in the dancehall that night. Carrying a gun was one thing, using it was another. Jenner had the bottle, he didn't. 'Go on then,' he whispered.

'What's the point of us fighting?' asked John. 'When we could work together.'

'Doing what?'

'Anything. You join my little firm and we can have Soho stitched up in a couple of weeks. Speed, dope, anything and everything.'

'And who is your little firm?' asked Maurice. 'Jack fucking Spot and his boys?'

'No,' replied Vincent. 'Me, Billy and Wally.'

Maurice sniggered.

'But there's going to be more soon,' said John, himself realising that he was hardly talking about an army. 'And you can be in on the ground floor.'

'I don't think so,' said Maurice. 'Nice as it is of you to ask.'

'I'm not asking, Maurice,' said John. 'I'm telling.'

'I'll think about it,' said the older man. 'I've got plenty of time.'

'You do that,' said John. 'And I'll be back.' He took another grape and popped it into his mouth before standing to go. 'And make sure you make the right decision. I'll see you later.'

John left the hospital and walked to the nearby tube station. Two things I need, he thought as he waited for the train to come rumbling and clanking up to the platform, a set of wheels and some good men.

The wheels were easy, he'd got some cash and he'd bumped into a young Irish bloke called Dev at a party. Dev reckoned he could get him something tasty if he wasn't too worried about the provenance. The men would be more difficult, but John's head was full of ideas and later that day he sat with Billy in a café in Streatham and shared some with his best friend.

'We need some more faces,' he said over a cup of tea and a sticky bun.

'Such as?' asked Billy.

'I was thinking of the Goon.'

Billy almost choked on his cream slice. 'The Goon. You're fucking joking, aren't you? He's mental.'

'That's why I want him. We need some mentals.'

'You're bloody mental yourself,' said Billy. 'Shooting Maurice. It was all over the papers.'

'Good, eh?' said John. 'That's what we need, a bit of public relations just like them pop groups.'

'And a visit from the bloody coppers.'

'Maurice won't grass,' said John.

'No, he'll wait until he gets out and come looking for you with his gun.'

'He was shitting bricks, Billy my boy,' said John with possibly a little more conviction than he felt. 'And that's why we need the Goon.'

The Goon's real name was Martin Forbes. He was in his mid-twenties, six four and weighed in only just less than Wally's Minivan. He was permanently unemployed and lived with his fifty-year-old mother in a prefab at the back of Brixton bus garage. He wasn't the brightest button on the blazer, but what he lacked in brains he more than made up with brawn and total fearlessness. Many had thought it funny to mock his size and lack of brainpower and most had regretted it as soon as the Goon had held them up by the throat until their eyes popped and their blood vessels swelled almost to breaking point. 'Don't take the piss,' the Goon would say. It was a foolish man who did it twice.

'I'll see him tomorrow,' said John. 'He'll be down the pie and mash shop at twelve.'

The Goon was pretty well known for his regular habits. Every Tuesday he went into the local pie shop, had his fill of pie, mash and liquor, generally about three portions, then took another portion in a basin with a spotted handkerchief on top back to his mum's for her tea.

The next day, it being Tuesday, John entered the cafe at twelve-fifteen. He thought it wise to let the Goon have his nourishment before springing his plan on him. He took the Webley, just in case. Jenner bought a cup of tea at the counter and, after some banter with the serving staff, took it over to the marble-topped table where the Goon was sitting alone. He plopped himself down on the wooden bench rubbed smooth and shiny by generations of pie eaters' bottoms, opposite the big man.

'Hello, Martin,' he said.

The Goon built a miniature wall of China out of mashed potato on the top of his fork, dipped it delicately into the greenish gravy and swallowed the portion. 'Hello, John.'

'How's it going?' asked Jenner.

'Not too bad.'

'How's Mum?'

'Same. Always moaning. Can't afford this, can't afford that.'

'Not working then, Martin.'

'Nah.'

'That's good.'

'Why?' The Goon's face darkened.

'Because I've got a proposition for you.'

118

'You?'

'Me, Martin.'

'Nobody calls me Martin.'

'They will if you listen to what I have to say.'

'Go on then.'

'I'm offering you a job.'

The Goon rolled the idea round the inside of his head like a pinball in a machine. 'Don't work,' he said. 'I get the dole.'

'What? A fiver a week? That don't go very far, now does it? 'Specially, Martin, when you're eating pies for three.' The Goon looked at him slitty-eyed.

'You taking the piss?'

'No.'

''Cos if you are...' He made to rise from his seat and John nudged his knee with the barrel of the revolver he'd slipped out from under his jacket. 'See that,' said John. 'Now, Martin, don't get me wrong. I'm only showing you this to make you listen.'

'Blimey,' said the Goon, peering under the table. 'Is it real?'

'Course it is.'

'Just like in the pictures.'

'Better. You want one?'

'A gun. Me?'

'Sure. Why not? Come and work for me and you can have one for every day of the week.'

The Goon sat back, ignoring his lunch, which John knew was a great leap, and ran that idea around the inside of his head too. 'Blimey, what do I have to do?'

'Look after me and Billy and Wally. Watch our backs.'

'What will you be doing?' The Goon wasn't entirely stupid. Just a bit slow.

John grinned. 'Making money. Making lovely money.'

'And you won't call me the Goon?'

'No fucker will ever call you the Goon again, I promise.'

'All right, John,' said the Goon, watching a skin form on the liquor on the side of his plate. 'You're on.'

And so the Jenner gang became four.

* * *

'You awake, boss?' Chas's voice interrupted Jenner's reverie, and looking at the clock, he realised he'd been lying half asleep, half awake for almost an hour.

'Yes,' he mumbled through gummy lips. 'Took my dose a bit late, that's all.'

'Got a nice cup of tea for you. And the papers.'

'Thanks, Chas,' said Jenner, pushing himself up. 'What would I do without you?'

'Make your own tea I expect,' said Chas as he put down the tray and drew the curtains on to another cheerless London morning.

'Yeah. That'd be right.' Jenner looked at his old friend as he fussed around the room, tidying piles of clothes and magazines. 'Jesus, Chas, you're getting more like your mum every day.'

'She was a good old sort, my mum,' replied Chas. 'She patched us up enough times.'

'God, but she did too. And hid us out from a few foes.'

'She loved it,' said Chas. 'Now drink your tea before it gets cold.'

'All right, mum.'

Chas pulled an ugly face and went to the door. 'Oh and young Mark's getting antsy about doing the drop later. You'd better come down and give him the full SP.'

'He's a good boy, Mark, isn't he?' said Jenner. 'He'll do.'

'He needs some back up. It's too much for one.'

'He must still know some geezers he can row in. What do you reckon?'

'I suppose,' said Jenner. 'I was just thinking about the old days. The Goon and Wally.'

'What a fucking pair they were.'

'Wally could never handle it.'

'He did his bit.'

'Yeah. But the Goon…'

'Martin, you mean.'

'I never could get used to calling him that,' said John.

'Me neither.'

'But you've got a lot to thank him for.'

Chas leant against the door jamb.

'He saved my life that time.'

'Yeah, and paid the price.'

'We should go visit his grave. We haven't been for ages.'

'And his mum's next door.'

'He always was fond of his mum.'

'Another fine pair.'

'We'll do it, eh, Chas?'

'Yeah. Soon as the weather improves.' And with that he was gone. Jenner drank his tea, got up, went to the lavatory where, as usual, it took him a few minutes to get a dribble of urine to flow. 'Fucking cancer,' he said to himself in the mirror as he shaved. 'It'll be a good job when I'm out of all this.'

He dressed and went downstairs where Mark was moodily watching morning TV. 'You all right, son?' asked Jenner as he entered the living room.

'Not too bad. But I'll be happier when that gear's out of the house and you've got your money.'

'All in good time, son,' said Jenner, looking at his watch. 'This afternoon will do it.'

'Where?'

'Cash and carry in Loughborough Junction. But this time you'll be doing the carrying and they'll be paying the cash.'

'How much?'

'Enough. A tidy little profit for all of us. You'll be able to get some new jeans.'

Mark looked ruefully at the faded pair he was wearing. 'These have got months left in them yet.'

'Get yourself a nice suit. Some white shirts and some knitted ties.'

'You've been watching them Quentin Tarantino films again, Uncle, haven't you?'

'No I ain't. I was watching Michael Caine the other night in *Get Carter*. What a bloke.'

'What? Fat and bloody useless.' Mark knew how to get Jenner riled. He'd teach him to take the piss out of his best Levis.

'Caine is king,' said Jenner.

'Used to be maybe. Now he's just a soppy old luvvie.'

'Bollocks,' said Jenner, easing himself into his armchair with a grunt.

'You all right, Uncle?'

'I will be. Where's Chas?'

'Sainsbury's. He took the Bentley.'

'He bloody would. Fancy making us a nice cup of tea then?'

'Yeah, all right. Then I want to know exactly what's happening after this. OK?'

'Done.'

Mark went about his chore and returned with two cups.

'Right,' said Jenner when he'd taken a sip. 'The cash and carry's run by a pair of Paki likely lads.' He told Mark the address. 'It's right behind the station at Loughborough. I've been doing business there for years. They're good as gold for ragheads.'

Mark smiled. 'Do you call them that?'

Jenner dismissed the question with a scowl. 'Tommo and Ali run the joint,' he continued. 'You'd think they were as poor as church mice from the way they carry on, but believe me these boys are minted. Both got nice houses in Southall. But they dress like tramps and they always try and beat down the price. But I've done a deal. Now the only problem is, sometimes they're a bit... you know... slipshod in their counting. So you're going to have to count the cash on the spot I'm afraid.'

'How much?'

'Three hundred thousand.'

'And I've got to count it?'

'Terrible job counting money, ain't it? What's the matter with you? There'll be a nice bonus in it for you when you come home, don't worry.'

'The geezer yesterday had a note counter. You got one?'

'Fuck off. Let your fingers do the walking.'

'All right, Uncle. Do I go on my own?'

'That's the plan. Don't worry, they ain't going to kill you and eat you. You ain't Halal.'

'Funny.'

'I try.'

'It weren't them who put the word out about the swap, was it?'

'No. Why would they? They want that stuff as bad as we want their money.'

Mark hung about the house for the rest of the morning, waiting for the time to pass until his appointment. At two-fifteen Jenner got the bag of cocaine out of the safe. 'I'll take the gun too,' said Mark.

'You don't need a gun.'

'I think I'll be the judge of that.'

'It'll show disrespect.'

'Only if I have to show it, and if I do, it'll be me that's being disrespected, won't it?'

'Fair enough.'

Mark strapped on the pistol and took the case of drugs to his motor. It was freezing out and his shoes slid on the pavement. He drove carefully to Loughborough Junction and parked the car on a meter in a side street close to the station. He checked the roads around the cash and carry for suspicious-looking people sitting in cold cars who could have been the Bill, but all seemed serene.

Eventually, as three o'clock struck from a church clock, he approached the old Victorian building with its sign: 'Ali & Tommo's Booze Emporium'. He could tell it had once been a school, the tall windows now either entirely covered with sheet metal or barred. The playground was a carpark/rubbish dump and he had to pick his way carefully through the garbage. Mark squeezed through the thick metal sliding front door and into a warehouse packed with boxes of cigarettes, wine, beer and spirits.

A little bloke in a turban was minding the store and Mark approached him. 'Tommo, Ali?' he said.

'Who wants 'em, geezer?' the Asian replied in a cockney accent.

'I got a delivery.'

'All deliveries at the back. Can't you read?' and he motioned with his chin to a sign on the wall that said just that.

'I can read,' said Mark. 'But I have to see them personally.'

'Where you from?'

'John Jenner.'

The Asian's face changed in a split second. 'Why the fuck didn't you say so, geezer?' he demanded. 'Come on. I thought it might be you, but I had to make sure. Can't be too careful.'

He slammed the sliding door shut and led Mark through the maze of shelves and halfopened boxes to an office in the back. Two middle aged Asians were sitting in front of a heater in a room that smelled of coriander, sweat and tobacco.

'Geezer for you from Mr J,' said Mark's guide.

The two Asians sat up and took notice at that. 'You're Mark?' said the older of the pair. He looked like someone out of a 1970s sitcom in his flares, skinny sweater and patchwork bomber jacket.

'That's right.'

'I'm Ali.'

'Nice to meet you.'

'Same here. Mr J says you the bizzo. Come in. Wanna drink?'

Mark shook his head and hefted the bag he was carrying. 'I've got this for you.'

'No problem.'

'And you've got something for me.'

'Sure,' said the other man in a suit two sizes too small. Mark assumed he was Tommo. 'Here.' He shifted a pile of newspapers to reveal a scruffy suitcase. He hauled it on to the desk and unzipped it. Inside it was packed with cash.

'I've got to count it.'

'No, geezer,' said the Asian who'd brought him through. 'It's all there.'

'Sorry, I've got orders.'

'Fair enough,' said Tommo. 'Take your time.'

Mark started sifting through the money. It was in all denominations from tenners up. Some was loose, some was banded and at the bottom there were a whole load of fifties in bank bags marked '£5,000'.

Even so, it took Mark what seemed like hours to count it all. When he was finished his fingers were stiff and his hands black with ink and dirt from the money. The Asians had long ago checked the contents of the bag Mark had bought and were celebrating by sampling the warehouse stock. 'I thought you lot didn't drink,' said Mark when he was finished.

'It's God's gift to us all,' said Tommo raising a bottle of white rum. 'Enjoy.'

'I'll pass for now,' said Mark.

'Is it all there?' asked Ali slyly.

'To the pound.'

The trio all crashed their various bottles and laughed uproariously. 'Told you. When Ali and Tommo make a deal it stays made.'

'Better to be safe than sorry,' said Mark, although he felt that somehow they were all enjoying a joke at his expense. 'I'll be off now.'

Suddenly all business, Tommo put down his bottle and said. 'Use the back way just in case.'

'Just in case of what?'

'Who knows?'

Shit, thought Mark. If some fucker's waiting outside...

But there was no one. Tommo let him out into a dimly lit alley and Mark slid his hand into his jacket and felt the warm and reassuring butt of this pistol. And even his car, although out of time at the meter, was ticketless when he got back to it.

Mark shoved the money into the boot and drove home.

'Everything all right, son?' asked John Jenner when he got back into the house.

'Couldn't be better.'

'All the dough there?'

'Every penny.'

'Diamonds those two.' Jenner opened the case and found one of the bags of fifties in the suitcase and tossed it to Mark. 'You've done well. Go out and spoil yourself.'

'Cheers, Uncle,' said Mark. 'Maybe later. Right now I'm going back to bed, it's been a stressful few days.

'Youngsters nowadays,' said Jenner to Chas, who'd joined them. 'No fucking stamina.'

TWELVE

S ean Pierce was summoned into his DI's office the next morning.
'Guv?' he said.

'You saw about this thing down on the motorway the other day,' said
Detective Inspector Alan Mobray once Sean was seated in the
uncomfortable visitor's chair in front of Mobray's desk. The DI didn't like
anyone to feel too comfortable in his presence, including his own troops.

'Thing, guv?' The DI was known to be a bit of a poet on the quiet and
didn't always explain exactly what he was thinking about, rather hoping
that his subordinates could read his mind.

'Drugs exchange at a Little Chef near Basingstoke. It's all in the
morning's orders. Someone told tales out of school. Local drug squad
nicked a couple of krauts with the dough. Some kid got away with the
gear and wreaked havoc on the M4.'

'Yes, guv,' said Sean. 'I saw it. What's it got to do with us?'

'Maybe nothing. But a whisper came up from the nameless, faceless
grass who's been feeding the drug squad information and whose identity
we're not privileged to know.'

'A whisper about what?'

'Who. An old villain who's been a bit quiet lately.'

'Guv?'

'John Jenner. Know anything about him?'

Sean felt his stomach lurch. Of course he knew about Jenner. His
father had been in his gang, and of course the father of Jenner's adopted
nephew, Mark, had been murdered by Jimmy. Then there was that
business with Linda…

'No, guv,' he said.

'Then you're just about to. Take anyone who's free and give our Mr Jenner a visit. Bobby Childs will probably be best.'

This was the moment Sean had been dreading since he'd been transferred to Streatham nick. A face to face with Jenner.

'Yes... Childs,' said Mobray looking at his watch. 'Dig him out of the canteen. That's where he seems to spend most of his time lately.'

Childs was a DC coming up to retirement. A good, solid, old fashioned copper which was probably why he'd been sidelined from promotion. Good, solid coppering was out of fashion in the new Metropolitan Police Service – as opposed to the old police force, which was what Childs continued to call it. Force being what he'd been used to wielding in the good old, bad old, days before PACE and when PC still meant police constable. 'He'll fill you in,' Mobray went on. 'They've had their share of run-ins in the past.'

'Jenner got much of a record, guv?' asked Sean, although he probably knew it as well as his own name.

Mobray shook his head. 'Slippery bastard,' he said. 'Never done a stretch. Time on remand is all. Then, before the trial, witnesses start forgetting such things as their own names or else relocate somewhere quiet and far away like the Hebrides.'

'I know the type.'

'Well, get to know this individual,' said Mobray. 'He may be a bit past it, but I'd still like to see him do some time.'

Sean nodded.

'Go on then,' Mobray said when Sean made no attempt to move.

'Sorry, guv,' he said, and left the room closing the door quietly behind him.

As Mobray had had predicted, Childs was sitting at a table in the canteen drinking a cup of something warm. 'Bobby,' said Sean.

'Yes, young man. What can I do for you?'

'John Jenner.'

'Christ. That's a name from the past.'

'Could be current.' Sean told him what the DI had told him.

'Beautiful,' said Childs. 'That's one fucker I'd love to see banged up before I go. Would make growing my sweet peas down in Kent even sweeter.'

For their retirement, Childs had bought himself and his wife a free-standing caravan on a site near Canterbury. He often showed photos around the squad room of its interior, all swagged curtains and etched glass. Outside was a large garden that Childs intended to turn into a new Eden.

'Let's see what we can do then,' said Sean.

They signed out for an unmarked car and headed towards Jenner's address. An address that Sean knew well, though he feigned ignorance. 'Nice gaff,' said Childs. 'The wages of sin. Had it for years. Used to live there with his missus Hazel. Fabulous woman, I've got to say. What she ever saw in that bugger I'll never know.'

'Children?' asked Sean.

'Strange one,' said Childs. 'One daughter. Martine. Like her mum. Then there's the lad.'

'Yeah?'

'Yeah. One of our own.'

'How do you mean?'

'The son of a copper. Billy Farrow. DS shot dead in Brixton way back in the early eighties. The boy was brought up by his mother. But she fell in with a bad lot. Started on the sauce, got married to a right bastard. Then she died and he disappeared. Meanwhile...' He let a moment pass. 'Meanwhile, the boy – Mark I think his name was – was being looked after by Jenner and Hazel and some old lag who drives Jenner about. Part of the family. Seems there was some history between Jenner and Farrow. Boyhood friends. I think the Met tried to intervene but the kid wanted to stay at Jenner's. All sorts of lawyers got involved.'

'Where is he now?'

'Who?'

'The boy.'

'Dunno. He took it on his toes too. Years back. All very strange.'

'So what about this Jenner then?' asked Sean, still feigning ignorance. 'What's his story?'

'What isn't? He's been a face locally since the 60s. Into everything. Drugs, protection, armed robbery. The whole nine yards.'

'But you've never been able to get him.'

'No. He had some help for a while from a bent copper named Sharman. Kept him one step in front of us for years until the bastard got found with his fingers in the drugs cupboard at Brixton nick and slung out. He was still around 'til recently, pretending to be a private detective. But now he's gone missing too.'

'A lot of people go missing round Jenner.'

'You can say that again. Vicious bastard. Here we are.' The car drew up outside John Jenner's house and the two coppers got out into the cold morning air. The black Mercedes was parked opposite with two up. Childs nudged Sean. 'What do you reckon about that?' he asked.

'God knows.'

'Maybe we will too. I've got the number.' Childs rang the bell next to the gate.

'What?' a voice demanded after a minute.

'If that's Chas,' said Childs. 'Be nice now.'

'Who is it?' the voice asked.

'DC Childs from Streatham nick and DS Pierce.'

'What do you want?'

'To come in?'

'Got a warrant?'

'Don't be silly. Just a chat. Nothing heavy.'

The speaker was silent for half a minute and Childs pulled a face. Then, without warning the gates swung open. 'Welcome to the house of fun,' said Childs and they walked up the drive past the cars parked there.

The door was opened by Chas, who stood like a statue with a sneer on his face. 'Childs,' he said. 'I thought you were dead.'

'Hoped more like,' said the detective.

'If the cap fits.'

'This is Detective Sergeant Pierce,' Childs said. 'New in the manor. Come to make your acquaintances.'

Sean just nodded.

Chas pretended that he didn't know the younger man, but he would've recognised him in a crowd. He was the spitting image of Jimmy Hunter at the same age, and it took all of his self control to keep his hands off him. Billy Farrow had been a friend of his, and Chas was a firm believer that the sins of the father should be heaped upon the son unto several generations.

'Come in then,' he said. 'Mr Jenner's in the living room.'

John Jenner was sitting in his armchair, a rug around his knees. 'I'd stand,' he said as the two policemen came in. 'But I've not been well.'

'I'm sorry to hear that,' said Childs.

'Course you are.'

'This is DS Pierce,' said Childs, introducing Sean. Jenner gave him a look that could have frozen meat, and Sean had a sudden intuition that Jenner knew exactly who he was. But how could he?

'Sit down,' said Jenner. 'You're making me dizzy.' The coppers sat on the sofa and Jenner said: 'So what brings you here?'

'Your name came up,' said Childs. 'With regard to a drugs deal. You might've seen it on TV or in the paper. Day before yesterday down near Basingstoke. There was a car chase...'

'Can't say that I have,' said Jenner. 'Don't read the papers much these days, the news is too depressing. And I prefer nature programmes on TV.'

'Yes, John,' said Childs. 'Of course you do.'

'Mr Jenner will do nicely,' said Jenner. 'I'm not your mate.'

'You can say that again.'

'So what do you want?'

'Just to see if you had any idea why someone would mention your name.'

'No idea.' But Jenner was very interested. Very interested indeed. He wanted to know who'd put his name in the frame so that he could deal out retribution. If not personally, at least through a third party. Mark Farrow to be precise. A whisper had reached him that the word was out about the exchange and the word had turned to to have been correct.

'So who was it?' he asked, hardly expecting an answer.

And he wasn't to be disappointed. Childs grinned and almost laughed out loud. 'Never you mind, Mr Jenner,' he said. 'Just let's say that someone doesn't like you.' Of course, he didn't add that neither of the coppers knew who the informer was either. But Childs had always pretended to know more than he did.

'Nothing new there then,' said Jenner.

'Fair enough. Mind if we take a look round?'

'Mind if I look at your warrant?'

Childs smiled again. 'No warrant. But as you're an upstanding citizen we thought you might like to help.'

'I'd like to help you leave,' said Jenner. 'All my life people like you have been coming here on the off chance. And what did you ever get to show for it? A few months on remand. I'm a businessman. My name is known. People don't like my success. They get jealous. They try and stitch me up.' He shrugged as if to say: 'What can you do?'

'Your name's not as well known as it used to be,' said Childs.

'Just as well. Keeps you lot out of my face.'

'Nice car,' said Childs, changing the subject suddenly.

'What?'

'The Bentley. Nice motor.'

'They're famed for it,' said Jenner.

'Expensive.'

'I can see you don't miss much. What are you driving these days? A Nissan or something?' Childs ignored him.

'And the Range Rover. Whose is that?'

'Mine. I took it in payment for a debt.'

'Something from Basingstoke, was it?'

'You've got bloody Basingstoke on the brain. No.'

'And who's in the Mercedes parked opposite?'

'Friends.'

'Not good enough friends to invite in?'

'Look, Childs,' said Jenner. 'And you, whatever your name is,' he added in Sean's direction. 'Come to the point or do one.'

Childs could see that they weren't going to get much from the interview and all Sean wanted to do was leave. Jenner had been giving him stony looks from the off.

'Well,' said Childs. 'Thanks for all your help, Mr Jenner. We'd better be on our way. We'll see ourselves out.'

'No you won't,' said Chas from the doorway. 'You wouldn't want to take the wrong turning, would you? Who knows what you might leave behind. Incriminating evidence. That sort of thing.'

'As if,' said Childs.

He and Sean got up and Chas shepherded them to the front door.

'Your mate don't say much, Mr Childs, does he?' he said as they left. 'Cat got his tongue?'

Childs said nothing and Sean ignored him too. Chas watched as they walked down the drive. He opened the gates for them to leave and closed them again firmly once they were through. 'Bastards,' he whispered when they'd gone, making a point of giving the Mercedes another look on the way.

He went back to where Jenner was sitting. 'What was all that about, boss?' he asked.

'A fishing expedition. Somebody talked about what was happening the other day just like we thought. But they've got nothing.'

Mark Farrow came quietly down the stairs. He'd been waiting for the police to leave, not wanting anyone to know he was back until he was ready. He heard his uncle and Chas talking and when he joined them he said: 'I was bloody lucky doing that pick up, wasn't I? They definitely knew it was going to go down.'

'They did. It goes with the territory these days. Fuckers will grass you up for the price of a packet of fags these days.'

'Sure,' said Mark, not convinced. 'But it should never have happened. I could've been captured, easy.'

'Plod from the sticks,' said John Jenner. 'No match for you, my boy.'

'But those two weren't plod from the sticks, were they?'

'No,' agreed Jenner. 'They weren't. Far from it. Did you recognise the quiet one?'

'No,' said Farrow.

'Jimmy Hunter's son.'

Mark almost literally felt his jaw drop. 'Never. What him, a copper?'

'Yeah. Amazing isn't it? Thought I wouldn't know him, little bastard. But I've been keeping up with his career. He's just moved over from north London to get a promotion. Living down Croydon way with his sister and her sprogs.'

'What?' said Mark, the colour leaving his face. 'What did you say?'

'Thought you'd be interested,' said Jenner. 'You fancied her once, didn't you?'

Fancied her, thought Mark. Jesus, that was putting it mildly.

It was a chance remark Mark overheard between John Jenner and Chas that had started it all off in the first place. One night, thirteen years earlier, the three of them were driving God knows where, and 'I see she's got married again,' was all that Jenner said.

'Who?' asked Chas.

'Marge Hunter.'

'No.'

'It's the truth. Bloke named Pierce, works for the bloody Gas Board of all things.'

'I didn't know her and Jimmy were divorced.'

'Yeah. Been seeing the bloke awhile. Gave the bold Jimmy the big E a bit back.'

'How do you know?' asked Mark from the back of the car.

'Blimey,' said John Jenner. 'I almost forgot you were there, you're so quiet.'

'So how do you know?' Mark pressed.

'I like to keep tabs on people,' said Jenner. 'Know your enemy.'

'Is she your enemy then?'

'No. But her ex is. And yours.'

During the drive and subsequently, Mark kept on at his uncle for details until eventually Jenner gave in. 'I know a private detective,' he said one sunny May afternoon. 'I keep him sweet with a few quid and he noses around for me. Nothing formal. Nothing in writing.'

'So tell me,' said Mark.

Jenner told him about Marge and the two children, almost grown then, called Sean and Linda, about Tom Pierce and the divorce, the subsequent remarriage and where the new family were living in East Croydon. 'One day,' he said, 'you'll have your revenge on that little mob.'

'Yes,' replied Mark. 'I will.'

Mark pondered on the information for a few days, and decided to do a bit of snooping of his own. By then he was nineteen and very much part of the Jenner organisation. He had money in his pocket and drove a new BMW.

The following Monday morning he got up early, dressed casually in a sweatshirt, jeans and loafers, took his car keys and headed south.

With the help of his A-Z he found the address that his Uncle John had mentioned and by eight o'clock he was parked up just down the wide suburban street, under a horse chestnut tree.

The morning exodus from the street was well under way and after just a few minutes an ordinary looking bloke in an ordinary looking suit carrying a briefcase – Mark assumed he was Tom Pierce – left the house, got into a Ford Sierra and drove off. Next, a young, good looking boy a few years younger than Mark came out of the front door, pulled a bike from the side passage, got on, and pedalled off. That must be Sean, thought Mark.

A few minutes later, two girls of about sixteen, dressed in school uniform, came chattering down the street, went up the front path and knocked on the door. It opened a moment later and Mark's life changed for ever. In the doorway he saw the most beautiful girl he'd ever clapped eyes on, dressed in the same school uniform with a school bag over her shoulder. She was taller than her friends and, even from a distance, Mark could tell she was the gang's leader.

She shouted something back through the open door, closed it behind her and the trio headed out into the street, Mark's way.

He sank down in his seat and watched them over the top of the dashboard. Linda Hunter, or Pierce as she now was, filled his eyes, making the others all but invisible. As she got closer he drank in her every

135

detail. All thoughts of revenge were forgotten and the only thing he could think of was how he could get to talk to her.

The three girls passed the parked BMW without giving it a second glance, turned the corner at the top of the street and vanished. Mark just sat where he was for ten minutes before switching on the engine and returning home.

It didn't take much research to discover which school the girls' uniform belonged to, and a couple of days later Mark headed back to Croydon. He left his car in the Pontins garage underneath the Whitgift centre in the middle of town and took a wander. The school, a massive mixed comprehensive, was close to East Croydon railway station and next to a park. Just before lunchtime, Mark was sitting on a bench with a good view of the school's main gates, as an ice cream van with its tones blasting out *Popeye The Sailor Man* arrived. At nineteen, Mark was an extremely handsome young man and he knew it. His dark hair was long over his ears, his skin was smooth and unblemished and that morning he hid his blue eyes behind dark glasses.

He was casually dressed again. A white T-shirt, leather jacket, skinny, faded Levis and black loafers.

He heard the sound of a school bell and the doors of the main building burst open and hundreds of youngsters aged between eleven and seventeen headed for their hour of freedom.

Suddenly Mark realised that maybe it wouldn't be as easy to spot Linda Pierce as he'd first imagined. Maybe she'd stay in for lunch. Maybe she was studying during her free time, or maybe she wasn't even at school that day.

Some of the kids headed for the centre of town, some hung around the playground and others came into the park where they grabbed what seating was there or else sat on the grass under the warm sun.

One kid, a boy of about thirteen, joined Mark on his bench. Mark lit a cigarette and the boy said: 'Got a spare fag, mate?'

Mark looked at him coolly through the dark lenses of his glasses. 'You're too young to smoke,' he said.

'Bollocks. I've been at it since I was ten.'

'I bet you have,' said Mark taking a cigarette from his packet and giving it to the boy. He offered him a light and the boy inhaled with obvious pleasure.

'Cheers,' he said.

'Don't let a teacher see you.'

'Fuck 'em.'

'Big school,' said Mark.

'Bleedin' dump.'

'Aren't they all?'

'Dunno. Ain't been to them all.'

Mark smiled at his cheek. 'Mine was.'

'Where was that?'

'Brixton.'

The boy nodded and smoked on.

'Know someone called Linda Pierce?' asked Mark casually after a minute.

The boy thought carefully. 'How old?'

'Sixteen.'

'She new?'

'Might be.'

'Good looking tart. Yeah, I know her. She's over there.' He indicated with his head to a crowd of girls just coming down the main drive, and Mark's heart raced as he saw her, a head and shoulder above the rest.

'Yeah, that's her,' he said.

'Your bird?' asked the boy.

'No,' said Mark.

'Fancy her, do ya?'

'Maybe.'

'Bit tasty.'

Mark agreed with a nod.

'You chatted her up?'

'Not yet,' said Mark as he got to his feet and walked towards the girls. 'See ya,' he said over his shoulder, and the boy nodded in reply.

The girls had entered the park and found a shady spot under a huge oak tree where they sat in a circle and produced sandwiches, snacks and drinks from various bags that they dropped in the centre of their camp. Mark watched for a moment and went closer, the sun at his back so that his shadow preceded him. One of the girls, a plump blonde, noticed his approach and nudged the one next to her.

Some boys of his age would have been intimidated by the young women, but Mark knew his worth. And he was no timid virgin. There were plenty of women camp-followers around the Jenner mob, and more than one of them had been happy to initiate a handsome young man into the ways of love.

Still keeping the sun behind him, Mark stopped by the group and, speaking only to Linda, he said, 'Hello.'

The blonde and one of her mates started giggling hysterically but Mark ignored them. 'Hello,' he said again.

Linda Pierce blushed as she realised he was speaking to her. 'Hello,' she said back. The blonde could hardly contain herself, rolling on the grass and showing off her knickers.

'Do you fancy an ice cream?' asked Mark.

The blonde almost burst at that.

'Oh do shut up, Bren,' said Linda. 'You'll wet yourself. And pull your skirt down. I can see everything you've got.'

This only made the girl laugh harder and Mark had to smile too. 'Well, do you?' he asked, hunkered down on his haunches, took off his shades and gave Linda the full effect of his eyes.

She thought for a second and twitched her nose. 'All right,' she said. 'If only to get away from her,' indicating the blonde.

'She's enjoying life,' said Mark, standing up and extending his hand.

'Too much,' said Linda and allowed him to pull her to her feet. At the touch of their skin, he felt an electric shock and knew she felt the same.

'My name's Mark,' he said.

'Linda,' she said, disengaging her fingers.

'Hello, Linda.'

'Hello, Mark.'

And as they walked in the direction of the ice cream van, he heard the blonde say through waves of laughter. 'Blimey, Linda's got a boyfriend. That's a first.'

'I can only be a minute,' said Linda. 'I've got some homework to catch up on.'

'That's OK,' replied Mark. 'I'll just get you a small cone.'

Linda just looked at him as if he was mad.

'If that's all right.'

'Yes,' she said.

'Good.'

'Tell me something.'

'What?'

'Why did you come over just now?'

'To talk to you, of course.'

'You've got a nerve,' she said as they stood in the queue, all the other kids' eyes upon them.

'I wanted to speak to you,' said Mark. 'Before you went.'

'Those girls will be taking the mick forever now,' said Linda.

'Your mates,' he said.

'Bunch of loonies more like.'

They got to the top of the queue and Mark ordered a pair of cones and gave one to Linda and they walked to a quiet corner of the park. 'I don't usually do this,' the young woman said.

'What?'

'Let blokes pull me.'

'Have I pulled you then?'

'You know what I mean.'

'So, will you come out with me?'

'I don't think so. My mum and dad are pretty strict.'

'Just for a walk or something. No big deal. Nothing heavy. I understand about the school work. I wouldn't want to mess up your education.'

'You talk like a teacher.'

'Do I?'

'How old are you, Mark?'

'Nineteen.'

'My mum would go spare.'

'Why?'

'You're too old for me.'

'How old are you then?' Although Mark knew.

'Fifteen.'

'And never been kissed.'

She coloured again. 'I wouldn't say that.'

'You got a bloke?'

She shook her head.

'Good.'

'Don't go getting any ideas just because I let you buy me this.' She held up her ice cream. 'It was just to get away from Brenda. I thought she was going to die laughing.'

'Me too. Is she your best friend?'

'One of them. I just moved to school here last term.'

'You live local?' It was half question, half statement.

'Yes. You?'

'Streatham.'

'What are you doing here?'

'Just on a wander. Sat down and saw you.'

'Don't.'

'Don't what?'

'You know.'

'Why not?'

'It's not right. Listen, I've got to go.'

Mark saw that the other four girls had stood up, collected their things and were looking in his and Linda's direction. 'Can I have your phone number?' he asked.

'No.'

'How about lunch tomorrow? We could get a burger.'

140

'No.'

'Please.'

'No.'

'What if I won't take no for an answer?'

'You'll have to.'

'Will I?'

'Yes.'

'I'm very persistent.'

'Don't be silly.'

'I'm not. And I'll be here waiting for you, come rain or shine,' he said as she walked away. 'Count on it.'

He waited to see if she turned, but she didn't. She joined her friends and they descended on her like a flock of bright birds. He imagined what they were saying and asking, but she never looked at him as they went back through the school gates and got lost in the crowd of school uniforms.

He was there the next day at the same time, but she didn't show up. He sat in the sunshine and knew he was being watched, but by whom he wasn't sure.

He came the following day and the day after, but there was still no sign of Linda Pierce.

The next day, Friday, May 14th. He'd never forget that day. It was raining buckets, but still he sat on the same bench at the same time.

The park was empty. No kids, no ice cream man. Just Mark Farrow sitting with the collar of his jacket turned up against the wet when a lone figure in a blue mac came out of the school, down the drive, over the road and across the grass towards him. She was carrying an umbrella and as she got closer he realised it was the laughing blonde. She stopped in front of him, a big grin on her face. 'She said that you were persistent,' she said.

'I am,' he agreed.

'She was worried you'd catch a cold. She sent you this.' In her hand was a scrap of paper. The blonde gave it to Mark and he opened it. 'Tomorrow, twelve, the Wimpy in the Whitgift,' it read, and was signed 'Linda'.

'Why didn't she come herself?' asked Mark, suspecting a gag.

'She's a bit shy,' said the blonde. 'But she'll be there. She likes you. She's seen you waiting every day.'

'Thanks,' said Mark. 'Brenda, isn't it?'

She blushed at the question. 'Yeah,' she said and turned to go. But stopped and looked back. 'Gosh,' she said, a faraway look in her eyes. 'I wish a bloke would wait for me like you are for Linda.'

'One will,' said Mark.

'You reckon?'

'Anyone who can laugh like you do will never be lonely,' he said.

'Cor, but Linda's lucky,' said Brenda, and she walked back to school.

Mark held the note for a moment before putting it in his pocket and heading back towards his car.

THIRTEEN

The following day, Mark was in Croydon an hour early for his meeting with Linda. He parked his car in the shopping centre garage again and joined the crowds looking for bargains in the Whitgift. He saw the Wimpy bar on the mezzanine and spent the next fifty minutes in a couple of book and record shops. He didn't buy anything. He was too preoccupied with the thought of meeting Linda Pierce. John and Chas had asked where he was going and where he'd been every lunchtime that week, but he just smiled and kept schtum. '*Cherchez la femme*,' John had said, and Mark hadn't disagreed.

'Got a bird?' asked Chas, never one to beat about the bush.

'Leave him,' said Hazel, ruffling his hair. 'You're only young once. Let him have his fun.'

'But no bun in the oven,' said Jenner.

'I said leave him,' said Hazel, and even tough John Jenner knew it was best to do what she said.

At quarter to twelve, Mark entered the steamy café that smelled of meat grilling, bought a coffee and sat at a table by the window. But he couldn't drink it. He just stirred the dun-coloured liquid, a hollow spot growing in his stomach as he convinced himself she wouldn't show, and had just sent the note to get rid of him. The place was just starting to fill with the lunchtime crowd and Mark watched the pedestrians walking by outside. Then he saw her and he had to take a sudden breath. She was wearing jeans and a sweater and carrying a small leather handbag, and he thought he'd never seen anyone look more wonderful in his whole life. She walked past the window where he was sitting and through the door, stopped and looked around. He couldn't help smiling as he raised his hand to attract her attention, and she smiled back when she saw him and walked over. He knew then that it was love and that he'd never forget the moment if he lived forever.

'Hello,' he said and stood up.

'Hello,' she said back, and they just stood looking at each other until Mark said, 'What do you want? To drink I mean.' Suddenly he wasn't so self assured as he normally was around women.

'A milkshake, please,' she said. 'Chocolate.'

She sat, and he went to the counter and ordered the shake and when he took it back it wasn't the only thing shaking.

He put her drink on the table and sat opposite. 'I wondered if you'd come,' he said to break the silence.

'I wouldn't have sent the note if I wasn't.'

'I thought maybe your friends were having a laugh. You know, sending me on a wild goose chase.'

'They wouldn't dare. Anyway, they've been talking about nothing else all week.'

Mark looked out of the window. 'Do you think they might come and see?' he asked.

'I told them not to. But that Brenda…'

'She seems all right.'

'She fancies you.'

'What about you?'

Linda blushed. 'I don't know. But when I saw you sitting there all alone in the rain…'

'I told you I'd be there, come rain or shine.'

'I know.'

'Ray Charles,' said Mark.

'Who?'

He smiled again. 'Brother Ray.'

She shook her head in a bewildered fashion.

'You don't know who Ray Charles is?' he asked.

She shook her head once more.

'I'll play it for you one day. You'll like it…' he hesitated. 'At least I hope you will.'

'I'm sure I will if you do.'

He felt ten feet tall at that. 'Thanks for the vote of confidence.'

'Actually, I didn't know if I should come.'

'Why not?'

'Family reasons. You know…' She didn't finish her sentence. 'My mum. She's not been well the last few years.'

Mark could easily guess why. It's not every woman's husband who gets life for killing a policeman.

'Does your mum know you're meeting me?'

'God no.' She put her hand over her mouth. 'Sorry. I didn't mean…'

'That's OK. So where are you supposed to be?'

'Meeting the girls for window shopping. I hate lying to Mum, but…' Once again she didn't finish.

'I didn't mean to cause you problems,' he said.

'It's not you. Any boy would be the same.'

'Thanks,' he said, but he grinned to show he didn't mean it.

'Sorry.' Then she saw his face. 'Are you teasing me?' she asked.

He couldn't think of anything he'd rather do right then. 'Yes,' he said.

'You are terrible.'

'No I'm not. So what do you want to do? Now, I mean.'

'Go window shopping like I said I was going to.' She stopped herself again. 'Sorry. Boys don't like window shopping, do they?'

'You might be surprised. I don't mind what we do. Just as long as I'm with you.'

She gave him a look that could have meant anything. 'Fine,' she said. 'But I hope you've got comfortable shoes on.'

They finished their drinks and left the restaurant and spent the next few hours wandering through Croydon, from the Mall to the market. By three they were both exhausted and Mark suggested a drink.

'Do I look eighteen today?' asked Linda. 'We've been thrown out of most of the pubs round here for being underage.'

'You bad girls.'

'We have our moments.'

'I bet you do, especially Brenda, eh?'

She frowned. 'Do you like her?'

'Why not?' Then he saw her look. 'I don't fancy her,' he said, 'if that's what you mean. But she seems like good company. Has she got a boyfriend?'

'One a week, our Bren,' said Linda.

They went into the Market Tavern and Linda sat in a quiet corner away from the staff and asked for an orange juice with ice. Mark went to the bar and ordered it, plus a pint of lager for himself. The place was buzzing and Buck's Fizz were loud on the jukebox.

'What are you doing later?' Mark asked casually when they were sitting comfortably.

'Revision,' she said.

'OK.'

'You don't mind?'

'Course not.'

'And they're expecting me for my tea soon.'

'They?' asked Mark, although he was well aware who they were.

'Mum and Dad. Well, he's my stepdad really, but I never really knew my real dad. And my brother.'

'What happened to your real dad?' asked Mark casually although he knew he was stepping on thin ice.

'He died,' said Linda. And by her tone he knew that she knew exactly what had happened to him.

'Mine too,' said Mark, not digging any deeper.

'I'm sorry.'

'I didn't know him either,' said Mark. 'I live with my uncle and his wife now.'

'Your aunt.'

'No. See, he's not really my uncle. I just call him that. He was a friend of my father's. They took me in.'

'And your mum. Is she dead too?'

146

'No. But she might as well be for all I see of her. She got into some bad ways. Drinking too much. Running with bad men. She's married now, but I couldn't live with them.'

'Why not?'

'He's a bit too fisty for my liking.'

'He hit you?'

'Me and Mum. I had to get out.'

'That's terrible.'

'I survived. But I worry about Mum. But she won't leave the bloke. He's had a few warnings, but… well, you know.'

'What kind of warnings?'

'From my uncle. But Mum's soft… Anyway, I don't want to talk about it.'

'My stepdad's great,' she said. Then hesitated. 'Sorry.'

'Don't be. It's not your fault my mum's a bloody fool. You're lucky.'

'Yes we are,' she agreed. 'He loves me and Sean.'

'That's your brother?'

'Yes. He's older than me. Nearer your age.'

'Almost a pensioner,' said Mark.

'Silly.'

'What does he do?' Mark asked.

'He's at college.'

'A smart boy.'

She nodded. 'So what do you do?'

'I work for my uncle.'

'Has he got his own business?'

'You might say that.'

'What kind of business?'

'Leisure.'

'And what do you do?'

'This and that.'

'You're a bit secretive.'

'No. It's just that I'm more interested in you.'

She blushed again. 'I'm not that interesting.'

'I think you are.'

'Tell me something,' she said after a moment.

'What?'

'Why did you come over to me last week?'

Mark thought for a moment. 'I told you that already.'

'Tell me again.'

'Because I thought you were beautiful.'

She shook her head. 'There are lots of beautiful girls in the world. Much more beautiful than I am. Why me?'

'That's it. I wanted to talk to you.'

She seemed satisfied by that. 'OK. Listen, I've got to go soon. The books call.'

'Can I see you again?'

'It's difficult.'

'I know. I'm too old for you and you've got your exams. When are they? Next month?'

She nodded.

'But I would like to see you.'

'And I'd like to see you too.'

'Give me your phone number.'

'No, I can't. It would be just too much of a problem. With Mum, you know. I know it sounds daft, but I've never had a boyfriend. Not a proper one. I'm sorry.'

'Well, I can't wait for it to rain so that you'll take pity on me again. Summer's coming.' She laughed at that.

'I'll give you my car phone number then,' said Mark. 'I'm out most of the time so it's easier than leaving messages at home.'

She seemed impressed that he had a car, let alone with a phone in. Those were the days before every hooligan had a mobile and they were still a bit of a novelty. 'I have to be around and about for work,' he explained as he jotted it down on a piece of paper from her bag.

'OK,' she said and tucked it away in one of the pockets.

'You will call me, won't you?'

'If I can.'

'Please, Linda.'

'All right, I'll call, but I can't say when.'

'Good.'

'Now I really must go.'

'Do you want me to give you a lift?'

'I can walk, it's not far.'

'I'd like to.'

'All right,' she said with a bit of reluctance. 'But you'll have to let me out round the corner. If my dad sees me getting out of a strange car, it'll be the Spanish Inquisition.' They finished their drinks and walked out into the Croydon sunshine and Mark took Linda's hand as they went back to the car park under the shopping precinct. She didn't object, and her warm fingers felt good intertwined with his. She admired the brand new car he was driving and he felt that everything was going his way. He put the problem of telling her how her father had gunned his down in a dirty gutter to the back of his mind. As he drove out of the garage he almost turned in the direction of her house before he remembered that he wasn't supposed to know where she lived, and asked directions.

She told him, and it just took a few minutes to get to the suburban streets on the outskirts of Croydon where she asked him to pull in about a quarter mile from her address. 'Call me soon,' he said.

'I'll try.'

'Please,' he said again, and he really meant it. He hadn't had such a happy afternoon since before Bobby Thomas had come into his mother's life and she'd taken him shopping up west for nothing in particular. Just a wander, as she'd called it. A look around the shops, and an ice cream for Mark on the way home.

'I will,' she said and kissed him quickly on the cheek before jumping out of the car and slamming the door behind her.

He watched as she trotted down the street in her high heels, her bottom swinging provocatively in her tight jeans, and he knew that one day they would be together.

She did call, but not for several weeks, and Mark had almost given up on her. 'Blimey,' he said, when he answered the phone and she'd identified herself. 'I thought you'd left the country.'

'I'm going to soon,' she replied. 'Two weeks in Spain with Mum, Dad and Sean.'

'Don't get arrested,' he said. 'You know what Brits abroad are like.'

'I won't. I'm going to be a good girl.'

'You're always a good girl as far as I can see.'

'Yeah, well.' There was a wistful tone in her voice.

'So, to what do I owe the pleasure of this call?'

'I've been thinking about you.'

'Have you?'

'You stopped coming round.'

'You made it pretty obvious you didn't want me to.'

'I never said that.'

'Not in so many words maybe.'

'You know what it was like…'

'No, I don't actually. You never let me get that close.'

'I'm sorry,' she said. 'It was exams, and Mum and Dad. Bren said I was barmy, and could she have your number.'

'She never phoned.'

'Because I wouldn't give it to her. You'd've had her knickers off on the first date.'

'Would that have worried you?'

'Course it would.'

'I never would've guessed.'

'Well, it would.'

'So are the exams over?'

'S'right.'

'How did you do?'

'Pretty well I think, but the results won't be through for ages.'

'So you're free now?'

'More or less. Until we go away.'

150

'Can I take you out then?'

'It's still difficult…'

'But can I?'

'Suppose so.'

'Don't sound so keen.'

'I am, honest.'

'So, let me take you for a meal one evening.'

'I've never been for a meal with a boy.'

'There was the Wimpy.'

'That's different.'

Mark laughed.

'Don't laugh at me.'

'I'm not. Tonight?'

'No. Saturday. There's a party for the girls. End of exams. I could go then, they'll cover for me.'

'Secret Squirrel.'

'No, secret Brenda.'

'She's all right, that Brenda.'

'I knew you fancied her.'

'I fancy you.'

'And I fancy you.' So there it was. She'd finally admitted it, and Mark felt like king of the world.

They went for their meal that Saturday. Linda looked even better than Mark remembered, and years older than her age. When he took her home, before eleven, like she'd promised her family, they kissed in the front of the BMW. But Mark didn't force anything.

They dated all that summer, with the exception of the two weeks Linda spent on holiday. She wrote him eleven postcards, which he kept for years.

Finally, on a warm September evening, Linda surrendered her virginity in the back of the car. Mark was as tender as any nineteen year old could be, and afterwards she cried, and he didn't know if she was happy or sad, and she never told him. She smoked her first cigarette that night too, sharing a Silk Cut with Mark on the drive home. 'Do you want to see me again?' she asked when they stopped at the usual place, just round the corner from her house.

'Of course I do. Why wouldn't I?'

'You've got what you wanted, some boys don't. After. You know. So I've been told.'

'I'm not some boys.'

'So you do?'

'Try and keep me away.'

'Because we'll have to do it all the time now.'

'No.'

'Why then?'

'Because I love you, Linda.' His mouth was dry and his hands trembled on the wheel as he said the words.

'Do you?'

'Since the first day I saw you.'

'In the park.'

'Yes,' he lied. Although it had been before, at her house that morning, but he'd never told her.

'You mean it?'

'I've never meant anything more.'

She started to cry again. Mark wasn't used to so much emotion, and he held her close. It was all he could think to do. 'I love you too,' she whispered.

He could hardly believe his ears. 'Do you?'

'Since the first day I saw you.'

'In the park.'

'Yes,' she replied. 'In the park.'

They stayed close for what seemed like hours. Mark was as happy as he could ever remember. There was just one problem. One day, and he didn't know when, he would have to tell Linda that her father had murdered his. And he didn't know how he was going to do it.

FOURTEEN

'D idn't you?' John Jenner said again to Mark. 'Didn't you?'

'What?' said Mark, suddenly jolted out of his reverie.

'Fancy her. That Linda Pierce. And she nearly screwed you up for life.'

Fancied her. Mark had loved her since that first time he'd seen her, and now, all these years later, it seemed that John Jenner knew something of her whereabouts. And as for the other, well that had always been his business. He tried to keep the tension out of his voice when he spoke. 'You know where she is?' he asked.

'Course I do. I've kept up with all of them. I told you that.'

'So? Tell me.'

'Why are you so interested?'

'I just am. Where are they?'

'Marje and Tom are both dead. You know, the bloke she married.'

Mark nodded.

'Little Linda got married, but her husband was killed in an accident.' Mark gave him a look. 'Oh don't be silly. I had nothing to do with it.'

Mark said nothing.

'She had a couple of kids. Luke and Daisy. And Sean moved in with her after the accident. She's got a nice place in Croydon again as a matter of fact. She didn't move far.'

'What's the address?'

'Mark.'

'What's the address, Uncle?'

'You're not going to…'

'I just want to see her,' Mark lied. 'I won't speak to her.'

John Jenner shook his head. 'OK, son. On your own head be it. But you remember what happened last time.'

'I was just a kid. So was she.'

Jenner gave him the address.

'Fine. I'm going out.'

'Christ, but I wish that bastard hadn't turned up this morning,' said Jenner, also wishing he'd kept his big mouth shut about it.

'But he did,' said Mark, and with that he went out to his car. He sat inside for a few minutes trying to calm the shaking in his arms and legs. Linda, he thought. Christ. I never thought I'd see you again.

He started the car, opened the gates and headed towards Croydon. Black clouds, like broken promises, loomed up before him as he drove. The road through Norbury and Thornton Heath had changed too in his absence, but he could have found his way there blindfold, so vivid were his memories.

He found the address John Jenner had given him without any trouble. It was a move up in the world from Tom Pierce's old place, in one of Croydon's smarter suburbs, a detached house with garage extension, with what looked like a tiny flat over it. He parked on the opposite side of the street and got out of the car and took a slow stroll, his eyes never off the building.

Parked on the short drive was a red Toyota Land Cruiser on a four year old plate. It was still in good nick, its paintwork gleaming. The thunderheads brought squally rain and Mark pulled up the collar of his overcoat as he walked. Just like May 14th, he thought. Me getting soaking wet waiting for Linda to show up.

He went back to the car and sat inside. Around three-thirty a procession of vehicles, mostly big four wheel drives like the Toyota, came down the street. It was the home from school run. He watched as a Fiat saloon pulled into the drive of Linda's house and a young blonde got out and unloaded a small boy in a red school sweatshirt, jeans and trainers. 'Luke,' said Mark to himself. The boy was dark haired and lively and ran to the front door which was opened by a dark haired woman. Mark was too far away to see the boy's face, but he knew he'd be the spit of his mother. It was something in the way he moved, and Mark felt a stab of jealousy that the boy wasn't his son. He peered through his rain -speckled windscreen and his heart turned over. It was Linda in the doorway. The boy jumped up at her and she swung him indoors and out of sight. The blonde, presumably a nanny or *au pair* or babyminder or whatever they called them these days, collected a kitbag from the car, followed the boy through the front door and closed it behind her.

Mark had seen enough. With all the kids about he felt even more out of place, like some kind of peeper, so he started the engine and drove home.

'Satisfied?' asked John Jenner when he'd arrived and slumped into an armchair. 'I assume you've seen her.'

'Yes, I saw her. And I'm going to see her again.'

The older man said nothing. Just walked out of the room and slammed the door behind him.

Mark sat where Jenner had left him, and his mind travelled back through the years.

*   *   *

That first winter he and Linda were together, they spent as much time in each other's company as possible. Around Crystal Palace and Anerley were a number of cheap hotels and motels, mostly used by reps and businessmen staying in London on a budget. Not that money was a problem to Mark, there was plenty of that available, but those hotels were convenient, and love didn't worry about its surroundings as long as they were clean and had a bed. So, whenever they could, they sneaked away for stolen hours of passion. But Mark knew, however wonderful the sex was and however much they pledged themselves to each other, he was living a lie. Eventually, it all got too much for him. He decided to tell Linda the truth.

He broke the news in a hotel room on Upper Sydenham Road. They'd made love all afternoon. Their affair was still new and they were both young. Mark, barely twenty, and Linda sixteen. The radio was on, playing something by Billy Idol. He'd never forget that, and he was sitting on the window ledge with a panorama that took in most of London behind him. Great views up there on the lip of London. Not that they had much time for looking out of the window in those days. Linda was sitting half on and half in the double bed they'd rented, her breasts bare and the sheet just about covering her legs. She lit a cigarette and Mark did the same, then said: 'You don't know who I am, do you?'

'Sorry?' said Linda.

'You don't know who I am,' he repeated.

'Course I do. You're Mark Farrow. Is this a joke?'

'Mark Farrow,' he said. 'Doesn't that ring any bells?'

She shook her head and he could see the bewilderment on her face.

'Billy Farrow,' he said. 'How about that?'

Nothing.

'Who are you then?' he asked.

'Mark, I don't like this.'

'Tell me your name,' he said.

'Linda Pierce. You know that. Don't, you're frightening me.'

Mark knew that he'd taken the wrong tack, but it was too late to turn back. 'No, you're not,' he said. 'You're Linda Hunter.'

Bewilderment was replaced by something else. A hint of awareness. Mark could see the emotions wash over her face, like the sea smoothing over a beach. 'What do you mean?' she asked.

'That's who you used to be before your mum got married again, isn't it?'

She nodded, and tears came to her eyes as she realised what he was saying.

'Billy Farrow was my dad,' said Mark, moving towards the bed. But Linda wouldn't let him touch her.

'And my father...' She couldn't finish the sentence.

Mark nodded. 'He killed him.'

'And you knew?'

'I always knew.'

'But why? Why come looking for me?'

'I wanted to see what you and Sean looked like.'

'Why?'

'Because... I don't know. I was curious. Then I saw you and fell in love with you.'

'In the park that day.'

Mark shook his head. 'No, before that. I came to your house. You never saw me.'

'And all this...' Her gesture took in the room, their affair, them.

'I couldn't help it. I had to tell you.'

'You lied to me.'

'I know, and I couldn't go on lying. I had to tell you the truth.'

'But how did you find me?'

'My Uncle John knew both our fathers. The things he does...'

'Being a gangster, you mean.' Linda was far from stupid and had long ago worked out what Mark and his family did for a living.

'That's right. But it's just a job.'

'You bastard.' Linda stubbed out her cigarette, scrambled off the bed and started to get dressed.

Mark sat where she left him and tried not to watch. 'Don't go,' he said. 'I couldn't help it.'

'All this was just lies,' she sobbed. 'All lies.'

'No,' he protested. 'No. I love you, Linda.'

She stopped getting dressed, and stood in her underwear on the thin carpet. 'But you never told me.'

'I just did. I couldn't live like this any more.'

'Like what?'

'Living a lie. I should've told you from the start, but you'd never have spoken to me. It was hard enough as it was.'

Linda slipped her dress over her head. 'I don't know, Mark,' she said. 'I don't know if I can handle this.'

He got to his feet and went to her, but she stiffened at his touch. 'Don't,' she said. 'Get me a cab, I want to go home.'

Mark knew better than to force it, so he picked up the phone and asked the receptionist to call a taxi.

Linda left him in the room, and he stood at the window as the cab arrived and Linda got in the back.

It was going to be some time before he heard from her again.

The morning after John Jenner had spilled the beans about Linda, Mark was up and about early. Even before Chas. He didn't bother with breakfast and left the house before seven. He stopped at a café in Norwood and bought a tea to go, which he drank as he drove down to Croydon. By eight o'clock he was parked in the same spot as the previous afternoon.

The house looked exactly the same, with the addition of a Ford Mondeo parked up next to the garage. There was no sign of the Toyota or the Fiat. Inside the garage, Mark assumed. But who did the Ford belong to? Mark hoped it wasn't some boyfriend of Linda's on an overnighter.

Just before nine the garage doors opened and the Fiat came out, driven by the nanny or whatever. The Toyota was inside and she didn't close the door, which probably meant that Linda was going to be coming out too. The nanny pulled the car round to the front door, which opened, and he saw Linda and the boy, Luke, standing in the doorway. He was dressed in cargo pants, trainers, the red school sweatshirt and a big jacket. Linda was in her dressing gown. Luke was carrying a lunch box, and Linda kissed him before he ran to the nanny's car, jumped into the front seat, belted up, and off they went. Linda closed the front door and all was quiet.

Next out was Sean Pierce, who Mark recognised from his visit to Jenner's house the day before. He came down the stairs on the outside of the garage from the flat, got into the Ford, let it warm up a minute and then drove off too. So that answered that question: John had said the brother was also living in the house. Mark had drawn back into his seat as he watched Sean leave for work. Unlike on TV, people did notice strange men sitting in strange cars in suburban streets. And they did phone the cops. And Pierce, being a cop himself, was more likely than most to be suspicious. Mark didn't look at him directly, just out of the corner of his eye, until the car had gone.

Nothing much happened for another hour. People came and went in the street, and Mark tried hard to look like he belonged.

Just before ten, there was more movement at the house. Linda entered the garage from the inside door, carrying a baby all swaddled up in a one piece, pink romper suit. Daisy. Linda was dressed in jeans and a leather jacket and Mark was pleased to notice she hadn't lost her figure during her pregnancies. She opened the back door of the Land Cruiser and strapped Daisy into the child seat in the back. She put a carryall next to her, got in the front, started the motor and drove on to the drive. She shut the garage door using a remote and headed off. Mark gave her a moment, then followed.

The high, bright, shiny truck was easy to keep in view. At first Linda headed towards London, then turned off at Crystal Palace and took a right into the Safeway carpark. Mark was right behind her and watched as she parked up, took out the baby and headed for the lifts. When she was gone, he followed.

Upstairs, in the warm supermarket entrance, he watched as she strapped Daisy into the child seat of a trolley. He helped himself to one and followed, keeping an aisle's distance between them. Mark couldn't believe he was so close to her after all this time. He only caught glimpses as she moved slowly along the shelves, but she seemed not to have changed one bit in all the years since they'd last met. But she must have. Getting married, having children. Losing a mother, stepfather and husband in such a short space of time. How long she'd been married he didn't know. It couldn't have been long: her hair was still raven black, her skin smooth. He could almost feel the former sliding through his fingers, and the coolness of the latter under his lips.

She shopped from a list she held in one hand, pushing the trolley with the other. Inside the shop she'd loosened Daisy's suit to expose a white T-shirt underneath. Mark shadowed her for ten minutes, occasionally dropping some item into his trolley. Eventually, he made his move.

Linda was reading something on a packet of cereal when he approached her, blocking her way with his trolley. She didn't look at him, just moved hers to one side. He blocked her again. 'Excuse me,' she said, trying to avoid him, but he didn't let her. She looked at him, annoyance on her face. 'I said excuse me…' she repeated. And then, for the first time, his face registered with her. He saw something click behind her eyes, her face paled, and he could almost see a lightbulb come on over her head, just like in a cartoon. 'Mark,' she said. Her hands whitened on the handle of the trolley, and for a split second he thought she was going to faint.

'Linda,' he said. 'Jesus. I'm sorry. I didn't mean to…' and he went to her and held her arm to steady her.

She stepped back, pulling her arm free angrily, and Daisy, who until then had been quiet, sensed something was wrong and began to cry. 'Now look what you've done,' said Linda. 'There Daisy, it's all right.'

The baby looked at them, and reassured, settled down again.

'Sorry, Linda,' said Mark. 'I didn't know how else to see you.'

'What do you mean?'

'I could hardly come round the house with a bunch of flowers and bottle of plonk, could I?'

'What house? What are you talking about?'

'Your house?'

'What about my house?'

'Your house in Croydon.'

'I don't understand.'

'I was watching you.'

'You what? Are you mad?' Her face was stormy now, the various expressions sweeping over it. He remembered that she could never hide her feelings, that he'd told her never to play poker for money.

'I don't know. Maybe. But I had to see you somehow.'

'Mark, what are you playing at?'

'I'm not playing at anything. I'm trying to talk to you.'

'Just like that. You never got in touch. Never called.'

'I know. I'm sorry. Listen. Can we talk?'

She didn't answer, just looked at him. Her face had become a picture of sorrow. He knew he'd hurt her, but he'd never realised just how much until then. They stood together like actors in a play under the harsh supermarket fluorescent lights and Mark knew that he was close to losing the most precious thing in his life for the second time. And for the second time he knew that he was entirely to blame.

He pointed in the direction of the exits. 'There's a tea place. We could sit for a minute.' She shook her head.

'No, you bastard. No.'

'Please, Linda. Just for a minute. I have to explain. I have to. If I ever meant anything to you, just give me that.' He knew that he was manipulating her, but he also knew that if he walked away now, he might never have another chance. 'Please.'

He saw by her expression that she was softening. 'What about my shopping?' she said.

'Bring it with you. I promise I won't keep you long. Then you can finish up.'

'I suppose.'

'Come on then. I'm paying.'

'Christ, I must be mad,' she said. 'All right. Just for a minute. You take my trolley. I can see shopping still isn't your forte.' She looked into his trolley which contained a jar of instant gravy granules, a pound of butter and a tea strainer.

'I was plucking up the courage to talk to you.'

Linda blew breath through her teeth as she unfastened the harness that held her daughter and lifted her out of the child seat. 'Come on then,' she said.

Mark abandoned his shopping and followed her, pushing the trolley.

Linda felt the baby's bottom and wrinkled her nose. 'She needs changing. Give me that bag.' She indicated the carryall that was hanging off the trolley's handle. 'There's a changing room next to the cafe,' she said. 'I won't be long.'

'You won't run away,' said Mark as she left him.

'No, Mark. I won't run away. I'm not you.'

He smiled thinly. 'What do you want to drink?'

'Tea'll do.'

'Something for Daisy?'

'You know her name then?'

He nodded.

'No. Nothing for Daisy. I've got some juice in here.'

Mark watched as she went into the mother and baby room, parked the trolley and went into the café.

The tea came in two stainless steel pots, with metal handles that he knew would burn their fingers, a tea bag in each. The milk was in those horrible containers that he always managed to shoot all over the table, and the sugar was cubed in paper wrappers. He wondered for a moment if he should get a cake for Daisy, but all the pastries seemed to be nearly as big as she was, so he left it. He'd never had much to do with children and he didn't want his ignorance to show.

He took the tray to a table in the corner near the window and waited. He could feel the itch of sweat under his arms and wondered what can of worms he'd opened by talking to her. What would she do?

Linda only took a few minutes and, although the place was almost deserted, he waved as she and Daisy entered and they came over and joined him. He stood as they approached and pulled out a chair for each of them. 'Good manners,' she said as she sat, Daisy on her knee. 'That really impressed me that first day in Croydon. The way you stood up when I got to the table. Nobody had ever done anything like that for me before.'

'You still remember?'

'Of course I remember. What am I, an amnesiac?' Mark thought from her tone that she might like to be. She went on. 'I remember how much of a mug I was. There weren't many good manners in evidence when you left without saying goodbye.'

'No,' he said as he pulled up his own chair and poured two cups of tea, after giving the bags a good squeeze with a spoon.

Linda meanwhile took a baby's cup from her bag, filled it with juice from a bottle and gave Daisy her drink, which she started to swallow with gusto.

'She likes that,' said Mark for something to say.

'Yes,' said Linda as she toyed with her cup. 'So come on, Mark. You didn't follow me here to talk about Daisy's likes and dislikes.'

'No. I came to see you.'

'Seems like you've seen me already. You told me you've been watching.'

He nodded. 'I only found out where you were yesterday.'

'So how did you know where to watch?'

'Uncle John told me.'

'Good old Uncle John. And what did he tell you?'

He told her.

'Seems like he knows me as well as I know myself.'

'He didn't do it to hurt you or your children. He was just keeping up.'

'Christ,' she said. 'You people. You can never leave things alone.'

'I'm sorry.'

'No you're not.' She took a sip of tea, keeping the hot cup well away from her daughter. 'Do you know what?' she said. 'I gave up smoking the day I found out I was pregnant with Luke. Six years ago. I've never touched a cigarette since. But by God, I'd love one now.'

He moved his head towards the sign on the wall. 'No smoking in here,' he said.

'Still the same, Mark. Still the jokes. Do you still smoke?'

He nodded. He would've given anything for a smoke too, but mums with babies didn't like it. That was another piece of information he'd gleaned from the papers.

'Andy gave up the same day,' said Linda. 'For what it was worth.' She paused. 'Andy was my husband.'

'I know.'

'Of course. Uncle John told you.'

Mark ignored the jibe. 'He sounds like he was a good man. I'm sorry about what happened to him.'

163

'He was,' she replied. 'And you're not.'

He didn't know what to say. Whether to ask how long she'd been married, how they'd met. What do you say to a widow you used to sleep with?

'But he wasn't you,' she said softly.

'What?'

'Nothing. Forget it.'

A long silence followed except for Daisy's drinking noises and the hisses from the hot water machines behind the counter. Mark looked at Daisy. 'She's beautiful,' she said. 'Your daughter. She looks just like you.'

'Oh please.'

'I mean it.'

'Yes, well, everyone says so. But I'd better go now.'

He knew that this was the moment. 'Can I see you?' he asked.

'You are seeing me. Here I am, in the flesh.'

'You know what I mean.'

'Do you think I'm quite mad, Mark? I've got a family. I've got my brother, who I'm sure you're aware is a police officer, living in my house. And you're, well, what you are. I'm a widow.' She shook her head. 'That's got nothing to do with it. What I have got is a life, Mark, and now you turn up out of the blue and expect me to drop everything and start up with you again. Christ, Mark, you're a bloody…'

'Don't say it,' said Mark, touching the back of her hand and feeling the same old electricity. 'Forget that. I just want to see you.'

'Do you?'

He nodded.

'Do you know how many times in the last… How long is it?

'Eight years…'

'Something like that.'

'Do you know how many times I've wanted to hear you say that?' He shook his head. 'Every bloody day,' she said. 'Even when I was married to Andy. Even when I was screaming my head off with pain as I had my babies. And now you're saying it, I'm not sure I'm ready.'

'Please, Lin.'

'Don't Lin me. A cup of tea doesn't get you back in my good books.'

'Please. Somewhere private where we can talk.'

The emotions rushed over her features again. 'There's a flat,' she said with a long sigh. 'In Balham. By the station. Over a shop. Andy and I bought it for an investment. To rent out. But each tenant was worse than the last, we always seemed to come out down. Of course it doesn't matter now. The compensation and insurance paid for it ten times over. But I'm sure Uncle John told you all about that.'

Mark nodded again.

'So when I got the last people out I had it done up and left it empty. I'll keep it until one of these…' she nodded down at Daisy. '…Wants to leave home and they can move in if they want to. It's appreciating like mad at the moment.'

'A hot spot,' said Mark.

'What?'

'Nothing.'

'Anyway. We can meet there. I don't know why I'm doing this, Mark.'

'When?' he asked. 'Today?'

'No, not today. What do you expect me to do? Turn my life around just to suit you? Oh, of course you do, I've always done it before, haven't I?'

'Sorry. Tomorrow?'

'OK. Tomorrow afternoon. I'll get the kids sorted. Greta can look after them.'

Greta, Mark imagined, was the blonde in the Fiat.

'What's the address?' he asked.

She told him. Then she finished her tea and got up. 'I'd better get the rest of my shopping,' she said. 'Though God knows I've lost the mood.'

'Sorry.'

'You keep saying that.'

'Sorry.'

She shook her head and smiled for the first time. 'Goodbye, Mark,' she said. 'Don't spy on me any more.'

'OK.'

'I'll see you tomorrow.'

'Tomorrow. Goodbye, Linda; goodbye, Daisy.' The little girl looked him long and hard and he swore she lifted her hand to wave.

FIFTEEN

Mark spent the rest of the morning driving the streets, just going nowhere, his mobile phone switched off. He checked out the address in Balham that Linda had given him. It was over a shoe shop next to a newsagents, with a green door that you could easily miss if you didn't know it was there. He looked up at the windows, blind against the day and imagined Linda and her husband eagerly discussing the pros and cons of buying, decorating and then letting the place out. They must have been innocents to keep getting turned over. Or at least Andy must have been. Mark knew how he would've dealt with reneging tenants. Go in and give them a bit of a surprise early one morning. Show them exactly what the terms and conditions of the lease meant. He'd met landlords before who would string your cat up or poison the goldfish just because the rent was a day late.

But then, maybe it wouldn't be so bad to be innocent. Mark tried to remember what that was like, but it was too far in his past to register. And maybe that was what Linda had needed. An innocent to become involved with. A bloke who went to work every day, came home clean, and whose idea of excitement was a Saturday night bottle of wine, a video and a beautiful woman to take to bed after. And he did get the girl, when all was said and done. At the same time Mark was moving around Europe, doing jobs that were dangerous or stupid or both, working with unreliable people, just to get money to live.

At this thought he started the car and headed towards Streatham. He parked up behind the six-screen cinema and spent the afternoon trying to forget who he was in the company of a Tinseltown hero who never had to deal with the consequences of his actions.

167

Mark got home just as Martine arrived back from work.

'Haven't seen much of you lately, handsome,' she said.

'I've been about.'

'I bet you have. I hear you've been messing around that Linda again.'

'Is that right? Who told you?'

She just grinned and shook her head. 'Not a good idea, Mark,' she said. 'She was never the right one for you.'

'And you'd know.'

'Course I would. I know you better than you think.'

'Yeah.'

'What are you doing?' she asked.

'When?'

'Now.'

'Nothing.'

'Come with me. I've got a couple of places to show you. We can have a drink.'

He shrugged. He wasn't doing anything, and it might take his mind off Linda. 'OK. Where are we going?'

'You'll see. Come on, it's important. Historically important.'

He allowed himself to be led out to Martine's Mini Cooper. She started it up with a roar and sped out on to the street, through the gates and past the inevitable parked up Mercedes. She accelerated hard up the hill in the direction of Streatham, then took a succession of narrow back streets, the blat of the car's exhaust bouncing off the fronts of the houses. 'Are you going to slow down?' asked Mark, one hand tight on the handle above the passenger door.

'Sure. When I'm dead,' she replied and put the little car into a four-wheel drift at the next corner, making a white van coming in the same direction mount the pavement to avoid them. 'Soft, fat fucker!' she screamed as she took the next corner on two wheels, sped down the white line, back on to the main road close to Streatham bus station and pulled up.

'Christ,' said Mark, the memory of his recent adventures on four wheels still fresh. 'Who taught you to drive like that?'

'Chas,' she said.

'I might've known. What are we looking at?'

She pointed at the building across the road. 'That's the old ice rink,' she said.

'I do know that.'

'Do you know that's where Dad met Chas and Hazel?'

'What? Skating?'

She shook her curls and laughed. 'No. Not Dad's speed at all. At the back there was a place called the Bali Hai. Sort of dance hall, disco, meat market, all done up like some Polynesian knocking shop. It was where all the likely lads and girls used to go Friday and Saturday nights back then. Chas had been in borstal for stealing cars. My dad and your dad were there one night scoping out the girls when they bumped into Chas. Dad knew him a bit. When he found out he was looking for a bit of villainy he asked him to join the gang. It was Chas who suggested that they branched out.'

'Doing what?'

'Have patience.'

'And Hazel?'

'That's another funny story. I'll get Chas to tell you. Now, how about that drink?'

'If you say so.'

She started the engine and roared off, up by Streatham Common and back the way they'd come, except she suddenly turned off up another side street, drove to the top, pulled in outside a small bar and killed the engine. 'Come on,' she said. 'I'm thirsty.'

'Why here?' asked Mark.

'Come inside and I'll show you.'

They got out of the motor and went into the bar. It was warm and quiet with an open fire in one corner and some moody Blue Note compilation playing on the stereo. There were a couple of other customers but no one paid attention as they took stools at the counter. Martine ordered two beers from the boy behind the jump and once they had them they went and sat by the fire.

'So?' said Mark, looking round. 'What's so special about this place?'

'This is where it started,' said Martine, taking a sip of her beer straight from the neck.

'What did?'

'Everything. This was where Dad started his protection firm.'

'Here?'

'Yeah. It used to be a pub, and it was the first one he got to pay up.'

'I thought it was drugs that got him started.'

'It was. But the pubs and restaurants paid the wages.'

'Jesus. How do you know?'

'Dad brought me here on my eighteenth. Showed me what could be done and then took me and a load of my friends up to Soho for dinner.'

'Amazing. I wonder what it was like then.'

* * *

The first pub John Jenner chose to put Chas's masterplan into action was a disreputable little boozer at the back of Streatham High Road, in a steep street full of terraced houses with a few shops at the top. It was called the Beehive and, like most pubs at that time, had a saloon bar, a public, a snug and a bottle shop. So small was the building that the three bars and off-sales seemed to be almost climbing on top of each other for space. The decoration inside was post war green and brown, the carpet in the saloon had a pattern that even an archaeologist would have had trouble finding, and the snug and public's floors were bare wood without a trace of polish. There were open fireplaces in each of the bars that glowed dimly with smokeless fuel. Legislation had been brought in to put a stop to the smogs that had killed so many Londoners over the previous century or so. It was a cheerless place, flyblown and miserable, and when John and Billy entered one chilly autumn morning just after the barman had opened the doors, it smelled of stale beer, old cigarettes and lavatory cleaner.

'Are you sure about this?' asked Billy as they sat at a wobbly table on the corner of the saloon bar. They had ordered two halves of bitter that tasted to both of them like piss.

'Sure I'm sure. Chas did collections for a bloke down Croydon way last year. Pubs, clubs, restaurants, the lot. They were coining it.'

'And Chas must be right,' said Billy. He was getting a bit pissed off with the most recent recruit to the gang. John was giving too much credence to his ideas. But the drugs were about all gone, and money was getting tight. John Jenner had walked out on his job at the printers, rented a flat in Brixton Hill and bought an old Pontiac convertible that was always breaking down, off a bloke called Dev.

Billy still wasn't working and Wally was getting stroppy. And as for Martin, the Goon… well, he was just Martin. And although he was good for putting the frighteners on customers who were disinclined to pay their debts, he was another drag on their finances, because John had insisted on giving him a regular weekly wage. He said it would be worth it in the end, and he was the boss.

'So what happened?' asked Billy.

'What?' said John.

'If they were coining it, what happened?'

'He got nicked for breaking into cars, that's what happened. And got sent to borstal.' Billy said nothing, just took another sip of his drink and looked at the old cat sat on the bar, regarding him with rheumy eyes. 'Don't worry,' said John. 'It'll all work out, you'll see.'

'But I do worry.'

'Too much, if you ask me.'

'So what do we do now?' asked Billy.

'Watch.' John got up from his seat and went over to the bar. 'Get much trouble in here?' he asked the barman.

'Do me a favour,' said the man, resting for a moment from putting bottles of tonic water on a shelf. 'Does it look like it?'

'Could be,' said John. 'See, I've got a proposition for you.'

The barman turned and leant on the counter. 'What? You a pop group? We've got no music licence.'

'No, no, no,' said John, although it was an interesting idea that he put away for later. 'See, we're a security firm.'

'In that get up?' said the barman. John was wearing a suit from Lord John in Carnaby Street. A blue pinstripe, with a waisted, tight-sleeved jacket, a pale blue pin through collar shirt, narrow black knitted tie and Chelsea boots. The reefer coat he'd been wearing over it had been carefully removed and folded neatly on to a seat when they'd first come in. That was another thing. Although money was tight, John insisted that his boys, apart from Martin who could never get anything to fit right, still dressed in the height of fashion.

'What's wrong with it?'

The barman shrugged. 'To each his own,' he said. He was wearing baggy flannels, a collarless, once-white shirt and a cardigan that looked like he used it to mop the gents.

'Anyway,' said John. 'What we do is, for a certain sum each week we make sure you don't get any trouble.'

The barman laughed out loud. 'Sonny,' he said. 'Drink your drink and get yourself and your mate out of here before I call the law.'

John thought for a moment. He knew that he'd meet resistance but hadn't considered what to do when it arose. We'll burn those bridges when we come to them, he'd always thought. Well, here was one.

'I'm sure you'll reconsider when you've had time to think,' was all he could say.

'I'm sure I bloody well won't. I fought the bloody Germans so's you could prance around in that suit, son. Do you think you can scare me? A spell in the army would do you lot a power of good. Why they stopped National Service I'll never know.'

Christ, thought John, he's just like my old man. Stupid git. But he left it, turned, and with as much dignity as he could muster, went back to the table and collected his coat. Without touching any more of their drinks, he and Billy left.

'Told you,' said Billy as they walked up to Streatham High Road and went into the Golden Egg restaurant to get the taste of the beer out of their mouths. 'Bloody told you, didn't I?'

'A little local difficulty,' said John quoting something he's heard some politician or other spouting on the TV a few days before. 'Martin, Wally and Chas'll see to it.'

'How?'

'I think it's about time those boys had a night out. A few drinks down the old Beehive should do the trick.'

Billy sucked at the straw in his coke. What had started out as a laugh was getting out of hand. He was tired of all the ducking and diving it involved. A few weeks earlier he'd seen a documentary on TV about young men joining the police, and what a good career it was. He'd watched it with interest. It seemed like a good, reasonably well-paid job, and it was on the right side of the law. Billy was no fool. He could see this whole gangster business ending in tears, with all of them in jail. He fancied a try at joining the police, but knew that John would go mad if he told him. 'Whatever you say,' he said. 'But I don't want any more trouble.'

'You like the money though, don't you?' said John.

'I don't care about the money,' replied Billy. 'You know if my mum finds out what I've been doing it'll kill her.'

'Mummy's boy,' said John.

Fuck me, maybe that's just what I am, thought Billy as he looked miserably out at the busy street. It was beginning to rain.

John caught up with Martin in the pie shop the same lunchtime. 'How's it going, son?' he asked as he took a seat and looked with disgust at the double portions of everything with liquor that the big man was digging into with his fork and spoon.

'Mustn't grumble.'

'Good. Got a job for you.'

'Yeah?'

'Yeah. You up for it?'

'What?'

'What I want you to do.'

'Suppose.'

'Good.' And he explained in words of one syllable.

173

When he'd finished, Martin swallowed some pie and asked with his mouth full: 'Can I get my gun soon?'

'Soon,' said John. 'Just be patient.'

The next evening, Friday, around eight-thirty pm, Wally, Chas and Martin walked into the Beehive, bought drinks and sat down. The pub wasn't much busier than it had been the previous morning. An old boy in a raincoat and trilby sat at the bar next to the cat who apparently hadn't moved in a day and a half. The barman had been joined by a slatternly looking woman who might have been his wife or might not. At the bar sat two men in their late twenties who'd missed the Swinging Sixties and who still dressed in the remnants of the Teddy boy gear of their youth. To Wally and Chas they looked like something out of the Middle Ages. Martin didn't have much dress sense. In the far corner, an ancient woman nursed a port and lemon which she sucked through a mouthful of gum with few teeth.

'Could do with some music in here,' said Wally.

'That could be the next thing,' said Chas. 'Jukeboxes. Lots of money in jukeboxes.'

'Mm,' replied Wally. 'Good idea. Have you told John?'

'First things first. Let's get us a few pubs under our belts before we expand.'

'Yeah.'

'Let's go then,' said Chas, picking up his pint jug and lobbing it at the few bottles on optic behind the bar.

The jug smashed a bottle of whiskey and went on to shatter the old fashioned mirror behind it. 'Yeah!' screamed Chas, as he picked up the table and hurled it at the man in the raincoat, who, agility belying his looks, ducked out of sight behind the counter as the cat fled.

'Oi!' shouted the publican, but by then the three boys were hurling chairs and tables everywhere. The two bar staff retreated through a doorway, slamming it behind them. Only the old girl with the port and lemon stayed still as Wally went behind the bar, rung up the till and took the few pounds inside it. Martin ripped a chair apart and demolished the glasses and bottles behind the counter. The two teds looked at the size of him and slunk out by the front door. A couple of faces peered in from the public and snug but didn't interfere. When the saloon bar looked as if a war had been fought in it and stank of spilled spirits, the trio fled, diving into Wally's van and losing themselves in the back streets of Streatham.

'Fuckin' hell, but that was great,' said Wally as they sped along. 'I could do that every night.'

'You might have to,' said Chas. 'Now where we going?'

'Pictures,' said Martin. 'John promised. There's a new Elvis on up at the Palace.'

'Jesus,' said Chas. 'I tell you what, we'll give you the ticket money and drop you off. I fancy a club. How about you, Wol?'

'I'm up for it.'

So that was what they did, giving Martin enough for a seat in the balcony and an ice cream in the interval. Two, in fact.

The next morning John and Billy turned up at the Beehive just as a uniformed constable was leaving. 'This could be fun,' said John as they walked into the remains of the saloon bar. Broken tables and chairs were piled up in one corner, the optics were empty and tape had been stuck over the mirror. The publican was mopping up the far side of the bar. 'We're closed,' he growled without looking up.

'Blimey,' said John. 'Had an accident?'

The publican turned his head and John saw a light come on behind his eyes as he recognised him. 'Oh, it's you,' he said.

'That's right, it's us. Looks like you had a spot of bother. Now what did I say?'

The publican didn't reply as John picked up the broken back of a chair, regarded it and dropped it on to the floor again. 'I've got some mates who could help you get straight like I told you,' he said.

'I might've met them last night.'

'Don't know what you're talking about,' said John with a straight face. 'Now, what about that insurance we were talking about?'

'That's down to the brewery.'

175

'No it's not. It's down to you.'

'The police have been here.'

'And gone. Now that's where we come in. See, the cops have lots of places to look after, but we give personal service. This would never have happened if you'd listened the other day.'

'I'll...' said the publicans.

'No, mate,' said John. 'You won't. You'll pay us what we want and we'll take care of everything for you. Won't we, Billy?'

Billy nodded.

'How much?'

'For a special introductory period,' said John enjoying every moment. 'A mere tenner a week. Blimey, it's bargain.'

'And what do I get?'

'Protection my friend. Protection from yobbos breaking up the place. We're just a phone call away,' and John took out one of the cards he'd had specially printed. On it was written 'SECURITY FORCE' in capital letters plus the number of the phone he'd had installed at his new flat. 'Twenty-four hours a day, seven days a week. What could be fairer?'

'I don't know...'

'Come on, son, cough up,' said John. 'You wouldn't want this to happen again, would you?'

The publican shook his head, no mention this time of the Germans or his part in their downfall, which had in any case consisted of being in the catering corps stationed at Aldershot for the duration.

'In advance,' said John. The publican took out a battered wallet from his pocket and counted out ten one pound notes.

'Cheers,' said John pocketing the cash. 'And you must have mates in the trade.'

The man nodded.

'Put the word around, we're looking to expand.'

Once outside, John Jenner put the money in his pocket and grinned at Billy. 'Easy,' he said. 'What did I tell you?'

'A lousy tenner,' said Billy. 'Not much is is?'

'Look around, son,' said John, encompassing the whole of Streatham with a sweep of his arm. 'Today, the Beehive, tomorrow the world. This is just the start. Once word gets around, we'll be laughing. Now come on, I'll buy you a Wimpy. We're in the money, son.'

*　*　*

'I don't really know,' said Martine in answer to Mark's question. 'Long before my time. I wasn't even born or thought of.'

'Exciting, though,' said Mark, finishing his beer.

'Oh yes,' said Martine. 'You eaten?'

Mark shook his head.

'There's a decent Indian just round the corner. Fancy a curry?'

'I don't mind.'

'Your enthusiasm is overwhelming.'

They left the bar and walked the short distance to the restaurant Martine had recommended. Once inside the warm, spice-scented room they were shown to a table at the back and Martine asked for beer and popadoms. When they were alone, Mark asked: 'Why did you show me those places tonight?'

'A history lesson, like I said. Thought you might be interested in where it all started, now you're taking over.'

'Who said I was?'

'It's obvious. Dad always wanted you to be the boss when he stepped down.'

'Boss of not much,' said Mark and watched as Martine lit a cigarette. 'A few old men past their prime.'

'There's more to it than that.'

'Like what?'

'I'll let Dad tell you that.'

'Thanks.'

'No problem.'

The waiter bought their drinks, the popadoms and the mixed pickles. They'd had time to study the menu and they ordered their main courses.

177

Once the waiter had left, Martine stubbed out her cigarette and dug in.

'I envy you,' she said.

'Why?'

'Being a bloke.'

'It's not all it's cracked up to be.'

'So you say.'

'Martine, I don't know what's annoying you, but if it's me, just say so.'

'Forget it,' she said.

'OK.'

When they'd finished the popadoms and the plates had been removed, Martine lit another cigarette. 'Want to sleep with me tonight?' she asked through a mouthful of smoke.

'What did you say?' said Mark.

'You heard.'

'Jesus, Martine, but you're full of surprises.'

'Look who my parents were,' she replied with a grin. 'Am I frightening you?'

'No.'

'Bet I am. So?'

'So what?'

'Don't piss about, Mark. Do you fancy it?'

'With your dad upstairs? No.'

'It'll be more fun that way.'

'I said no.'

'Is it because of Linda?'

'It's nothing to do with her.'

'Course it is.' Mark could see she was beginning to get angry as the volume of her voice rose. 'Why do you want to sleep with her again? She's had a couple of kids, hasn't she? You fancy stretch marks, do you?'

'Keep your voice down,' said Mark.

'Don't tell me what to do.'

The other diners were beginning to notice their argument as Martine got even louder. 'Just calm down,' said Mark.

178

'Bollocks to calm down,' she shouted as the waiter arrived with a trolley loaded with food which he began to set out on their table.

'Martine,' said Mark.

'Don't Martine me,' she spat back. 'Will you or won't you?'

'I couldn't,' said Mark. 'You're like my sister. It'd be like incest.'

'Incest, you bastard!' She was screaming now, and heads were popping out of the kitchen to see what all the fuss was about. 'You're just a fucking pussy.'

Mark didn't reply.

'Piss off, you wus,' she yelled, threw her napkin at him, got up and flounced towards the door, turning before she left. 'I only ask once, and that's it. You'll be sorry, I promise. And you can bloody well walk home or get Linda to give you a lift.'

The door closed behind her with a draught of cold air and Mark was left to face the other customers and the staff. He calmly asked for the bill, paid in cash, abandoned the food cooling on the table, and left the restaurant.

Martine's car was gone and he did walk home through the frozen streets, to calm himself down. When he got back to the house the Mini was parked on the front. He tried the key that John Jenner had given him, but the door had been locked from the inside and he had to ring the bell and wait for Chas to come from the back to open it. 'Had a bit of a row?' he asked, but Mark just thanked him and went upstairs to his room.

That night he didn't lock the door, and afterwards asked himself if he'd forgotten, or if he expected what happened to happen. It was a tough call.

He fell asleep quickly, but woke up again at that strange hour between two and three in the morning, when the winter night was at its darkest and bodies were more likely to give up their souls.

As soon as he opened his eyes he knew someone else was in the room. Someone warm and fragrant and female who had pulled back the covers of his bed and was stroking his naked body to arousal. He was on his back, his cock was hard, and she was ready to lower her wetness on to him and make her his. But Mark held her waist and lifted her off, dropping her

179

on to the floor by the side of his bed with a thump and a gasp. 'I told you no,' he said, suddenly wide awake.

'You bastard,' she said back.

'And I thought you only asked once.'

She hit him then, a hard blow to the side of the head, but he'd suffered worse and just laughed in the silence of the room. 'You'll have to do better than that,' he said. 'Now piss off.'

'You'll be sorry,' she hissed. 'Sorrier than you'll ever know.'

'Then do whatever you're going to do and get it over with.' He was suddenly tired again. 'But let me get some sleep, will you?'

He saw her naked form glowing whitely in the darkness, the darker triangle between her legs, before she got up, gathered her dignity and her dressing gown around herself and left, slamming the door behind her.

Mark got up, went to the door, locked it, then went back to bed where he lay awake much longer than he intended to.

SIXTEEN

'Sean. In here.'

It was shift change early the next morning and Sean had just arrived at Streatham Police Station where his DI was waiting. The previous evening he'd spent in the company of his sister who had been in one of the strange moods that overtook her sometimes. He knew that the loss of her husband had affected her badly, but sometimes he thought he could see light at the end of the tunnel of her grief. But not last night. She'd drunk too much and had gone to bed sobbing. His heart went out to her, but he knew that when she was in that kind of mood there was no reaching her.

'There's been a shooting in Loughborough Junction,' said Mobray, when Sean had sat down. 'Three Asians shot and killed. All known to us. And all known to John Jenner...'

Sean could hardly believe his ears. Jenner again. It seemed like the man was haunting him.

'...I know it's not our manor,' Mobray went on, 'but it all seems to be too much of a coincidence that his name's popped up again.'

You can say that again, thought Sean.

'Anyway, that's what the source says, and right now the source is God. So get down to the scene and liaise with Superintendent Bowers from AMIP. He's in charge of the murder squad. Area drugs is there too. These bastards have been playing fast and loose with Class A for years and now it looks as if the chickens have come home to roost. Take Childs with you. And tread carefully, boy. The Chief Super at Brixton doesn't like his corns being trod on.'

'I'd like to meet this source,' said Sean.

'So would I,' said Mobray. 'And maybe one day we will. But right now I want to know if Jenner had anything to do with this latest incident. From what I can gather it's like a butcher's shop down there and I'd dearly like to get him off the streets if he fits the frame.'

'Why us, guv'nor?' asked Sean. 'Seems like a waste of time to me. Haven't we got enough going on here without going outside our jurisdiction? Sounds like the world and his wife are already dealing with it. We'll probably just get in the way.'

'And you're an expert on the use of manpower from this station now, are you?'

'No, guv. It's just a bit thin, that's all. This Jenner bloke looked like he had one foot in the grave to me. And his sidekick wasn't too fast on his feet either.'

'They've been a thorn in my… our side, for too long,' said Mobray. 'If there's a war kicking off, I want to know all about it. Just go. And then come back and tell me what's going on. Simple enough for you?'

'Yes, guv.'

'Then get out of here and do your job.'

Sean found Bobby Childs at his usual table in the canteen, chewing on a pastie. 'You and me, Bobby,' he said. 'We're off to Loughborough Junction. I hope you can keep that down. A bit of a nasty one by all accounts.'

'I thrive on them, son,' said Childs swallowing the last piece of tough pastry filled with gristle. 'What's it all about?'

Sean explained what little he knew as they went, plus the theories about Jenner and Chas.

'Those bastards will never quit until they're dead,' said Childs, lighting a cigarette as they walked to Sean's car. 'Don't smoke in my car, Bobby,' said Sean.

'Health police,' mumbled Childs, but he dropped the quarter-smoked cigarette and ground it into the tarmac of the carpark before he climbed aboard. 'By the way,' he said en route, 'I checked the numbers of those motors outside Jenner's house that day.'

'And?'

'The black Merc belongs to a security company up west. Top drawer. Look after the likes of Madonna and Tom Cruise when they're in town. Ex-SAS, you know the sort of thing. Wouldn't tell me a dicky bird. As soon as I said who I was they put me on hold. I listened to twenty minutes of *Bridge Over Troubled Waters* easy listening style before I hung up. The Range Rover was more interesting. Belonged to a dotcom – or should it be *dotcon* – company based in Lisle, France. Went down the tubes with the rest of them a couple of years back. I spoke to interplod. No trace lost or stolen. No trace at all, so I suppose Jenner *could've* taken it as part payment for a debt.'

'Dead end?' said Sean.

'Yeah. And the Bentley's legit. Registered to Jenner.'

'So nothing.'

'Apart from the fact he thinks he needs a couple of heavy duty, heavy money minders, no. The Rover could be of interest to Customs and Excise. I gave them a bell, but they didn't seem too keen, so I left it.'

'We'll catch them on the flip side,' said Sean.

They drove to the warehouse in Loughborough Junction, which was already a hive of activity by the time they arrived. The whole place had been cordoned off with blue police tape and there were the usual collection of plain and marked police vehicles parked around the perimeter, inside which white-suited SOCOs were busily searching every cranny. Outside the cordon, a crowd had gathered, with several recognisable journalists already there and at least two television crews setting up.

Sean showed his ID to a uniformed sergeant who pointed him in the direction of a soberly attired, iron grey haired man talking to a young woman by a skip that was being searched by uniformed officers.

'Superintendent Bowers?' said Sean, as he and Childs approached them. The grey haired man frowned. 'Who wants him?'

'Sergeant Sean Pierce from Streatham,' said Sean. 'And DC Childs. My guv'nor DI Mobray sends his compliments. Seems like all this could have something to do with a target we're investigating.'

'Name?'

'John Jenner.'

'John Jenner, eh? I thought he was dead.'

'So did a lot of people apparently, sir, but he's still with us. Although not looking too good.'

'Well, that's improved my day. I always did fancy dancing on that particular individual's grave.'

'Something for us, sir?' asked the woman, a tall blonde wearing a woollen hat and a puffa jacket over jeans and boots.

'Maybe,' said Bowers. 'Pierce, is it?' Sean nodded. 'This is DI Cooper. Sally Cooper. My good right arm. Have a chat with her. If you're lucky she might let you have a look inside although it's not something I recommend. Me, I'm going for a scout round. Sally, look after these two, but make sure they don't step into anything that might be important.'

'Understood,' said Cooper, and Bowers moved off, looking around as he went, as if for important clues.

'What exactly happened?' Sean asked Cooper as they walked towards the building.

'The two blokes who run this place, Ali and Tommo – that's Ali Gulati and Tommo Alahan – plus their warehouse manager, Jimmi Faress, also known as Geezer, were all shot and killed here sometime during the last two days. Ali's wife eventually called us in. Apparently none of them were exactly what you'd call pipe and slipper men. They came and went pretty much as they pleased. They liked a drink and girls and a game of cards. Some of these card games went on for a week or more. So when none of them showed up for their teas the other night, no one was particularly worried. But then a few customers turned up to collect orders and found the place locked up, so, eventually, Mrs Ali came down with a spare set, found the remains of the three of them inside and went into one big style. She's in King's College now, under sedation.'

'When exactly was this?'

'Early this morning. The sparrows were still coughing.'

'And the bodies are still *in situ*?'

'Nice turn of phrase,' said the young female detective inspector. 'Yep, still there. Want to take a look?'

'If we must.'

'Up to you. But you'll have to dress up.'

'Bobby?' said Sean.

'We'd better. The guv'll want the full SP.'

So, the trio, once dressed in white paper coveralls, hats and overshoes, went inside, through the warehouse and towards the office door. Cooper took the two men to one side where they had a view through the glass front of the office. 'Better not go inside,' she said. 'Forensic will do their collective nuts. But you can see pretty well from here.'

'Too well,' said Sean. 'Christ, it's like a bloody massacre.'

'Yep,' said Cooper, which appeared to be her word of the day.

Inside it was carnage.

The heater had been turned off but it was still warm in there and the air now stunk of blood and bodily waste as well as the other odours that Mark had noticed on his visit. Three bodies were sprawled haphazardly across the floor. Ali had lost half his head to a shotgun blast and the rest was spread across one wall like so much brown porridge. Geezer was half on, half off a secretary's chair, his innards in his lap as though someone had tossed several kilos of sausage there. Tommo was in the doorway, flat on his back, staring up at the ceiling with open eyes. There were several bullet wounds in his chest and Sean could see the whiteness of bone through the dried blood.

'So, what do you reckon?' asked Sean.

'At least two weapons used, maybe more,' said Sally Cooper. 'Those two...' she pointed at Ali and Geezer, 'shotgunned, and him...' she indicated Tommo lying on the floor, 'handgun, I imagine. So that means there were at least two, maybe three or more, who knows? We'll have a better idea after the PMs.'

'Quite a party,' said Sean.

'Anything found?' asked Childs.

'Like?' said Cooper.

'Money or drugs. Weapons. Anything really.'

'Not so far. But there's plenty of illicit fags and booze from the Continent.'

'So you think this was something to do with smuggling?' asked Sean, hoping that it was.

'I dunno,' said Cooper. 'No. My gut says drugs. I know French contraband is big business, but it doesn't smell right. Anyway, Customs are coming down later. They might have some ideas. What about you?'

'We'll go and talk to Jenner again. By the way, are Area Drugs about?'

'In the cafe on the corner. They want the bodies out of the way before they'll soil their dainty little hands.'

'Sounds about right,' said Childs. 'Always were squeamish buggers.'

'Yeah, I know,' said Cooper. 'I was with them for three years.'

Sean smiled. Nice one, Bobby, he thought.

The three of them divested themselves of their coveralls and went looking for the drugs squad. They were indeed ensconced in a greasy spoon just across the road, two rough-looking individuals in scruffy clothes and two days' growth of beard who welcomed Cooper like an old friend. 'Christ, Sally. Be careful, they don't serve croissants in here,' said the most raggedy of the pair in a broad Welsh accent.

'Graham, you look as lovely as ever,' she said to the one who'd spoken. 'Going to get me a cup of tea?'

'Earl Grey?'

'It's getting old, Graham. Leave it.'

She introduced Pierce and Childs. Graham was Sergeant Graham Jackson, and his companion was DC Paul Brant.

Jackson sent Brant to the counter for refreshments and when he returned, the five of them huddled around a single table. 'So,' said DS Jackson. 'What do you reckon?'

'We've heard that a drug deal that went pearshaped down near Basingstoke three days ago was run by a bloke called John Jenner and that this is where the gear ended up,' said Sean. 'But you know all about that.'

Jackson shook his head. 'It's news to me.'

'What?' said Sean suddenly confused. 'But it's your snout gave us the info, surely.'

Again Jackson reacted negatively. 'No mate, sorry. We've been rummaging around in Hackney for the past week helping out Operation Trident. We just got a call to come see what's been did and what's been hid with that trio of likely lads over the road. This is murder squad business. We're just here to annoy Sally really.'

'Christ,' said Sean, looking at Childs in bewilderment. 'Then whose fucking snout is it then? Sorry,' he said to Sally.

'I've heard the word before, DS Pierce.'

'Sean, please.'

She smiled and Jackson, Brant and Childs all exchanged looks that Sean didn't notice.

'John Jenner, eh?' said Jackson. 'Bloody hell. I thought he was out of our hair for good.'

'How come?' asked Childs.

'He's got cancer,' said Brant. 'Terminal.'

'Shit,' said Childs. 'And they told me there was no truth in the power of prayer. No wonder he looked so rough the other day.'

'You've seen him?' said Jackson.

'Just for a minute. Renewing an old acquaintanceship, as it were.'

'Do you reckon he's got it in him to do that over there?' Jackson stuck his thumb in the direction of the warehouse.

'Doubtful,' said Sean.

'It doesn't take a lot of strength to pull a trigger,' said Sally Cooper.

'No. That's true,' said Sean. 'And it looks like there were at least two of them.'

'He always had a gang,' said Childs. 'And that sod Chas has a mean streak.'

'I don't believe it,' said Jackson shaking his head. 'They were old mates, him and Ali and Tommo. They've been working together for more years than I've been in the job.'

'When thieves fall out...' said Sally.

'No. It just doesn't make sense, unless Ali or Tommo or both of them suddenly decided to turn Jenner over. But why would they? They've all been feathering their nests very nicely since God was a child, thank you. Why now? When Jenner's on his last legs?'

'Precisely,' said Brant. 'Now would be the best time.'

'I still don't see it,' said Jackson. 'I know it makes sense if you look at it that way. But Jenner's is just a name that's come up from Christ knows where. He's been quiet for ages. There's plenty of other villains who'd do those three over there for fourpence and never turn a hair.'

'Well, we'd better get on, I think,' said Sally Cooper, finishing her tea. 'There's going to be a mobile HQ on the carpark over there as soon as. My guv'nor and I will be running that in tandem with Brixton nick. You boys are more than welcome to hang around but you might be better served checking on your own snouts. What do you say?'

'We say good riddance to the lot of them,' said Graham Jackson. 'We've got plenty enough to do without worrying about dead drug dealers. It's the live ones we're interested in. But we'll keep in touch, Sally. Anything we hear we'll pass on.'

'That'll be a first then,' said Cooper,

'Funny,' said Jackson, and with a nod to each, he and Brant left.

'Not much help, were they?' said Childs.

Cooper wrinkled her nose. 'Not much, but they've got some good intelligence and when they're prepared to share they might come in useful.'

'Did you believe that about it not being their snout who gave up the info?' asked Childs.

'I do, as it happens,' said Sally Cooper. 'Graham never was one for hiding his light. If it had been one of his, he'd've let us know soon enough.'

'It's a bloody mystery then, isn't it?'

'I don't think there's much for us here,' said Sean. 'We'll leave you to it, Sally. But we're going to have a good nose round over the next few days and we'll check back.'

'Thanks,' said Sally Cooper. 'You do that.'

The three of them went out into the freezing morning and parted company by the police lines. 'Don't be a stranger now, Sean,' said Sally Cooper as she ducked under the tape.

The two cops watched her walk away and even under the thick clothing she wore they could see that her figure was quite something.

'You've pulled there, son,' said Childs.

'Don't be daft,' said Sean, but he'd felt it too. He'd have to do some checking on Sally Cooper to see if she was available or just flirting.

They drove back to Streatham in silence. 'Shall we have a word with Jenner again?' asked Childs on the way.

'No,' said Sean. 'Lets see what's going on back at the factory first.'

'Do you think it is contraband?' asked Childs. 'Don't forget the French -registered Range Rover Jenner's got.'

'Could be. Mention it again to Customs if you like.'

'Fuck 'em,' said Childs. 'Miserable bastards won't return my calls. Let them work it out for themselves.'

* * *

Mark stayed in bed late that morning. He didn't want to face anyone. All he could think of as he lay in his bed was his meeting with Linda that afternoon and what had happened the night before with Martine. Maybe he should've been kinder in his rejection. Or maybe he should've let her have her way with him. He knew it wasn't the end of the matter, and whatever way he'd played it, trouble would surely follow.

Around twelve, his door burst open and John Jenner came in waving the early edition of the *Standard*. 'What the fuck did you do?' he demanded.

'What?' said Mark, sitting up in bed, assuming Jenner was talking about the previous evening's disaster with Martine. But he threw the paper on to the bed open at page three. The headline read:

SLAUGHTER AT LOUGHBOROUGH JUNCTION

Mark picked it up and read the piece. 'Christ,' he said. 'Is this who I think it is?'

'Yes,' said Jenner. 'And they were killed the day you collected the cash. Did you do it? You were carrying.'

'No,' said Mark. 'Course I bloody didn't. What do you think I am?'

'I know what you are,' said Jenner. 'Did you do it?'

'What? Kill the lot of them? I don't think so.'

'Get up and get dressed. I want to talk to you downstairs,' said Jenner and he stomped out of the room.

Mark read the story again and his stomach churned as he took in the details. Christ, he thought. It must've happened just after I left.

He could still smell Martine's musky perfume on him, so he went to the bathroom and washed and shaved, before getting dressed and going down to the living room where John Jenner and Chas were waiting for him. Before he left his room, he stripped the bed and threw the sheets into the washing basket.

'Look, Uncle,' he said when he got down there. 'This was nothing to do with me.'

'Course it wasn't,' said Chas, but Mark could see that Jenner was still in a rage.

'Don't you believe me?' Mark asked him. 'What possible reason could I have for doing it?'

'A quarter million quid's worth of charlie,' said Jenner. Suddenly he exhaled. 'Sorry, Mark,' he said, 'I know it wasn't you, it's just I've known those three for more years than I care to remember. It was a shock. We were friends. I even went to Tommo's youngest's christening or whatever they call it in Muslim.

'I know, Uncle,' said Mark. 'But it must've happened just after I left. It didn't say anything about any drugs on the premises in the paper.'

'Fat chance. Whoever did this had them away.'

'Who do you reckon?' asked Chas.

'Dunno,' replied Jenner. 'But I'm bloody sure I'm going to find out. Mark, I want you to go and have a look see.'

'What? With half the Bill in south London on site? I don't think so. Anyway, what the fuck will I be able to find out?'

'I don't know. I just want you to go. This afternoon.'

'I can't.'

'Why not?'

'I've got an appointment.'

'What? With the bloody dentist? Cancel the fucker.'

'No.'

'It's that fucking Linda Pierce or whatever she calls herself now, ain't it?'

'That's none of your business.'

'But this is our fucking business. If they killed Ali and the rest they could come here next.'

'That's what you haven't been telling me about, isn't it, Uncle? Whoever's out there, killing people. That's why you've got a car full of security parked outside night and day. Well, if you're not prepared to fill me in, I'm not prepared to run your sodding errands for you.' And with that, Mark grabbed his coat and keys and left.

It had started raining again and the bare branches were dripping. Mark felt as if it rained every day of his life. A few days ago, things had been simple. The scruffy flat in Canvey, his battered TV and his record collection. Fish and chips and a harmless flirtation with the girl behind the counter. No worries, no stress, as long as he didn't dwell too long on the past. But now the past had come back and hit him four square between the eyes. He could just piss off and get lost again, or he could face up to who he was, and what he was and maybe make something of his life at last.

He arrived at Linda's flat in Balham at the appointed time and pressed the bell. The traffic on the main road made hearing anything inside impossible and he wondered if she'd stood him up. He jiggled from foot to foot nervously as the rain fell.

Suddenly the door opened and she was there, dressed in a long dark blue overcoat. 'You came,' she said.

'You knew I would. I just wondered if you'd be here.'

'When did I ever let you down?'

He didn't answer.

'Well, are you coming in?' she said. 'It's freezing out.' He entered and she shut the door behind him. They were standing in a small hall no bigger than a telephone booth. In the corner was a stack of envelopes thrown higgledy piggledy. Mail for previous tenants, he guessed. A flight of carpeted stairs led upwards. 'Come on up,' she said. 'Mind you, it's freezing indoors too. I've put on the heating but it'll take a bit of time to warm up.'

'I don't mind,' said Mark.

He followed her up the single flight, then through another door, down a corridor and into a simply furnished living room. Linda felt the radiator by the door and said, 'That's better. It'll be all right in a few minutes.'

She sat on a sofa and Mark, divested of his coat, took the armchair opposite. The curtains were open and the rain bounced off the window sill outside. The windows themselves had been fitted with double glazing, which muted the sound of the traffic and the rain.

'Nice place,' he said.

'No it's not,' she replied. 'It's a cheap conversion, the floorboards are warped and the roof leaks. But I don't care. Why should I?'

Mark felt there was no answer to that.

'So,' she said. 'You wanted to talk to me.'

'That's right.'

'Well, go on then. I'm listening.'

'I don't know where to start.'

'Start with you coming looking for me when I was fifteen and still at school.'

'I wanted to see what the children of the bloke who'd killed my father looked like, you know that.'

'You wanted revenge. And I fell for you, and you so kindly broke the news to me one afternoon after we'd made love.'

'I blew it.'

'And making me fall in love with you, then dumping me, was that the revenge you were looking for?'

'No. I fell in love with you too. The first day I saw you. You know that too.'

'You had a funny way of showing it, I must say.'

'I showed it by keeping on at you to come back.'

'You did, didn't you.'

Mark had refused to give up after Linda had walked out on him that day at the hotel.

192

He'd never had her home phone number, since she wanted to keep their affair secret from her family, and she'd always called him. So, at the beginning of the new term, he started hanging around the school again, parking his car outside the gates. Stalking, they'd call it now. Mark couldn't have cared less: he wanted her back and intended to get her. But she ignored him. The school even called the cops, and Mark had to stand ignominiously in the fine drizzle one January morning as two uniforms spun his car in front of an interested audience of school kids. Not that there was anything to find. Mark was smarter than that. But it was a drag all the same, the cops grinning at the state of him and taking the piss big time.

But it was the ever dependable Brenda who saved the day once again. She phoned him one afternoon in February. 'How did you get my number?' he asked.

'I looked in Linda's book,' she said. 'You two, what are you like?'

'I messed up, Brenda,' he said. 'It's my fault.'

'What happened?'

'That's a bit personal,' he said.

'All right, don't tell me. But she's missing you like mad.'

'She told you that?'

'She doesn't have to. She's lost weight, and her school work's gone down the pan.'

'So what do I do?'

'Come round my house Saturday night. My folks are away, and Linda's sleeping over. You can see her then. If she'll let you, that is.' She gave him an address in Purley and he wrote it down.

'And she will be there?' he said.

Brenda giggled. 'Do you think I'm inviting you round to have my evil way with you? Don't flatter yourself.'

'Sorry, Brenda.'

'Not that I wouldn't, if it was anyone else but Linda. But you're safe. Come about eight.'

Mark presented himself at the door the next Saturday evening, eight on the dot, still half expecting that it was a practical joke. Brenda answered the door and said: 'She's in the kitchen. I'll be upstairs. Don't break any furniture or crockery.'

He kissed the girl on the cheek and she blushed. She wasn't half bad, as it happened, but she wasn't Linda.

Linda was in the kitchen drying up some dishes when Mark walked in. 'Who is it, Bren?' she asked. When she turned she dropped the plate she was holding, and if Mark's reflexes had been any slower, crockery indeed would have been broken. But he caught it a foot from the floor and handed it back to her.

'Surprise,' he said.

'What are you doing here?' demanded Linda, then light dawned. 'That bloody Brenda.'

'I had to see you.'

'I thought the police warned you off.'

'Bloody Old Bill. Whose idea was that, anyway?'

'The headmaster's. Mr Barnes.'

'You've lost weight,' he said.

'I'm smoking too much.'

'I miss you, Linda.'

'Do you? The daughter of your father's killer?'

'Christ, I'm sorry I told you. Or at least I'm sorry I told you the way I did. It was stupid.'

'Unfeeling, I'd call it.'

'I know.'

'Then why?'

'Because I couldn't go on lying to you.'

'Oh, Mark.'

'Linda. Can we try it once more? It's all out in the open now.'

'You hurt me.'

'I know. Do your folks know?'

'Only Sean. He was the only one I could tell. He wanted to go round and bash you up.'

'I deserved it.'

'At least you didn't come to my house.'

'I wouldn't do that.'

'Barnes wanted to tell my dad, but I begged him not to.'

'What did you say?'

'That you were just a boy who wouldn't take no for an answer.'

'And I won't.'

Linda put the plate carefully on the draining board. 'Where's Brenda?' she asked.

'Upstairs, I think.'

'Probably eavesdropping outside.'

'Let's give her something to listen to then,' and Mark took Linda in his arms and kissed her. He felt her relax in his embrace and he knew that things were going to be all right.

But, of course, he was wrong.

* * *

'I'm sorry, Linda,' said Mark as they sat together in the flat in Balham. 'You don't know how sorry. I've lain awake a thousand nights since trying to make sense of it.'

'And I haven't, I suppose.'

'I don't know.'

'Well, I have. Even with my husband lying next to me asleep, I thought about you. You fucking bastard, I hate you.' She was crying.

'Do you?' He moved to sit next to her and she slid as far away from him on the sofa as she could. But he moved closer and took her in his arms. She fought him for a moment and then hugged him close. He breathed in her perfume, almost gasping, like a man suffering from smoke inhalation taking in oxygen, and he kissed her. On her mouth and on her cheeks where the tears tasted like salt and he drank them as if his life depended on it.

She kissed him back and they both knew that they were lost. 'Take me to bed,' she said.

They stood, and she took his hand and led him out of the room and upstairs to the top floor where there were two bedrooms. They went into the larger of the two, where there was a double bed. It was cold in the room and the rain beat on the roof and ran down the window like a mother's tears. For all the evidence to the contrary, they might have been the only two people in the world.

They got undressed quickly. 'Don't look,' she said. 'It's not like the first time. I'm afraid everything's going south.'

'You're still so beautiful,' he said. 'The most beautiful woman I've ever seen. It's exactly like the first time. Remember in the car?'

'Bloody romantic,' she said.

'It was as far as I was concerned.'

'Hush,' she replied. 'Don't talk.'

Afterwards they lay together. 'You knew this was going to happen, didn't you?' said Linda. 'All part of your plan.'

'There was no plan.'

'Don't give me that. You get the full SP from Uncle John, come snooping round my house. Follow me to the supermarket. Tell me we've got to meet somewhere private. Well, at least me having this place saved you the price of a hotel room for the afternoon.'

'Don't, Linda,' said Mark, touching her face gently. 'Don't make it like that.'

'What is it like then?'

'I just wanted to be with you.'

'And I wanted to be with you a thousand nights and daytimes too, but where the bloody hell were you? Running bloody riot somewhere, I suppose.'

She reached for her bag, rummaged around inside it and came out with a packet of cigarettes. She stripped off the cellophane, opened the box, ripped off the silver paper and fished one out. 'Look what you've made me do,' she said.

'I'm sorry,' he said, taking the cigarette from between her fingers and putting it on the bedside table. 'I was lots of places. Horrible places mostly. But I always wanted to be with you.'

'Well, here we are. Older, but no wiser. So what's next?'

'I don't know. All I know is, that after today I want to be with you all the more, and all the time.'

'A new daddy for my children, is that what you mean?'

'They could've been our children,' said Mark.

'Are you kidding?' she asked. 'Don't you ever say that. For Christ's sake, Mark. You're a villain, my brother's a copper. Your bloody uncle's a gangster. My father's a bank robber who's in prison for killing your father who was a copper too. Christ, we're almost bloody related.'

Mark could hardly believe that what she was saying was almost exactly what he'd said to Martine the night before. 'Is what we just did? Commit incest then?' he asked.

She didn't reply, 'I've got to go,' she said, getting out of bed and grabbing the duvet to cover her nakedness. 'Luke'll be home from school soon. I'll have a shower. The water'll be hot.'

'Do you have to go?'

'Why? Want seconds?'

'Don't be like this, Linda,' he said. 'You're only hurting yourself.'

'Makes a change from you doing it then,' she said. After she'd left the room and he heard the sound of running water from the bathroom, Mark lay back in the bed and sighed. Good move, he thought to himself.

She was back in minutes, a towel now wrapped around her waist. She found her scattered clothes and began to dress. He watched her every move.

'You're lovely,' he said.

'Oh, Mark,' she said, sitting next to him on the bed. 'Why did I let you talk me into this?'

'Because you wanted me to?'

'Course I did. I haven't had a man touch me since Andy died. I was drying up inside. When I saw you yesterday I almost passed out, I wanted you so much. How come you can still do that to me after so long?'

'Because we were meant to be.'

'Meant to be what?'

'Together, of course.'

'We can't be. Don't you understand? It could never work. Not now. Not after all the things you've done.'

'And how many women do you think I've had since I left?'

197

'Loads, probably.'

He shook his head. 'Only one.'

'Sure.'

'It's true, I promise you.'

'Don't promise me, Mark. You break promises.'

He shrugged. 'Yeah, I know.'

'So who was she?'

'A Vietnamese girl I met on my travels.'

'You've been to Vietnam? I don't believe you.'

'No. It was in Paris. I worked for her grandfather.'

'Doing what?'

'Bad things.'

'What was her name?'

'Lan.'

'Was she beautiful?'

Mark nodded.

'What happened to her?'

'We split up. Culture clash.'

'And there's really been no one else?'

'No. You can believe me or not. But it's the truth.'

She looked at him long and hard through narrowed eyes. 'OK,' she said. 'I believe you. I'm bloody amazed, but I believe you. Got any more revelations?'

'Your father gets out of prison soon.'

'Thanks, Mark. Now you've really made my sodding day. Shall I meet him at the prison gates with Luke and Daisy in tow? Look kids, here's grandpa. What a surprise.'

She started to cry again and Mark took her in his arms. 'I know I was wrong coming to see you, but I couldn't not do it. Not once I'd seen you again. I love you, Linda, always have, always will. Maybe it's wrong or foolish or whatever, but it's the truth. At least let me have that.'

She turned and looked him in the eye: 'Oh dear, Mark. But God forgive me, I love you too.'

SEVENTEEN

Mark and Linda stayed in the flat for a few minutes more. She insisted that she had to leave, he begged her to stay. His only thought was that, once they were apart again, she would change her mind. Something terrible would happen and she'd stop loving him, or worse, because so many people he'd known were dead, that she would die too.

He knew that he was being morbid and Linda laughed at his fears when he told her. 'I'll be fine,' she said. 'We've found each other again, and whatever happens I don't intend losing you for a second time. It'll all be fine. Trust me.'

'Will it?' he said.

'Yes. It will if we want it. But we have to be strong. You'll be strong for me, won't you?'

He nodded, but he knew they would be faced with almost insur-mountable problems. 'I just wish we could stay here forever and never leave,' he said.

'Me too. But we can't. Now I've really got to go. They'll be wondering where I've got to. I said I was only going to pop round IKEA to look for some bits and pieces for the kitchen.'

'And you're going home empty handed.'

She smiled. 'I'll tell them I met a nice young man in the bedding department who kept me occupied.'

He smiled at that. 'So when can I see you?'

'Soon, I promise.' It all seemed too simple to Mark. Too easy.

But eventually they left the flat with the rain still pouring down. Beside the tube station they parted to find their respective cars. Mark held her close and smelt the water in her hair before he watched her walk across the main road and disappear down a side street. A few minutes later he was still standing by the station entrance being buffeted by the wind when the Toyota appeared, turned in the direction of Streatham and vanished into the traffic. He watched until its red taillights disappeared before walking back to his motor.

Instead of the elation he should have been feeling, his mind was full of dread. He sat behind the wheel of the cold car for five minutes before he switched on the engine. The rain was coming down even harder and it was impossible to see anything except the jewels of the street lamps and car lights through the water on his windscreen. His breath fogged the inside of the glass, and in his hand, like a talisman, he held a piece of paper with Linda's mobile phone number written on it. They'd exchanged numbers before leaving and he'd made her promise to ring him as soon as she'd arrived safely home. Eventually he started the engine and turned on the air conditioning and wipers. The world suddenly came back into focus and he carefully pulled out into the traffic.

Just before he reached Jenner's house his mobile rang. He pulled into the kerb and answered it. 'I'm back,' said Linda. 'Safe and sound.'

'Is Luke all right?' asked Mark. He already felt like part of the family, but knew it could be a big mistake.

'Perfect. They just got home.'

'And Daisy?'

'She was sleeping like a baby – well, she would – in the back of Greta's car. Everyone's fine, Mark. You mustn't get paranoid.'

'I know. Will you ring me tomorrow?'

'Of course.'

'Are you going shopping?'

'I might.'

'Perhaps we could have a coffee again.'

'That would be nice.'

'Ring me before you leave.'

'I will.'

'I love you,' said Mark.

'I love you too,' and after a moment's silence she disengaged.

Mark sat with the car's engine running and his phone in his hand for another few minutes before continuing his journey.

* * *

Deep in the bowels of Brixton prison, Jimmy Hunter heard about the Loughborough Junction shootings that same afternoon, via his transistor radio, permanently tuned to the London news and talk station, LBC. He listened to the report as the rain lashed down outside. His only view was a square foot of sky through a double thickness window that distorted his vision until he thought he might go blind. Jimmy Hunter loved the outside. He loved those precious minutes when he was under an open sky, and would have welcomed the rain on his face.

It was just another shooting as far as he was concerned. There seemed to be more and more of them every year, and what were three Pakis' lives to him? Good riddance, he thought, if he thought anything at all. But when Terry the Poof brought him his supper he had more information. The prison grapevine was as reliable, if not more so, than any of the outside media. Terry had the names of the deceased before they were reported in the news. 'Christ,' said Jimmy, his tea and toast forgotten. 'Are you sure?'

'Sure I'm sure,' said Terry, sitting on Jimmy's bed, before a look made him stand and lean against the wall. Jimmy didn't like his bed disturbed unless he asked for it.

'I used to run with those fuckers years ago,' said Jimmy. 'When I was webbed up with John Jenner.'

'Is that right?' asked Terry. He knew when to show interest in what Jimmy said, and when to keep it buttoned.

'Bloody right. It was all a bit up in the air at first because some cunt tried to stitch us up over a deal. It all involved Ali and Tommo, see. But Johnny always was a bleedin' diplomat, so when he susses out that the Pakis can shift gear for us, we made our peace.'

'When was this?' asked Terry.

201

'Early 70s. We had a bit of a name by then, the Jenner mob. There was half a dozen or so of us. We were supplying spliff, speed, downers and a bit of coke all across south London, and uptown too. But we had to be careful. North of the river there were a lot of faces that didn't like anyone dabbling in their business. We was all tooled up of course. Guns were easy to get then, and Johnny especially wasn't frightened to use 'em. Good days. The only fly in the ointment was Billy Farrow. He'd joined the filth by then. What a fucking surprise that was. And believe me, Johnny wasn't best pleased. None of us were. The thought of some copper who'd once been one of us was enough to freak anyone out. But Billy had sworn he'd never let on. Just as well that he was walking the beat right on the other side of town. Me, I wanted to top the fucker soon as I heard, but Johnny wouldn't have it. Course I did in the end, but that's the way it goes. See, they'd been mates, Billy and him, since junior school. But to be fair, I think Billy kept his promise. Mind you, he'd've been dead meat if he hadn't. He knew that. You didn't cross Johnny and come out ahead, let me tell you.

'Anyway, we were selling dope to a couple of bands, and Johnny sussed that vans loaded with equipment might be the ideal way to bring the gear into the country. It was simpler then. There weren't sniffer dogs at every port like now. So John gets hold of a tour manager for one of these groups. Quite famous they were, as it goes; Bad City Blues, they were called.'

Terry shook his head. He'd never heard of them, but then UK Garage was more his style. And who gave a fuck about what some group of long hairs had done practically before he was born?

Jimmy ignored him. 'It was a Saturday,' he continued, 'in the summer of '71. I remember because there was a big concert on up at Crystal Palace Park that afternoon. I think Jeff Beck was playing and we were going. Celebrating the deal, if you get my drift. We had comps. Johnny organised them. He always could get in anywhere could Johnny, I'll give him that. Anyway, the band's roadies were due in that day from Germany. They'd been on tour for a couple of weeks and Johnny had arranged for the tour manager bloke to pick up a load of hash on the border. A couple of grand's worth. And you've got to remember, in those days people were still buying two quid deals, so that was a lot of money.' Jimmy smiled at the memory. 'Now, the tour manager was a bit of a lad, clever with his hands. Into electronics, if you know what I mean. He'd split some speakers and amps and stashed the stuff inside. All was sweet. We were due to collect it from the place they stored their equipment at in Wandsworth. An old shop the band had rented with a garage at the back for the truck. One of those big Mercedes, it was. Really plush, with aircraft seats and space for amps, speakers and instruments right at the back. A nice little package.

'We were due to collect at three o'clock, as I remember. Me, this bloke Chas, Johnny's number two, Johnny himself and a big twat called Martin drove round in Johnny's Jag. Mark Ten, beautiful set of wheels, maroon with black leather interior. Johnny loved that motor. Stacks of room.

'So anyway, we're all tooled up like I said, except for Martin who you couldn't trust with anything more powerful than a pea shooter, though he'd been promised. But promises are like little fingers - easily broken. And Johnny wanted to be early. He had a nose for a stitch up and he was bloody well right, as always. It was real hot and quiet that afternoon, as I remember. We'd been in the pub and had a few whilst we were waiting and I'd taken a load of speed. Always was a fucking mug for amphetamine in those days. Coke's OK, but you can't beat a real nosebleed load of speed. So there's the four of us in the Jag. Me and Martin in the back, Johnny driving, Chas next to him in charge of the music. Cassettes only, of course, and I remember he'd got a tape he'd made of the Who. Banging it was, and Johnny'd fitted about eighteen speakers all round the inside of the motor. So we've got the windows down and the music real loud. Bunch of stupid kids really, because if we'd got pulled we'd've been for it. One stop and search and we'd've been well nicked.

'So we get to the Wandsworth Road about two-thirty and there's a little alley round the back of the shop by the garage that's just wide enough to take the truck. We drift round and it's parked up and empty. But there's another motor there as well. An old Cortina 1600E. Well, Johnny boxes them both in and we go and have a shufti. Inside the garage is this tour manager bloke and another long haired git who's the driver of the Merc, plus some German hippy bird they'd picked up in Dortmund or some God-forsaken hole and she'd come along for the ride. Well handsome she was, with one of those floaty dresses they wore then, nearly see through and not much on underneath.' He smiled at that memory.

'But what was more interesting was that there were a couple of young Paki blokes there too. Ali and Tommo, not more than bloody seventeen either of them. But of course I didn't know who they were then. And the tour manager's got all the equipment broken down into bits and he's pulling out lumps of black all wrapped in cellophane like there's no tomorrow, and the Pakis are so into it they're nearly dribbling, and nobody notices that we're on the plot. So we pull out our weapons and burst through the door and the tour manager and the roadie nearly shit their pants. But the Pakis are cool. Fuck me if they don't pull out a couple of pistols themselves and for a minute it looks like it might all go off big time. I'll never forget being in that hot little shop and wondering if any of us are going to get out alive, when Johnny says, "Hello Ali, hello Tommo, how's tricks?" Fuck me, you could've knocked me down with a feather. "Hello John," says the bigger of them, that was Ali. "We're just here to do a little deal."

'"Trouble is, it's our deal," says Johnny. And he says, "Come on boys, we're all friends here - let's put up the guns and see what can be done." So we do, and it turns out that Johnny met Ali at some party months ago, and they'd sussed out that each of them was a bit of a chancer and that maybe sometime down the road they could do a bit of business. And it also turned out that Big City Blues are off to America for six months that very evening, to make an album and God knows what, so the tour manager fellah has done a bit of a double cross and arranged to sell our drugs to Ali and Tommo for twenty per cent more than we'd paid. I suppose he reckoned that by the time he got back to London we'd've forgotten all about him or maybe we'd be banged up out of the way.

'As you can imagine, this doesn't go down particularly well with Johnny Jenner. Say what you like about the geezer, and I've said plenty, he was always fair in his dealings. His motto was that to live outside the law you've got to be honest. A bit soft if you ask me, but then he's on the out and I've been stuck behind bars for nearly twenty years.'

Terry decided it might be safer to make no comment about that remark.

'You see, he'd paid up front to the Krauts who were bringing the hash into Europe. Gone over with a bag of our dough. Risky business, but we trusted the Germans, at least up to a point. We'd been doing business with them for a couple of years. Normally it was COD, but no way were we giving that cash to the tour manager, and the Germans weren't parting with a joint until they got paid. They didn't know the tour manager guy any more than we did, and as it goes they were dead right. So, Johnny and Ali go outside to have a pow wow about what's to be done, and the rest of us are left in the shop with the bird and the two cunts who've tried to rip us off. And you can tell what rank amateurs they are as they're babbling on about what a big mistake they've made, and how sorry they are, but to be honest I'm more interested in the hippy bird who you could tell got a bit excited when we all pulled out guns and it looked like there was going to be a massacre. She's giving me the old eye and by Christ she's not half bad, so I give her a wink and I reckon I'll be in her pants, if she's wearing any, by teatime.

Anyway, a few minutes goes by and Ali and Johnny come back and tell us what's going to happen. In order to keep everyone happy, they were going to split the deal fifty-fifty. We'd take half and Ali and Tommo would do the same. The two Paki boys would pay us ten percent more than we'd paid, which gave both of us an instant profit, and besides that, we didn't have to give those bastards from the band anything for their trouble, so we were quids in. Anyway, we sort the gear out, money exchanges hands as good as gold and everything's sweet. "So what about these two?" says Chas whose been very quiet up to now. "We teach 'em a lesson," says Johnny. "Just let us go," says the tour manager, "and we'll say nothing".

'"Dead right," I says and shoots the driver in the foot. Bang! he's wearing big platform shoes and the one of them just about explodes and he's on the floor crying his eyes out and bleeding like a pig. Then Martin gets sent out to put our share of the gear into the motor and Johnny picks up a hammer that's lying on the work bench and gets Chas to hold the tour manager, Mr Fucking Electronic Genius's right hand, and he smashed every fucking bone in it, so that he wouldn't be doing any delicate work for the next few months, if ever. And all the time I'm eyeing this bird up, and the more violent things get, the more she likes it. So we've got money and drugs and time's getting on, so Johnny asks the Pakis to come up to the Palace with us and listen to the music. "Fine," says Ali, "we were going up there anyway," and I say to the bird, "Do you want to come too?" and fuck me if she doesn't say yes, so we all had a right result and the only losers were those greedy buggers with the band.'

'What happened to them,' asked Terry.

'Never heard of again, mate.'

'Seems fair.'

'Don't it?'

'And the girl?'

'Gave me a blow job in the Jag whilst Jeff Beck was playing. Lovely.'

'A good time was had by all then.'

'That's right.'

'So why did you fall out with Jenner?' asked Terry. 'In the end I mean.'

'Long story mate, I'll tell you another time.'

* * *

When Mark got home that evening, he could sense the atmosphere in the house. And it wasn't good. Chas, Martine and John Jenner were sitting in the living room. The air smelt of dope and Jenner's eyes were red rimmed and looked like they might pop out at any moment. It was then that Mark realised just how sick his adopted uncle was. 'Had a good time?' asked Jenner when he walked in.

'Not bad.'

'Well, while you were out with your bit of skirt we got some news.'

'Yeah?'

'Yeah. It was those fucking niggers.'

'Exactly what fucking niggers are you referring to?' asked Mark.

Chas took over the story as Jenner poured himself a liberal hit of dark rum. 'A little firm that's got a bit big for its boots since we started to take it easy.'

'Black bastards,' said Jenner and lit a joint. Mark could tell it was going to be a fun evening.

'Yardies,' said Chas.

'Yardies, my arse,' interrupted Jenner. 'Just some black fucking chancers think they can operate on my territory. And kill mates I've had for years.'

'Who are they?' asked Mark.

'There's loads of 'em,' said Chas. 'But the main men are called Beretta, Karl and Moses.'

'And how do you know it was them?'

'We asked around. Apparently they were down some shebeen getting tanked up and smoking crack and they started boasting about taking out Ali and Tommo. They're stupid, those cunts. Can't ever keep their fucking mouths shut. The only reason they haven't been nicked ages ago is that they'll kill anyone they think is grassing them up without a second thought.'

'But someone grassed them to you. Are you sure it's legit?'

'Sure we're sure,' said Jenner. 'Now what are you going to do about it?'

'Me?'

'Am I talking to anyone else?'

'I'm on my own. And they're mobhanded.'

'You scared?'

'Yeah.'

'Then call up that old firm of yours and get them back in the saddle.'

'I've lost touch with that lot.'

'Then get in touch again.'

'I don't even know where they are.'

'Then find 'em. You found Linda, didn't you?'

'You told me where she was. If you hadn't talked about her I wouldn't even have thought of her.'

'It was that fucking brother of hers coming round here.'

'Why not tell him?'

'I've never been a grass.'

'Piss off, Uncle, it's not the fucking 60s. Get real, man. This is a new century. Someone's obviously whispering about you. Sean and his mate made that bloody obvious, didn't they?' Jenner sat as still as a statue, but Chas nodded. 'So spread a little happiness,' said Mark. 'Do the same to this mob. They'll be off the streets and out of your hair in no time.'

'I want them dead.'

Mark blew air out if his mouth in exasperation. 'So what do you want me to do?'

'Kill them.'

'And if I won't?'

'Then the past could jump up and bite your arse,' said Jenner.

'Are you blackmailing me?' Mark could hardly believe his ears. 'Is this what you bought me back for?'

'Whatever it takes,' said Jenner.

'Jesus,' said Mark. 'I could just get lost again. Walk away and vanish. For good this time.'

'No,' said Jenner. 'Not this time. This time I'm calling in the favours you owe me.'

'He's lost it, Dad, look at him.' For the first time, Martine spoke. Mark said nothing. It was happening. Everything he'd feared when he and Linda had parted that afternoon. His life was falling apart again and there was nothing he could do about it.

'Be quiet, Martine,' said Jenner, and she jumped up from her seat and stormed through the door, slamming it hard behind her.

'A woman scorned,' said Chas.

'All right, John,' Mark said when the echoes from the slammed door had ceased. 'Solve the mystery for me. What did you do to these people to get them so worked up at you?'

'We made a bit of a ricket a couple of months back,' said Chas, answering for Jenner who sat very still as if looking inside himself.

'What kind of ricket?' asked Mark, already fearful of the answer.

'The worst kind.'

'Tell me.'

'We took on some muscle to sort out a little problem and everything went arse upwards.'

'Chas. Are you going to tell me straight or what?'

'We sold some coke on credit to a bloke called Jimmy Hop. A black geezer who lived on the Aylesbury estate at the Elephant. He was a good customer, always paid up, no worries. But then he took a big consignment and vanished off the face of the earth.'

'How much?'

'About ten grand's worth. Then we heard he was hanging out at his brother's in another block and we sent these blokes to sort it out.'

'And?'

'And it all went pear shaped.'

'Who were these geezers?'

'They'd been recommended. A little firm from Kent. Jed, Fish and Benny.'

'And what happened?'

'Well, as far as we can tell, they got a bit over-fisty.'

'Tell me.'

So he did.

* * *

The trio sat in the car for a minute and Fish, who was driving, let down his window and took a deep breath of the warm October morning air. It was just before dawn and the birds who spent the night in the trees that grew on the public parts of the estate were just coming awake. Fish looked like a fish, with popout eyes and a mouthful of sharp, grey teeth. 'Right,' he said. 'When we go in, we're coppers, right?'

The other two nodded. Jed sat next to him. Jed was a big man. Brawny, he spent too much time in the gym and thought a day without anabolic steroids was a day without sunshine. Benny was in the back. He was small and mean and gobbled Valium to keep his meanness in check, except today he hadn't had any and was feeling ready for some violence, ultra as possible.

'Just like we've got warrants,' Fish went on. 'We make a lot of noise and sod the neighbours. When they hear us shouting they'll just be glad that it isn't them getting the early morning call.'

More nods.

'Come on then. Let's go.'

They left the car as the sun began to rise over the river behind them, turning the windows in the tower block they were heading towards golden. Jed took a sledgehammer, Fish carried a pump action shotgun loaded with six rounds and Benny held his Colt .45 down by the side of his leg.

They walked in single file to the entrance to the block and up the two flights of steps to the first floor. They saw no one, and as far as they could tell, no one saw them. The Aylesbury wasn't a place of early risers. Late returners possibly, but that particular morning no one seemed about. It was ten past five by his watch when Fish tapped Jed on the shoulder and said, 'Do it.'

Jed hefted the sledgehammer and whacked the reinforced door with all his strength. The metal boomed and he hit again, the door sagged and he kicked it open with the steel-reinforced toe caps of his boots. He dropped the hammer, pulled the Glock 20 out of his coat pocket and ran into the hall screaming, 'Police! Everyone stay where they are!'

They slammed open doors as they went into the interior of the flat. Bathroom clear, kitchen clear, living room clear, but full of the detritus of a night on the toot. The glass-topped coffee table was smeared with white dust, a crack pipe made out of a coke can and the barrel of a cheap ballpoint pen lashed together with sticky tape, stood to attention amidst a scattering of rocks. There were roaches, beer cans and dirty cups and glasses everywhere, but no one was in the room.

The two bedrooms were in the back of the flat looking out over the courtyard and the trio thundered towards them, Jed hitting light switches as he went. There was a bedroom door on either side of the hall. Jed took the left hand one and Benny the right. Inside Jed's, a black man was sitting up in bed and reaching for a pistol on top of the bedside table as the door hit the wall and bounced back. 'Steady,' said Jed and the man froze. The black woman in the bed beside him wailed as she pulled the covers over herself. 'Police,' yelled Jed again as he kicked over the table and the Browning automatic bounced across the carpet. 'Don't fucking move.'

The black man lolled back against the bedhead as if this sort of thing happened every morning. A sort of wakeup call if he forgot to set the alarm.

Simultaneously, Benny smashed the door opposite and found it occupied by a young girl, just a teenager, with a baby in a crib next to her bed. Of Jimmy Hop there was no sign. 'Shit,' said Benny as the baby started crying and the girl threw a hairbrush at his head.

'Don't be bloody silly,' he said and dragged her from under the sheets. She was naked except for a pair of red knickers. He yanked her though the door and across the hall into the other bedroom where its two occupants were under the twin gun barrels of Fish and Jed. 'Where is he?' demanded Fish.

'Who?' replied the black man.

'You know bloody well,' said Fish. 'Jimmy Hop. Your fucking brother. Where is he?'

Benny walked across the room dragging the girl behind him carrying the Colt in one hand. The woman in the bed was still squealing and the baby was crying and Fish knew that things could go very wrong at any moment should a bunch of real policemen arrive on the scene. Not that it was likely, he knew. A call from the Aylesbury being no copper's priority, the response time wouldn't exactly be record breaking.

'Gone away,' said the black man, almost seeming to enjoy the scene being played out in his bedroom.

'Where?'

'None of your business.'

Blimey, thought Fish, this isn't going the way it was planned. So he clouted the black man around the face with the barrel of his gun. Some blood flew from the wound and dappled the sheets. The black man touched his hand to his head. 'You ain't five oh,' he said. 'Who the fuck are you?'

'Never you mind,' said Fish. 'We've come for the gear.'

'No gear here,' said the black man.

'Bollocks,' said Jed, raising his gun. 'Give it up.'

'All gone,' said the black man. 'Just like Jimmy. Gone away.'

'You're lying,' said Fish. 'We want the dope or we want the cash and we ain't got all day. What do you think this is? A fucking debating society?'

The black man sucked his teeth and shook his head.

'Get that fucking baby,' Fish said to Jed. 'Let's get this bloody show on the road.'

The girl Benny was still holding began struggling even harder and he threw her down on the bed. 'Don't make us,' he warned.

Jed came back with the carrycot the baby had been sleeping in. He put it on the floor and Fish stuck his gun against the baby's chest, which started it screaming even louder. 'I'll do it, you fucks, if you don't talk.'

The girl in the red pants said: 'There's nothing here, honest.'

'You don't know the meaning of the word, love,' said Fish and pulled back the hammer on his gun to emphasise the remark.

'OK man.' said the black man, 'Leave the baby. What are you people anyway? Even I wouldn't threaten a little child for a few quid.'

'More than that, I think,' said Fish. 'Now tell us.'

'In the kitchen, pull out the fridge. It's all there.'

'Jed,' said Fish, 'go see.'

Jed went back into the hall to verify the truth of the black man's story. It only took a minute and he came back and nodded, carrying two ASDA carrier bags which sagged under the weight of their contents.

'Now, that was wise,' said Fish. 'But we need the money too. Christ knows how much you've used out of this little lot.'

'We've got no money, man,' said the black man, but Fish knew that he was lying. Every black man lied, as far as he was concerned. That was a constant.

'You fibbed about the dope and I know you're fibbing about the cash. You've been selling gear out of here and I don't reckon you take Barclaycard, so produce the cash, black boy, or the baby gets it.'

The young woman in the red pants was producing a keening noise from her mouth that was getting on Benny's nerves. 'Shut it,' he said and backhanded her across the face. The keening increased in volume instead of abating and he punched her hard, which seemed to have the desired effect as she collapsed silently to the floor, piss running down her leg.

'Leave her, man,' said the black man. 'Check the bathroom. The cabinet comes off the wall.'

Jed did as he said, ripping the glass-fronted cabinet from its screws and sending it crashing into the bath. Behind it, a cavity had been made in the plasterboard and inside that were blocks of money in plastic sandwich bags. Jed pocketed the lot, figuring it was about five thousand pounds. He went back into the bedroom and gave Fish the thumbs up.

'Fine,' said Fish. 'We'll be going now. Give Jimmy our regards and tell him we're sorry we missed him.'

'Who shall I say called?' asked the black man, regaining his cool now.

'Just a few mates looking for a line or two.'

'OK,' said the black man. 'But I'll remember you, my friend, and one day we'll meet up again.'

'You sure?' asked Fish.

The black man nodded. 'And I got a memory like an elephant. Believe me.'

Fish pondered for a second. Him and his mates weren't local, but did a lot of business in south London, and who knew when the black man or one of his women might catch a glimpse? 'I do,' he said. 'I'm afraid I do. I wish you hadn't said that.'

'You should've worn a mask, white man,' said the black man.

'Yeah, we thought about it but decided to pass,' said Fish.

'And he knows my name,' said Jed.

The black woman in the wet red panties decided at that moment to wake up and get back in the show. She jumped to her feet and ran towards the door. Fish brought up the shotgun without really thinking and fired a round into her back which severed her spinal cord and blew her stomach and its contents across the wallpaper, where it steamed like half-cooked stew and stank like a backed up toilet.

There was a stunned silence. Then the black man dived for the Browning. Jed shot him behind the ear before he could get there, the powerful handgun blowing it clean off his skull. It flew on to the carpet and lay there like a piece of thick cut bacon.

Benny, almost at exploding point by then, smiled, walked over to the woman in the bed and put three rounds into her chest. The dirty white sheets turned crimson and he said: 'What about the baby?'

'Leave it,' said Fish. 'The social will look after it.'

'Serves the fucker right for being born,' said Benny, and without a backward glance the three stepped over the two bodies on the floor, walked through the smoke and stink of cordite and bodily fluids and left the flat. Incredibly, only a few minutes had passed since they entered, and the estate was still snoozing the early morning away.

'Better go and tell Mr Jenner what occurred,' said Fish.

'Do you think he'll get all humpity?' asked Jed.

'Fuck his luck if he does,' said Fish. 'He's got his gear and his dough back.'

And carrying their weapons and the bags quite openly they returned to the car and drove away.

* * *

'We don't know exactly what happened,' said Chas. 'But those fuckers left three dead in that flat.'

'And they know you instigated it?' asked Mark. 'The Yardies, or whatever they are, I mean.'

'I think even lemonades can add two and two,' said Chas.

'Well, fuck me,' said Mark. 'You certainly know how to pick 'em.'

'They were the best we could do at short notice.'

'But business is business,' said Mark. 'They knew the risks.'

'But this got a bit personal.'

'How come?'

'There were three Hop brothers,' said Jenner. 'Jimmy, who owed us the dough. Benny, who got offed in the flat, and Cy.'

'Yeah?' said Mark, but he'd already guessed.

'Cy goes by the street name Beretta,' said Chas.

'Well, of course he does,' said Mark. 'And he's got the hump, right?'

'Just a bit,' said Jenner. 'Won't be happy until we're all brown bread. And he means it.'

'Terrific. No wonder you've got tight security here.'

Chas shrugged. John Jenner was still gazing into the distance.

'I'm going upstairs,' said Mark. 'I need to make some phone calls.'

'So you're going to help?' said Jenner, turning his head slowly in Mark's direction.

'Looks like I don't have much choice, do I?' he replied and left the room.

EIGHTEEN

Mark went straight to his room, closed the door and sat on the bed. The curtains were open and, although there was no light on, the garden shone from the frost that had settled on the lawn.

Wearily, regretting his return south of the river more with every moment – aside from seeing Linda again – he switched on the bedside lamp, found his bag and fished out a battered black leather-bound notebook. He held it in his hand for a moment before opening it at the first page and reaching for his mobile. It had been a long time since he'd used the book. A lifetime, for some.

The first number he tried rang and rang into the bitter night, and he looked at his face reflected in the black mirror of his bedroom window. Eight years, he thought. What're the odds?

The second number was unobtainable, but the third rang for just a few seconds before it was answered with a grunted, 'Hello.'

'Is Diz there, please?' asked Mark, realising as he said it how ridiculous it sounded.

'What?'

'Diz. Dizzy. Dizzy Dawes.'

'Christ. No one's called me that for years. Who's this?'

'Is that you Dizzy?'

'It's Eddie. Who's this?'

'Mark.'

'Mark who?'

'Mark Farrow.'

'It can't be.'

'It is.'

'Mark Farrow?'

'Yeah.'

'Christ.'

'It is. Dizzy.'

'It's Eddie now. Always Eddie.'

'Sorry. I can't believe you're still there.'

'You can't believe me. Bloody hell, man, it's been… how long?'

'Eight years, more or less.'

'And you can't believe it's me. I can't believe it's you, Mark.'

'It is.'

There was a long pause. 'So?'

'I'm back, Eddie.' It sounded strange to Mark's ears to call his old friend that. It had been Dizzy Dawes since school.

'So what do you want me to do? Dance, sing?'

'Listen, I know I just vanished, but I had my reasons.'

'Reasons to be cheerful part three.' An old Blockheads hit.

That was more like Dizzy, thought Mark. 'Yeah.'

'So? Why the call?'

'I was wondering what you were doing.'

'Sitting here in front of the telly, smoking spliff, drinking strong lager, same as every night.'

'Where's Bren?' Bren was Brenda. Eddie's wife. A sweet girl, if a little simple, Mark remembered.

'Gone. Took the kids and pissed off with a driving instructor from Cheam.'

Mark didn't know if he was being serious. 'Kids?' he said.

'Two now. One you met in his bassinet, the other came later, after you split.'

'Boy or girl?'

'Does it matter, Mark? They might as well not exist as far as I'm concerned. They're living in Nottingham or Birmingham or some bloody ham or another now, I don't know.'

'I'm sorry, mate.'

'Yeah, sure. So what's the real reason for this new year communication? Forget to send me a Christmas card? Want to know what I got from Santa? What?'

'I'm trying to find the boys.'

'What boys?'

'Our boys. The old crew.'

'Christ, Mark, where you fucking been?'

'Around. I'll tell you if you let me. We could meet.'

'That'd be good. Talk about old times. Old mates who never call.'

'Listen. I'm sorry, Diz. I mean it.'

'I told you, it's Eddie these days. Don't call me Dizzy. I don't answer to that name anymore.'

'OK Eddie. Are you working?'

'Me? Fuck no. That's one of the reasons Bren did a runner. No gainful employment. No regular fucking income. I can hear her saying it now, the cow. No, mate. I'm sitting here in my flat waiting for the bailiffs, living high on what the government supplies every fortnight in Giro form.'

'Maybe I can do something about that.'

'Like what?'

'Put a little work your way.'

'What kind of work?'

'Dirty work.'

'Real dirty work?'

'The dirtiest.'

'Are you kidding me? You ain't seen the state I'm in.'

'It's well paid.'

'How much?'

'Not on the dog, mate. Like I said, we could meet.'

For the first time, Edward 'Dizzy' Dawes sounded interested. 'When?' he asked.

'Tomorrow.'

'Sounds all right. I've nothing else to do.'

'Fine. I've got someone else to see first, I think. How about late afternoon?'

'Whenever.'

'I'll call you…'

'What? In eight years time?'

'No. Tomorrow lunchtime. We'll make a meet. You're still in Stockwell?' Course he was. Stupid question.

'No. I'm at Claridges, but I've had my calls diverted.'

'Sorry mate. I'll bell you, all right?'

'You do that.'

Mark clicked off the connection and put the phone on the bed. He decided to wait until talking to Dizzy, or Eddie, or whatever he was calling himself these days, before trying to find more old friends. His welcome in that quarter could hardly have been called warm. Only the mention of money had made Eddie soften up, and even then it was little more than a faint thaw of the chill that had gripped his voice when he'd discovered who was calling. But who could blame him? Mark had been the leader of the firm and he'd just split without warning. They hadn't known what had caused him to leave – and they never would as far as he was concerned.

Mark switched off his mobile and went downstairs. Both Chas and John Jenner had gone up to their respective rooms and Martine's absence made him suppose that she was on one of her boozy nights out. Thank God for that, he thought. The last thing he needed was a rerun of the previous night's events. Or the recriminations he was sure it would eventually bring.

He switched on the TV, found a bottle of brandy in the cupboard, poured a decent glassful and lit a cigarette before sitting in front of the box and staring mindlessly at the screen.

Shit, he thought, I wonder where all this grief is going to end. He couldn't know what the future held, but perhaps if he had, he would have just got up and walked out into the cold night, never to return.

He thought about Linda. On the screen, an old James Bond film reeled in front of his eyes, and ridiculous people did ridiculously violent things to each other, then got up and carried on as if nothing had happened. In real life it wasn't like that, Mark knew. He killed the volume and used the landline to call Linda on her mobile. She answered quickly.

'Is it all right to talk?' asked Mark without identifying himself.

'Yes.'

'I've been thinking about you,' he said.

'Me too. Thinking about you, I mean,' she said.

'Good.'

'Don't be too pleased. You don't know what I've been thinking.'

'True. But you're talking to me, so it can't be all bad.'

'Don't you believe it.'

'I meant what I said.'

'About what?'

'About you. And me.'

'Mark. Seems to me I've heard that song before.'

'Yeah, I know. But you'll end up believing me.'

'So you say.'

'So I mean. Anyway. Tomorrow. How about lunch? We can't keep meeting in Safeway's - people will talk, and my grocery bill will go through the roof.'

'Suppose so.'

'Where then?'

'Somewhere where no one will know us.'

'Know you, you mean,' she said.

'If you like.'

'Sneaking around, like we used to?'

'Linda. I've explained.' He watched the images on the screen flicker in front of him like cardboard cutouts in glorious Technicolour.

'But that doesn't make it right, Mark.'

'I know. But tomorrow. You'll meet me?'

'Yes. You know I will. I'm just a fool.'

'You're not.'

'I wonder, would you have pursued me if Andy hadn't died?'

'Would you have let me?'

'The trouble is, Mark, I don't know.'

He sighed. He didn't know either.

'So where do we meet?'

'Remember the Horniman Museum?'

'How could I forget?'

'There's a restaurant there. It's open for lunch. It's pricey. You can treat me.'

'I'd treat you to lunch on the moon if there was a restaurant there,' said Mark.

'Don't lay it on too thick, Mark.'

'Sorry. What time?'

'One-ish. We should be able to get a table without booking. I'll leave Daisy with Greta.'

'You can bring Daisy if you want,' said Mark. 'I liked her, and I think she liked me.'

'Dangerous territory. I don't want you bonding with my children, then taking off. They've suffered enough loss, thank you very much.'

'I won't take off again.'

'Don't make promises you can't possibly keep. You promised me you'd never leave me once before, and look what happened.'

He couldn't think of anything to say that wouldn't make it worse, so he said nothing.

'So, I'll see you there,' said Linda after a moment's silence.

'Sounds fine.'

'Wait till you see the bill and you'll wish it was just your groceries you were paying for.'

'I can handle it.'

'And me, Mark. You always could handle me. Isn't that right? Now I've got to go.'

When she switched off, Mark replaced the phone in the cradle. He realised that Martine had entered silently, her shoes in her hand. She was drunk. 'The bird,' she said. 'Has to be. Got a date?'

'How long have you been there?'

'Wouldn't you like to know?'

'Not really.'

'You're a fucking prick,' she said, the words slurring together.

'I think you've already made that clear.'

'Piss off.'

'Why bother, Martine? Why don't we just coexist peacefully?'

'And why don't you help my dad?'

'That's just what I intend to do.'

'What? Between shags with that bitch?'

'Why do you hate her so much?'

'Because she rules you, you bloody fool.'

'And does that make you jealous?'

'Jealous?' she almost screamed. 'You think I give a shit about you or what you do?'

'If last night was anything to go by.'

'Bollocks,' she said and walked out. Mark looked at James Bond and envied him his way with women. When he'd finished his drink he shut off the TV in the middle of the dramatic finale of the film and went to bed. If only the rest of his life was that simply sorted, he thought.

The next day he hung around the house all morning communicating with no one and staying in his room. At noon he set off for Dulwich and the Horniman Museum. He'd taken Linda one Saturday afternoon when they'd been going out together. Maybe not the obvious place for a date, but the Horniman had captured Mark's attention when he was a boy. It had been founded by the tea magnate of the same name and contained items he'd discovered on his travels to India and China. The dark exhibits excited something in Mark's soul and he wanted to share it with his first real love. But outside in the grounds their passion had gotten the better of them and instead of ancient artifacts, Mark and Linda had found a quiet corner to make love. It was the first time in the open air for both of them and they often laughed at the memory, especially the part when one of the attendants had come out for a smoke break and had stood not two yards away from where they'd hidden in the undergrowth.

Mark arrived early, found a parking space and went to find the restaurant. It looked very smart from the outside and he didn't know if it would work out in the wilds of south London. Still, he was prepared to give it a try, if only for old time's sake. And the fact that Linda had suggested the place made him think things could be going his way.

Outside the building, only a few feet from where they'd hidden together on that long ago summer afternoon, Mark took out his mobile and keyed in Eddie Dawes's number. The phone was answered in a moment. 'Eddie,' said Mark. 'How you going?'

'Hungover. Nothing new there.'

Mark hated to hear his old friend talk like that. 'Are you about later?' he asked.

'Yeah.'

'Where?'

'The Four Feathers in Stockwell,' replied Eddie. 'Our old hangout, remember?'

'Sure,' said Mark, walking around to keep warm.

'Only it ain't the Four Feathers no more,' said Dawes. 'It's the Rat and fucking Parrot now. Times change.'

'They do,' agreed Mark.

'And people,' said his old friend.

'True.'

'What time?' asked Eddie. 'Though I don't know why I'm asking as I'm in there all afternoon, every afternoon. In fact, I was just on my way there now. I was just waiting for your call. Not that I really expected it, as you've been known to let me down before.'

Mark ignored the jibe and the self pity in Eddie's voice. There was plenty of time to sort that out later. 'Will you be there around four?' he asked.

'If the money holds out.'

'Make sure it does. I'll bring a live injection.'

224

'How come you're in the money?'

'I'll tell you later,' said Mark as he saw Linda's car coming down the drive. 'Someone's here.'

'Wish I could say the same,' said Dawes, and he dropped the phone down with a bang.

Mark waited as Linda parked her car and got out. She was wearing a long leather coat and looked fabulous. He walked towards her and they embraced. 'Just like old times,' he said.

'But I'm not getting my knickers off in the bushes if that's what you mean,' she said. 'It's too chilly. Besides it'd ruin my coat.'

'I think we're both too old for that,' he said.

'Speak for yourself.'

They laughed, and arm in arm walked into the restaurant.

The place was quiet. They were offered a table by the window, where they ordered bottles of wine and mineral water. The menu was pricey and the room was warm, with white linen on the tables, and glasses and cutlery sparkled in the subdued lighting.

'Who would ever have thought it?' said Mark as he looked around. 'A place like this out here in the boonies.'

'All sorts of things have changed round here,' she replied.

'So I've noticed.'

'Good. You should.'

'I was thinking about you last night,' said Mark when the drinks had been brought to the table, the wine tasted, announced satisfactory and poured.

'And me you, like I said.'

'And?'

'And I've come to a decision.'

He didn't like the way the conversation was going. This is where she tells me she doesn't want to see me anymore, he thought. 'And?' he asked.

'Simple. I will keep on seeing you, but...'

He cocked his head like a dog.

'...But I don't want you involved with my family. I don't want you seeing Luke or Daisy, and I don't want Greta to know what we're up to.

And I especially don't want Sean to find out. I'll go out with you when I can, but nowhere where I'm known. I'll sleep with you when we can at the flat or wherever, but that's it. I don't want a boyfriend. I don't want a relationship.

'You just want a shag now and then, is that it?'

'If that's how you want to put it, yes.'

'And I have no say in the matter.'

'Course you do. You can take it or leave it, Mark.'

He took a sip of wine which now tasted like vinegar. 'So I'll just be your bit on the side.'

'If you like.'

'I don't like.'

She shrugged. 'Please yourself. I made out for eight years without you, and I daresay I can make out for a lot more. My family is what matters to me now. I enjoyed the other afternoon more than you'll know. I miss having sex. I enjoyed it with you years ago and and I enjoyed it with Andy. But I made do without it after he died… and I'll make do without it when you go away again.'

She gave Mark a long, cold look.

'Who says I'm going to go away again?' he said.

She smiled. 'Mark. One thing you taught me is that people like you always go away.'

'But I'm here now.'

'Don't get hissy. You pissed off once before and I expect you'll piss off again. I'm not going to build my life around you for a second time only to be left high and dry. So why don't we order?'

They did as she said, but Mark wasn't interested in the food. When the waitress left them alone he played with his glass and said: 'OK. You win. I'll play along.'

'It's not a case of winning or losing. It's simply a case of being pragmatic. I've got a life and I don't intend to let you spoil it.'

'I don't want to spoil it, I want to make it better.'

'Then do what I ask.'

There was no answer to that that he could think of.

The rest of the meal passed pleasantly enough, but afterwards Mark couldn't remember much about it. He ate little, but Linda tucked in mightily. Their roles seemed to have reversed since his return.

Afterwards they sat in her car, as she ran the engine for the heater.

'So?' she asked.

'So what?' he asked back.

'Are you sure you want to carry on, now you've had more time to think?'

'Play it your way?'

She nodded.

'You know what I'm going to say,' he said.

'No I don't.'

'Yes, I'm sure.'

'Good.'

'So when can I see you?' he asked, feeling like a little boy as he did so.

'Call me on the mobile tonight. I'll see what I can get organised for the weekend. I'll get Greta or my other regular babysitter to look after Luke and Daisy on Saturday evening. We could meet at the flat.'

Mark felt like he was about as important as the babysitter in her life. If she couldn't get one then he was on the out.

'OK,' he said and opened the car door. 'I'll call you tonight.'

'Give me a kiss then,' she said.

He did, and she was careful not to muss her lipstick. Mark got out of the car and went back to his own where he sat and watched her leave. Once upon a time he could have had her for life but he'd messed up, and now she was getting her own back, and there was nothing he could do about it except walk away – and that was the last thing he wanted to do.

He looked at his watch and started his car. The hours had flown and it was time to get to Stockwell to catch Eddie Dawes.

He intended to park in the same cul de sac close to the Four Feathers where he'd parked in the old days. But when he turned the corner he didn't recognise the old pub where he and his little crew used to plan their many exploits. Gone was the miserable facade and in its place was a new name and a smart new frontage, even hanging baskets just waiting for the spring to arrive so they could burst into bloom.

He opened the door and walked across the polished floor to the bar. At that time of day the place was almost empty, just a few drinkers sporadically dotted around, sitting as far away from each other as they possibly could. The in house music system was playing a Van Morrison album and the lunchtime specials were chalked up on a blackboard. In the old days, the Christmas decorations would still have been up mid January and the lunchtime 'specials' would have been restricted to ham or cheese rolls, with or without pickle. Things had certainly changed. Mark scoped the room for Eddie, and twice his gaze passed a big man in dirty jeans and an anorak sitting on a stool and gazing at his own reflection in the mirror behind the bar. Mark looked at his bearded face. Somewhere lost in there was his old friend.

'Eddie?' he said, once he'd walked up to him.

The big man turned. 'Mark Farrow,' he replied. 'Christ, I'd recognise you anywhere.'

Which was more than Mark could say about Eddie, and once again he realised how much things had changed in his absence. Dizzy Dawes had been the sharpest dresser of any of the boys but now his appearance was that of someone who didn't care what he looked like. And he was half cut into the bargain. Shit, thought Mark, this isn't going to work.

He sat at the next bar stool and nodded in the direction of Eddie's glass, which just contained the dregs of a pint. 'Drink?' he asked.

'That's what I'm here for.'

'Lager?'

'Bitter. And a chaser. Scotch. Bells.'

Mark ordered Eddie's drinks from the girl behind the jump and a pint of lager for himself, although he really didn't want it. When the drinks were brought and paid for he suggested they sit at one of the booths at the back of the pub. They carried their drinks over and sat down.

'So, Mark?' said Eddie when he'd downed half his pint and wiped the foam from his moustache. 'Tell me all about yourself.'

'Not much to tell.'

'In eight years? I don't believe you. I bet you've had some fun.'

'That's not how I'd describe it.'

'So how would you describe it then?'

'Another time, Eddie, eh?' said Mark. 'I'm looking to find the boys if I can. I need them.'

'And when we needed you?'

'I was gone, I know. I'm not proud of what I did, but that's in the past.'

'The past is all I've got.'

'We can change that.'

'We, white man?'

Eddie's favourite expression. And for the first time Mark felt that his old friend was hiding somewhere inside the unwashed mess of a man sitting in front of him.

'Got any fags?' asked Eddie.

Mark pulled out his packet but there was only one left. He offered it to Eddie, who said: 'Typical. You never had any bloody smokes. Hold on, I'll get some.' He got to his feet, staggered, smiled self-consciously and hunted in his pockets for change. He came up light and said: 'Got any dough, Mark? I'm temporarily embarrassed. I was nursing that last pint waiting for you. Didn't you say something about a live injection?'

'Sure,' said Mark. He pulled out a wad of cash and peeled off a tenner. Seeing Eddie's eyes on the money, he said: 'How much do you need?'

'That lot wouldn't even start to cover it.'

Mark peeled off another forty quid, added it to the tenner and put it on the table. 'There you go, mate. And there's plenty more where that came from if you're interested.'

'Always interested,' said Eddie and picked up the small pile of notes with dirty hands tipped with bitten fingernails. 'Always interested.'

He went to the bar for change and Mark saw that he ordered a swift scotch whilst he was there, downing it in one, before going to the cigarette machine. Mark had seen some problem drinkers in his time and it looked like Eddie Dawes was one of them. Just another little local difficulty to overcome, he thought as he waited for Eddie to return.

When he sat down again, Mark said: 'So do you see any of the others these days?'

'You are out of touch,' replied Eddie through a mouthful of smoke.

'Put me back in touch then.'

'OK. Andy's dead.'

'What?'

'Dead.'

'What happened to him?'

'Car crash, about three years ago. You remember him and cars.'

'Course.' Andy had been a car thief extraordinaire. He'd even managed to steal a Maserati Spyder worth about two hundred thousand pounds from the lockup belonging to a main dealer. Exactly the same specs as the one driven by Don Johnston in *Miami Vice*, the TV series from which the boys got most of their fashion ideas at the time. They'd enjoyed burning up London until he'd piled it into a set of traffic lights in the Kings Road.

'What was he driving?' asked Mark.

'Funnily enough, a bog standard Ford Sierra. He was mini cabbing at the time.'

'Stroll on. Elvis?'

'He's inside. Doing a double handful in Parkhurst for dealing smack.'

'Bloody hell. What about Tubbs?'

'He's about.'

'Where?'

'Managing a KFC in Holloway.'

'I don't believe this.'

'What did you expect? That we were all doing well in your absence?'

'I didn't know.'

'So what's the job?'

'I need to take care of some spades who're getting above themselves.'

'How much care?'

'Intensive care. Undertaker care.'

'Heavy.'

'We did it before, remember?'

'How can I forget? I still dream about it sometimes.'

'Yeah.'

'So where did you get to, Mark?'

'Long story.'

'You keep saying that. Enlighten me.'

'Not now. I need to think.'

'You talked about money. How much?'

Mark thought about the case full of cash in John Jenner's safe and plucked a figure from the air. 'Ten grand.' He'd worry about getting it later.

'For what?'

'A couple of days' work.'

'Sounds all right.'

Mark looked at the state of Eddie Dawes. 'I don't think so, Eddie. I don't think you're up to it.'

'But I could use the money. And I've still got my little baby.' He was referring to the topped and tailed sawn-off double-barrelled Remington shotgun he'd used to great effect in the old days.

'I would've thought you'd've dumped that years ago.'

'Sentimental value.'

'Listen, mate, I don't mean to be personal...'

'But you're going to be.'

'OK. Look at you. Man, you were the sharpest of the lot of us. What happened?'

'Life happened. Bren leaving happened. Being out of work happened. You leaving happened.'

'You can't blame me...'

'I do. We were great, the five of us. We had a future. And look what went down. One dead, one banged up, one doing some stupid job

231

for not much more than minimum wage, and me on my arse in an empty flat.'

Mark didn't know what to say.

'Then look at you. Nice clothes. Probably got a decent motor outside and talking grands. Something's wrong somewhere.'

'Yeah.'

'So?'

'So?'

'So let me get in touch with Tubbs. It'll be just like the old days. Only three of us instead of five.'

'These people killed three friends of Uncle John's the other day and nicked three hundred thousand quid's worth of coke. This is fucking heavy, Eddie. Not to be played about with. You could die.'

'I'm already dead, Mark, if you hadn't noticed. I'm just walking around a little bit longer than most corpses. I don't give a shit about that. But for ten grand I'm prepared to do anything. It could be a whole new start for me.'

'And what about Tubbs? These are black geezers.'

'He always was an equal opportunities villain, Mark, remember? He wouldn't care if they were red, white or blue.'

'And you still speak to him?'

'Every now and then I go up Holloway and pig out on free chicken. It's his only perk.'

'Where's he living?'

'In a bedsit a couple of streets away from the shop. He always smells of fat.'

'Lovely.'

'So?'

'All right, Ed, get in touch. Let's make a meet. It can't hurt.'

'You got any more dough? I've got expenses.'

What, a bus pass? thought Mark, but he didn't say it. Instead he peeled off another fifty quid and passed it over to Eddie Dawes. After giving him his mobile number, he left him to his drinking.

Christ, he thought, when he returned to his car. Talk about the gang that couldn't shoot straight. But he only needed them for backup, and they'd been good as gold in the old days.

So what could go wrong?

Everything. That was what.

NINETEEN

'S o where do these spades hang out then?' Mark asked John Jenner and Chas on his return to the house.

'On the Ashworthy,' growled John Jenner. 'Niggers like to stick together in their little tribes. Gather round the cooking pot at night and eat their stinking goat curry.'

'Nice, Uncle,' said Mark. 'A very modern outlook. We had goat curry at Tootsies, remember? I need to take a look. Suss out the ground.'

'I'll give you the guided tour,' said Chas. 'We'll take your motor. It looks like a drug dealer's car, so it'll be well at home up there. How long's it been since you saw the place?'

'Years.'

'You won't recognise it.'

Mark had been familiar with the Ashworthy estate on Brixton Hill. It was an immediate post-war project, although he wasn't sure if it had been built on bomb sites or whether it was part of the great slum clearance that had taken place in the late 1940s. Homes fit for heroes being the intention. No huge high rises there, the tallest buildings being perhaps ten stories, like large matchboxes laid out on their sides, almost Stalinist in their brick and window regularities. There were low rise blocks too, and maisonettes, and even studio-type flats for single people. Utopia in south London had been the architects' aim and, for a while at least, it had been. Mark always imagined the planners of the Ashworthy to be out of some post-war black and white British film. Good looking boys back from the conflict, full of liberal feelings, dressed in baggy flannels and pullovers, smoking pipes and untipped cigarettes over their drawing boards, still using military slang. He'd had friends from school who'd lived on the Ashworthy, and often he'd visited the place to while away the school holidays, playing music, smoking dope, and hanging round the open areas looking for girls. It had been all right then, he remembered. But as he and Chas cruised the winding streets in the Range Rover, he realised it had changed for the worse.

Homes fit for heroes had turned into homes fit for crack whores. The Community Centre, once the hub of the estate, where residents' committee used to meet, had been burnt out. Graffiti scarred what smoke-stained walls remained. Next door was an off-licence, its windows and door covered with metal sheeting and its entire stock seeming to consist of strong canned lagers, cheap cigarettes and cut price vodka. What a career move to get to manage that dump, thought Mark as they cruised slowly by. 'Shithouse,' grumbled Chas who was driving. 'Filthy fucking shithouse.'

The tarmac on the roads was cracked and weeds sprouted through the gaps. The whole place was seedy, dirty and depressing. Black sacks of garbage spilled out smaller supermarket bags that had been torn by dogs or cats or rats, and evil-smelling rubbish tumbled into the gutters, propelled by a sharp wind that blew across the muddy spaces where once grass had been religiously shaved by council workers. No one cut the grass any more and what was left of it sprouted in unhealthy clumps, dotted with faeces – both animal and human. 'Christ,' said Mark. 'I wouldn't fancy wandering round here after dark.'

'Let's hope our motor doesn't break down then,' said Chas. 'It wouldn't last the night up here without being picked clean and burnt out.'

'You're so cheerful, Chas,' said Mark. 'Is that what keeps you going?'

'Something like that,' replied Chas, but he laughed as he said it. 'Sorry, mate. But things seem to be going from bad to worse.'

'Since I got back, you mean?' said Mark.

'No.' Chas shook his mighty head. 'It's been going pear-shaped since John was diagnosed with the big C.' He stopped the car and pointed to one of the smaller blocks. 'Moses lives in number five with his mum.

Slag's been on the game since the old king died. Seen more pricks than a secondhand dartboard.'

Mark smiled at the old joke and reflected that the old firm wasn't suited to the modern world. 'Beretta lives behind us in that tall block. Top floor. He's got some white trash slapper sucking his dick every night after she's sucked on the crack-pipe. And young Karl is in the maisonettes on Brixton Hill. Handy for the chip shop and the pub. Life's good for these fuckers, ain't it?'

'It's about to change, Chas, I can promise you that,' said Mark. 'Drive around a bit more. And then let's go and have a pint.'

They settled in the Telegraph pub on the Hill. A huge old boozer that had gone through so many style changes over the years, it was a wonder it still retained its original name. Mark bought two pints of lager and they sat in a corner away from the boisterous, mixed race crowd around the pool table.

'This place has changed,' said Mark.

'Changed,' said Chas. 'I'll say it's fucking changed. Used to be a nice old pub, but it's gone downhill.'

'What hasn't, in your opinion?' asked Mark.

'Don't be funny. You think things have got better?'

'Some things. Technology. Would you still like cars with no heaters and wind-up gramophones and having to use a payphone to get in touch?'

'We managed,' said Chas. 'And, for your information, I never had a wind-up gramophone.'

'Dansette, was it?' asked Mark with a grin.

'Yeah. It was, as it goes, and I had to work all summer holidays in the grocers to get it.'

*　*　*

It had been a magic summer for Chas. Nineteen fifty nine, and he had been fourteen. He'd been in long trousers a couple of years and loved the sound of the music he listened to every night on Radio Luxembourg and the

American Forces Network, under the covers in the bedroom in the attic of his parents' house in Streatham Vale. Boy, he loved that music. The record that changed his life was *Rockin' Through The Rye* by Bill Haley and The Comets. He'd heard it on *Two Way Family Favourites*, a request show on the old Light Programme, whilst eating his Sunday lunch – or dinner as they called it then –three years before. He'd practically felt his balls drop at the first notes and almost choked on a piece of hot roast potato as his father leapt to his feet to turn off 'that bloody jungle music' as he called it. Chas shared his old dad's racist views, but was somehow blinkered about black musicians and the white ones that aped them. He adored them from that moment and still did. Lonnie Donegan, Jerry Lee Lewis, Elvis, The Drifters, Coasters, Platters *et al*. He ate them up over the next few years, but his father wouldn't let him near the Bush radiogram where he stored his Ronnie Hilton, Mantovani, Alma Cogan and Ted Heath LPs. 'If you want to play that rubbish, get your own,' he'd said.

So Chas hunted out boys of his own age who were equally besotted with rock 'n' roll, and spent hours around their houses listening to everyone from Tommy Steele – just OK – to Cliff Richard – awful – in the hope of the occasional Little Richard record floating to the top of the pile.

As he sat in the pub with Mark, Chas yearned for those simpler days when he was an innocent and not yet the gangster he was to become. He'd broken his mother's heart when he'd first been sent away in the early 60s, even though she'd slowly come round to the way he ran his life later on. His father, of course, had long washed his hands of the long haired lout that his son had become. That's what he'd called him when he'd thrown Chas out of the house at age sixteen, with little more than the clothes he stood up in. His father had smashed up his record player and destroyed his precious vinyl that day and, although he could forgive him for the disownment, the records were another matter. They'd never spoken again. Not even at his mother's funeral. When his father died a few years later, Chas didn't even bother to attend his cremation. Burnt before he got to hell, was his opinion. And good riddance.

But that summer of 1959 had been the dog's bollocks for Chas. He'd grown tall and strong over the previous winter playing football for the school and spending hours in the gymnasium building muscle. He'd done some boxing and won every bout he'd taken part in, making him quite a star with the girls. He'd lost his virginity that spring to a little raver called Sally from St Martin's School For Girls, who must've worn twenty stiff petticoats under her brown gingham school dress. Fourteen. Early for those days, but now… pretty much average, he imagined, or maybe – looking at the little girls in the street dressed like tarts – it was as old as the hills.

Just before the summer holidays, he'd toured the shops and cafés close to home looking for part time work. The shop where his mum bought her groceries was run by an elderly Jewish man and his wife, and he'd offered him a couple of hours' work a day, plus all day Saturdays, for the princely sum of a pound a week. Chas jumped at it. He'd yet to become the hardened thief he would be before too much time had passed, but he'd earned his spurs shoplifting small items at Woolworths, and he knew that on top of his wages he could probably nick enough fags and sweets to make his pay up to something decent. And if they left that old till unattended from time to time, he could lift a few bob as well. His pocket money from home was five shillings a week; that, plus the quid, plus whatever else he could scavenge, would soon get him that Dansette record player in the window of the electrical shop that he yearned for and admired every day on his way to school. Chas'd also noticed that the attached record bar, as they called them then, wasn't too security minded. He was sure that he could nick a few forty-fives when it got busy in there.

So all summer he worked in the shop, delivering boxes of groceries on a broken down bicycle that the proprietor supplied, pocketing tips and stealing bits and pieces until, two days before school was due to start, he took twelve and a half quid into the electrical shop and purchased the machine. Laughable by today's standards, the record player was made of cheap boxwood covered in red and white plastic, with a BSR ten-record autochange, a four-inch speaker and a single tone control. But it became the centre of his life. He begged, borrowed and stole records from wherever he could and, although the sound was as lo-fi as could be, it played those little plastic discs to perfection. Something that his recently purchased multispace CD player could never do. Maybe it was his age, he thought. Maybe you had to be a teenager.

It was the time of teddy boys. Italian style was just creeping into the shops. To go with his music, Chas needed a pair of Levi 501's, a box jacket and some winklepickers. His father wouldn't hear of it. 'Stout shoes,' he said. 'Stout shoes for school that will last. And if you want jeans -' he almost spat the word '- Ladybird do a perfectly good pair for ten and six at Woolworths.' So Chas had to rob the money from his mother's purse and his father's wallet. Then hide them in the garden shed and change out of his hated Ladybirds before hitting the hot spots of Streatham and Croydon. It was at these coffee bars and record hops that he met the people he admired. Young villains with money in their pockets: he dreamed of emulating them, and did so until he was caught and sent down.

* * *

'Drink up, Chas,' said Mark, shaking the big man out of his reverie and back to the present, where rap music was pumping out from the pub jukebox. 'We'd better be getting back.'

If only I could, thought Chas. Get back to simpler times. Duller times too, for sure. But they fitted his skin. Not like now, when he felt like he had ants running around inside his body all the time. But he only grunted, drained his glass and followed Mark back to the car. They drove home in silence.

Once there, Mark said to John. 'I need to know more about these people. I'm going to wander up and have a look round on my own. Nobody knows me. I'll buy some spliff and make myself busy.' Then he had a thought. 'Or maybe I'll send somebody else.'

'You take care,' said John. 'It's the badlands up there.'

'I'll be fine, Uncle. And soon they'll be out of your hair.'

John Jenner touched his receding pate and smiled for the first time. 'Good. You do that, son and I'll owe you.'

'And get Martine off my case will you, Uncle?' said Mark. 'She's getting to be a pain in the arse.'

'Getting?' said John Jenner.

'You know what I mean.'

Later on his mobile rang. It was Eddie Dawes. 'I've made a meet with Tubbs,' he said.

'When?'

'Tomorrow. It's his day off.'

'Where?'

'A pub in Holloway.'

'What time?' asked Mark.

'Twelve.'

'Fine. I'll pick you up at your place. Elevenish.'

'I'll be waiting.'

Mark arrived in the familiar street just before the allotted hour, left the car at the kerb and went to Eddie's door. He still lived in the top flat in a terraced house off Stockwell Road. It hadn't weathered well: the front door was battered and looked like it had been busted open several times and repaired by a blind man. A blind man had painted it too, sometime back in the last century, and the paint was peeling and blistered. Mark rang the doorbell marked 'Dawes', and a few minutes later Eddie appeared, pulling on his anorak. 'I'd ask you up,' he said. 'But it could do with a tidy.' If the flat was anything like the outside of the house, or indeed Eddie himself, Mark thought, a tidy was the least it needed, but he said nothing. They went to the Vogue and Eddie said: 'I knew you'd have a nice motor.'

'It's stolen,' said Mark.

'Yeah?'

'Yeah.'

'Good for you. Nick it in France, did you?' asked Eddie after examining the plates.

'Something like that.'

'Good on you, Mark. Andy would be proud of you.'

Mark nodded. 'When things are sorted, I'll get something of my own.'

'Lexus are good,' said Eddie. 'Always fancied a Lexus myself.'

'We'll see,' said Mark as he started the car and headed towards the river.

241

They were mostly silent on the drive until Eddie directed Mark into the back streets of Holloway and pointed out their meeting place. It was another theme pub. Mark was getting heartily sick of the idea. This one was a taste of blarney; the name picked out in gold script on the sign, with shamrocks instead of punctuation marks, and enough Irish memorabilia inside to dam the Liffey. There was a hockey match playing on the TV, the sound low and an Irish tenor bleating from the sound system.

'Bloody hell,' said Mark. 'I hate these places.'

'They're all the go,' said Eddie as they went to the bar and Mark ordered two pints of Guinness. What else?

There was no sign of Tubbs; the entire clientele, what there was of it, was white. A few hard looking gentlemen sat around getting the feel of the auld sod, and a couple of ladies of rather dubious virtue sat at the bar sucking on glasses of the black nectar. Behind the bar counter a young man with short hair, dressed in black trousers, a white shirt and a black waistcoat busily polished a glass, occasionally taking surreptitious drags on a cigarette he had hidden behind the till. 'Nice,' said Mark. 'You bring me to the best places.'

'It'll do,' said Eddie. 'It serves booze and the music's not too bad.'

Mark gave him a funny look. 'So where's the man?'

'He'll be here.'

Mark looked at his watch.

'Speak of the Devil,' said Eddie as the door opened and a huge black man appeared. 'Christ,' said Mark. 'Tubbs has got tubby.'

The black man walked to their table and Mark got to his feet. 'Tubbs,' he said.

'Crockett,' said the black man, his face splitting open to show two rows of even white teeth. 'I never thought I'd see you again.'

'Well, here I am,' said Mark. 'And if he's not Dizzy, I'm not Crockett. Mark'll do.'

That had been their names in their youth. Crockett and Tubbs from *Miami Vice*, Dizzy Dawes, Elvis and Andy. What a crew. And how times had changed.

'Drink?' asked Tubbs.

'I'll get them,' said Mark. 'It's my treat.'

'Rum and coke,' said Tubbs. 'With plenty of ice and a slice.' Eddie Dawes pointed at his almost empty Guinness glass. Mark went to the bar and suddenly it was the 80s again.

*　*　*

The *Miami Vice* boys had all gone to Tulse Hill Comprehensive together, just a few yards up the road from John Jenner's alma mater, the Strand. It hadn't been a good school and Mark was glad when John had showed him that it had been demolished. It fact it had been a dump. A sink for all the losers in south London as far as he could remember. Him included.

The boys were all the same age and had entered their secondary education in 1981. The five had teamed up early on, in fact, just before Mark Farrow's father had been murdered. It made him something of a celebrity at the school, that his policeman father had been gunned down only a couple of miles away. They didn't start out to be villains, but circumstances, and Mark's deteriorating home life, had led them into a life of crime. He was their leader and where he went the others followed.

Tubbs, at the time known simply as Winston McLeash, was one outcome of the marriage between a Scottish merchant seaman, Angus McLeash, who had carrot-coloured hair and the palest skin that Mark had ever seen, and a young Nigerian woman who was black enough to almost vanish in a darkened room. Winston, the eldest of their five children, all born neatly nine months after Angus's various shore leaves, had fared well by the match. He was black, but not completely, and his hair was thick and shiny as if oiled. Life was not kind to redheaded black people, Mark had noted, so Tubbs had been lucky. He'd been a slim boy despite his nickname, but now his waistline had expanded. He toasted his two old friends when Mark brought their drinks over.

'To good times,' he said.

'Looks like you've had more than a few lately,' said Mark, tapping him on the belly.

243

Tubbs roared. 'Too much fried chicken, my friend. Doesn't do much for the figure.'

'Well, it's good to see you, Tubbs,' said Mark. 'I've missed you.'

The black man suddenly became serious. 'No man,' he said. 'You want something, just like the old days. But me and Eddie have fallen on hard times, as you can see. So what do you need, and how much is it worth?'

Mark looked at Eddie. 'I thought I'd leave it up to you to tell him,' said the latter.

Mark nodded. Probably for the best, he thought. 'A little job,' he said. 'Like the old days.'

'What kind of job exactly?' asked Tubbs.

Mark made a pistol out of his right hand and dropped his thumb like the hammer but said nothing.

'It's been a long time, man,' said Tubbs. 'Me and Eddie, we're out of practice. What's the fee again?'

'Ten grand each. Cash. Unmarked notes out of sequence. A little reconnaissance and it should be all over by the weekend.'

'Sounds good,' said Tubbs. 'Maybe too good. Who we going to fix?'

'Some bad black boys from Brixton,' replied Mark.

'How bad?'

'About as bad as they come.'

'Ten grand each you say?'

Mark nodded.

'Eddie?' said Tubbs.

Dawes shrugged. 'I've already said I'm in if you are.'

Tubbs smiled again. 'I wish Elvis was here.'

'Me too,' said Mark.

'What the hell,' said Tubbs. 'I can go home to the islands with that much dough.'

'You've never been to the islands in your life,' said Mark. 'Closest you've been to the West Indies is a week in Lanzarote in 1989.'

'Sure,' said Tubbs. 'You're not wrong. But a man can dream can't he?'

Mark nodded and went off to order another round.

TWENTY

'You got a motor, Tubbs?' asked Mark Farrow, upon his return.

'An old banger. Vauxhall Astra. You can't afford much on my wages.'

'Not like some,' said Eddie.

Mark ignored him. 'You can get a new one if you do the job,' he said to Tubbs. 'Unless you blow it all on "the islands".'

'Might never come back,' said Tubbs. 'Open a fried chicken restaurant on the beach and spend my days drinking rum and chasing women.'

'You'll have to lose a bit of weight,' said Eddie. 'Otherwise you'll never catch them.'

The big man rocked with laughter again. 'You can come too, man,' he said to Eddie. 'Swim every morning in the sea before we open up.'

'Nice idea,' interrupted Mark. 'But we've got business to discuss here first.'

His two old friends hushed up and listened.

'There's a bloke called Beretta up on the Ashworthy estate. You remember it?'

They both nodded.

'He deals dope and whores from what I've heard, and last week him and his two main men went in and killed some business associates of Uncle John. And by the way, had it off with a pile of charlie. Now, apparently they've been hassling the old firm for months, after a bit of trouble over some money owed. It's time they were sorted. There's a lot of aggro floating around and it has to end.'

245

'And we're going to do it?' said Eddie.

'Let the man finish,' said Tubbs, visions of blue seas and white sands still floating around inside his head.

'It'll be fine,' Mark reassured them. 'They think Uncle John is finished, running scared. He's not well.'

'What's the matter with him?' asked Tubbs.

'Cancer. Terminal.'

'So what's he worried about then?' asked Eddie. 'He'll soon be out of it, won't he?'

'Thanks for your sympathy, Ed,' said Mark.

'Sorry. But you know what I mean.'

'And you know Uncle John,' said Mark. 'He never gives in.'

'What started the aggro?' asked Tubbs. 'As I remember, everyone had their own patch, stayed out of each other's way and rubbed along pretty well.'

'Times change,' said Mark. 'And three other people got dead a while back.'

'Friends of Beretta, was it?'

Mark nodded. 'An unfortunate overreaction from some geezers from Kent employed by Uncle John.'

'And this mob got the hump about it.'

'That's about it.'

'And we've got to sort it.'

Mark nodded again.

'For ten grand.'

'That's the deal. But I've had another idea.'

'What?' asked Tubbs.

'If we can get the dope back, I'll up the ante.'

'How much?' asked Eddie.

'Depends on how much is left. I reckon you two can cop for a third between you.'

'And it was worth how much?' asked Tubbs.

'Three hundred thousand.'

246

Eddie whistled between his teeth.

'Sounds OK,' said Tubbs. 'But if they've got rid or we can't find it, we get ten grand each, right?'

Another nod from Mark.

'No,' said Tubbs. 'Let's make it twenty.'

'You don't want much, do you?'

'Man, it's risky. These guys are stone killers, right?'

'Right,' said Mark.

'And they might have other friends?'

'Almost certainly.'

'So twenty sounds about right. Eddie?'

It was Eddie's turn to nod.

'I dunno,' said Mark. But he knew he'd agree in time, he just didn't want to seem like a pushover.

'Take it or leave it,' said Tubbs, echoing Linda's words the previous day.

'And you'll do what needs to be done?' said Mark.

Tubbs nodded.

'Eddie?' said Mark.

Eddie Dawes looked at Tubbs and grinned, and suddenly Dizzy was back in the room, conjured up from some far off place where he'd lain dormant for years. 'And we fuck off after, Tubbs, you and me?'

'That's the plan, my man,' said Tubbs. 'Just think about it. Cheap rum, cheap spliff and cheap women. We'll be kings.'

Eddie Dawes looked at Mark. 'OK,' he said. 'Fuck this country. Fuck this winter. Let's do it, eh?'

'Great,' said Mark.

'So what's the plan?' asked Tubbs.

'Simple,' said Mark. 'You, my friend go down to Brixton and make like you've got a lot of dough and are in the market for a big buy. We find out where they've got the dope and get it back, taking no prisoners. We organise a buy and fuck them up.'

'Then I'm going to need some flash,' said Tubbs. 'My Vauxhall Astra ain't exactly some big drug buyer's car of choice.'

'We need Andy,' said Eddie.

'Yeah,' agreed Tubbs. 'He'd get me a fucking Roller, no danger.'

'I'll organise something,' said Mark. 'Don't worry.'

'And my flash cash?'

'There's no problem there either,' said Mark.

'Sounds good,' said Tubbs.

'Eddie,' said Mark.

'Man, for that sort of loot I'll do anything.'

'Don't forget they might've got rid of the gear already,' warned Mark. 'Don't be getting your hopes up too high. And these geezers are dangerous. Really dangerous. Uncle John's got twenty-four hour a day security.'

'So why don't they get the dope back?' asked Tubbs. 'His security, I mean.'

'They're legit,' said Mark. 'They're bodyguards, not fucking assassins.'

'But we are,' said Tubbs. 'Remember, Eddie?'

'I'll never forget it.'

'And you'll do it again?'

'Just once more.'

'And then we'll be set for life,' said Tubbs.

Eddie grinned, and Mark could see the boy he used to be.

*　　*　　*

It had been a year before Mark vanished and the boys were full on rogues and vagabonds. Mark was with Linda, but the others preferred to play the field. Mark liked having a steady woman. It made him feel older and more responsible. He had to take a fair amount of piss taking from the others, but he was the boss and if it got out of hand, he soon sorted them. The 80s were almost over. The age of excess had peaked and fallen back, the pastel-coloured clothes had been replaced by darker, more sombre colours, but the boys were still up for whatever larks could be found. Mark was a busy man. Apart from working for John Jenner, he supplemented his income with money from the many and varied tricks the boys got up to. He was on coke, big style. Coke and booze and love.

That was what kept him going and he thought the good times would never end. There was still the problem of his mother and Bobby Thomas. But he tried to ignore that as much as possible. Every night was a party and every day was grafting, but he had a beautiful woman, a wardrobe full of clothes, money in the bank, and his BMW parked out front for all to admire.

Life was sweet, but it was about to turn sour.

The boys were ambitious in their villainy. Andy Styles was a renowned car thief and, with help from Dev at the breaker's yard and the garage he ran in Herne Hill, he was ringing motors like a trooper. The rest were flogging drugs the length and breadth of south London. By then, John Jenner had moved out of that market, not really understanding the changing tastes and styles of the younger generation, so Mark and his boys had taken over. Jenner meanwhile was huge in the protection racket, taking money from what seemed like most of the pubs, clubs and restaurants from Greenwich to Twickenham. Later, of course, he went back into dope, but for the moment he was happy to see Mark doing well, as long as there was a cut in it for him. It was all working out nicely. But of course, there was always someone ready to put his oar in and spoil a sweet operation.

At that time, the particular someone was a young black man called Neville Lloyd. Neville lived at various addresses from the Elephant and Castle through Camberwell, all the way down to South Norwood. The boy was a bit of a beast with women, and had girlfriends stashed away all over the place. Most had children by him, all boys. Rumour was, he wanted to start a football team. He revelled in his reputation as a 'babyfather'. And, despite the fact that his women knew there were others in the frame, they were desperately loyal to Neville, running errands, taking messages and letting him stay with them whenever he felt the need. Another rumour was that he had identical wardrobes in all the girls' flats so that it didn't matter where he was on any given night, because he could discard one designer suit and leave in top nick the next morning. Aside from his sexual prowess, Neville liked to think of himself as a bit of a style king.

He also had a chain of boys on bicycles and motor scooters running around the estates and up and down to pubs and clubs, delivering all sorts with huge bricks of mobile phones stuck up their jumpers, ready to take orders and collect from one of Neville's safe houses where the drugs were stashed.

Mark had no argument when Neville was flogging weed. As far as he was concerned, weed was the black man's natural stock in trade. And if he moved a little smack or cocaine on the side to his regulars, no problems. But suddenly, as club culture took off in a big way, the demand shifted to ecstasy. E's were the next big thing, and at anything up to £25 a hit, were extremely lucrative. The Old Bill really didn't know what was going on. All these kids stoned out of their minds on bottled water didn't make any sense to them. But it made sense to Mark. Perfect sense. And when he linked up with a couple of geeky college students from Sussex called Paul and Dennis, who were producing thousands of the pretty little pills in all the colours of the rainbow and decorating them with cutout logos of comic characters, they knew their time had come.

Business was booming. Until, that is, the day Elvis came in with a handful of their pills and a black eye. Dennis was in tow, looking like he'd lost a quid and found a twopenny piece.

'What's the problem?' asked Mark.

'These fucking well are,' said Elvis, throwing a handful of pills on to Mark's desk. 'They're fucking rubbish.'

'What?' said Mark. 'Show.'

The pills looked OK to him, but Dennis shook his head. 'Not ours,' he said.

'What?' said Mark again. 'What do you mean?'

'We got one analysed,' said Dennis. 'Mostly chalk with a tiny bit of speed.'

'And you made these?'

'Do me a favour, Mark,' said Dennis. 'We wouldn't let rubbish like this out of the door.'

'So?' said Mark.

'So someone's bootlegging our product,' said Elvis. 'And there's more than a few pissed-off punters out there. Two of them caught up with me last night and I got this. He stuck his face over Mark's desk and pointed to his swollen eye.

'Shit,' said Mark.

'Shit's right,' said Elvis. 'I had a right ruck. They wanted to rip my head off. Lucky Tubbs was with me.'

Mark sat back and looked at Dennis. 'There's no chance that Paul's been at it?'

'Christ no,' said Dennis. 'Paul's even more of a perfectionist than me. He just wants to love up the whole world.'

'Yeah,' agreed Mark. 'But they've got our logo on them. Our guarantee of purity and value.'

Dennis looked a little hinky.

'What?' said Mark.

'I think the bloke who makes our pill stampers might have gone native.'

'How d'you mean?' said Mark.

'Well, he's an old mate from uni. You know we more or less make these by hand?'

Mark nodded.

'I mean we can do thousands, but we ain't Glaxo Wellcome.'

'Yeah... ?'

Dennis wasn't happy. 'I think the bloke who made our stamper dies made one for someone else and put our little logo in it.'

'Fuck,' said Mark. 'So someone just produces any old shit and people think they're buying off us?'

Dennis nodded. 'Or someone we've supplied.'

'But they could put anything in them.'

Dennis nodded.

'Poison, all sorts.' Mark knew all about drugs cut with strychnine, scouring powder and even ground glass. 'Christ, people could be dying out there and it's down to us.'

'Well, not on these,' said Dennis. 'Like I said, it's mainly chalk, a little baby laxative and some amphetamine.'

251

'But you don't know what else is going on.'

'No,' said Dennis.

'Who is it?' Mark said to Elvis.

'No idea, mate.'

'Well, you'd better find out. All of us had better get on the case. I don't want no fucker saying I killed anyone. At least, not unless I meant to.'

Elvis nodded.

Finding out who was behind it wasn't hard. The boys went to all the haunts where drugs were freely available, but instead of selling they were buying. Pretty soon they started to turn up more of the bootlegged E's, all of them bought from Neville's runners.

'Bastard,' said Mark late one night at Tubbs' flat, where the boys had gathered.

'Well, he's not really doing much damage,' said Dennis.

Paul nodded.

'Except to our reputation,' said Dizzy. 'No one's bleedin' buying at the moment. This stuff's so duff we have to give the bloody things away to prove they're good and that just wastes our time and makes no profit.'

The rest nodded.

'So we have a word with Neville,' said Mark.

'He needs more than a word,' said Tubbs. 'Black fucker.'

'But no one can ever catch up with him,' said Andy, lifting his nose out of a manual for the latest Volkswagen Golf. 'He's got more homes than Barretts.'

'We'll catch up with him,' said Mark. 'I'll make a couple of calls.'

Which he did. Posing as a punter looking for a couple of thousand tabs of E.

It took a couple of days, but eventually he connected with one of Neville's lieutenants and made his bid.

'Perfect,' he said to the boys when they met in the Four Feathers. 'Greedy fuckers can't wait to meet me. Promised me pure E for a fiver a tab.'

'Bloody cheek,' said Paul. 'Our stuff's worth twice that.'

'So I jumped at the offer,' said Mark.

'Where and when?' asked Elvis.

'Saturday night there's a rave on up Waterloo way. You know, in those old arches under the railway? They want to make a meet.'

'Will Neville be there?' asked Dizzy.

'Oh, for sure,' said Mark. 'I'm supposed to turn up with ten grand in readies.'

'And he believed you?' asked Dennis.

'Course he did. I told him I'd been buying off us big time. But I heard that he'd starting supplying the same merchandise for half the price.'

'Didn't he wonder about you?' asked Andy.

'No. Why should he?'

'But he knows you,' pressed Andy.

'Yeah,' said Mark. 'But he doesn't know Paul and Dennis. They go in and meet the boy and we're right behind them.'

Paul looked at Dennis and Dennis looked at Paul, and neither of them looked happy. 'You know we're scientists, not gangsters,' said Paul.

'You don't have to do anything,' explained Mark. 'Just be there and get a sight of the merchandise. He'll be at the bar, he said. There's a door at the back. Go outside. Tell him you don't want to flash the cash where everyone's watching.'

Mark knew the layout of the place well, having done regular business there.

'Then we go after them mob-handed?' said Dizzy.

'Spot on,' said Mark. 'That bastard needs teaching a lesson.'

Saturday night came and the boys met in the same boozer. They looked as if ready to party in jeans or combat trousers, desert boots and loose sweat tops and T-shirts. They stayed in the pub until past closing time then trooped out to their cars.

At that time Suzuki jeeps were all the rage. Andy could unlock and start one as if by magic, and the boys were making a little extra spending money by ringing a couple a week in Dev's garage. That week Andy had stolen two, resprayed them, changed the VIN number on the engine and replaced the registration. They were both soft tops, one now red, the other white. Dizzy was driving the red one, Andy its white twin, and they let the tops down before driving off. It was still a bit early for the rave to really get going so they took a diversion down the Kings Road to see what was happening down there. They stopped at a coffee shop and soon had a crowd of admiring young women collected around their motors. Dizzy was rolling spliff in the back of the red car and Mark was snorting coke with Tubbs and anyone else who was interested in the front of the other. Everyone was kicking back and happy, but Mark was keeping an eye on the clock and at one-thirty he went round reminding the boys that there was work to be done. 'Shit,' said Dizzy. 'I was just getting off with that bird in the blue dress.'

'Get her phone number,' said Mark. 'We've got heads to break.'

That cheered Dizzy up no end, and a minute later he was ready to go, the young woman's telephone number written in red lipstick on his belly.

'That'll wear off,' said Mark as he got into the car next to Andy.

'Let the boy have his fun,' Andy said. 'You know what he's like.'

They set off again, running the cars over the river on Battersea Bridge and heading east across the top of south London in convoy. Dizzy was off his nut and kept nudging Andy's Suzuki with the bumper of his motor, and Mark, who was trying to snort coke off the dash, kept spilling the powder on to the carpet. 'Fucking bastard,' he said as Dizzy drew level with them just past Vauxhall Cross and then tried to run them on to the pavement. 'He'll have us nicked.'

'Who the fuck cares?' said Andy.

'You will if Old Bill takes a look at the gear we've got in the back.'

In a roll of carpet stuffed into the luggage compartment at the back of their car were four baseball bats, a couple of tyre irons from the garage and Dizzy's sawn-off shotgun. And Mark was carrying a small .38 five - shot Colt revolver he'd borrowed off John Jenner tucked into his boot. Jenner hadn't asked him why he needed a shooter, just given him the usual advice: 'If you use it, lose it.'

'No, mate,' screamed Andy above the slipstream and the music booming out of the sound system. 'We're minted. Magic. Old Bill can't even see us. We're invisible.'

'Have you had too much coke?' yelled Mark in reply. But he knew what Andy meant. They were untouchable. The boys were out for revenge and no one could stop them.

So on they raced, bumping and tailgating each other, cutting off other drivers, jumping red lights and going the wrong way around roundabouts until they reached the mean streets of Waterloo.

Before the rave scene took off, those streets would have been deserted at that time of a Saturday night/Sunday morning. Previously, all the action had been in the west end, various spots of north London and down the Old Kent Road. But then entrepreneurs discovered that they could make lots of money by leasing or squatting railway arches and playing Acid House music at ear-splitting levels – the bass could be turned up so high it made the dancers' ribs vibrate inside their bodies – and tiny bottles of water that cost pennies in any cash and carry store could be sold for fortunes.

Of course, the emergency exits and toilet facilities were almost non-existent, there was always danger from falling masonry and unsafe staircases, and taps were always turned off, which meant that kids who couldn't afford the expensive bottled water dropped from dehydration. Oh yeah, and if you thought about bringing your own refreshment, there were always plenty of bouncers at the door to confiscate it. The raves were advertised by flyer, word of mouth and mentions on pirate radio, sometimes nothing more than a mobile number to call. The venues were cheap or free, and the entrance fee was enough to ensure that the organisers always drove the latest motors and wore the most fashionable clothes. Then there was the drug franchise. And that's where Mark and the boys had been given pretty much free rein until Neville had stuck his beak into the action.

Not that they minded competition. After all, there was plenty to go round. But like John Jenner before him, Mark Farrow treated south London as his own. He didn't care what went on north of the river. Whoever wanted it was welcome; to Mark it was another country. But south of Old Father Thames was his – a massive cash cow that was there to be milked by him and his mates alone. And Neville was taking the piss. It wasn't on, and Mark was determined to make an example of him. How much of an example none of them was going to realise until it was too late.

Eventually they found a couple of parking spaces and dumped the cars. They didn't bother putting up the tops as they didn't intend being around for long, and Andy had fitted a couple of devices that made the cars almost impossible to drive away unless you were... well, Andy.

They gathered around the back of the white car and Mark handed out the weapons. 'You two go in first and find Neville,' he said to Paul and Dennis. 'I'll be right behind you. The rest of you follow on.' He gave Paul a briefcase full of newspaper cut to the size of fifty pound notes, with the real thing top and bottom which would convince Neville it was ten grand if he wasn't allowed to examine it. 'Don't let him get too close to this,' he said. 'Tease him until you're outside.'

Again Paul didn't look happy about the deception, but wisely stayed silent. Mark was bopping from his cocaine intake and the boy knew he'd brook no argument. 'Don't leave us with him too long, will you?' Paul said.

'Trust me,' said Mark, grinding his teeth. 'I'm a fucking doctor.'

'What about the bouncers?' asked Tubbs.

'Depends who's on and if we know them.'

'We'll know 'em.' Tubbs again.

'Chances are,' said Mark.

'So.'

'So we ask them to take a break and give them a few quid.'

'What happens if they're not keen?' asked Dizzy.

'You've got your shooter. Convince them that discretion is the better part of valour.'

'I can do that,' said Dizzy, slipping the gun inside his combat pants and down one leg.

'You only do that to impress the girls,' said Mark.

'No. I can do that without,' replied Dizzy. 'Remember the bird in the blue dress just now?' And he lifted his shirt to show the red smears on his skin.

'And she thought you were just pleased to see her.'

'That's the truth. And I intend to see her again.'

'Come on then,' said Mark. 'Let's do it. And let's do it properly.'

The bouncers, two black guys and one white, were easy. They all knew Mark and the boys and let him, Paul and Dennis go to the front of the short queue. 'The rest of my lads are behind me,' Mark said as he slipped each a score.

'No worries,' said the head man.

'And I wouldn't worry too much if you hear a bit of a do in a minute. There's someone inside who's been taking the piss.'

'Never seen a thing,' said the security man as he let them through.

The brick railway arches, three in all, were black with years of accumulated muck and were connected by a series of short tunnels. The main entrance was through a small door let into larger double doors that were chained shut. Once inside, the noise hit Mark like a hammer. The bass beat at Mark's chest as he looked through the mixture of strobe lights and a fog of dry ice that made visibility all but impossible. Perfect, he thought as he moved around the edge of a floor that was filled to capacity with dancers in various stages of undress, all moving spastically in the heat they generated. It must've been close to a hundred degrees inside and sooty water dripped from the ceiling on to the crowd below. That night the DJ was known as Phil The Lodger for no reason Mark could fathom, and he was perched on a small stage made of scaffolding in one corner of the largest arch, with music relayed through to the others by a series of speakers the size of small cars.

In the smallest of the arches where the volume of the music was marginally lower, a bar had been set up and sweaty individuals doled out overpriced water, beer and soft drinks. That was where Mark had arranged to meet Neville and do the deal.

Mark stood in the shadows and scoped out the bar. Christ, but the music was heavy. Mark enjoyed House music when he was stoned, but he actually preferred the Jazz and R&B that John Jenner had collected in the 60s and 70s.

Mark spotted Neville straight away. He was wearing a leather suit with a huge gold chain around his neck and enough rings to stock a jeweller's shop. He was leaning on the jump like he owned the place, flanked by a couple of heavy-looking black guys acting as security for him and for the metal attaché case that stood at his feet.

Wanker, thought Mark as he grabbed Dennis by the elbow and pointed out the tall black man. 'Go,' he said.

Dennis and Paul both shrugged and moved into the bar area. Mark hung back until he saw them speak to Neville, a short conversation ensued. And then all five men walked behind the bar and out through a small door in the back wall. Mark smiled to himself and moved in the same direction, body swerving through the crowd, followed by the rest of his boys.

Mark went behind the bar and through the door that led into the yard where the organisers and staff parked their vehicles. Outside, it was cool and quiet and Mark felt the sweat begin to dry on his body. Neville and his minders were showing Paul and Dennis the contents of the metal case, the bag of fake money lying on the bonnet of a Ford Granada.

'Neville!' Mark yelled as he got close.

Neville turned and said: 'Hey man, what you doin' here?'

'Is that the gear?' Mark asked Paul, who threw the handful of pills he was holding on to the ground and nodded.

'Rubbish?' asked Mark.

'Well, it ain't ours,' said Dennis. 'Though they're all tricked up with our logo.'

'You're having a laugh, aincha?' said Mark, who stuck his foot on to the bumper of the Granada, tugged the little pistol out of its hiding place and stuck it into Neville's face, just as the rest of the boys approached from the building in a flying V pattern, weapons at the ready.

'Whassa matter, my man?' said Neville, seemingly little perturbed.

'What's the fucking matter, you cunt?' said Mark. 'The matter is you're selling duff gear on our patch.'

'No, man,' protested Neville like butter wouldn't melt.

'You're taking the rise, Neville,' said Mark. 'Bootlegging our product and ruining our good name.'

'No, man, just a bit of friendly competition.'

One of Neville's minders, freaked by the sight of Mark's pistol, decided to even things up by bringing his own weapon into play and stuck his hand inside his jacket. Tubbs hit him on the outside of his leg joint with the Louisville Slugger he was carrying and the man dropped on to one knee, the pistol clattering to the ground.

'I'm going to kill you, Neville,' said Mark, almost incandescent with fury that Neville didn't seem scared.

'No, man. We meant no harm.'

Just then, one of the bar staff came out of the door carrying a crate of empties which she dropped with a scream and Neville took off.

He ran across the yard and up a ramshackle metal staircase towards the top of the viaduct where the railway ran. 'Shit,' said Mark, giving chase, closely followed by Dizzy and Tubbs. The rest of the boys were left to sort out Neville's two bodyguards, the barmaid, the case of pills, the gun and the money.

The staircase was attached to the wall with long bolts that had long since loosened, making it wobble and bang against the brickwork as Mark and the other two chased Neville to the top. Old paint and rust showered down on them as they clattered up.

At the top, Neville leapt over the lip of the wall and started to run in the direction of London Bridge station, jumping from sleeper to sleeper. The line was shadowy, with only the occasional bright white light from above giving illumination. It was quiet up there, except for the heavy breathing of the pursued and the pursuers. And then, in the distance, they all heard the heavy cough of a diesel engine starting up.

'Give it up, Neville,' yelled Mark. 'You're done.'

Neville stopped and leant forward as he tried to regain his wind, and Mark and the two others stopped too. 'You're fucked,' said Mark. 'Too much nooky.'

'Fuck you,' said Neville.

In the distance they heard the train's brakes being released and its headlights came on.

'Mark,' said Neville. 'We can come to some arrangement. There's plenty out there for everyone.'

'Piss off,' said Tubbs. 'We don't do business like that.'

The train had started and was coming closer, picking up speed as it headed towards Waterloo East.

Mark raised his gun. He'd never really thought that he'd use it, but Neville wouldn't listen to reason.

The train's headlamps picked out the four young men and their shadows lengthened along the rails.

'Don't be silly,' said Neville. 'You ain't got the nerve.'

Mark squinted down the short barrel of the pistol and for the first time Neville realised he was serious.

'No, Mark,' he said,

'Go on,' yelled Dizzy. 'Do the fucker.'

The sound of the engine was like a scream and the driver sounded the horn. Neville looked around and realised he was directly in its path and he made as if to jump out of the way, but slipped on the smooth metal of the rail and fell backwards. The great engine, its brakes full on, making the metal screech and the viaduct shake, cut across the young black man's body. Neville's scream merged with that of the train, and Mark, Tubbs and Dizzy moved back against the brickwork.

'Fucking hell,' said Mark as they watched Neville's decapitated body being dragged over the sleepers. 'Let's get the fuck out of here.'

TWENTY-ONE

Even before the train driver managed to bring the engine to a halt, dismount and run back to Neville's body, the three boys had vanished down the side of the viaduct and back to the yard.

Although it seemed to Mark as if years had passed since they had set off after Neville, when they returned to the yard, everything looked the same as it had when they had left. Andy, Dennis, Paul and Elvis were standing over Neville's mates, holding their weapons – including the pistol the black man had dropped – with the barmaid looking on.

'Let's go,' said Mark grabbing the case of pills and the bag of fake money. 'It's time we weren't here.'

'What's up?' demanded Elvis. 'Why'd that train stop? What happened to it?'

'It's relatively undamaged,' said Mark. 'Which is more than be said for Neville. Now let's get out of here before someone calls the cops. If they haven't already.'

'Where's Neville?' said one of the black men.

'Gone to a better place,' replied Mark. 'Which is exactly what we're going to do, and I reckon you should too. He's brown bread up there.' And he hustled the boys out of the yard via the back gate to their cars.

Neville's death made headlines for a few days locally and it took a lot of John Jenner's money and more than enough favours to get the boys off the hook. The official verdict was death by misadventure. A prank that went too far. Just a bunch of young men having fun which went disastrously wrong. But the wounds between the black and white gangsters never fully healed. Even now, Mark realised, what was happening in south London might have its roots in that dreadful night.

*   *   *

'We done him good, didn't we?' said Eddie as he sipped his second beer.

'He slipped,' said Mark. 'It was his own stupid fault.'

'Those spades – sorry Tubbs – didn't reckon that,' said Eddie. 'They always said we murdered him.'

'Yeah. And if my uncle hadn't given away most of his protection business in Brixton to keep them sweet we might've ended up in jail or worse.'

'Have you done anything like it since?' Tubbs asked Mark.

'Don't ask,' he replied.

'Was that why you fucked off like you did?'

'Long story. I'll tell you sometime, but not now.'

'Fair enough. So when do we do it?'

'Sooner rather than later,' said Mark. 'I'll need to organise a motor and some cash for you. Have you got a mobile?'

'No problemo,' said Tubbs. 'Plenty of those about. There's always kids in the caff trying to sell them. I got this…' He pulled a smart new Nokia from inside his jacket. 'Ten quid, fully chipped.'

'Give me the number,' said Mark, and he wrote it down on the back of Eddie's empty cigarette packet. 'Right,' he said. 'I'm off to get things together. You coming, Eddie?'

'No. I think I'll stay here for a few with Tubbsy.'

'Well, don't get too pissed. And both of you, keep your mouths shut about this.'

'Who's to tell?' said Tubbs.

'Fair enough,' said Mark. 'But schtuum it, all right?'

The two men nodded and Mark made his leave, still wondering how it would all end.

He drove back to south London and found John Jenner rolling a spliff in his front room. 'Leave that for a minute,' said Mark. 'I've got something we need to talk about.'

'Talk away,' said Jenner, and Mark explained his plan.

262

'That's the best you could do?' said Jenner when he'd finished. 'A pair of losers like them?'

'They're all right,' said Mark, defending his old mates, although he was inclined to agree with Jenner. 'Trust me.'

'That's what the bloody doctors said to me when I went in for a check up,' replied Jenner. 'And look what happened.'

'Hardly their fault, Uncle John,' said Mark.

'Bloody right,' said Jenner, wincing from pain. 'Now do you mind if I finish this?' he indicated the half-rolled joint in the table in front of him. 'My insides are killing me.'

'Go ahead,' said Mark. 'Just give me the keys to the safe. I need some dough.'

'Don't spend it all at once,' said Jenner, licking the glue on his Rizla. 'We might need it.'

What for? thought Mark, Funeral expenses? But he said nothing.

He went down to the cellar and counted out forty grand from the bag of cash he found there. Not that he intended to pay more than the minimum up front, but he wanted money of his own around in case everything went up the pictures.

He took the cash back to his room and stashed it behind the wardrobe, a hiding place that he'd always trusted in the old days, just keeping ten thousand back. Then he phoned Tubbs on the number he'd been given.

Tubbs was still with Eddie and they were still in the pub – or another pub for all he knew – judging by the noise in the background. 'Are you pissed, Tubbs?' asked Mark.

'Just a bit. It's the thought of all those island women.'

'Forget that for now. We need to meet. But I want you sober. Can you get away tomorrow morning?'

'Sure. I've got a good kid as assistant manager. University graduate, would you believe?'

'I'd believe anything right now. So, tomorrow.'

'Sure, I'll phone him later. If I could drop him a few quid…'

'Yeah, that's sorted. I've got money here. But it's not for spending in boozers.'

'I'll be as sober as a judge.'

'Sure. I've had experience with judges and that doesn't fill me with confidence.'

'You know what I mean.'

'And try and keep Eddie on the straight.'

'No worries. He can stay at my place tonight. You want him there tomorrow?'

'Course. There's a boozer in Waterloo. Quiet. Round the back of the station. The Little Red Engine. Know it?'

'No. But I'll find it.'

'Be there tomorrow at eleven. We'll talk then.'

'No problem Mark.'

'Good.'

'And Mark...'

'What?'

'Thanks. Thanks for giving us a chance.'

'You might not end up thanking me. This isn't a joy ride.'

'We know that.'

'Eleven then. The Little Red Engine. Look up the address in the phone book.'

'We'll be there.'

Mark nodded, although he knew no one could see and pressed the 'End' button on his mobile.

He was at the pub dead on time and ordered a mineral water while he waited. Tubbs and Eddie arrived about eleven-fifteen, complaining about the lack of parking spaces. They both looked a little the worse for wear and again Mark wondered about the wisdom of using them in his plan. But needs must, he thought as he carried them over two bottles of overpriced water.

Eddie looked disgusted. 'I need a proper drink,' he moaned.

'Drink it or leave it,' said Mark. 'But I need you on top.'

Eddie sipped at the drink and pulled a face but kept quiet.

'What about wheels?' asked Tubbs.

'I've spoken to Dev. Remember him?'

Both men nodded.

'He's still in the game and thinks he knows where he can lay hands on some fancy BMW. You know the sort. Red, with black windows, lowered and flared.'

'Sweet,' said Tubbs. 'I've always fancied one of those.'

'Typical,' said Eddie, grinning like a monkey.

Tubbs grabbed him in a neck lock. 'Don't disrespect me, mon,' he said in a heavy West Indian accent. 'Me chop your balls off and wear them for earrings.'

'Leave it out, you two,' said Mark. 'This is serious.'

'Sorry, baaas,' said Tubbs and even Mark had to smile. He took an envelope of money out of his pocket and slid it across the table.

'There's five G's in there,' he said. 'Four for you and one for him.' He pushed Eddie on the shoulder. 'Exes, right? Not just for booze, Eddie.'

Eddie pulled a 'what, me?' face and Mark smiled again. If he had to trust anyone he supposed that these two were as good as any, for all their faults. 'I'll know about the motor later. Keep in touch. Tubbs, you'd better take some proper time off. I don't want you frying chicken when you're supposed to be a player.'

'I've got some holiday due,' said Tubbs.

'Use it. You've both got my number. Use that too. But don't say anything on air that anyone could use.'

'We'll be OK,' said Tubbs.

'Yeah, I know,' said Mark. 'And get some clothes more fitting to your new occupation, Tubbs.' He looked at his nylon jacket embossed with a cartoon chicken looking aghast at the sight of a flaming barbecue, teamed with a pair of baggy jeans. 'I don't think that's the look of the day for a man looking for a big score of coke.'

Tubbs looked down at himself too and nodded his head in agreement. 'You could be right. Fancy a trip to Camden, Eddie?'

'Sure.'

'And when you've done that, why don't you both go home and get some sleep,' said Mark. 'You look like you need it.'

For once they did as he said. Obviously the sight of so much cash had made the pair of them realise who was boss. Or maybe they were both tired.

Later that afternoon, Mark tried Linda on the off chance. 'Can you talk?' he asked when she answered the phone.

'Yeah. The kids are upstairs in the playroom with Greta. I'm doing some housework, would you believe?'

'Not really.'

'Well, I am.'

'It's good to hear you got domesticated.'

'After you've had two children, it's hard not to. For me anyway.'

'So you're doing a bit of dusting.'

'Something like that.'

'Got your apron on?'

'Not the kind of apron you'd like, part of a French maid's outfit.'

'Shame. Can I see you?'

'What? In a French maid's outfit?'

'That would be good, but seriously, can we meet?'

'Suppose so.'

'Don't sound so keen.'

'Mark. We've been through this. I want to see you, but I don't trust you an inch.'

'I suppose I deserve that.'

'You do.'

'How can I prove to you how sorry I am?'

'Just stick around. Be a nice bloke. Pay me compliments and tell me I look great even when I don't. Just be a man. Not a shadow of one.'

Mark was silent for a moment. 'So I suppose a blow job is out of the question?'

Linda laughed out loud. 'You're a dirty boy, Mark, but you're getting me excited.'

'So let's meet.'

'Not tonight. It's Greta's night off. I'm being a real mum. We've got the new Disney DVD and I'm ordering in pizza as a treat.'

'You really are domesticated, aren't you?' said Mark.

'That's me.'

'Tomorrow then?'

'Yes. I think I can manage that.'

'Where?'

'Come to the flat again. I'll even cook for you.'

'I don't believe it. You've never cooked for me in your life.'

'Maybe that's where we went wrong. Maybe I should've.'

'We never had the chance. Not with one thing and another.'

'And that's the really sad part.'

'Don't get morbid,' he said, clutching his phone tightly.

'With all the things that have happened to me, it's hard not to.'

'I'll cheer you up.'

'That's what I was hoping you'd do.'

'What time? Tomorrow, I mean.'

'About seven. I'll go round early and get the place sorted. Greta can look after Luke and Daisy. I'll tell her...well, whatever I decide to tell her.'

'I'll be there.'

'Fine. See you then.'

'You will.'

'Goodbye.'

'Bye, love.'

And she hung up.

The next morning Mark went to check the car that Dev had found. It was perfect. A bright red BMW 5 Series with plenty of chrome. The body had been lowered, and the wheel arches were flared over wide wheels with low profile tyres. Inside was a multichange CD player with a huge amplifier and a dozen speakers. The seats were black leather and a little fir tree air freshener hung from the rearview mirror.

'What do you reckon?' asked Dev.

'Good,' said Mark, walking round the car before inspecting the interior. 'All it needs is a coke spoon in the glovebox for it to be perfect.'

'Where's it going?' asked Dev.

'Keep it here for now,' said Mark. 'I'll have Tubbs pick it up later. Do you remember him?'

'Sure. The black fellah.'

'That's the boy.'

'I hope he dresses the part,' said Dev.

'Me too. I sent him off shopping yesterday with a pile of Uncle John's money.'

Mark called Tubbs right away and told him to get over to south London pronto.

'No problemo,' said Tubbs. 'What about Eddie?'

'Leave him. I just need you right now.' And remembering what Dev had said added: 'And wear something in character. You kick off today.'

'Got just the thing.'

The thing was a long leather overcoat over a black tracksuit with a thick gold chain around his neck. 'How do I look?' asked Tubbs an hour or so later, once he'd appeared at the Half Moon pub, just around the corner from Dev's garage.

'Like you're auditioning for a part in the Wesley Snipes story,' replied Mark.

'Is that good?'

'At least you left your leather hat at home.'

'It's in my car.'

'I think it'd better stay there for now, don't you?'

Tubbs shrugged. 'I love that hat. Cost you a lot.'

'Where is it?' asked Mark, ignoring Tubbs's last comment.

'On the back seat.'

'The car I mean, fool.'

Tubbs grinned, showing a lot of white teeth. 'By the station, on a meter.'

'Right. Let's get it and dump it at Dev's. From now on, you're a bad boy from the frozen north of Highgate looking for a new source of snow.

I'll show you where these people hang out, then you're on your own. Last chance to change your mind, Tubbsy boy.'

'No, man,' said Tubbs. 'You're going to change my life.'

'One way or another,' said Mark, too quietly for his friend to hear.

They collected Tubbs's ancient smoker of a car and drove to the garage. Dev looked at Tubbs in his new clothes and pulled a face at Mark, who shook his head in reply. This wasn't the time for Tubbs to feel self-conscious. Not that it looked like he would be. He strode over to the BMW as if it had been made for him, which well it might have been, so perfectly did his new clothes fit the ostentatious motor. He shrugged his mighty shoulders in the huge coat and slid behind the wheel, turned on the ignition and altered the electric driver's seat to accommodate his bulk. 'Nice, man,' he said to Dev. 'Mark, my friend, pass me some CDs will you? They're in the glove compartment of mine.'

Mark went back to the Vauxhall and collected a handful of discs and took them to Tubbs who fitted them into the player in the boot before returning to his seat and fiddling with the controls on the dash. After a second, the sound of Snoop Doggy Dogg burst from the speakers and Tubbs danced on the seat. 'Cool,' he yelled above the din.

Mark leant in and turned down the volume. 'Bit ancient, isn't it?' he said.

'Good old school rap,' said Tubbs defensively. 'Kill the bitch, kill the bitch,' he sang.

'Christ,' said Dev. 'What's he all about?'

'Don't worry,' said Mark. 'Just store that banger of his well out of sight and we'll be off.'

'Now you take care of that car,' said Dev. 'It's not paid for.'

'You amaze me,' said Mark as he got into the passenger seat next to Tubbs. 'I never would've believed it.'

Tubbs switched on the engine, listened to the grumble from the twin exhausts, stuck it into first gear and shot off the forecourt into the traffic with a screech of tyre rubber. The last Mark saw of Dev was through the side mirror: he had a look on his face that said he thought he'd never see them or the car again.

Mark directed Tubbs to Brixton Hill, then down a couple of back streets past the pub where Beretta and his mates did their business during the day. 'They're supposed to be there from lunchtime onwards,' he said. 'You can drop me off and then pay the place a visit. Just suss it out. They'll come on to you as soon as they see this motor and what you're wearing, I reckon. They'll want to know the full SP. Just play it cool. There's plenty of time. But you're going to have to fly solo, Tubbs. They're bound to know me, and I want you to get matey before they meet Eddie. So be careful.'

'Man, I'll be as cool as ice.'

'That's good. Now drop me off here and I'll walk the rest of the way home.'

'No problem,' said Tubbs, bringing the car to as tyre-smoking halt.

'And listen: drive carefully. This car with you inside it dressed like that might as well have a big arrow over it saying, "Mr Plod, please give me a pull". So try and leave a little tread on the Dunlops, will you?'

'I'll even stop at zebra crossings,' said Tubbs with a big grin.

'Yeah, sure. Good luck and call me soon.'

'Roger and out.'

'Whatever.'

'Man, I'll be safe as houses.'

Mark got out and slammed the door behind him, then watched as Tubbs spun the car on its axles and headed back to Brixton. 'Sure,' he said to its retreating back. 'But there's such things as earthquakes.'

TWENTY-TWO

Tubbs sped away from Mark, accelerating fast through the gears, the fat tyres of the BMW gripping the damp road like a dog with a juicy bone. It felt good to drive a motor like the Beemer after the rust bucket he owned and he wanted to get a feel for the car. Sure, Mark was right. It was an open invitation for a pull from the filth, but right then Tubbs felt on top of the world.

Funnily enough, he'd always had a secret desire to be a copper, ever since he was a kid. But there hadn't been many black police when he'd been of the right age and he'd heard about the way they were treated by both the public and by their own colleagues. Not well. Not well at all. But maybe if he'd joined up he'd've made commissioner, he thought. Or maybe sodding not.

Undercover would've suited him, just like his namesake in *Miami Vice*. And now he was undercover, and if everything went OK, he'd have enough money to get out of this bitch of a cold city that had never treated him any more than rough, and get to the islands and make something of himself.

Sweet dreams, he thought as he pulled up outside the boozer Mark had pointed out to him. But first he had to convince these fools that he was who he was pretending to be.

He got out of the car, operated the central locking and alarm and worked his shoulders before pushing through the pub door.

His first impression was that the stink of weed seemed to permeate every surface. Smoke hung low over the few drinkers inside, even at that early hour. The jukebox was on and Dandy Livingstone was warning Suzanne to beware of the Devil. Very apt, thought Tubbs.

All heads turned as he entered. 'Mornin',' he greeted the clientele. Without getting an answer, he headed to the bar, which seemed to be under the control of a small black individual in an Hawaiian shirt and jeans, perched on a high, chrome stool. 'Gimme a beer, man,' said Tubbs. 'It's been a long, aggravatin' drive.'

The black man pulled a Red Stripe from the cooler, uncapped it and stood it on the bar. 'Glass?' he asked. He didn't usually offer, but Tubbs was a big man and he didn't want to antagonise him.

'No,' said Tubbs and sank three quarters of the liquid with one swallow.

'Two sixty -five,' said the barman and Tubbs pulled a wad of Mark's cash from his coat pocket and dropped a twenty on the bar. 'Another, my man, if you please,' he said, as he finished the first bottle and belched loudly.

The little man did as he was bidden and delivered a second bottle which Tubbs sucked on briefly before hauling out a packet of cigarettes. 'Got a light, my friend?' he said to the nearest punter who produced a box of matches which he handed Tubbs. 'Cheers,' said the big man as he got the cigarette lit to his satisfaction and handed the box back. 'I heard that this place was a friendly environment.'

'Who you hear that from?' asked the man.

'Just friends, business acquaintances. You know.'

The man sucked on his cheek. 'Like?'

Mark had known that this would happen and had supplied Tubbs with the name of a drug dealer presently doing time up north on category A. Another one of John Jenner's old enemies. There seemed to be a lot of them about. 'This is fucking risky, Tubbs,' he'd said. 'But it's all we've got. I hate to send you in cold like this, but if you want to earn…'

'So who am I?' asked Tubbs.

'That's the problem. You are who you are. I can't give you a false identity and an alias. You'll just have to wing it.'

'And if they check?'

'Listen, man,' said Mark. 'These are bad fuckers. They're not going to be able to get a look at the police national computer. They're fucking animals. Even the bentest copper in the Met would think twice before webbing up with them. They won't have a fucking clue, man. Losers, each of them. The only way they get ahead is with ultra violence. Fuck 'em. You can do it.'

Tubbs said to the black guy at the bar: 'I shared a cell with a geezer called Blakey, up in Brum. He told me to look for a face named Beretta. I'm just out and I need supplies.'

'They fed you well inside,' said the black man, looking Tubbs up and down.

'Prison gym,' he replied. 'And it's amazing what extras you can get in the shovel these days with mates on the out.'

'So why don't your mates help you now?' asked the black man.

'You know I took all the questions I could stomach from the pigs,' said Tubbs. 'I didn't expect the same when I came in here for a quiet drink.'

All of a sudden the door burst open and three more black men entered and the barman scuttled to get drink on the counter before they reached the jump. They were trouble, Tubbs didn't have to be a genius to spot that. And it looked like they'd been too long on the toot. Their skin was the grey of elephant hide and all three seemed to have heavy colds. 'Whose wheel's in our space?' the biggest of the black men demanded. 'We had to walk.'

'What car, man?' asked the man Tubbs had been talking to.

'Flash Beemer. Red,' the other replied.

'That's me, man,' said Tubbs. 'I didn't see no double yellows.'

'Red route, boy,' said the first man. 'Our red route. Now get it moved.'

'You a traffic warden, boy?' said Tubbs. 'You left your pretty uniform at home?'

The three men looked at each other and then Tubbs. 'Who the fuck are you?' said one, a handsome man with a shaven head. 'This is our pub.'

'Just popped in for a drink,' said Tubbs. 'I heard good things about the place. But I reckon they was wrong.'

'Who the fuck is this cunt?' said the third black man to no one in particular, a cadaverous type with huge hands and feet. 'Let's kill the fucker.' And with that, he pulled a handgun from the pocket of his overcoat.

'Hey, man,' said Tubbs, stepping back sharpish. 'Chill. I'll move the fucking car. I was just looking for someone called Beretta.'

'Looks like you found it,' said the man with the gun. 'This is a fucking Beretta, you cunt.' And he pointed it at Tubbs's head.

Everyone in the pub had moved out of the line of fire and Tubbs suddenly decided that maybe undercover wasn't such a good place to be after all.

'Why you looking for me?' asked the first man pushing his companion's gun down. 'I'm Beretta, man. Who the fuck are you?'

'My name's Tubbs,' said Tubbs. 'I've been away. I heard that you could help me.'

'With what?' said the first man, his brow wrinkled in thought.

Tubbs looked round. 'In private, man,' he said.

'We're all friends here,' said Beretta. 'At least I hope we are.' His tone was menacing, and Tubbs tried hard not to swallow and give his nervousness away. 'Now who gave you this information?'

'A geezer called Blakey.' Tubbs repeated his story. 'We shared a cell for a few months in the Green.'

Beretta's forehead wrinkled even further. 'How long you been out?'

'A month or so,' said Tubbs. 'I took a holiday after.'

Beretta nodded. 'Moses. Chop one out,' he said, and Tubbs almost heaved a sigh of relief.

The man with the gun put it away, went to the bar, wiped it down with a pristine white handkerchief he'd taken from his pocket, produced a fat baggie of white powder, poured a hefty pile on to the bar, then chopped it into lines with a one-sided gold razorblade. 'We the kings here,' said Beretta. 'No go zone for coppers. Are you a copper, my friend?' he said to Tubbs.

The pub went very quiet, the jukebox died and everyone seemed to hold their breath, including Moses who was making pretty patterns on the bar with the cocaine.

'What the fuck…?' said Tubbs, his voice rising. 'Fuck you, man. You call me out as five-oh in front of these people. I got a reputation to think of. I'm leaving.'

'Cool it, big man,' said Beretta. 'Stay and have a snort. It's cool. Moses….'

Moses went back to his task and once the lines were out, the three took turns, using a gold tube that Moses supplied. Then it was Tubbs's turn and he took a monstrous hit, which just about turned his brain to jelly.

'Christ,' he said, 'That's fucking good.'

'Only the best for us and our friends,' said Beretta.

'You got any of this for sale?' asked Tubbs, after he'd lit a cigarette and taken a hit on his beer to cut the metallic taste of the drug. 'It's just the sort of quality I could use.'

'Maybe,' said Beretta. 'And Blakey's dead.'

Christ, thought Tubbs, Mark never told me that, the bastard. 'What?' he said. 'How? When?'

'Got shanked in the shower a few weeks back,' Beretta went on. 'Thought you might've heard.'

'He was fine when he used to spot for me in the gym,' said Tubbs. 'We looked out for each other.'

'Sure you did. Shame you got out then. You could've watched his back.'

'Man, that's too bad,' said Tubbs.

'He never should've dropped the soap,' said Moses, and all three laughed, like it was the best joke they'd heard in years.

'Funny you never heard,' said Beretta. 'You being best mates and all. I wonder about you. Moses, you take this fucker to the shitter and check him out.' He turned to Tubbs, squinted at him and said: 'You wired?'

'No man,' said Tubbs. This geezer is as changeable as the weather, he thought. One minute all friends, the next as paranoid as fuck. Too much sugar on his cornflakes probably.

'And?' said Moses.

'If he is, flush him.'

Moses, and the third man – Karl, Tubbs surmised – hustled Tubbs to the gents, which stank equally of piss and chemicals.

'Strip, boy,' said Moses. 'Right down.'

Tubbs removed his new clothes, slowly draping them over the door to the sitdown.

'You respect your threads.' said Moses. 'I like that in a man.'

'You like peeping too,' said Tubbs when he was naked. 'You've been inside, I can tell. Whose bitch were you?'

Moses hit him hard with the barrel of his gun and Tubbs had to hold on to the wall to prevent himself falling. Meanwhile the third man was going through his pockets. 'No ID,' he said. 'Man of mystery, huh?'

'I don't carry anything with my name on, ever,' replied Tubbs, who'd purposefully dumped anything that could identify him before meeting Mark. 'Strictly cash.'

Karl riffled through the notes he found and pulled an approving face. 'You can say that again.' Then to Moses: 'He's clean. No wires, no weapons. Just cash, and plenty of it.'

'Gimme,' said Moses, and the third man handed him the money. 'Get dressed, boy,' Moses said to Tubbs.

Tubbs did as he was told, looked in the stained mirror and touched the bloody lump on his head. 'Here,' said Moses and handed him the handkerchief he'd used to wipe down the bar. 'No hard feelings.'

'None taken,' said Tubbs, dabbing at his face.

'Outside,' said Karl, and Tubbs, now fully dressed, walked back into the bar.

'He's clean,' Moses said to Beretta. 'And he brought us a present.' He handed the cash over and Beretta slid it into his pocket. 'How much?' he said to Tubbs.

'Two grand or thereabouts.'

'What you need all that for?'

'Just walking around money.'

'Nice place to take a walk. Fair enough. Now what did you want with me?'

Tubbs looked at the other faces in the bar and said: 'Like I said, it's private.'

'Yeah.'

'So?'

'Siddown,' said Moses, then to the barman. 'And get him what he's drinking. And another round for us.'

The quartet moved to a spot behind the pool table, out of hearing of the rest. Once the barman had brought them their order and was safely back on his perch, Tubbs said: 'I need some powder.'

'Who doesn't?' asked Moses. 'Where you from again?'

'North London,' replied Tubbs.

'That's a big place,' said Beretta.

'Holloway.'

'How long were you away?' asked Moses.

'Two years.'

'For what?' Beretta again.

'Weed. Got captured with a big bag. Cops didn't take kindly to it.'

'They tend not to,' said Moses.

'Now it's bloody almost legal,' said Tubbs.

'Wrong time, wrong place,' said Beretta and sniffed loudly, which was the cue for Moses to bring out the coke again, and all four hit on a line each.

'This is good stuff,' said Tubbs. 'You got more?'

'More than you can afford,' said Beretta.

'How much?' asked Tubbs.

'How much we got, or how much is it?' said Beretta.

'Both.'

'You might be grass,' said Moses. 'Why should we tell you?'

'You've got my two grand. And there's plenty more where that came from.'

'Our two grand now,' Beretta corrected him.

'OK, your two grand. Take it as a down payment.'

'We're taking it anyway,' said the third man. 'Sort of a gesture of faith on your part.'

'Whatever,' said Tubbs. 'You got any now?'

'You've got no money,' said Moses.

'I can get more.'

'When?'

'Tonight.'

'Maybe,' said Beretta. 'You got a phone number?'

Tubbs reeled it off and Moses made a note of it in a little book. 'We'll think about it, Mr Tubbs,' he said. 'We'll ring you later. Or maybe tomorrow. Or maybe never. We need to check a little. Make sure you ain't five-oh. You get my drift?'

Tubbs nodded. He wondered what they'd turn up, if anything. He had a small record from way back, but that was under his real name, which he hadn't supplied.

'Now go,' said Beretta. 'We'll talk later.'

Tubbs left the bar and climbed into the BMW, which he drove through the narrow streets of Brixton, before parking up and calling Mark Farrow on his mobile.

'I met 'em,' he said. 'Not nice people. They told me Blakey was dead. Thanks for telling me. I felt like a right wanker.'

'I never knew. Sorry, mate. So what happened?'

'They gave me some lumps and took the two grand I was holding.'

'And?'

'And nothing. They're doing some checking on me. But they're so stoned I don't reckon they'll even remember my name in half an hour.'

'It's risky, Tubbs. If you want to pull out, do it now.'

'No, Mark. They've got lots of dope, and I want us to get it.'

'This is crazy,' said Mark.

'No worries,' said Tubbs. 'I'm going round to Eddie's. They're going to phone me.'

'When?'

'Whenever. Could be they're dialling now, could be next week, could be never. I'm sorry about the cash, Mark.'

'No problem. Did you make a fuss about it?'

'No. One of them had a gun on me at the time. But I told them there was more where that came from.'

'Good.'

'You figure they'll try and take the rest?'

'Yeah. That's why we hit them first.'

'But I want that gear.'

'Sure you do. We'll work something out.'

TWENTY-THREE

Tubbs went round to Eddie's flat, dug him out of bed and told him what had occurred at the pub. Eddie sat, bent over his first cup of tea, listening, then said: 'Christ, Tubbs, this is getting heavy.'

'We knew it would.'

'They could've killed you.'

'No pain, no gain, my man.'

'So what now?'

'Now we wait.'

And wait they did.

Meanwhile Mark was looking forward to his date with Linda.

Looking forward to it more than he thought he should, especially as he knew he'd put Tubbs in harm's way. The day dragged by like a snail on downers. He kept checking that his phone was switched on, but he heard nothing from Tubbs, so when the appointed hour arrived, he arrived at the flat in Balham and rang the bell. Linda answered the door wearing a simple black dress and black nylons, with high heeled, strappy shoes. She'd curled her hair slightly, her eyes were mascaraed and her lips a deep shade of red. She looked wonderful. Mark stood in the doorway until she offered him her hand. 'Are you going to stay out there all night?' she asked.

'No,' he replied. 'I just can't believe how great you look.'

'Takes longer every year,' she said.

'I don't believe you,' he said. 'It's natural.'

'Tell that to Estée Lauder. Now are you coming in or not? It's getting chilly and I'm not dressed for it.'

'That's true.'

'But I'm dressed for something.'

'What?'

'Don't be naive. I went shopping this afternoon.'

'Where?'

'Soho.'

'Really?'

'Yes. A little shop I know called Agent Provocateur.'

'What do they sell?'

'You have been away for a long time,' she said, dragging him in, slamming the door and pulling up the hem of her skirt to show off stocking tops and pink, lacy suspenders. 'Underwear,' she said. 'The most outrageous in London. I blushed when I bought it.'

'For me?'

'No. For the milkman. Of course for you, silly.'

'I'm flattered.'

'You should be. They cost me an arm and a leg. Now get upstairs. And you go first. I don't want you looking at my bum.'

'Isn't that why you bought the underwear?'

'Maybe. But later. I've cooked.' They went upstairs, Mark in the lead. At the top he stopped and turned.

'Wait a minute,' he said. 'Now you're looking at my bum.'

'And why not?' she said. 'It always was your best feature.'

'Charming.'

'All the girls at school thought so, and it hasn't gone south – yet.' Mark smiled and went into the living room where the table was set for two and was full of warm odours from the kitchen next door.

'Hmm,' he said. 'Smells good.'

'So it should. I've been slaving over the oven for hours.' Mark suddenly felt a constriction in his chest and his eyes filled with tears. What a waste of all those years - we could've been together, he thought. Years we'll never have back. Years wasted.

'Are you all right?' asked Linda.

'Fine,' he replied. 'Never better in fact.'

'Then take off your jacket, sit down, have a drink. Anything. You look like you've seen a ghost.'

'No. Just thinking.'

'Well, don't think. It's bad for the brain. Just enjoy.'

'I'm sure I will. I'm starved.'

'Good. I'll open the wine.' She was as good as her word and produced an expensive bottle of Pinot Grigio from the fridge.

'I'll do it,' said Mark.

'I love a masterful man,' said Linda and kissed him, handing him the bottle. Her perfume was subtle but powerful and Mark's head swam as he inhaled it.

'Like it?' she asked, noticing his reaction.

'Love it. Smells even better than dinner.'

'Seventy quid an ounce,' she said. 'No rubbish here.'

'I know,' he said and made a grab for her, but she danced out of his reach.

'The wine,' she said. 'Quick, before it warms up.'

'Yes, OK, the temperature is rising.'

'So I noticed, big boy,' she said. 'And that ain't the only thing, is it?'

Mark reddened at her remark. 'Don't tease me,' he said.

'That's just what I intend to do. I've got a late pass tonight and I mean to make the most of it.'

Mark felt for the switch on his mobile phone, then pulled his finger away guiltily. He had to stay in touch with the outside world, much as he would have liked to put it out of his mind. 'We will,' he said.

'We'd better. Now open that bottle whilst I check on the potatoes.'

Mark did as he was told and filled the glasses waiting on the table. He picked up his as Linda came back. 'About another fifteen minutes,' she said.

He reached for the other glass and handed it to her, that old, familiar electricity sparking as they touched. 'A toast,' he said. 'To us.'

'To us,' she echoed and they clinked their glasses and drank. Mark's mouth filled with the smoky taste of the wine.

'That's beautiful,' he said. 'Perfect. Just like you.'

'Thank you,' she replied. 'Now why don't you sit down,?' You're making the place look untidy.'

Once again, he did as he was told, sitting on the sofa whilst Linda took one of the dining chairs. 'Sit by me,' he said.

She shook her head. 'Not now. The way I feel the dinner might burn.'

'Would it matter? There's plenty of takeaways in the street.'

'Don't be so bloody cheeky, Mark,' she said. 'I've not worked my fingers to the bone all afternoon for us to have lamb korma out of a foil container. There's starters, roast lamb with green beans, and a pudding.'

'You're the only pudding I need,' he said.

'You bad boy. Just remember that everything comes to him who waits,' and she crossed her legs provocatively, once again showing her stocking tops and the soft white thighs above.

'It is getting warmer in here,' said Mark. 'Do you think we could open a window.?'

She blew him a kiss, put down her glass and went back into the kitchen, swinging her backside as she walked, and Mark wondered whether his appetite was greater for the food or for her.

Dinner was a great success. A simple smoked salmon terrine followed by noisettes of lamb with new potatoes and mange tout with a light rosemary jus, then tart tatine with cream.

'You've outdone yourself,' said Mark as he cleared his pudding plate.

'I'm glad you like it. Delia helped.'

'Who's Delia?' asked Mark mystified.

'I keep forgetting you've been away so long,' said Linda. 'She's a TV cook.'

None the wiser, Mark helped her stack the dishes in the sink before they returned to the living room. This time Linda sat on the sofa next to him. She'd already poured them a large brandy each. 'Coffee?' she asked.

'Maybe later. After.'

'After what?'

He put his brandy glass on the coffee table then took hers and put it next to his 'After this,' he said, gathering her into his arms and kissing her.

She wriggled around in his arms, her skirt riding up her thighs and he put his hand between her legs which she clamped tight. 'Gotcha,' she said.

And then from inside his jacket he heard his phone ring.

'Leave it,' whispered Linda.

'I can't.'

'You can.'

The phone chirped on and he removed his hand, stood up and recovered it from his pocket. He checked the display, it said TUBBS and he pressed the receive button.

'Shit,' said Linda.

'Hello,' said Mark. 'This better be important.'

'I got a call from Beretta,' said Tubbs above the sound of traffic.

'He wants a meet.'

'When?'

'Now. As soon as possible. And he wants money.'

'How much?'

'Ten grand he said. He wants to do a deal.'

'Shit,' said Mark to himself. 'I'm busy.'

'He said if not tonight, not ever,' said Tubbs. 'Come on, Mark, this is what we've been waiting for. How busy can you be?'

'Enough,' said Mark, pulling a 'I'm sorry' face at Linda. 'Where's the meet?'

'Outside Brixton Town Hall. I've got to call him when I've got the dough.'

'I'm not with it,' said Mark. 'I'll have to go home and get it.'

'How soon?'

'Where are you?'

'With Eddie in Stockwell.'

'Meet me at John's place. You remember where it is don't you?'

'Sure I do. That big old house in Tulse Hill.'

'That's the one. I'll be there in half an hour.'

'Me too.'

'Wait a minute. He's got security outside. They may not be too pleased to see you.'

'Shoot first and ask questions after?'

'That's about it. Park up the hill. I'll drive down and you can flash me.'

'I might get arrested.'

'Fuck off Tubbs, I'm not in the mood for your jokes. You know what I mean.'

'Chill man. Sure I do.'

'So look out for me. You know my motor.'

'Yeah.'

'See ya,' said Mark and he clicked off the phone.

'You're going,' said Linda, her face pink with anger.

'I've got to.'

'Always. You always go.'

'This is important.'

'And this isn't.' The sweep of her hand took in the whole room and herself.

'Of course it is.'

'But not more important than a phone call.'

'You don't understand.'

'I understand only too well. I've made every effort for you, Mark. New knickers, food. What more do you want?'

'I'm sorry.'

'Always sorry. Always disappearing. Always leaving people who care for you hanging out to dry…'

'It's not like that,' he interrupted. 'There's something I have to do for John…'

'And always John,' she spat. 'Bloody John Jenner. He's your god, isn't he? When John calls, Mark goes running. You even left your mother for him.'

The remark nailed Mark's heart like the bolt from a crossbow. 'Don't say that,' he said.

'It's true, Mark, and look what happened to her.'

'Please, Linda.'

'No,' she said, getting up from the couch. 'Go on, Mark, piss off. But just remember what you're missing,' and she pulled her dress over her head revealing froths of pink lace around her hips and breasts, showing off her figure so beautifully that Mark's eyes goggled. 'And this was your last chance, I promise,' and she threw the dress to the floor and slammed out of the room.

Mark put on his jacket and left. Standing on the landing he could hear her sobs echoing through the building. 'Shit,' he whispered to himself, but instead of going upstairs he went down and out into the cold street with what she'd said about his mother ringing in his head. Mum, he thought. Jesus, Mum, I'm so sorry.

* * *

The last time Mark Farrow had seen his mother alive was on April 9, 1989, a date he'd never forget. It was also the first day he saw her dead. He was paying one of his rare visits after she'd called him up on the phone the day before. She'd sounded awful when they'd spoken. Things were going from bad to worse, she told him. She was drunk. Nothing new there: by then she was drunk most of the time. She begged him to come round, so he told her he'd be there the next day about seven, as long as Bobby Thomas wasn't at home. He wouldn't be, she told him. He hardly ever was these days, pubbing it mostly, or with some old slapper he'd pulled in one of the boozers he went to.

The next evening, Mark drove to the house in East Dulwich where Thomas and his mother rented their flat. Or at least his mother rented the flat and Thomas stayed there, rent free. It was a dump, but it was all she could afford. The top floor of a three-storey terraced house just off Lordship Lane, lined with pizza and fried chicken and hamburger take-outs. Mark sent money and would've sent more, but he knew it just got spent at the off licence and in betting shops.

Mark was on his way to a restaurant up west, where some dodgy mates were throwing a birthday party for another dodgy mate. Mark couldn't remember any of their names now, but he could remember exactly what he was wearing. An Armani suit, Hugo Boss shirt and tie combo, Calvin Klein underwear and shoes by Church. He was a real little gentleman, as some old Dickensian character might have remarked. Under those smart clothes beat a heart of solid stone, or so he thought. But even stone can sometimes shatter when tapped from an unexpected direction. And, as tough as Mark might think he was, he would never be the same again after that dreadful night.

The front, party door was open when he arrived at the house. He shook his head and walked up the six dusty flights of uncarpeted stairs that led to his mother's flat, past bicycles, a roll of carpet and mail that had gathered and seemingly multiplied with time, addressed to tenants old and new, present and departed. The door to her flat was open too. It was still light outside, but dismal indoors, and the bare bulb in the short hallway of the apartment glowed dimly. Mark gently pushed open the door, as if he expected an ambush. 'Mum,' he called, but all was quiet, except for the reverberation of reggae music from somewhere nearby. 'Mum,' he called again, walking down the hall. 'You there?'

Still no answer. The kitchen was empty, so was the living room. Mark knocked on the bedroom door. He hated the thought of his mother and Bobby Thomas sleeping in there together, but when his knock went unheeded, he opened it and peeped inside. Empty too. He wondered if she had gone out for cigarettes or booze and forgotten he was coming. That left only the bathroom. The light was off and the door was ajar, but Mark pushed it open anyway and reached for the switch.

Afterwards, he wondered if he'd realised in the split second between the connection being made and the fluorescent fixture springing to life what he was about to find. He'd never know, but as his eyes adjusted to the light he saw the terrible truth. The bath was full of what looked at first sight like thin tomato juice and what he could see of his mother's naked body lay in the mixture of blood and water, her white skin streaked with gore. Her head was tilted back, her eyes shut, and one arm hung over the edge of the porcelain, the wrist cut from palm to elbow in one vertical line – there was no hesitation marks. Blood had dripped on to the floor, making a sticky pool that had run over as far as the toilet bowl, but now it was clotting and hung like red strings from her fingertips. Water was still dribbling out of one of the taps, and the bath was almost full. His mother appeared to be floating, the water lapping around her chin and mouth, bubbling slightly when she breathed.

She was still breathing, that was all that Mark could think of. 'Mum,' he said, his mouth so dry it hurt to speak. 'Oh Christ, Mum. What the hell have you done?'

The room seemed to contract: the walls and ceiling bearing down on him as if he was in a coffin.

He knelt beside the bath, the blood soaking the knees of his trousers. He tried to pull her upright and keep the water out of her nose and mouth. He wanted to get her out of the bath but she was a dead weight and he could feel panic growing inside him. Phone, he thought, he had to phone.

He left her and ran into the living room. Please God, don't let it be cut off, he thought, then remembered that she'd called him the night before and felt blessed relief when he heard a dialling tone when he picked up the receiver. He dialled three nines with a shaking hand and said aloud, 'Come on, come on,' as it rang. It seemed like hours, but they picked up on the fourth ring.

'Emergency. Which service do—'

'Ambulance,' he interrupted. 'An ambulance, quick.'

'Your number and address please, sir,' said the voice.

Mark told the operator, and added, 'It's my mother. She... she's cut her wrist.'

'An ambulance will be with you as soon as possible,' said the voice, but Mark had already dropped the handset on to the floor and raced back to the bathroom.

Nothing much had changed. His mother was lying in the bath, still breathing – just – and blood ran slowly from her wrist.

Mark grabbed a hand towel and wrapped it around the wound on her right arm, then stuck his hand into the pink gruel in which she lay and pulled out her other wrist. That too was cut and Mark hastily wrapped a towel around it, knotting it tightly. He didn't know if he was doing the right thing or the wrong thing, but at least he was doing something. Something to help.

He looked at his watch, its face stained with blood, and reckoned it was three minutes since he'd called 999. Three minutes that might have been three years, so slowly was time passing. 'Come on,' he said again, squeezing his mother in his arms.

And then, just as he did hear the klaxon getting closer, she opened her eyes and looked straight into his.

'Blue eyes,' she said. 'Such beautiful blue eyes... Mark, promise me you'll take care of everything...' She stiffened, he heard a rattle in the back of her throat and she closed her eyes for the last time. He felt her spirit leave with her last exhalation of breath, and she died in his arms.

'Mum,' he cried, not believing what he saw. 'Mum! Don't go. Oh, Christ, why did you do it?' He let her body drop and walked up and down the bathroom floor, trailing blood and water in his wake.

He raised his arms and lowered his head. 'Why?' he kept saying. 'Why? Why? Why?' He wanted to cry but no tears came. He stamped and wailed and beat his arms on his head, but still no tears came.

The ambulance men arrived, a minute or so late, thundering up the stairs, shouting as they came. But they were too late.

The paramedics did their best to revive Susan Thomas, but to no avail. Mark went with her in the ambulance, but it was hopeless, and they turned off their siren for the trip to Kings College Hospital.

An hour later, Mark was sitting outside the Accident and Emergency department in his damp, bloodstained clothes when John Jenner, Chas and Hazel arrived.

Hazel took him in her arms and held him tightly. 'Mark,' she said. 'I'm so sorry.'

'She waited for me before she died,' whispered the boy. 'She told me to take care of everything. How could she?' and he sobbed into the collar of Hazel's jacket.

'It was all too much for her,' Hazel said back. 'She couldn't cope.'

'But to do that...' said Mark.

'Have the police been?' asked John Jenner.

Mark nodded. 'There's one somewhere. I didn't say much.'

'Good,' said Hazel.

'Has anybody seen Thomas?' asked John Jenner.

Mark looked up at him and shook his head. 'He wasn't there. I said I wouldn't go round if he was...' Once again he couldn't finish the sentence.

It was then that Bobby Thomas arrived through the doors of A&E. He was pissed and belligerent. Mark had left a message with the neighbours downstairs, who'd come out to see what all the fuss was about. 'Where is she?' he demanded in a voice slurred from alcohol and God knew what else. 'Where's my little Susie?'

Mark lost it. He pulled away from Hazel, and before anyone could stop him, his blue eyes dark and wild, he pulled back his tight fist and hit Bobby Thomas full in the face. Thomas's nose burst and more blood speckled Mark's suit jacket. He went down hard and curled himself up into a ball and stayed there.

Chas grabbed Mark in a bear hug before the boy could follow through, lifting him clear off the floor and pushing him hard against the wall. 'No, son,' he said. 'Not here, not now.' Mark struggled for a moment, but the bigger, older man kept whispering in his ear for him to be calm, and, after a few seconds, he was.

A nurse, alerted by the commotion arrived and shook her head as she surveyed the scene. 'Can't you people take it outside?' she said. 'We have enough trouble here as it is.'

Hazel went to her, apologising profusely. 'Sorry, nurse,' she said. 'The boy just lost his mother.'

'I know,' replied the nurse. 'Now are you going to stop or do I go and get that policeman?'

'It's stopped,' said Hazel. 'It's all over.'

The nurse went to Thomas's prone form and turned his head to look at his nose. 'It's broken,' she said. 'Come on, get up. I'll fix it.'

Thomas staggered to his feet and, giving Mark a look of pure loathing, followed the nurse back into the ward.

John Jenner went over to Mark who was leaning against the wall looking at his swollen knuckles. 'Come on, son,' he said. 'Let's go home. There's nothing we can do here except get nicked. We'll come back tomorrow and sort everything out.'

'Susan was Thomas's wife,' Hazel reminded him. 'The arrangements are down to him.'

'No,' said Mark. 'I want to do it.'

'And so you shall,' said Hazel. 'Tomorrow. Things will look different tomorrow.'

Different, thought Mark as she led him out to their car. Not better – different. And that's how it's going to be from now on.

Bobby Thomas didn't press charges against Mark, and because he was skint as usual, he allowed Mark to arrange the funeral and John Jenner to pick up the bill. Mark didn't see him again until the inquest – the verdict was suicide – and again at the funeral in Greenwich cemetery. John Jenner paid for the headstone too, but Mark rarely visited his mother's grave. It brought back too many painful memories. Just once every twelve months, when he was around, on the 9th of April, with a bunch of flowers to replace the dead ones that had lain there all year.

Mark assumed that he would never see Bobby Thomas again after that, but he was wrong. They were to meet again quite soon, and once more it would be a life-changing event for Mark Farrow.

It was a beautiful spring evening in May when it happened. One of those perfect days in London when everything fits together perfectly. The temperature was in the low 70s, with a warm breeze blowing in from Africa, pollution was down and the grass was green and sweet.

Mark got a call at a pub where he was collecting money for John Jenner. Mark tried to make the extortion as pleasant as possible. He'd have a mineral water with ice and lemon and engage the publican or his wife in some conversation. The owners of this particular boozer went along with the fiction that Mark was just another customer, unlike some of the calls on his list where he was treated with as much caution as one might afford a rabid dog. With respect, but no friendship, and most of them were more than happy to see the back of him as quickly as possible. It was just part of the job, and Mark had stopped caring long before.

'Call for you, Mark,' said the barman, holding up the phone.

Mark went behind the jump and took the receiver.

'Mark?' said John Jenner's voice.

'Yes, Uncle.'

'What are you up to?'

'Usual.'

'Right. I need to see you.'

'When?'

'Now.'

'Where?'

'Dev's scrap yard.'

'Why?'

'You'll find out. How long will you be?'

'Half hour. Maybe less.'

'Good. Just toot your horn when you get there, Chas'll let you in.'

'What's all this about, Uncle?' asked Mark.

'I told you, you'll find out when you get here.' And he hung up.

Mark replaced the receiver, smiled a thanks to the barman and went back to his drink. The brown envelope stuffed with cash was in his pocket and he finished the water, wished everyone a pleasant good night and left. What they said about him when he was gone was irrelevant as far as he was concerned.

He went out to his car and headed towards Herne Hill and Dev's railway arch.

It was around eight when he arrived, and the evening had taken on a lavender tinge. The yard was up a half-demolished street of ancient slums, next to a council tip. The whole area was up for redevelopment and, at that time of night, was deserted. It stood behind high walls topped with razor wire and the only entrance was a pair of chain-link metal gates.

When he got there, Mark bipped his horn. After a few moments, Chas appeared and the gates swung open. He waved Mark through and closed them tight.

Mark got out of his BMW and joined Chas. 'What's going on?' he asked.

'Got a surprise for you,' said Chas.

'I don't like surprises.'

'You'll like this one.'

They walked together through the piles of old motors, thirty and forty feet high, that always seemed to Mark to be on the verge of toppling down and crushing anyone underneath.

At the back of the yard was a huge structure like a wallless barn, the roof supported by eight metal braces, each as thick as a tree trunk. In one corner was a Portakabin that Dev used as an office, and in the other, the crushing machine. It was a huge beast of a thing, battered and black with oil from countless engines, with a crane at one end to lift the hapless motors to their destruction and eventual end as three-foot-square cubes of metal, glass and rubber.

In the centre of the barn was a sunken drain to take the effluent from the cars and wash it away to God knew where. All in all it was a very iffy concern and Dev only managed to keep it running because of the compulsory purchase order that was on the land, and a few well chosen backhanders that kept council and environmental health officials turning a blind eye to what hazards went on behind the closed doors.

John Jenner's latest motor, a new Jaguar saloon, was parked up empty next to the Portakabin.

'Inside,' said Chas.

Mark turned the handle of the cabin and went in. It was dark apart from one dim bulb burning in a desk lamp, but Mark could still see who was there. John Jenner was perched on one edge of Dev's untidy desk. In front of it, in a swivel chair, was Bobby Thomas. His arms were tied behind him with rope, and his ankles were constrained with more of the same. His mouth had been taped shut. 'Hello, Mark,' said Jenner. 'Glad you could make it. Look what the cat dragged in.'

Thomas strained at the ropes.

'Stop it,' said Jenner, who got down from the desk and slapped him hard round the face.

'What's he doing here?' asked Mark.

'Went out for a walk and didn't go home,' said Jenner.

'He was going down the pub,' said Chas. 'Drowning his sorrows.' Then he looked at Mark and said: 'Sorry.'

Mark shook off the bad choice of words. 'I thought he'd left London.'

'I told him to,' said John Jenner. 'At the funeral I explained what would happen if I saw him again, but he must've thought I was joking.'

'Bad idea,' said Chas.

'Let's hear what he's got to say,' said Jenner and ripped the tape off Thomas's face, leaving tiny blood bubbles in the pores on his lips and chin.

'You bastards!' ranted Thomas. 'If you don't let me go I'll have you for kidnapping!'

Jenner laughed. 'Kidnapping. Hear that, Chas? He says he'll do us for kidnapping. What do you think he'd say if I cut his dick off and shoved it down his throat?'

'Not much,' replied Chas. 'With his dick in his mouth and all.'

'From what I've heard, the size of it, he'd hardly notice,' said Jenner.

'Mark,' said Thomas. 'Tell 'em. It wasn't my fault your mum killed herself. She wasn't well.'

'And whose fault was that?' said Jenner. 'Anyway, you won't be missed. Remind me, what do you do for a living?'

'I'm unemployed at the moment,' said Thomas.

'At the moment,' said Jenner. 'You ain't done a day's work since you met Susan. You lived on her pension and the dole. Well, the pension's finished now, and so are you.'

'What are you going to do?' asked Mark.

'That's up to you, son,' replied Jenner. 'What do you think?'

Mark said nothing.

'Now where's that...' said Jenner. 'Ah, here it is.' And he moved some papers on the desk revealing an automatic pistol with a silencer screwed to the barrel. He picked up the gun and worked the action, forcing a round into the breech. Thomas went white and the smell of shit filled the room. Sure enough, a dark stain spread over the crotch of his trousers.

'Oh dear,' said Jenner, sighting down the barrel of the gun. 'He's messed his pants. What a shame.'

'Don't, please,' begged Thomas.

Jenner handed the gun to Mark. 'Here you are, son, it's all yours.'

Mark hefted the front-heavy weight of the pistol in his hand. This was what he'd been waiting for for years. A chance to get even with Thomas. But looking at the flabby, scruffy, shit-stained alcoholic sitting in front of him, he couldn't dredge up enough energy to pull the trigger.

'Get him outside,' said Jenner, and Chas lifted the man, seat and all, and carried him through the door of the Portakabin and dumped him on the filthy concrete outside.

'Are you going to do it?' asked Jenner. 'He's all yours.'

'He's pathetic,' said Mark.

'Yeah. He is now. But if we let him go, he'll be boasting about it in some boozer before the week's out. Saying we've gone soft, and we might never have the chance again.'

'Can't we just let him go? Get him out of London?'

'I've done that once, like I said. He's taking the piss. Do you want me to do it?'

Mark shook his head. He knew that Jenner was right. And he also knew that whatever happened, whether Thomas walked or not, the night would haunt him forever. The same way the sight of his mother dying in the bath had filled his dreams every night since the night he'd found her.

'What did she tell you?' pressed Jenner. 'When you found her?'

'She told me to take care of everything.'

'So do it,' said Jenner. 'Do it for her.'

Mark nodded and stepped outside to find that Chas had knocked Thomas off the chair. He was lying on the ground squirming against his bonds like a slug in salt.

Mark walked over to Thomas and turned him over with his foot. 'I remember everything you did, Bobby,' he said quietly. 'I remember how you spoiled my mum's life. And mine.'

'No, Mark,' begged Thomas. 'We had some good times. Going to football. You remember...'

Mark shook his head. 'We never had one good time, Bobby,' he said. 'From the day you met her it was all crap. It all went to hell.'

'Please, Mark...'

Mark raised the pistol in his fist as if it weighed tons instead of pounds and said: 'How many rounds, Uncle?'

'Nine,' came the reply.

Mark smiled and pulled the trigger half back and Thomas crabbed across the concrete as if he could somehow escape. 'You're not going anywhere, Bobby,' said Mark, adding a slight pressure with his finger. The gun fired. The first bullet hit Thomas in the thigh and he screamed. Then Mark pulled the trigger again, and again, hitting the prone man in his torso and his groin, until finally he blew half his head off and kept firing until the action blew back and the gun's magazine was empty. But even then he kept trying to pull the trigger.

'Get the car,' said Jenner to Chas. 'And start the crusher.'

'He's going to leak all over the place,' moaned Chas.

'Then get the fucking hose and sluice it down. Come on, Mark. I'll take you home. Chas'll bring your motor.' Jenner gently extracted the gun from Mark's hand and gave it to Chas. 'And make this disappear.'

Chas nodded and walked from under the roof of the barn to where an ancient, once red Vauxhall Viva was parked up. He got in, started the engine after a couple of tries and drove it up next to the crusher.

'Time for us to go,' said Jenner, leading the younger man to the Jaguar and helping him into the passenger seat before getting in behind the wheel and driving back to the gates.

The last Mark saw of Bobby Thomas was Chas loading him into the boot of the red Viva.

Mark was opening the gates for his uncle's car when he heard the crusher start up.

TWENTY-FOUR

Sitting in his car, looking up at Linda's living room window, still lit through drawn curtains, Mark shook his head at his own stupidity as he thought back. Inside that flat was heaven. The only heaven he'd ever known or wanted. And the chance of a future with the one woman he'd ever really loved. But he'd turned his back and walked out, possibly never to return. And for what? To get back to the killing – and there'd already been too much of it in his life.

He started the engine and drove off with just one backward look into his rearview mirror at the tightly closed front door, wondering if he'd ever see her again.

He drove the short distance to Tulse Hill and slowly drifted his car down the hill towards John Jenner's house. He quickly saw the gleam of the reflected street lights on the red cellulose of Tubbs's BMW and its lights flashed once briefly.

Mark parked behind the Beemer and joined Tubbs in the front.

'What's the story?' he asked.

'Beretta called me an hour ago. He'd got ten grand's worth of coke and wants to do a deal.'

'And has to be tonight?'

'Right.'

Mark shook his head wearily. 'Fucked up my evening, I can tell you.'

'Sorry about that, but I thought you'd want to know.'

'Course I do. Right, come on, let's go inside and get the cash. You going to be all right doing this on your own?'

'Gonna have to be, ain't I?' replied the black man.

'Where's Eddie?'

299

'At home. I could've put him in the boot with his sawn-off, but he gets claustrophobic. And they told me to come alone.'

'They would. What do you reckon, Tubbs? Are they going to rip you off?'

'They might try.'

'That's what worries me. You're going in blind with a lot of money. These fuckers are mental. They'll kill you soon as look at you.'

'Nice thought. But they want money. And they've got all that dope to shift. What they're not sticking up their own hooters. And believe me, they're doing plenty of that. I reckon this is a try out. See if I can come up with the money sharpish and if there's more where that came from.'

'I hope you're right.'

'If I'm not, I'm in trouble. You got a gun?'

'Several.'

'Good. Handy?'

'With the cash.'

'Thank fuck for that.'

'You've got to be so careful, Tubbs. How long is it since you used a firearm?'

'Not since you pissed off. But you never forget.' He paused and Mark saw fear flash in his eyes. 'Do you?'

'Like riding a bike. But I hope you don't have to find out. We need to know where the stuff is being kept. Who else is about. What security they've got and what they're carrying themselves. It's bound to be heavy duty. These fucking Yardies judge their manhood by the calibre of their weapons. They're toting fucking Uzis around London, shooting anything that moves.'

'I know. I read the papers. Now listen, are we going to do this or sit here all night?'

'I like your enthusiasm,' said Mark. 'Come on, we'll go in mine.' They left the BMW, walked over to Mark's car and he drove the short distance to the gates of the house. Mark opened them with the remote Chas had given him. The black Mercedes was parked across the street still, and he could dimly see two shadowy bodies inside.

'What's all that in aid of?' asked Tubbs.

'The fuckers you're going to make a buy off tonight and their mates.'

'Uncle John was always good at making enemies.'

'You can say that again.'

They left the car and crunched across the drive to the front door, which Mark opened with his key. From behind the living room door he could hear Michael Caine's voice. 'Come and say hello,' he said, opening the door and pushing Tubbs inside.

John Jenner was alone watching *The Italian Job* on DVD. 'You still into this old crap, John?' said the black man, looking at the screen. 'They don't get away with it you know.'

'Christ,' Jenner said when he saw Tubbs. 'The return of Django.' He killed the movie with the remote.

'Hello, John,' said Tubbs. 'Long time.'

'Christ, but it is. Too long,' said Jenner. 'I'd get up Tubbs, but my legs are bad tonight.'

'I heard about your troubles,' said Tubbs who went over and shook the older man's hand. 'I'm sorry.'

'That's what life's all about,' said Jenner who pulled the big man closer for a clumsy embrace. 'You look well. I can see you're eating regular.'

'Fried chicken,' said Tubbs. 'Always been my problem. Now I cook it for a living.'

'But not for much longer, I hear,' said Jenner. 'You're back in the world.'

'If I can hack it.'

'That's why we're here, Uncle,' said Mark. 'Tubbs is off to make a buy. We've come for the money and a little something to keep him healthy.'

'Buying back our own gear, it don't seem right.'

'It wasn't really our gear, Uncle,' said Mark. 'We'd already been paid for it once. It belonged to your mates at the cash and carry. If you want us to leave it…' He didn't finish.

'No,' Jenner almost shouted. 'No,' he said again more quietly. 'Sorry, boys. I'm upset by the way things are going. So tell me all.'

Mark quickly filled Jenner in on what had happened during the day and the older man frowned. 'Dangerous,' he said. 'Bloody dangerous. They'll pop you for ten bob, Tubbs, let alone ten grand.'

'That's the chance I've got to take,' the big man said.

'You going with him, Mark?'

'Not in his car. He was told to go alone. Besides, they might know me, and even if they don't, any white face is going to set them off. But I'll be close.'

'Good,' said Jenner. 'When're you going?'

'Now. As soon as Mark gives me the money,' said Tubbs.

'Go on then, son,' Jenner said to Mark. 'I'll keep Tubbs company.'

Mark left them, went down to the cellar where he made up a parcel of ten thousand pounds in a plastic supermarket bag and picked out the Browning 9mm he'd carried himself, checked the clip and took it all back upstairs. 'Here you go, Tubbs. Now be careful. I'll be about but I don't want to crowd you.'

Tubbs nodded, looked inside the bag and riffled the notes. 'All here?' he asked.

'Course. And this bugger's loaded with hollow points,' replied Mark, handing him the pistol.

Tubbs dropped the magazine out of the Browning, checked that the chamber was clear, replaced the clip and racked a round into the breech, weighing the gun in his massive hand where it looked like a toy. 'Feels good,' he said. Then he took out his phone, dialled a number and waited for an answer. It was picked up quickly. 'It's me,' he said. 'I've got what you want.'

He listened for a moment.

'About twenty minutes. I'll be there,' he said, then killed the connection. 'It's on.'

'Then let's go,' said Mark. 'Later, Uncle.'

'I wish I was going with you. I'd show those spades what for. No offence, Tubbs.'

'None taken, John.'

'I'll wait up. We'll have a drink when you get back.'

'Sounds like a plan,' said Mark, glad he'd said 'when' rather than 'if'.

'He looks bad,' said Tubbs, once they were outside.

'He is,' was all Mark said.

He dropped Tubbs off at the BMW and watched as he drove off before following. He knew where Tubbs was going so he kept well back, the bright colour of his friend's car being easy to spot even after dark. Tubbs drove up to Streatham High Road, took a right down Brixton Hill, past the prison where Jimmy Hunter slept the sleep of the unjust, and along to Brixton Town Hall, opposite where Mark's life and so many others had changed all those years before. But he thought of none of this as he followed his old friend on what could turn out to be the last drive of his life.

Back at the house, John Jenner was dozing in front of the TV. He hoped the boys would be all right. Mark was OK, but he didn't know about Tubbs. He'd been too long out of the game. They needed an ally. If only his old friend Nick Sharman was about. He was the kind of bloke they needed. Sharman. Bloody hell, what a chancer.

Jenner remembered the first time they'd met. It had been on the recommendation of John's brief, when he'd been looking for an easy way out of a sticky situation.

In those days, the early 80s, the pubs shut at three in the afternoon and the landlord of the Three Dials in Kennington Lane called time on the dot and made short shrift of the few remaining drinkers, so that by three-fifteen the bar was empty except for John Jenner, Hazel, Chas and David Lawson, Jenner's lawyer. On the face of it, Lawson was a pillar of the establishment, with his handmade shoes and an office in St James's, but deep down he was as bent as they come. A corrupt and evil man, he hid his dishonesty under suits from Savile Row and shirts and ties from Jermyn Street. Jenner and Chas were wearing jeans and leather jackets, and Hazel looked stunning in a black leather suit and black nylons, her red hair coiled about her shoulders like electric snakes.

The four sat together and waited for DC Sharman to arrive. At three-thirty on the dot there was a rap on the back door and the landlord went through and answered it.

'Punctual. I like that,' said Jenner.

'I think there's a lot about Nick you're going to like,' said Lawson.

'We'll see,' said Jenner.

The man who followed the landlord through into the bar was young, tall, lean, dark haired, and wearing a slim-cut grey sharkskin suit, black, chisel-toed shoes, a white, tab collared shirt with a skinny black tie. His hair was thick and quiffed with gel, and he moved lightly on his feet, sussing out the room as he entered.

'Who the fuck does he think he is?' asked Chas. 'Bryan fucking Ferry?'

Hazel shushed Chas as the young policeman came over to the table and stood silently in front of the quartet, a slight smile on his handsome face.

Lawson stood and shook his hand. 'Nick,' he said. 'Good of you to come.'

'David,' said Sharman in reply. 'Not a problem. Always a pleasure to see you.'

'Gentlemen,' said the lawyer. 'May I introduce Detective Constable Nick Sharman? Nick, this is John Jenner, his wife Hazel, and one of his associates, name of Chas.'

'Delighted,' said Sharman, solemnly shaking hands all round. When he got to Hazel he held her fingers for just a beat too long.

She didn't seem to mind, but John Jenner's eyes narrowed. 'Nick,' he said. 'I wonder if you'd mind Chas making sure it's only us who're going to hear this conversation?'

'You think I might be wired?' asked Sharman, seeming greatly amused at the prospect.

'It's a possibility.'

'Fair enough.' The policeman raised his arms and Chas patted him down, then stepped back and shook his head. 'Clean,' he said.

'My apologies,' said Jenner.

'No problem,' came the reply.

'Please sit,' said Jenner.

Sharman did so, pulling a packet of Silk Cut and a brass Zippo from his pocket. He offered them round, and all but Lawson accepted. He flicked on the lighter, lit all four, Hazel's first, and dropped it back on the table. As he did so the cuff of his shirt slid back revealing a Rolex watch with a metal bracelet. Sharman saw them notice and smiled.

'Drink?' asked Jenner.

'Scotch,' replied the detective.

'Four large ones,' Jenner said to the landlord. 'And a vodka and orange for Hazel. Then get lost.'

The landlord set about making the screwdriver just as Hazel liked it. Lots of ice, a slice of lemon, a large vodka and a bottle of Britvic orange in a tall glass. He served her first then went back to the bar, brought over four clean glasses, a bottle of malt and a jug of water on a tray, set them out, cleared away the dirty pots, put them on the counter, and left.

'And don't come back 'til you're told,' added Jenner without thanks. 'And don't be fucking earwigging or Chas'll have your legs.'

When the men's glasses were charged and 'cheers' had been exchanged, Jenner leant forward and said: 'We've never met, but David here has said good things about you, Nick. You don't mind me calling you Nick, do you?'

'No problem,' replied Sharman around the edge of his glass. 'But we did meet once.'

'When?' asked Jenner with a frown. He didn't like not knowing.

'A couple of years back, when I was in uniform,' said Sharman. 'I gave you a parking ticket round the back of the Elephant. Nice old Aston Martin, as I remember.'

'And we spoke?'

'Yeah. You tore up the ticket and threw it at me, called me a cunt too. Excuse my language, Mrs Jenner.'

There was a moment's silence, then the company roared with laughter. 'Did I pay it?' asked Jenner.

'David did, as I recall,' replied the cop.

'Probably,' said Lawson. 'Just one of the perks of the job. Clearing up after John.'

'No hard feelings, I hope, Nick?' said Jenner.

'I could've done you for assault,' said Sharman. 'But when I checked out the registration and found out it was you I decided not to. I reckoned one day we might meet again, and maybe to our mutual advantage.'

'And here you are,' said the older man.

'Here I am,' said Sharman.

'And David says you've got something to sell.'

'Well, not exactly sell,' said the policeman. 'More like hire. When you need them, if you know what I mean.'

'Maybe,' said Jenner. 'What is it exactly?'

Rather than answer immediately, Sharman said: 'I've only been married for a little while. And wives are expensive.' He smiled at Hazel who smiled back. 'And she wants to have a baby. Even more expense. And I've got a few other expenses too.'

'Like what?'

'I like nice things. Clothes…' He touched the lapel of his jacket that was so sharp it almost cut him '…and a decent motor.'

'And a decent watch,' said Lawson.

'Exactly.' Then he sniffed exaggeratedly.

'And a bit of hokey cokey, I'll bet,' said Chas, entering the conversation for the first time.

'There is that,' said Sharman and, as he said it, the sun went in and the bar darkened and the four others at the table saw that there was something of the night about the young policeman. But something of the night was a trait they all shared.

'So,' said Jenner.

'So, what I earn isn't enough to keep me and my new missus in the way we'd like to become accustomed.'

'So?' said Jenner again.

Sharman reached into the top pocket of his jacket and fished out a leather folder and tossed it on to the table. It flipped open and inside was his warrant card. 'So that's for hire,' he said. 'And this.' He put his foot on

306

an empty chair next to him, pulled up his trouser leg and pulled out a short-barrelled .38 revolver from an ankle holster and gently placed it beside his glass and cigarettes as the three men stiffened and Chas went as if to reach inside his coat. Hazel put a restraining hand on his arm.

'Relax,' she said. 'We're all friends here, I hope. Or, will be soon. And you can call me, Hazel, Nick.'

Sharman smiled at her again, then turned to Chas. 'You missed that,' he said. 'Could've been a transmitter.'

Chas just sat in his seat and seethed.

'You can use that?' asked Jenner, nodding at the gun and ignoring Chas's discomfort.

'I can.'

'Have you ever?'

'Used it? Of course. On the range. I'm a bloody marksman.'

'But not in anger.'

'That's for me to know.'

'And they just let you walk around with one?'

'There's an operation on later. I told them I was off to see a snout and had this issued early. But I could use one of my own.'

'I think we might be able to help you there,' said Jenner. 'But how much will all this cost us?'

'Depends,' said Sharman thoughtfully. 'Depends what you need doing.'

'Like a sliding scale?' said Lawson.

'Exactly,' the policeman replied, slipping the gun and the warrant card back from where they'd come. 'A sliding scale. That'll do nicely.'

'As a a matter of fact, there is something,' said Jenner, topping up his glass. 'I'm up on charges at the Bailey in a few weeks.'

'I know,' replied Sharman.

'Serious charges. I only got bail thanks to the work of my friend here.' He gestured at Lawson who grinned like the Cheshire cat. 'I've done a little remand and I don't like it inside.'

Sharman nodded.

'And if your lot get a result I'm going away for a while.'

'A long while,' said Sharman.

'Yeah, maybe,' said Jenner, narrowing his eyes. 'And I wouldn't like that. I'd miss my family. But that's not the point.'

'I would've thought that was exactly the point,' said the Detective Constable.

'There's a witness,' said Jenner. 'A young man who took advantage of our good natures and then reneged.'

'Laurie Skinner,' said Sharman.

Jenner smiled. 'You have been doing your homework.'

'Word gets around. Gossip, you know.'

'More than gossip, I would've thought.' Jenner again.

Sharman nodded once more.

'The young man in question, I can hardly bear to mention his name, has gone to ground. I think perhaps your lot think he might be interfered with if he was walking the streets,' said Jenner.

'A possibility,' agreed Sharman.

'Any ideas where he might be?' asked Lawson.

Sharman shook his head. 'Need to know,' he said.

'And you don't,' said Jenner.

Sharman shook his head for a second time.

'You see, it would be ideal if the charges just went away,' said Jenner.

'Something nasty would have to happen to the witness for that to occur,' said Sharman.

'Very nasty.' Jenner again.

Sharman smiled. 'But of course, you'd need the address where he's at for that to happen.'

Jenner nodded.

'And that could be arranged?' asked Lawson.

'If the price was right,' said Sharman.

'What could you do?' interrupted Chas. 'You're just a DC. The lowest of the low.'

Sharman smiled. 'Like I said, if the price is right, all sorts of things could happen.'

308

'And the price would be?' asked Jenner.

'Ten.'

'Ten what?' said Chas.

'Well, not ten pence,' the copper said.

'Ten grand,' said Lawson.

'That'd be right.'

'And you could sort it out for us?'

'I could try.'

'Trying's not good enough,' said Chas.

'I think you'd find it was if it was me trying.'

'David,' said Jenner.

Lawson picked up his briefcase, laid it on the table, opened it and produced an envelope which he tossed on the table. 'There's five thousand there in small, used notes,' he said. 'Have that for now and let's see what happens.'

Sharman picked up the bulging envelope, peered inside but didn't count the money, then slid it into his inside jacket pocket. 'You came prepared. You must've been sure of me. That's fine. Thanks. I'll be in touch.'

'Make sure you are,' said Chas. 'That's a lot of bread.'

Sharman acknowledged him with a nod. 'Well, I've got to be getting back,' he said after a few moments. 'Like I said. We've got an operation on today.'

'Nothing we should know about, I hope,' said Jenner.

'No,' said the policeman. 'Nothing for you to worry about.'

'Good. 'Cos if it was…' Jenner didn't finish the sentence.

'You'd be the first to know,' said Sharman. 'As long as…' He paused, rubbed the first finger and thumb of his right hand together.

'Naturally,' said David Lawson.

'Well, cheers then, gentlemen. And Mrs Jenner… Hazel,' Sharman finished his drink in a swallow and pocketed his cigarettes and lighter. 'I'll be in touch.'

'Soon, I hope,' said Jenner.

'As soon as,' said the policeman, and with a merry wave he went out the back way.

'What do you think?' Lawson asked, addressing his question mainly to John Jenner.

'He's a flash bastard,' said Chas.

'You're just pissed off because you missed his gun. You should be more careful, son,' said Jenner.

Chas said nothing in reply, but they could all see how tightly his teeth were gritted, and how red his face was getting, a mixture of anger and embarrassment.

'Getting old, mate?' asked Jenner with a grin. 'But I'll give you that, Chas. Flash, he certainly is. Maybe too flash for comfort.'

'But useful,' said Lawson. 'Potentially very useful.'

'He's very handsome,' said Hazel.

'I saw you noticed,' said her husband. 'And he noticed you. All teeth and smiles. "You can call me Hazel." Sometimes I don't believe you.'

'So I should hope he noticed me,' she said. 'Being the only woman in the room.'

'I'm surprised you didn't volunteer to shake him down yourself,' said Jenner.

'Maybe I should've done,' replied his wife. 'I might've found his gun.' She winked at Chas, but his face just got redder.

'So what does your woman's intuition say?' asked Jenner.

'He'll do,' she replied. 'He's got an eye for the ladies, that's for sure. Clothes, coke and cars probably aren't his only expenses.'

'I believe there are a couple of mysteries in his life,' said Lawson. 'Of the female persuasion.'

'That's handy,' said Jenner. 'A little something we know that he won't want his new wife to. Something to keep him in line. Have you used him yet?'

'Just for small things,' replied Lawson. 'Penny ante stuff. Getting a few addresses. Things like that.'

'So let's see how he does with Skinner.'

'I reckon he might be doing us up,' said Chas. 'He'll be noticed, wearing clothes like that and a watch like that. I reckon he's on the cross.'

'A double agent, you mean?' said Lawson.

'Yeah.'

'Maybe, maybe not,' said Jenner. 'He's flash, you're right there, Chas. But I reckon he's corkscrew. Double bent. He reminds me of us ten years ago. Let him have his head, David. And when he's in too deep we'll have him.'

'No problem, John,' said Lawson. 'No problem at all.'

It was only a matter of days before the bent brief heard from the young policeman. 'Got a bit of news for you,' said Sharman when he called Lawson on his private line.

'What exactly?'

'Not on the dog. Let's meet.'

'When?'

'Soon as you like.'

'Tomorrow,' said Lawson, and he gave a time and location. Lawson met Sharman alone at the Sweet Bird Of Youth public house in Mayfair the following lunchtime. 'Nice place,' said the policeman as the lawyer joined him just after two.

'One of my locals,' said Lawson, ordering a gin and tonic for himself and a refill for Sharman's scotch, before they found a quiet corner table in the busy pub.

'It's all right for some. My locals leave a lot to be desired.'

'That's police work for you.'

'Too true.'

'So what's the news?'

'It's a tricky one. The robbery squad have got Skinner tied down tight.'

'Where?'

Sharman grinned, showing white teeth. 'A safe house in Canonbury. But I warn you, there's armed response on hand 24 hours a day, seven days a week. No one wants to lose this fish.'

'Address?'

Sharman told him.

'Good, Nick,' said Lawson.

'Listen,' said Sharman, grabbing him by the cuff of his jacket. 'I don't care about that little shit Skinner. You can do what you want with him. But there's coppers in there with him, and I won't have them hurt, get me?'

'A touch of conscience, Nick?' asked Lawson, freeing the expensive wool and mohair mixture and smoothing the material.

'If you like.'

'Don't come across all pious with us, Nick. If you're in, you're in. If not… Well, John won't be pleased. Chas wasn't keen in the first place, I should warn you. Thought you were too flash.'

'Is that right?'

'It is.'

'How about Mrs Jenner?'

'She liked you fine.'

'Good. And I'm not in the least bit pious, David. Just careful. Just like you should be. A grass – even a supergrass – gets offed, no big deal. There's a bit of a stink for a few weeks, an inquiry, then it's business as usual. But a copper gets hurt and it's like putting on a blender with the top loose. All sorts of shit flies around, anyone in the way gets covered. Tell John to take it easy. Pick his time.'

'I see what you're saying, Nick. You're very careful.'

'I try to be. That's what keeps me in the job, and I'm no use to you out of it.'

'Too true. But who said anything about offing him?'

'What? You're going to send him flowers and a note asking him to change his evidence?'

'Hardly.'

'Exactly.'

'So?'

'So what?'

'Are you going to go in easy?'

'We will.'

'Good.'

For all his flash ways, which didn't endear him to his male colleagues at Kennington nick but set the hearts of the female officers aflutter, Nick Sharman knew how to keep a low profile. At work he wore a Timex, and had swapped the fake Rolex for it after seeing Lawson and his clients at the pub after their first meeting. And he knew that by accepting their money that day, and supplying the address of the safe house to Lawson a few days later, he was walking on thin ice. But needs must when the Devil drives, and his new missus, Laura, was used to the best. He'd already forked out a deposit he couldn't afford on their little two up two down in Camberwell, and she'd demanded the most expensive furnishings she could find in the Fulham Road boutiques she favoured. And now she was talking about babies, and Sharman knew that Peter Jones was going to be favourite for all the bits and pieces that that entailed. And the two young women he saw on a casual basis didn't come cheap either. Trouble was, he just couldn't leave skirt alone. As it happened, he wouldn't have minded having a pop at Hazel Jenner. But even he wasn't that big a fool. Pity though.

Shit, he thought as he tubed back south of the river for the afternoon shift. I hope this one doesn't go up the pictures.

It was three days later that he got the news, sitting in an ancient Ford keeping obbo on a suspected car ringing firm in darkest Waterloo. The passenger door opened with a bang and he narrowly missed spoiling his sharply creased khakis with drops of coffee from a Styrofoam cup in his hand. 'What the...?' he yelled.

'Sorry, Nick,' said his new companion. 'Didn't mean to make you jump.'

'Jesus, Sarge,' said Sharman. 'Where did you spring from?'

'I thought you were supposed to be keeping a keen eye out.'

'I am. Over there.' Sharman pointed at the undistinguished front of a garage built into an old railway shed round the back of Waterloo station.

'I could've been a bad boy creeping up on you to deliver a killing

313

blow,' said Detective Sergeant Jack Robber with a leer, as he helped himself to one of Sharman's cigarettes from the packet on the dash. 'Got a light?'

'Forgotten to buy fags again, Sarge?' said Sharman.

'Why bother, when you've always got loads?' said Robber.

Sharman sighed, lit his superior's cigarette and cracked the window on his side another inch.

'Heard about what happened at Canonbury?' asked Robber when his cigarette was burning to his satisfaction.

'What?' said Sharman and felt his stomach clench.

'A grass got blown away by a sniper whilst he's taking a constitutional in the garden.'

'Do what?'

'Yeah. Just having a wander, smelling the daisies, when some shooter on a tower block puts one in his head. Nasty business, from what I can gather. Not enough left of his loaf for his mum to recognise, by all accounts.'

'Christ.'

'Christ is right. It's gone right off over there. He was the main witness in the case against John Jenner, and now it's gone all to cock.'

'Who did it?'

'Nick, sometimes you can be very naive. Who do you think?'

'Jenner?'

'Course. But not in person. That fucker never gets his own hands dirty these days. As it happens, he was on the golf course all afternoon. A bloody QC as his partner.'

'So, an airtight alibi.'

'Exactly. So that's a lot of the tax payers' money wasted.'

'I'm sorry to hear it.'

'Not as sorry as the prosecution team. But that's life.'

'Case dismissed.'

'Got it in one. Bad day for the Met.'

'Anybody else hurt?' asked Sharman casually.

'No. His minder hit the dirt. Messed up his suit by all accounts. Blood and grass stains are buggers to get out. Grass stains. Geddit?'

'Very funny. But at least there's that.'

'At least. Now, what about this bloody ringing team? Anything happening?'

'Not a sausage, Sarge,' said Sharman, and lit a cigarette of his own. He noticed that his hand was as steady as a rock.

TWENTY-FIVE

When Tubbs parked on a double yellow outside the old church opposite the Town Hall, Mark let the Range Rover drift past, took a right through the one way system and stopped in a side street next to the library. He stepped out of the truck and crossed the road heading south, squinting through the railings at the red BMW. Tubbs was standing next to it when he was approached by a man in a long leather jacket and hooded sweatshirt with the hood up. They spoke for a moment and then both climbed into the car. Mark sprinted back to his own vehicle, did a hasty U-turn and rejoined the one way system.

As he'd surmised, the BMW was just in front of him, heading back towards Streatham and the Yardies' estate of flats. Just as well they like to keep things on their own patch, Mark thought, otherwise he could easily have lost his friend in the maze of south London streets.

The BMW turned left just opposite the Telegraph pub, where he'd drunk with Chas just a few days before, then turned again into the estate.

Mark dumped the Range Rover on the corner, set the alarm and hoped it would still be there when he returned. He pulled up his coat collar, jumped over the low wall that acted as boundary for the estate and strolled through to the block that Beretta called home.

Just as he'd surmised, the red car was parked outside, empty.

Mark stood in the shadows beside a ripe rubbish chute that rustled with vermin, and mentally crossed his fingers that his old friend would be OK.

Inside the flats, Tubbs had been taken up to the top floor in a lift that creaked with age and neglect and which smelled all right provided he didn't breathe through his nose. Then he was led down a windowless corridor lined with doors reinforced with metal, to flat number 80. Moses, the man who'd met him down in Brixton, had checked the money on the short ride back to the estate and had almost cracked a smile at the amount, but said little.

Tubbs was getting nervous. He didn't know if Mark had managed to follow him, and even if he had, what could he do if things kicked off?

Moses rapped on the door of the flat, gave the thumbs up to the spy-hole in the metal and, after a moment, with a rattle of chains and the clicking of at least three locks, it swung open. Moses held up the plastic bag of money and said 'Result,' to Karl, who was standing in the hallway with a machete in his fist.

Charming, thought Tubbs, who could feel the reassuring weight of the Browning down the back of his strides. He wondered how often Karl had used his weapon.

Tubbs was hustled in to the flat and to the living room, which was surprisingly neat and tidy. He'd expected a crack den at least, but in fact it was more like his old Aunty Hilda's place in Peckham, where he'd been raised. The carpet was thick and red, a three piece suite in front of a widescreen TV that came with satellite, video and DVD hookups. A huge music centre sat on a dark wood sideboard, and vinyl albums and CDs were stacked on each side. Aunty Hilda wouldn't have had all the high tech equipment but she would have approved of the picture of Jesus nailed to the cross on one wall. Very religious was Aunty Hilda, and he hoped she was with the Lord right now looking down on her favourite nephew and keeping him from harm.

Curtains were drawn across what looked like balcony windows. Beretta was sitting in one of the armchairs, watching football. He was dressed in black suit pants, an unbuttoned black waistcoat and a gleaming white dress shirt, open at the throat. He looked a bit like a preacher on his day off, thought Tubbs, and, aside from the greyish tinge to his face, he appeared as healthy as a horse. A young black woman looking just too thin and scrawny in her short skirt and top was stretched out on the sofa. This must be the crack whore Mark had told him shared the accommodation. Between Beretta's chair and the TV set was a large glass coffee table, upon which sat a couple of crack pipes, a bag each of rock and powder, and the makings of spliff. A large ashtray in the centre was full of roaches and cigarette ends and the air was filled with the aroma of marijuana. Next to the ashtray was a foot-square mirror upon which half a dozen chunky lines of powder had been neatly cut.

Beretta stood as the three men entered the room. 'Lulu,' he said to the girl. 'Get lost baby. We got business.'

'Oh honey,' she said, looking round at Tubbs with lowered eyelashes. 'Do I have to? *The Simpsons* is on in a minute.'

'*The Simpsons* is always on in a minute,' said Beretta. 'Go watch it in the bedroom. Take a rock. Have fun.'

She made a disgusted sound with her tongue, but seeing Beretta's expression change, she got up, took a yellowish piece of crack from the bag, a cheap plastic lighter and one of the pipes and flounced out, slamming the door behind her.

'Stupid bitch,' said Beretta. 'But she gives good head. Maybe you'd like to try her out, Tubbs.'

'Another time maybe,' said Tubbs. 'We're here for business, ain't we?'

'Business and pleasure can always be mixed,' said Beretta with a wolfish grin. 'My Lulu is a good earner when she's in the mood.'

'Fine,' said Tubbs. 'But what about the powder?'

'No problem. You searched this boy?' he said to Moses who shook his head.

'Do it.'

Fuck it, thought Tubbs as Moses gave him another shakedown, this time coming up with his mobile and the niner.

'You don't trust us, man,' said Beretta when Moses passed the gun to him and tossed the telephone on to the floor. Beretta pressed the button on the butt of the pistol to release the magazine, put it on the coffee table then slid back the action and caught the shell which popped out and dropped it into his waistcoat pocket. 'Souvenir,' he said.

'Nothing personal,' said Tubbs. 'But I was carrying a lot of cash.'

'You're safe with us,' said Beretta. 'No one messes with our bidness.'

'I'm glad to hear it,' said Tubbs.

'Sit down, man,' said Beretta, all at once the perfect host. 'Take the weight off your feet. And you sure got some weight there.'

Karl laughed as Tubbs sat in the seat that Lulu had vacated, Karl next to him, Moses standing by the sideboard counting out the money from the plastic bag.

'Drink, smoke, coke?' said Beretta also sitting again.

Tubbs shook his head. 'Where's the stuff?' he asked.

'Patience, man,' said Beretta. 'Moses?'

'All there, boss,' said Moses. 'Nice dirty notes.'

'That's good,' said Beretta, swooping down on the mirror and snarfing up one of the lines. 'I like a man who's exact.'

Although he was being friendly, Tubbs felt the tension in the atmosphere like water running down the walls and wondered if he'd walk out of the flat alive, or be carried out dead and dumped in some obscure and deserted part of the city.

Moses brought the money to Beretta who sat up and wiped his nose on his sleeve. He tossed it on the table and some slipped on to the carpet which he ignored. 'Two thousand quid this morning, ten tonight,' said Beretta lighting a cigarette. 'You've got access to lots of bread, Mr Tubbs.'

'I told you, I got backers.'

'Anyone we know?'

'I doubt it. City folks. More money than sense and a big liking for cocaine.'

'How'd you meet these city folks, you just out of the slammer and all?'

'I made contacts inside.'

'Yeah?'

'Yeah.'

'But you was in there for weed, am I right? It's a big jump from weed to powder. You talking serious Class A here.'

'Might as well be hanged for a sheep as a lamb,' replied Tubbs. 'If I ever get nicked again I go away for a long time. I mean to make some money and go back home.'

'Where's home?'

'JA.'

'You ever been there?'

Tubbs shook his head. 'But I think about it all the time.'

'We all do, man,' said Beretta, looking at the wall as if he could see though it and picture white sands and blue sea. 'But not many make it.'

The atmosphere had lightened as the men talked, but suddenly Beretta was all business again. 'Karl,' he said. 'Fetch the gear.'

Karl stood and left the room. A minute later he returned with another supermarket bag, this one weighed heavily down. He gave it to Beretta who reached inside and brought out two plastic bags full of white powder that Mark might have recognised as being part of the consignment he'd delivered to the warehouse at Loughborough Junction. 'I'm giving you a good deal here, Tubbs,' said Beretta. 'Two K for ten K.'

Tubbs pulled an approving face.

'See, we kinda got this through the back door,' Beretta went on. 'A bargain.'

Not for the three poor bastards you gunned down in cold blood, thought Tubbs, but only said: 'Cheers.'

'But I expect more business from you, big man,' said Beretta. 'This won't last an hour in the city. They got Hoovers for noses, those bastard suits.'

'You can say that again,' said Tubbs. 'May I?' And he reached out his hand.

'What a polite boy,' said Beretta. 'Sure, Mr Tubbs. Have a sample.'

Tubbs picked up a single-sided razor blade from the table and made a small slit in the plastic. He dipped in one sausage-like finger and licked the powder off it. He made a sour face as his mouth numbed out, and Beretta laughed. 'Good or what?' he said.

'Better than good,' replied Tubbs as he made saliva to try and get some feeling back into his dead lips and tongue. 'Man, that's prime.'

'I told you, didn't I?' said Beretta, hardly able to keep the pride out of his voice. 'When I say my product's good I mean it. Now, you want a beer, man?'

All that Tubbs wanted was to leave in one piece and find Mark, but he could feel that to make too swift an exit might set Beretta off. Besides, he reckoned that the Yardie wanted to talk, and any information would be useful. He only hoped that Mark would be patient.

'Sure,' said Tubbs. 'A beer would taste good.'

'Karl,' said Beretta, and Karl went out of the room again. He was obviously low man on the totem. The gopher. Messenger boy.

He returned with four bottles of Red Stripe, moisture condensing on the glass. He passed them round. 'To business,' said Beretta, and he tapped Tubbs's bottle with his own.

'And pleasure,' replied Tubbs, remembering the start of their conversation.

'Sure, pleasure,' said Beretta. 'You want to go see Lulu, make her forget about the fucking *Simpsons*.'

Tubbs was just about to make another excuse when his mobile rang. The room went silent except for the electronic trilling.

He reached for it but Beretta was too quick for him. He snatched it off the floor, pressed the answer button and said: 'Mr Tubbs's phone. How can I be of assistance?'

He listened for a moment. 'I'm afraid he's in conference at the moment. Can I ask who's calling?' He was as polite as a secretary, and Tubbs could see that Beretta was not one to be underestimated.

'I'll see if he can come to the phone,' he said. Then to Tubbs. 'A Mr Marks for you.'

'Cheers,' said Tubbs, taking the instrument and feeling the sweat on his palm. 'Hello,' he said.

'It's me,' said Mark. 'You OK?'

'Never better,' said Tubbs.

'Thank Christ for that. I thought you were dead. I'm outside.'

'No problem,' said Tubbs, smiling at Beretta as he said it. 'Everything's just dandy here.'

'Good. You going to get out all right?'

'A perfect meeting,' said Tubbs. 'I'm just having a beer.'

'I wish I was,' said Mark. 'I'm freezing. This place stinks and I'm starting to get some funny looks from the residents.'

'Then just chill, my friend,' said Tubbs. 'I should be free and clear within the hour.'

'I'm already chilled to the fucking bone, thanks very much,' said Mark. 'Get back to mine, and make sure you're not followed.'

'Sweet,' said Tubbs, and clicked off the connection.

'You got friends waiting?' said Beretta. 'Checking you out?'

'They worry,' said Tubbs taking another swig from his bottle. 'You know how it is.'

'City boys,' said Beretta. 'Don't trust anyone an inch.'

'That's life these days,' said Tubbs. 'And I'd better be moving. Things to do, people to see. Money to make.'

'Sure,' said Beretta and Tubbs knew that this was going to be the toughest part. 'Karl. See Mr Tubbs to his car. Make sure he walks unmolested through our brethren. He's carrying a serious and valuable cargo.'

'Sure, boss,' said Karl, sliding the machete up the sleeve of his jacket.

Tubbs shook hands with Beretta and Moses, picked up the carrier bag and made to leave.

'Ain't you forgotten something, Mr Tubbs?' said Beretta and Tubbs felt sweat break out all over him. Was this the sting? The bit where they took him down and ended up with money and drugs?

Beretta pointed to the table where the Browning lay. 'You may need that,' he said. 'Those City boys take no prisoners, I hear.'

Tubbs breathed a sigh of relief and picked up the gun and the clip and stowed them in separate pockets. 'Nearly forgot,' he said. 'Glad my head's screwed on or I'd forget that.'

'Keep it screwed tight, my man,' said Beretta. 'And keep in touch. I'm only a phone call away.'

'Will do,' said Tubbs. 'Thanks.' And with that, he and Karl left the room. Karl opened the fortified door to the flat and they went down to the car. Many eyes followed their progress, but no one made a move. Tubbs drove the Beemer off the estate and down the first side street he came to. He stopped at a gap by the kerb and sat shaking for fully five minutes before he headed back to John Jenner's house.

Eventually he was calm enough to drive and made the short journey in minutes, calling Mark on the way to open the gates. When he'd parked the car he went to the front door where Mark hugged him hard. 'You did well, son,' he said.

'Nearly needed new underwear,' replied Tubbs as he followed Mark into the living room. 'Thought for sure I'd go caca when they found my gun.'

'You're the man,' said Mark.

'Too right,' agreed John Jenner from his seat in front of the fire.

'Let's see what we've got here,' said Mark taking the plastic bag of dope from Tubbs. 'You got a good deal, son.'

'Fucking good,' grumbled John Jenner. 'It cost them nixes.'

'I think they need readies,' said Tubbs.

'That suits us,' said Mark. 'And we know where they live, who's about and the layout of the place.'

'We sure do. It's imprinted on my mind for ever.'

'You did so good, Tubbs,' said Jenner. 'Reminds me of another bloke I once knew, name of Sharman. He went into a flat for me too, but it didn't work out so well.'

'What happened?' asked Tubbs, glass in hand, reclining in the armchair.

'It's a long story.'

'We've got time.' There was nothing Tubbs liked better than old war stories. John Jenner knew that and he sat back and filled the boys in on the story so far.

'So he came good with the grass,' said Tubbs. 'Earned his bread.'

'Ah, but it gets better.'

*　*　*

Sharman got another call from Lawson the next day. This time the meeting was at a bar in St Catherine's Dock, all chrome and leather, and foliage-filled coloured drinks. 'A bit poncified,' said Sharman, when he joined the lawyer.

'Suits me,' said Lawson.

Sharman made no comment.

'You heard what happened?' asked Lawson.

Sharman nodded.

'John's very pleased.'

'Good.'

'And no policemen involved.'

'I heard one's got a big bill at Sketchley's.'

'He'll get over it.'

'I expect so.'

'So what now?' asked the policeman.

'There's something else you can do for us.'

'What?' asked Sharman, lighting a cigarette.

'Simple. We need someone to mind one of our boys going into a very nasty place.'

'Like?'

'You know the Lion Estate?'

'Jesus, do I.'

'We're making a drop there on Thursday next. The person we're delivering to owes John a great deal of money. Now he wants more supplies and has promised to make good the whole debt when we deliver the next consignment.'

'And you think maybe there's going to be a rip off.'

'Precisely.'

'How much are we talking?'

'Altogether, fifty grand's worth.'

'That is a lot of money. Specially round there. People kill their grannies on the Lion for a quid.'

'Exactly.'

'And who's the face you're delivering to?'

'Lionel Godey.'

'Lionel? Bloody hell, I thought he was inside.'

'He's out on bail.'

'And what bent brief arranged that?'

Lawson smiled.

'I thought as much,' said Sharman. 'You do mix with the cream.'

'I have to earn a living.'

'Sounds to me as if you're running with the hare and hunting with the hounds.'

'Is that the sound of the pot calling the kettle black? My loyalties always have and always will lie with John. But I'm the best there is, and besides, he couldn't collect if Godey was on remand.'

'Fair enough,' said Sharman.

'So you'll do it?'

'How much?'

'What?'

'How much for me when I collect the dough?'

'You don't have to collect. They don't know you. Tony Wiltse is the courier. He works for John.'

'I know him.'

'Excellent. He's a good lad with a clean record.'

'So how much?'

'Five hundred pounds.'

'A monkey to go up against Lionel and Christ knows how many others on the Lion? Do behave.'

'Scared, Nick?'

'Bloody terrified.'

'Good. That's how you keep sharp in this line of business.'

'A grand,' said Sharman.

'Funny. That's exactly what John said you'd ask.'

'Then he's smarter than you.'

'In some ways.'

'And you owe me for Skinner. The other half. And I'll need to be tooled up.'

Lawson put his briefcase on the table and said, 'It's all been taken care of. Open it.'

Sharman smiled, put the case on his lap, flipped the latches and opened the top so that only he could see inside. He smiled as he saw a Beretta nine millimetre semi-automatic pistol, a stack of banded ten pound notes and another brown envelope.

'There's five hundred in each bundle,' said Lawson. 'Plus the other five K. Old notes. Non-consecutive. There's also instructions on where to meet Tony and what time on Thursday. I take it you're free that afternoon.'

'You take it right, David,' said Sharman and he shut the case. 'Another drink?'

'Lovely. But be warned, Nick. You're getting in deep. Make sure your waterwings are on tight.'

'No problem,' said Sharman as he rose to go to the bar. 'I can walk on water, me.'

Lawson grinned. 'That's over eleven grand you've had since we started working together. Now maybe you can get rid of that piece of junk on your wrist. Another drink?'

Sharman reddened as he looked at the fake Swiss watch he was wearing. On his way home that night he dropped it down a drain.

The Lion Estate was in Deptford, between Evelyn Street and the river. There was a fine view of The Isle Of Dogs from the upper floors of the four tower blocks, which stood guard over the lowrise flats and the playground in the centre. 'Playground' was a euphemism for a muddy area in the middle of the place where the disaffected youth played football among dog shit and used syringes.

Sharman met Tony Wiltse at the Traveller's Rest boozer in Deptford High Street at ten-to-three as instructed. Not that any sensible traveller would wish to rest in its dilapidated bars at that time in its history.

Sharman went to the bar, ordered a pint and looked at Wiltse in the mirror behind the jump. Wiltse rose and walked over to him, carrying a Head sports bag. 'Nick,' he said.

'Tony,' said Sharman. 'How's it going? Drink?'

'I'll have a goldie.' Sharman ordered a large scotch from the slattern behind the bar and they took their drinks to a table as far away from the counter as possible. 'You carrying?' asked Wiltse.

'Yeah. You?'

Wiltse shook his head. 'Not me. Not my style. I work in the office mostly, doing the accounts. That's why you're here.'

Sharman nodded. 'And there's just you and me?'

'No. We've got a driver. Ricky. He's in the car outside. You parked up?'

'On a meter. Two hours.'

'That'll do. I hate this kind of fucking job,' said Wiltse.

'I would've thought they'd have sent in a team,' said Sharman. 'There's a lot of cash involved.'

'John didn't want Lionel to think he didn't trust him.'

'But he doesn't.'

'That don't matter. It's all down to respect.'

Shit, thought Sharman. I'm being set up here. A number cruncher and a bent copper. If we never come out, who's going to miss us?

Sharman swallowed the rest of his drink and looked at his watch. The Timex. He still hadn't got over Lawson recognising the snide Rolex for what it was. 'Three o'clock,' he said. 'There's only fifteen minutes. We'd better go.'

Wiltse nodded, sunk his whisky, grabbed the bag and they left the pub together.

Ricky was sitting behind the wheel of a navy blue Jaguar XJ illegally parked opposite the pub. Wiltse got into the front passenger seat and Sharman climbed in the back, the Beretta digging painfully into his groin as he did so. 'Ricky, this is Mr...'

'Nick,' interrupted Sharman. 'Just Nick.'

'Oh, sure,' said Wiltse.

Ricky didn't seem to care either way, he just started the engine, engaged drive and pulled into the traffic without a word.

The Lion was only a few minutes away and it had started to rain by the time they drove on to the estate. Sharman peered through water streaked windows at the water-streaked buildings and shook his head, wondering how anyone could live in such a place. I don't like this, he thought as he eased the automatic from his belt and quietly pulled back the slide, putting a bullet into the chamber and pulling back the hammer. He slid it gingerly back into place, thinking that this was not the time to put a bullet into his balls.

Ricky steered the car through the potholes and pulled up outside one of the tower blocks. 'First floor,' said Wiltse. 'Just as sodding well. The lifts never work and they're full of shit, anyway.'

Sharman just grunted a reply and they got out into the rain and went for the front door.

The foyer was dank and gloomy and Sharman mentally agreed it was just as well that they only had to go up two flights of stone steps to the first floor.

The door of the flat was halfway down a graffiti-covered corridor and Wiltse banged on it. Once there had been a square of glass in the door, but it had been replaced with plywood. Two bare wires protruded from where a doorbell might have been and the letterbox and knocker had been ripped off, leaving a toothless mouth of a hole that was now backed with metal.

After a minute, Wiltse grimaced and hammered again, harder this time.

Eventually the two men heard the sound of locks being disengaged and the door opened on a heavy steel chain.

'Come on, Lionel,' said Wiltse. 'Open up. It's me.'

'Who's that with you?' demanded a voice from the darkened inside.

'Nick.'

'Nick who?'

'Nick It-doesn't-matter,' said Sharman. 'Just open up for Christ's sake. It stinks out here.'

'Not much better inside,' said the voice, but the chain came off and the door opened to reveal a shell-suited figure.

Wiltse and Sharman slid inside and the door was locked and bolted behind them.

In fact, the interior of the flat was a good deal sweeter than it had looked from the hallway. The walls were painted pale blue and there was a carpet on the floor on which the pattern was still discernible. 'Down here,' said the man who'd opened the door.

Sharman recognised him from some mug shots he'd seen back at Kennington Police Station as Lionel Godey.

He led them into the living room where thick curtains covered the windows. Sharman went over, pulled one aside and looked straight down into Ricky's eyes behind the wet windscreen of the Jag.

'Oi,' said Lionel. 'Don't take fucking liberties.'

'Just checking we hadn't been towed away,' said Sharman.

'Fat chance of that round here.'

'Joke,' said Sharman.

'I don't like jokes,' said Lionel. 'Or the people who make them.'

'Forget it,' said Wiltse. 'We're here for business.'

'Yeah,' said Lionel, giving Sharman a dagger look. 'Show.'

'The money,' said Wiltse.

'It's here.'

'Show,' said Sharman, already tired of the whole deal.

'Who is this mug?' said Lionel.

'A friend,' said Wiltse.

'Well, he wants to watch himself.'

And you want to watch yourself, if I ever get you in the cells one fine night, thought Sharman, but said nothing. 'He will,' said Wiltse and shot Sharman a glance that said 'keep your mouth shut'. Sharman nodded.

'All right,' said Wiltse. 'He'll keep it buttoned. Now come on, Lionel, let's get on with it. We haven't got all day.'

'No problem,' said Lionel, now sure of his place in the pecking order. 'Jack!' he shouted.

After a moment, another man, heavily built, wearing a leather jacket and jeans, entered the room carrying an identical bag to Wiltse's. He put it on the table and unzipped it. 'There you go,' he said.

Wiltse put his bag next to it, and opened it too. Inside were a number of tightly bound, clear plastic bags containing white powder. 'It's good stuff,' said Wiltse.

330

'It had better be,' said Lionel.

Wiltse opened the first bag and looked inside. When he looked up there was a puzzled expression on his face. 'What's this?' he said.

'The money,' replied Lionel. 'Twenty thousand.'

'What about the rest?' asked Wiltse.

'A bit of a problem,' said Lionel. 'Cash flow.'

'Fuck cash flow,' said Wiltse. 'The deal was you paid up to date. Fifty K. You taking the piss or what?'

Sharman saw the look between Lionel and Jack and knew that it was all starting to go wrong. Or at least that's what his instinct told him. He unbuttoned his jacket.

'You see, last time the merchandise wasn't up to scratch. Whoever walked on it had big boots,' said Lionel.

'It was good gear,' protested Wiltse.

'Once upon a time,' said Lionel.

'Are you saying we're doing you up?' demanded Wiltse.

'It's all in the mix,' said Lionel. 'We want to make sure this lot is OK before we part with any more dough.'

'John isn't going to like this,' said Wiltse.

'How about this then?' said Jack and pulled a small revolver from the pocket of his leather.

Fuck, thought Sharman, reaching for his gun.

What happened next changed him from the man he was — a small-time chancer with an attitude — to what he was to become for the rest of his life: a man who went to sleep at night with ghosts around his bed.

The first shot from Jack's pistol went wide, digging plaster from the wall beside Sharman's head, as the copper fired back hitting Jack in the shoulder and spinning him round. Then Lionel tugged a big automatic from somewhere inside his shellsuit and Sharman fired straight into his face. The man tripped over his feet and the gun went off and a huge gout of blood exploded from Wiltse's neck and he fell to the floor. Jack shouted something Sharman couldn't understand and brought his gun up and Sharman finished him with a shot to the chest. He stood in the smoke-filled room, ears ringing from the gunshots, and looked at the three dead men on the floor. 'Fuck,' he said aloud as he lowered his warm gun. 'That's me fucked.'

* * *

'They were his very words when he told us the story,' said Jenner to the two young men.

'What happened?' asked Tubbs. 'Did he go down?'

'Sharman? You're having a laugh, aincha?' said John Jenner. 'Slipperiest fucker in all Christendom was our Nick. And still is, from what I hear.'

'So?' asked Mark who hadn't heard that particular story before.

'He stuck his gun in Tony's hand, fired it again using his finger, cold blooded bastard, so that the body would have powder residue on it. Then took the dough and the gear and strolled down to the motor, cool as you like, and made Ricky drive him up to Lawson's office. Dumped the lot on David's desk and asked for another two grand. One each for both the geezers he'd shot. Never looked back after that.'

'Christ,' said Tubbs.

'Christ is right,' said Jenner.

'But of course you only had his word for it,' said Mark.

'Do what?' Jenner said.

'How do you know that he didn't collect the whole fifty, shoot everyone and keep the thirty grand for himself?'

'You're a cynical bastard, Mark,' said Jenner. 'And I do like that in a man. In fact, it did cross my mind at the time. But I don't think so. Sharman was cold, but not that cold. Maybe later it would've been something he'd do, but that was early days. Anyway, it's all water under the bridge now. Over twenty years ago. Who cares? Not me. He more than made up for it later with little jobs he did for us. I wish he was here now.'

'Don't you trust us, Uncle, is that it?' asked Mark.

But before Jenner could answer, Tubbs's phone rang.

TWENTY-SIX

The trio looked at each other, then Mark nodded and Tubbs fished his phone out of his pocket. 'Yeah,' he said. 'Oh, it's you, Eddie. No. Everything went fine.' He looked at Mark who gestured for the phone which Tubbs passed over.

'Hey, Eddie,' said Mark. 'How you doing?' he listened. 'Good. Tubbs did great, but he could've been in big trouble. So next time, we do the biz, OK?' A pause. 'Fine. Look, let's meet up tomorrow at the usual place in Stockwell. We'll talk then. Right. Midday. See ya.' And he closed the phone.

'Listen,' said Tubbs, when Mark gave him the phone back. 'I'd better be off.'

'OK, Tubbsy?' said Mark. 'You heard that?'

Tubbs nodded.

'Twelve o'clock in the Four Feathers. We'll plan our strategy.'

'Sounds good,' said Tubbs and got to his feet. 'Later, Mr Jenner,' he said.

'Be careful driving home,' said Jenner. 'You did well tonight. I owe you.'

'I'm being well paid,' replied Tubbs.

'Money isn't everything.'

'Only rich people say that,' said Tubbs. 'You take care too,' and Mark saw him to the front door.

'He's right,' said Mark as they stood in the hall. 'You were the business.'

'Like riding a bike,' said Tubbs. 'Just what you said. I miss the old days, and this is just the same.'

'If you say so, Tubbs,' said Mark and he hugged his old friend before opening the front door. 'Be safe.'

'I'll try.' Tubbs went to his car and headed home.

Mark went back to where John Jenner was rolling the latest in a long line of spliffs. 'So far, so good,' he said.

'Yeah. But the hard part's still to come,' warned Jenner. 'The killing bit.'

Mark went upstairs and called Linda on his mobile, but her machine picked up. He didn't leave a message.

The next day, Mark was early for the meet in the pub, but Eddie had beaten him to it. He was sipping Guinness and looking longingly at the tightly skirted backside of the barmaid who was bending over the lower shelves, too busy bottling up to notice his glances.

'You'll go blind,' said Mark, once he'd joined him at the bar.

'Jesus, but that's a work of art,' said Eddie. 'Just look at those buns.'

Mark grinned and when the barmaid noticed he ordered a lager. 'Why don't you ask her out?' he said when he'd been served.

'Fat chance.'

'You never know until you try.'

'I ain't been out with a woman for… Christ. More than two years.'

'So your old right hand gets plenty of exercise?'

'Not really. After a bit you don't miss it anymore.'

'But if you get this money…'

'I'll clean up my act. Lose some weight. Go to the gym. Buy some decent clothes and a car.'

'Or go to JA with Tubbs and cook chicken.'

'It's an option. You say the boy done well?'

'Oscar-winning from what I can gather. I was outside hiding in the garbage. It was a solo effort on his part.'

'He's got some bottle.'

'Always had, remember. It's not something you forget.'

'I dunno, Mark,' said Eddie. 'I'm shitting myself — straight up.'

'You'll be OK, Ed,' said Mark. 'Trust me.'

'I do.'

Just then Tubbs himself came in through the front door and joined them at the bar, ordering a small lager for himself. 'They've been on.'

'Who?' asked Eddie.

'The pros from Dover,' said Tubbs. Taking in his mystified expression, he added: 'Beretta.'

'That was fast,' said Mark.

'Tell me about it. It was six this morning.'

'Don't he ever sleep?' asked Eddie.

'With all the charlie he's got, I doubt he does,' said Tubbs. 'Probably sits up all night in that flat with his bird sucking him off and wondering what next for world domination.'

'What's he want?' asked Mark.

'See if I wanted more.'

'What'd you say?'

'That I was working on it.'

'Good,' said Mark. 'That means the ball's in our court. We name the time and place, then we take them down.'

'In the flat?' said Tubbs.

'No. Too confined. Too many places they can lie low. Remember what Uncle John told us about that geezer Sharman.'

'Who?' asked Eddie.

Mark summarised Jenner's tale of the previous night. 'We take them outside, clean.'

'What about the cops?' asked Eddie.

'Cops,' said Mark. 'Fuck 'em. What do they know? These days they're only interested in catching speeders and making money. We'll be gone before they know what's happening.'

'But what about the dope?' said Tubbs. 'And their dough? It'll be up in the flat.'

'So we do them in the street, then go get what we need.'

'We don't know where they keep it.'

'It's a small council flat. Where are they going to put it? How long did it take – Karl, was it? – to fetch it?'

'A minute.'

'There you go. It was probably on the kitchen table in clear sight.'

These fuckers think they're fireproof.'

'You make it sound so simple.'

'It is.'

'And then we split the profits.'

'That's the game,' said Mark. 'And then Eddie can ask that barmaid out on a date.'

'Fuck off,' said Eddie. 'If I'm rich I want to go out with someone with class as well as arse.'

'There's no answer to that,' said Tubbs. 'So when do we do it, Mark?'

'Soon as. Give them a day to think you've been working hard at shifting that gear, then we go.'

'Sounds like a plan,' said Tubbs.

And it was. A simple plan. But even the simplest plans have a habit of going awry.

Though not at first.

As Mark had instructed, Tubbs held fire for twenty-four hours. He'd received a few calls from Beretta, checking on how things were going, but he just played it cool, telling him things were progressing nicely and that the product was going well, that everyone involved was happy with the quality. More than happy, in fact.

Then, early on the following morning, the three met at John Jenner's house and put the second part of the plan into operation.

Tubbs called Beretta on his mobile. 'Hey man,' he said. 'It's me, Mr Tubbs. Things are going better than expected and I'm almost dry. What's the chance of a meet?' He nodded. 'That's good. I'm holding large.' He nodded again at what was being said on the other end of the connection. 'Twenty-five. Yeah. You can do that today? Fine. No more on the phone. How about a drink in that boozer where we first met, later? Yeah. Last orders? That'll be fine. Around eleven then. See you there. And maybe we can go on and celebrate. That'll be dandy. Later then.' And he pressed the kill button. 'You heard,' he said to Mark and Eddie. 'We're on.'

'Perfect,' said Mark.

When eleven pm rolled around, Tubbs parked his BMW behind

Beretta's silver Lexus outside the pub. Inside, things were winding down after a quiet weeknight session. Tubbs pushed open the door and saw Beretta, Karl, Moses, and a woman he hadn't seen before but who was cut from the same cloth as Lulu, sitting at a corner table that was covered in dirty glasses and overflowing ashtrays. The £25,000 that Mark had given him from the fast depleting stash in John Jenner's safe was in a shoulder bag, the Browning down the back of his pants, and his mobile phone, charged up, live and connected to Mark's in the top pocket of his jacket. From where Mark and Eddie were sitting, up on the estate, in an anonymous and untraceable Ford Escort – courtesy of Dev – they could hear everything that was said. Both were dressed in black, gloved up, with balaclava helmets rolled up over their heads, like watch caps.

'Mr Tubbs, my man,' said Beretta as Tubbs approached the table. 'Good to see you again. Did I not say that you'd be back soon?'

'You did, and you were right,' Tubbs agreed.

'You know everyone except for Comfort. She's my number two woman.'

Comfort looked to be so out of it, she didn't care what number she was. Or maybe she just knew better than to argue. She just looked up at Tubbs with unfocused eyes, then buried her face in her drink.

'A line, my man?' asked Beretta, but Tubbs shook his head.

'Later,' he said. 'Let's get down to business.'

'Not before you've had a drink. Hey Shorty, another round here and…?' he made a quizzical face at Tubbs.

'Lager,' said Tubbs.

'A lager for my friend.'

The same little barman put down the cloth he'd been using to dry a row of glasses, and busied himself with the order.

'Sit down,' said Beretta. Tubbs complied and Shorty rushed over with a tray of full glasses which he distributed around the table before starting to clear away the empties. 'Leave them,' said Beretta, and he did.

Tubbs placed the bag of cash between his feet and lifted his glass, toasted the quartet and drank.

'So business is good,' said Beretta.

Tubbs nodded.

'Like I said it would. And you have money?'

Another nod from Tubbs.

'Fine. We'll finish this and go back to mine. Lulu's sleeping one off, but I'm sure we can scare her out of bed, and then we party.'

'Sounds good,' said Tubbs.

Inside the Escort, Mark gave Eddie the thumbs up and pressed the mute button on his phone. 'They'll be coming soon,' he said. 'Get ready.'

Eddie reached round for the sawn-off shotgun he'd owned since the 80s, broke it open and inserted two twelve-gauge shells into the breach. Then he snapped it shut and pulled back the hammers.

For the first time, Mark recognised the boy who'd run wild on the streets of south London all those years ago, and he knew that everything was going to be fine. He himself was carrying one of the guns that he'd kept hidden in a secret compartment built into the Range Rover he'd driven back from the Continent — a twenty-shot, fully automatic, drumloaded shotgun, known as a 'street sweeper'. He'd alternated buckshot and solid shells when loading it and Eddie's eyes had almost popped out of their sockets when he'd shown it to him. 'You hardly need us,' he'd said, and Mark had just grinned and winked at him. It felt good to hold the heavy weapon in his hands and smell the old gunpowder that never went away, despite almost constant cleaning.

Mark dropped the gun on to the back seat, started the car and drove closer to Beretta's block. He killed the engine and clicked off the mute button on his mobile. 'Let's get this show on the road,' he heard Beretta say, and gave Eddie the thumbs up again.

Back at the pub, the five at the table were the last customers in, the jukebox was turned off and the lights dimmed. Behind the bar, Shorty stood hesitantly, wondering if Beretta's crew were looking for a lock in, or whether for once he might get to see his bed before dawn.

Bed it was. As the four men rose, Beretta pulled Comfort to her feet and they left without saying thanks. Shorty shook his head and went to the door and locked it.

Outside, the five of them split up to their separate cars and set off towards the estate.

'We're on our way,' was all Tubbs said before surreptitiously switching off his phone.

'They're coming,' said Mark to Eddie, and did the same.

The silver grey Lexus slid like a big fish through the streets of Brixton, its headlights casting long shadows into the night, closely followed by Tubbs's BMW. Inside the lead car the three black men and their woman sat back, secure in their own invincibility, as the CD player pumped out loud garage music.

The BMW drew up outside the block of flats where Beretta kept his safe house. The engine died and the music and lights were extinguished. The Beemer pulled in two car lengths behind it.

Opposite, in the Ford, Mark said: 'They're here.'

He and Eddie looked at each other, pulled the balaclavas down over their faces, pushed opened their doors and stepped out. 'Oi, junkie!' Mark shouted over the top of the car. 'Hold on a minute.'

All four turned as one. Moses and Karl one side of the car, Beretta and the woman the other. The woman hadn't been in the equation originally, but it was too late to worry about her now. Just another innocent victim. Collateral damage. Tubbs's driver's door opened too and he emerged, the Browning in his right hand.

'Just stand still,' said Mark and his words rang out clearly into the night air, but Beretta and his men paid no attention. 'Go Dizzy,' yelled Mark as he pulled the trigger on the streetsweeper and Eddie fired too, the double blast from the two shots that sounded as one echoing around the flats.

The twin blasts cut Moses and Karl down, one load of buckshot hitting Moses in the chest and the other smashing into Karl's side. They fell against the body of the Lexus in tandem and bounced back on to the road, their bodies ripped and torn by the lead, both of the car's side windows imploded into crystal dust.

Tubbs aimed at Beretta, pulled the trigger, but nothing happened and he cursed and slapped at the safety catch on his pistol as Beretta ducked behind the car reaching into his coat for the gun hidden there. The woman just stood, her hand going to her mouth to cut off the scream that was growing in her throat.

Mark fired again and almost blew her head from her shoulders. The hand covering her face was severed from its wrist and flew across the pavement, landing on the scruffy grass verge in front of the block.

Beretta, meanwhile, crabbed himself away from the car, attempting to take shelter behind the low wall that separated the estate from the public road. He produced a handgun as he went. In fact, he would've been better employed staying where he was and engaging the gunmen, but the sight and sound of the attack had momentarily panicked him and he'd lost his usual cool as the woman's blood had splashed over his clothes.

Lights were coming on all over the blocks, and a young white couple heading out to buy a late fish supper at the chip shop round the corner were suddenly illuminated as they crossed the grass, and Eddie turned and aimed his shooter in their direction.

'Leave 'em,' yelled Mark, high on adrenalin, and Eddie put up his gun.

That was his mistake. Although dying, Karl had managed to haul the Glock he carried in a holster underneath one arm and fire it once before slumping back on the bloody road. More by luck than judgment, the bullet hit Eddie in the forehead and he was dead before he hit the ground.

'Shit,' screamed Mark, firing at Karl; his body jumped and was still, his gun sliding across the street into the gutter.

Tubbs was firing at Beretta, who was sheltered by the wall. Beretta returned fire and knocked Tubbs to the ground. It was all going wrong. Mark kept pumping slugs and shot towards Beretta, sending lumps of brick off the wall, but otherwise producing no effect. Then Tubbs climbed to his feet, blood pumping from his wound and he ran towards Beretta, crossing between Mark and his target and forcing him to hold fire.

'Get down, Tubbs!' Mark shouted, but it was too late. At point blank range Beretta fired at Tubbs and he crashed to the ground, blood pooling black under his body. Beretta snaked along the ground to the front door of the flats. As he entered, Mark fired once more and saw a hit, but Beretta double tapped a response and forced him to duck down behind the Ford.

Mark peered over the bonnet, but all he could see was the door swinging shut behind Beretta. Things had gone from bad to worse. A cursory glance at the bodies of his friends confirmed their demise, and he considered getting into the Ford and leaving but he wouldn't give Beretta the satisfaction. Instead he ran across the street and into the front of the block.

As Mark hit the cracked and filthy frosted glass doors with his shoulder, ready to take his revenge on Beretta in a blast of fire, he saw the lift doors closing.

Shit, he thought. Just my bad luck: this would be the night the sodding lift works. Ten fucking floors. And the only way is shanks's pony. He carefully opened the door to the stairs, just in case Beretta had tried to fool him and was waiting, but the well was empty. Empty, dark and smelly, it echoed with every step and he climbed up.

Wet with sweat, his legs shaking at the unaccustomed exercise, Mark listened out in case Beretta was lying in wait at the top stairwell, but it was deserted. Must get a bike, he thought. Or, if I get out of this alive, maybe I'll join a gym, thinking of what Eddie had said in the pub the last time they'd met. No exercise for him now, or romantic nights in the arms of an Irish barmaid. Mark paused for a moment before entering the tenth floor corridor, his ears waiting for the sound of sirens which must eventually come. Surely someone had called three nines after the fire-fight in the very public street outside? But all was quiet.

Gently once again, Mark pushed open the door at the end of the short landing and he peered down the tunnel. All was still and quiet: the lift doors were open and the car was empty.

Mark walked down the corridor on tiptoe until he came to flat number 80. The door was locked and he didn't have a key.

'Knock, knock,' he said, then stood at an angle to the door, raised his weapon and fired at the lock. The sound of the explosions was deafening in the confined space and sparks and smoke filled the hallway. But after the fourth round the reinforced door sagged and he booted it open with his Doc Marten shod foot. 'Beretta,' he yelled, although he could hardly hear his own voice after the concussion from the powerful shotgun. 'Give it up, you bastard. I'm coming in.'

There was no reply that he could hear, so he flattened himself against the wall and peered through the doorway. The flat's small hallway was empty and the centre light was out, making it dark and shadowy. A thin glow shone under the bottom of the door at the end. He tried to remember how Tubbs had described the interior of the apartment. Must be the living room, he thought. But where was Beretta? And how badly was he hit?

Still there was no sound of the cops. But by now, Mark was so deafened by the gunshots and concentrating so deeply on every sound and movement inside the flat that, for all he knew, there could be armed response coppers on the stairs right now toting H&Ks.

Fuck 'em, he thought, as he fully reloaded the streetsweeper, dropping empty, smoking cartridge cases into his pocket. Leave nothing except the dead had always been his motto. He padded across the carpet, bent almost double and leaning to one side to leave as small a target as possible. There were closed doors on both sides of the hall but he ignored them. Go to the light, was all he could think. Go to the light and kill the bastard who had killed his friends.

And then he was there.

At the closed door, behind which, God only knew...

He raised the gun to the door and pulled the trigger. The wood bowed immediately and a huge opening appeared in the centre. Mark dodged back into the closest doorway as more holes were punched into the cheap wood – this time from inside and from a handgun.

Yes, my man, thought Mark. You're there, and I'm going to huff and puff and blow your house down. Once again his finger found the trigger of the shotgun and he pumped half a dozen rounds at the door, which literally blew off its hinges. He ran to the doorway and tumbled inside, hiding behind a chair. After a few seconds he took a look. The place was a mess, smoke wreathing around a single lamp burning in the corner.

On the coffee table bags of cocaine and stacks of cash were piled high and on the sofa beyond, half sitting, half lying was Beretta, his face grey and old-looking, one hand covering the bloody wound in his side, blood soaking through his white shirt. In his other hand, he held his gun, the weapon almost slipping from his gore-covered fingers.

'Gotcha,' said Mark standing, and Beretta looked up through hooded eyes and raised the pistol as if it weighed a ton. 'Too late,' said Mark. 'This is for Tubbs and Eddie,' and he fired once again over the table at Beretta's chest, the spread of the buckshot blowing the drugs and money into the air in a cloud of powder and torn paper before ripping another hole in the black man's torso.

Mark stood in the smoke and dust, licking at the coke that settled on his top lip and laughed out loud. All for what? he thought. All for fuck all. And, just as he was about to turn and leave, he felt a terrible blow to his back. He turned and saw a young black woman standing behind him, a long kitchen knife in her hand streaked with blood, about to stab him again. Lulu he thought. The beautiful Lulu. Bloody hell, I forgot all about her, and there she was hiding, all the time waiting to stab me in the back. How typical of a woman. He pushed the barrel of the streetsweeper deep into her skinny stomach and fired, almost cutting her completely in half and sending long trails of hot blood up the wall behind her. She doubled up, dropped the knife and fell on to the carpet hard, twitched twice and was still.

'Stupid bitch,' Mark said aloud to her bloody corpse, as the pain from the stab wound wracked his body and he knew he was in trouble. He looked at the wreck of the room, the cocaine settling on every surface like snow, making Beretta's face as white as a circus clown's and contrasting surreally with a thin dribble of blood that trickled from the side of his mouth. Mark knew he had to get out of there, quick. And empty handed, at that.

He went back down the hall into the corridor. A couple of the front doors were cracked open slightly as the inhabitants checked out the results of the short battle that had intruded on their late night telly viewing, but when he raised his gun they slammed shut in his face, one by one.

And then, through his battered eardrums he finally did hear the sound of sirens getting closer, and knew that his troubles might only just have begun.

He ran to the still open lift and pressed the button for the first floor. Slowly the doors closed and it descended, and he could hear nothing but the creaking of its old machinery. Finally, after what seemed like forever, the doors opened to the sound of sirens right outside and he knew he'd have to abandon the bodies of his friends, as well as the Ford and the BMW, to the forces of law and order, and all that that entailed.

When he'd been hiding in the rubbish chute a couple of days earlier, he'd noticed that the opening on the first floor was big enough for a man to slide down. Now he ran down the corridor and pushed himself out through the gap, his legs dangling, and breathed in the first fresh air in what seemed like hours. It didn't matter that this was 'fresh' air fouled by the stink of the inhabitants' garbage. All was quiet at the back of the flats, the commotion of cops and civilians exclusively at the front. Mark took another deep breath and jumped down to the ground below, landing awkwardly, the shock shooting up to the wound he could feel was still bleeding into his clothes. But how badly he was hurt he had no idea.

He limped off over the scrubby grass towards the edge of the estate. Behind him he heard a shout, which only made him run faster, although the pain of the wound in his back made him feel weak and dizzy.

If I can get to the road, he thought, I'll be all right. Just the road. Dear God, let me make it to the road.

By this time sirens were coming from all directions and Mark knew that he was close to capture and a life sentence. Not fucking likely, he thought. I'm not going inside, not with Jimmy Hunter due out any time now. I want that bastard, outside, for myself.

Mark jumped over the low wall of the estate before he realised he was still carrying his gun. Not something to be seen with, he reckoned, and straight away saw a skip outside a terraced house being done up by some optimist, convinced that Brixton was going to be the 'new Notting Hill'. He stuffed it and his balaclava deep into the building waste that littered the skip. And blessing the fact that his dark clothes would disguise any blood stains, he straightened his shoulders with an effort, and walked confidently along the pavement. Just then a squad car came screaming round the corner, seeming to slow at the sight of him, then picked up speed, blues flashing and two-tone sirens yelping, heading back the way he'd come.

Mark breathed a real sigh of relief, even though it hurt, turned the corner, and headed for John Jenner's house.

It wasn't much of a walk, but Mark had to stay in the shadows, ducking down behind parked motors whenever a police car showed, which was often, and by the time he got there, he was weak and dizzy from loss of blood. He rang the bell by the front gate, and after what seemed an eternity, Chas buzzed him in.

'Christ, what happened?' asked the big man once they'd arrived in the kitchen, Mark sinking into a chair.

'Gone to shit,' said Mark. 'Get me a drink will you? Something strong.'

'You look like death,' said Chas, doing as he was asked, and pouring Mark a large brandy from a bottle of Remy on the counter.

'Not me,' replied Mark. 'Tubbs, Eddie. All the spades. She stabbed me.'

'Who?'

'Beretta's bird. Get Uncle John.'

Chas rushed out and reappeared a moment later with John Jenner. 'Oh my God, Mark,' he said. 'What's happened to you?'

'I've been stabbed. Uncle, I'm sorry, it all went…'

'Never mind about all that now,' said Jenner. 'Let me see.'

Mark slumped forward in the chair and the older man looked at his back. 'Hospital,' he said. 'Chas get an ambulance…'

'No,' said Mark. 'You fix me up.'

'This is serious,' said Jenner.

'No,' repeated Mark. 'If it'd hit anything vital, I'd be dead.'

'You look like you almost are,' said Chas.

'I'll be all right. I just need patching up.'

'Martine,' said Jenner. 'She's upstairs. She'll do it. She knows some first aid. Get her, Chas.'

345

'Not Martine,' protested Mark.

'Yes, Martine,' insisted Jenner. 'Go on, Chas.'

Once again the big man left the room. In a few minutes he arrived back with Martine in tow. 'What the hell?' she said, seeing Mark's parchment-white face and the blood that was now beginning to drip on to the floor. 'What have you done?'

'You should see the other fellah,' said Mark with a humourless grin. 'Can you stop the bleeding?'

'Let's see,' said Martine. 'Take off your top.'

With difficulty and some help from her, Mark managed to strip down to his bare skin. The blood had started to clot, but pulling away his shirt and T-shirt started it off again. Meanwhile Chas had found a box of medical supplies, including bandages and tape. 'Haven't needed this for ages,' he said. 'But we're always prepared.'

'Right, you two,' said Martine to Chas and Jenner. 'Out.'

Reluctantly the two men left the room and Martine said: 'I've got you all to myself again,' she said. 'And half naked too.'

'But not capable,' said Mark.

'Don't you believe it,' she replied. 'I can make the dead dance.'

'I'm not dead yet.'

She reversed the kitchen chair and made Mark sit facing the back and examined the wound. 'You should get this seen to properly,' she said. 'It's deep and there's some fabric been pushed inside. It could get infected.'

'I'll survive. Just patch me up so's I can go and speak to Uncle John. And I'm afraid he's not going to like what I've got to tell him.'

'Not a bad bod,' she said, ignoring him. 'A bit scarred up. This isn't the first time you've been in the wars, is it?'

'I've had my share.'

'I never saw it properly the last time, in the dark.' She ran her hand down his spine and said: 'And I could've been all yours. Instead of that cross-eyed bitch who always fucks you up.'

'Martine,' said Mark. 'Just do it, will you?'

'Sure.' She busied herself cleaning up the wound and got hold of the

346

bottle of brandy. 'This might sting,' she said and splashed the spirit into the cut.

'Fucking hell!' Mark yelled, almost passing out from the shock. 'Careful.'

'Don't be such a baby.' And then, much more gently than Mark expected, she taped the wound together with butterfly strips of tape and bandaged his shoulder, running the fabric under his armpit. 'That should do,' she said finally. 'Not *Casualty* exactly, but it's the best I can manage with what I've got.' She handed him a bottle of pills. 'These are painkillers. A bit past their sell-by date, but they might help.'

Mark undid the bottle and swallowed a couple of pills, washed down with brandy. 'Thanks,' he said. 'I'd better find some clean clothes.'

'I'll go,' said Martine, gathering up his bloodstained garments. 'And I'll get Chas to burn these.'

'Thanks again,' said Mark.

'You know, we could've been magic,' said Martine as she left the room. 'But it's your loss, you moron. You'll regret it, I promise.'

Maybe it *is* my loss, thought Mark, as he sipped more brandy from the bottle. And maybe I will regret it, but that's life.

When Martine returned with a shirt and sweater and helped Mark put them on, he said: 'I've got to give Uncle John the bad news now,' and got to his feet.

'He'll get over it.'

'I hope so.'

'And you take care, darlin',' she said and jumped up and kissed him full on the mouth.

'You'll have me over,' he said, grabbing the chair for support.

'That's always been my plan. Anyway, I'm off upstairs. I don't want to be there if Dad goes into one.'

'Nor do I,' replied Mark. 'But I'm afraid he might.'

She looked at him one more time. 'When will I see you?' she asked.

He shook his head. 'I don't know.'

'Nothing new there then,' she said and left him alone.

Painfully he left the room after her and went up to find John Jenner and Chas. They were sitting together in the living room in silence as he entered and sat gingerly in one soft armchair.

'So what happened?' asked Jenner.

'It all went wrong,' said Mark and briefly filled them in on the events of the night.

'You lost the money and the drugs,' said Jenner when he'd finished.

'And Eddie and Tubbs,' said Mark.

'But you killed the spades.'

Mark nodded. 'And the two women.'

'So five dead niggers,' said Jenner. 'No loss.'

'Six if you count Tubbs,' said Mark.

'You know I didn't mean that.'

'So what if you did. But I just left them. There was nothing I could do.' Mark felt like crying but knew it was just a waste of time and tears both.

'Those things happen,' said Jenner.

'But not to me. And I left the two motors and weapons and my DNA on the knife in the flat. It's fucked, Uncle John.'

'One of those things.'

'No,' said Mark. 'I've got a really bad feeling. I'm going to split.'

'In your condition?'

'I can manage.'

'Where are you going to go?' asked Chas.

'I'll find somewhere. You've got my mobile number. We can keep in touch. I don't know what I'm going to do.'

'I'd try and convince you to stay…' said Jenner.

'Don't,' interrupted Mark. 'I'll get my stuff and I'll go.'

Jenner nodded and Mark left the room, went upstairs and packed a few things in his bag. His back was killing him, but he knew he had to go and go that night. He closed his bedroom door behind him and went back downstairs. Chas was waiting in the hall. 'You don't have to do this, you know,' he said.

'Yes I do,' said Mark and went back to say goodbye to Jenner. 'I'm off now, Uncle,' he said.

'Be careful,' said Jenner.

'You too. This isn't going to go away.'

'What the hell,' said Jenner. 'What can they do? Give me cancer?' He stood and embraced the younger man, being careful not to touch his wound, and then, both with tears in their eyes, they kissed once and Mark went out to his car and drove away.

TWENTY-SEVEN

Mark spent the night in the Range Rover in a back street in East Dulwich. It wasn't the first time that he'd slept in a car in his life, and he doubted that it would be the last. It had been too late to find a hotel or B&B without causing unwelcome interest, and that was the last thing he wanted to do. He hardly closed his eyes all night, he just lay curled up in the back, with the radio tuned to a local news station. Reports of the killings in Brixton filled the bulletins, but shootings were so prevalent in London those days that, by morning, it was the second item after something about a pop star's birthday party at a hotel in Park Lane.

But Mark knew that the cops wouldn't lose interest so quickly. He drove to an all-night supermarket, purchased some toiletries and used their gents for a wash and brush up, then breakfasted at the diner attached to the store. He wasn't hungry, but he knew he had to eat. His wound was hot and sore, but if it hurt too much, he'd munch painkillers until the pain subsided. But what next?

After eating, he drove up to Crystal Palace and booked into one of the very same hotels he and Linda had enjoyed afternoons of passion in, all those years before. It had been refurbished since and he hardly recognised the place, but it still brought back memories. Some good, some bad. Once inside his room, he drew the curtains, took more pills and fell into bed. He slept for hours and it was only the ringing of his mobile that eventually woke him. It was Chas. 'Bad news, son,' he said. 'They came for your uncle this morning and he had a bit of a turn. He's in hospital.'

'Oh, Jesus,' said Mark. 'What happened?'

'A stroke. He's in intensive care in King's.'

What more can go wrong? thought Mark. 'I'll go and see him.'

'I wouldn't if I were you. Your name was mentioned.'

'Shit.'

'Shit's right. And what happened last night is all over the telly and the papers. You're famous again.'

'Oh Christ, Chas. Can we meet?'

'Sure. Course. There's a pub near the hospital. O'Neill's. It used to be the Station. It's on the bridge over the railway at Denmark Hill.'

'I'll find it.'

'Are you up to it? How do you feel?'

'Like I've been hit by a bus, but I'll manage. How's Martine taken it?'

'Not well. She blames you.'

'She blames me for the war in the Middle East. But we'll worry about her later. When?'

'I'm at the hospital now. Outside, having a bit of a walk. I can see the pub from here.'

'I'll be there within an hour. Wait for me.'

'I've got nothing else to do.'

'See you then.' He killed the phone.

In the bathroom he looked at his face in the mirror. He was pale and drawn and looked ten years older than he had just a few days previously. But who could blame him? Old friends had died. He'd killed some people and had been injured. He turned and craned his neck to look at his bandage. There was a dark stain visible through the white material, but no blood had seeped all the way through. Maybe while I'm near the hospital, I can get it checked, he thought. Or maybe not.

He left his few things at the hotel and motored down to Denmark Hill, found the pub and parked in a back street. When he pushed through the doors into the almost deserted saloon bar, he saw Chas sitting at a corner table, nursing a beer. 'Want a refill?' he asked once he'd walked over.

'No,' said Chas. 'Don't even want this one, really.'

'Fair enough. But I need a livener. You woke me up.' Mark went to the bar and ordered a Beck's with a brandy chaser and took the glasses over

352

and joined Chas who was staring gloomily out of the window. 'What happened exactly?' asked Mark once he was seated.

'Cops came just after five and rousted the house. They wanted John for questioning about the shooting, and they wanted to find out where you were. That fucking Hunter's son was there, the little shit. And they brought Customs with them. Something about Ali and Tommo importing duty frees from the Continent. And them seeing your motor parked up outside with French plates. They put two and two together and got seven, as usual.'

'Is that how they knew about me, the motor?'

'Dunno. They never said. But apparently Interpol or whatever it's now called want to talk to you about some killings in Germany.'

'Yeah. They would.'

Chas nodded. He'd heard worse in his life.

'So what happened to Uncle John?'

'They took him up Streatham nick, stuck him in an interview room and he just keeled over. Course, they thought he was trying it on, but eventually they called an ambulance and the paramedics brought him to the cardiac unit here. Best in London, supposed to be.'

'And?'

'And he's not good, Mark. Not good at all. They did some tests and the cancer's spreading fast. He's riddled with the shit. Liver, kidneys, lungs. The lot.'

'What are his chances?'

Chas shook his head. 'Poor. You'd better be prepared for the worst.'

'And Martine's with him.'

'Been there all day.'

'Any Old Bill about?'

Chas shook his head again. 'They put a copper on the door at first, but they tugged him off a couple of hours ago. John ain't going nowhere, mate.'

'That bad?'

Another nod and Mark blew out a sigh and downed his brandy in one. 'What about Customs?'

'Dunno. They sloped off sharpish when there was no sign of your motor.'

'It's all gone to shit, Chas.'

'I know. So what are you going to do?'

'Not go to Germany is top of my list. But I'm going to have to leave the country, and I want to see Uncle John first. Do you think I can get in?'

'Don't see why not. Security's not up to much and, like I said, the Bill's gone walkabout.'

'Did they charge him?'

'No. Just helping with enquiries. They only had to look at him to see he wasn't wandering the streets the other night killing folks.'

'And Martine blames me?'

Yet another nod.

'Bloody hell,' said Mark. 'I don't want her starting a scene in there. Drawing more attention to us. Can't you do something?'

'I'll go over and suggest she come home and get cleaned up, maybe sleep for a bit.'

'Do you reckon she will?'

'She's taken it hard, Mark. She loves the old man.'

'I know she does. So do I.'

'So do we all.'

Now it was Mark's turn to nod.

'Give me a few minutes and I'll see what I can do,' said Chas and, leaving his glass, he walked out of the pub.

Mark sat where he was until his phone rang.

'It's me,' said Chas.

'Yeah.'

'I'm dragging her back home to get changed and have something to eat. We'll be gone for a bit so you can get in. She's in the loo… No, she's coming. See ya.' And he cut the connection.

Mark gave them a few minutes before he finished his drink and went over to the hospital. ICU was on the third floor and he took the lift, keeping an eye open for anyone who looked like a copper. Once there, he found a nurse and inquired about John Jenner.

'Are you family?' she asked.

'Nephew,' he said. 'Can I see him?'

'Let me look,' she replied. Then: 'I'm afraid it's not good.'

'I heard,' he said. 'That's why I came.'

'He's been sleeping a lot,' she said. 'I'll speak to the doctor.'

She vanished in a swish of starch, and Mark stood by the enquiries desk trying hard to look like he belonged.

'You can go in and see him now,' said the nurse. 'But don't be too long, and don't let him get excited. He's awake but very woozy from the drugs we've administered.'

'I won't be long,' said Mark. She nodded and she led him into the private room. John Jenner lay very still and there was an oxygen mask over his face. His skin was the same colour as his pillow, tubes and wires were attached to every inch of skin, and machines bleeped and whirred beside him. Mark knew deep inside that his uncle would probably never leave the hospital. He pulled up one of the two chairs in the corner and sat by the bed. Jenner turned his head and reached up and pulled the mask off his nose and mouth. 'Mark,' he said. 'You shouldn't have come.'

Mark ignored his comment and said, 'Uncle John. How are you feeling?'

'Not too clever. How do I look?'

'Honestly?'

'Of course.'

'Not too clever.'

'Fair enough.' He looked round. 'So this is what it all comes to,' he said. 'If I'd known all those years ago I don't think I'd've bothered.'

'Yes you would.'

'I don't know so much, son. I mean, is this all there is? The sum total.'

'You've done loads. Dragged yourself up and made something of yourself.'

'Are you kidding me? Do you know what I am?'

'Yes.'

'I don't think so, Mark. No one ever knows anyone else. Well maybe me and Haze.' He smiled. 'God, but I wish she was here.'

'Perhaps she is.'

'Perhaps. You know never a day goes by without me thinking about her. Talking to her. She was the only one for me from the minute I laid eyes on her.'

'I know, Uncle.'

'I had other birds, you know. It was all there on a plate. Tarts. And ladies too, sometimes. She always knew but she never made a fuss. Just treated me so good I forgot about them. I wish now I hadn't though.'

'We always wish we were better than we are.'

'And we are, you know, son. We're all better than the worst things we've ever done.'

'I wish I could believe that.'

'I saw her when she was dead,' Jenner said. 'They had a special room in the hospital. It was bloody horrible. She still had one of those pipes in her mouth. Have you ever seen anyone you've made love to, dead?'

Mark shook his head.

'It's bloody horrible. You don't want to.' He looked at him suddenly. 'I know you saw your mum dead,' he said. 'And I know what that must've been like, but I think this was different. I slept with her for so long. I used to watch her asleep sometimes.' He smiled. 'I knew she'd never tell me to piss off again. Or that she loved me. Or even ask me what I wanted with my eggs. It was over. Finito.'

'I'm sorry, Uncle,' said Mark.

'Is my wallet here?' Jenner asked suddenly.

Mark saw it on a side table. 'It's here,' he said.

'Show.'

Mark leaned over, picked it up and put it on the bed. Jenner found it, opened it without looking and pulled out a photo of his late wife. 'I've carried this with me for ten years,' he said. 'Put it on the table where I can see it.'

Mark did as he was told, and Jenner turned his head painfully, then smiled. His lips were white and Mark offered him a drink. He sucked at the straw greedily, then lay back. 'That was good,' he said. 'You know, when she died a bit of me died with her. It's never been the same since. I tried other women afterwards too, but they never knew what I was talking about. Not like Hazel. So I gave up. Christ, but I was lonely, but you can't force things like that. Did you ever read a story called *The Ice Queen*?'

'When I was a nipper.'

'It frightened me when I read it when I was a kid,' said Jenner. 'The fact that someone could have their heart replaced by a sliver of ice. I hated that. But when Hazel went, it happened to me. It's still there. Sometimes it's so cold in my chest, it hurts. So you see, I'm not scared of dying. I'm scared of being in this place, but dying, no. In fact, I rather look forward to it. Do you believe in heaven and hell, Mark?'

The young man shook his head. 'No, Uncle. I don't think so.'

'People who do, say there's many gates to hell,' said Jenner. 'And I've looked at some of them. I've killed people, Mark. Looked in their eyes and just blown them away. I wish now I hadn't done that too. But I could never have stayed in the job I had, all those years ago. I was always a wrong 'un. Your dad got it right. He joined the police to make things better.'

'It didn't work though, did it?'

'Maybe not. But he tried.' John Jenner lay back on his pillow and his eyelids fluttered. 'You won't leave me, will you?'

'No, Uncle.'

'Where's Chas and Martine?'

'He took her home for a bit. She blames me, you know.'

'No, she don't. She loves you, Mark.'

'Not any more, Uncle. I think I spoiled that, like I spoiled so many things.'

'Don't be so hard on yourself. You're a good boy, Mark.'

'I doubt the cops would agree with that.'

'Bloody coppers. What do they know? They done me up in the end, didn't they though?'

'Yes, Uncle John. They did. But I didn't help.'

'Forget it, son. I love you. Always have. You've got the same eyes as Billy. He always was my best mate. Apart from Hazel, of course. I'm tired now, son. I want some kip. Will you stay?'

Mark nodded.

'Hold my hand, son and I won't feel so lonely.' And his eyes shut and he slept, and the only sound in the room was the gentle bleeping of the machines he was connected to. Mark leant over and replaced the mask on his mouth and sat with his uncle's hand in his.

John Jenner dreamt of his ex-wife as he lay there. In his dream it was that first Friday night at the Bali Hai in Streatham. He was all done up in the latest King's Road fashions. Sharp suit, flowered shirt and tie, and zip up boots with a slight heel. And Chas was there. And Chas's sister too, and her mates. And one of them was Hazel. Red hair in a bob, the shortest skirt he'd ever seen. Bare legs because it was a warm night, and high boots with stiletto heels. He'd never seen anyone like her before or since. The minute he clapped eyes on her she had to be his. And the feeling was mutual. He'd bought her champagne and they'd ended up on the back seat of the big old Pontiac he'd been driving that year. He never could get the stains off the leather. Jenner smiled in his sleep. And the machines kept up their bleeping.

Mark saw the smile and was glad, until he heard a commotion in the corridor outside. Chas's deep voice and Martine's too, almost hysterical. The door burst open and she came in like a small whirlwind. 'What are you doing here?' she shouted. 'It's all your fault!'

Mark disentangled his hand, stood and saw Chas in the doorway with the young nurse he'd met earlier behind him. 'Leave it out, Martine,' he said.

'Leave it out?' she shouted even louder. 'Leave it out, you bastard? You came back and look at the state of him.'

'I didn't mean…'

'Didn't mean?' she interrupted and began to beat on his chest with her tiny fists so that the pain in his back came flooding back and he winced.

'Please!' called the nurse from behind Chas's huge back. 'Please don't. You'll only make it worse for him.'

'She's right,' said Chas and almost lifted Martine off her feet, dragging her into the corridor and marching her to the relatives' room which, thankfully, was deserted, followed by Mark. 'In here,' he said.

They all went in and Chas closed the door firmly in the nurse's face. 'Stop it, both of you,' he said quietly. 'Let's give the old man some respect.'

Martine sat on a chair, head in hands, and tears leaked through her fingers. Mark put his hand on her shoulder, but she shook him off. 'I'm so sorry, Marty,' he said. A name he hadn't called her since they were much younger. 'If I'd only known.'

But it was no good and he could see that.

John Jenner went flatline alóne. No family, no medical staff in the room. The nurse heard the panic siren go off and called a code but it was no use. His body couldn't take any more and it just shut down. He was still smiling when he died. Still dreaming of Hazel and better times.

The trio in the family room heard the commotion too and, differences forgotten, rushed to Jenner's room. But they were forbidden entrance and had to watch the doctors and nurses attempt a resuscitation through the window. When it was all over, Martine staggered, and Chas helped her back to the relative's room where she curled up on the uncomfortable sofa there. She was inconsolable and, after a few minutes, he left her and joined Mark, still looking through the window at Jenner's still body.

'Did you talk to him?' asked Chas.

'Yeah. He was talking about Hazel.'

'He never did get over her dying, you know.'

'I know. Martine said that he met her through you.'

'Yeah, that's right. She was a friend of my sister's. I fancied her like mad, but I was too young. Then when she saw John, it was all over. You couldn't get a cigarette paper between them.'

'It was at some club, wasn't it?'

'Yeah. the Bali Hai in Streatham. What a place. We had some laughs there, I can tell you.'

'You met him there too, didn't you?'

'Yeah. I was just out of borstal. I got nicked for stealing motors. Blimey, what a sodding place. Long shorts, vests and cold showers there, my boy. And they chopped all your bloody hair off. And the buggers who ran the place... All ex-army who'd give you a good hiding for looking at them sideways.'

'How long were you there?'

'Three months with no time off for good behaviour. Then when I came out, I got all booted and suited and went to the Bali to see what was happening. All the young villains went there. But there wasn't much trouble. It was like an open city in a war. We left our differences at the door. Well, most of the time anyway.'

'So how did you meet him?'

'He made some comment about the barnet being so short. His was halfway down his back then. Hard to believe now, I know. He reckoned I looked like one of the Krays. I had this smashing navy blue suit, see, with a white on white shirt. I thought it was the business. He was like some kind of rock star. But we had a drink and he asked me to help him out with some villainy. I was skint, so I said yes. Anyway, who turns up but my sister and some mates including Hazel. She was a bit posh see, but the family had fallen on bad times. Anyway, she's got the shortest mini you've ever seen and John asked her to dance... the rest's history.'

'You fancied her?' asked Mark.

'Every fucker fancied her, but she was particular. When she found out that John was a naughty boy, she liked him even more. She liked spending money, see. And she didn't have any. But John promised her the world and he come good.'

'I never knew.'

'John don't talk about it much. He's never really been the same since she died. Always blamed himself.'

'But it wasn't his fault, was it?'

'No. You don't expect a young woman like that to have heart problems. And she'd never let on. She never even went to the doctor 'til it was too late to do anything. John called in all the big guns to try and do something for her but she was too far gone.'

'I thought she was the business, too,' said Mark. 'It all fell apart for me after she died.'

'For a lot of us.'

'Listen, Chas,' said Mark. 'I've got to go. I shouldn't be here. It's screwing up Martine.'

'Whatever you think,' said Chas.

'I'm staying in a hotel in Crystal Palace. Keep in touch by mobile. Let me know when the funeral is.'

'I'll do that.'

'And Chas…'

'Yeah.'

'Look after her. She's special.'

'You can say that again. She's got both of them in her.'

Mark smiled a rare smile for that day. 'I know.'

And then he left.

Once back in his car, he sat for a while and let the tears flow. But who was he crying for? he wondered. For John Jenner or for himself? He was truly an orphan now. Alone and on the run. Eventually he dried his eyes on a tissue from the glove compartment, shrugged, grinned a wry grin, and drove back to the hotel.

* * *

It was the biggest funeral south London would see for years. Maybe decades. Maybe ever. John Jenner had been well known in the area, and well liked. At least by people who hadn't crossed him and paid the price. And, as if to join in the mourning early on that Friday, less than a week after he died, the rains came. But it did little to dampen the enthusiasm of the locals. The service wasn't until noon, but as early as ten am, the first spectators had begun to line the route between the funeral directors in Camberwell and the church beside the cemetery in Greenwich where Hazel was buried. When his wife had died, Jenner had bought adjoining plots so that one day he could lie next to her, for eternity.

That part of the capital has never been the most attractive, even in bright sunshine, but as the clouds thickened and the rain became heavier and the street lamps clicked on, it took on the air of desolation that suited the mood of the day for the mourners.

Jenner's body had been lying in rest at a funeral home in Walworth, and Chas, Dev and Martine drove there in Jenner's Bentley, with Chas at the wheel.

A few reporters and cameramen from the local papers and TV, who had been outside Jenner's house, followed the car in convoy. Dev suggested shooting a few tyres out to detain them, but Chas put the block on the idea. 'Not very good PR,' he remarked.

When they arrived at the undertaker's premises, it was like a circus outside. As if to underline the gloominess of the occasion, the rain had become heavier and, as they ran from the car to the entrance, they sheltered under a massive golf umbrella, its red and white stripes and the flashes from the photographers' cameras, contrasting with the greyness of the day.

Inside the funeral home, the chief director was waiting, wringing his hands. 'Miss Jenner, gentlemen,' he said as they entered. 'My sincere condolences.'

'Thanks,' said Martine brushing by him. 'Is everything ready?'

'Of course. The vehicles are in the back.'

He showed them through, past the other main mourners who had congregated there. It was an eclectic bunch. Old friends and enemies from the past. Old villains, some geriatric pop stars and a few footballers from pre-Premier Division days, plus business acquaintances of John Jenner, who – as Martine whispered to Chas – were only there to make sure he was dead.

In the service area at the back of the funeral parlour, the hearse and the cars for the mourners were parked in a circle, like a wagon train waiting for an indian attack.

The hearse in which Jenner's body was waiting was horsedrawn, with a pair of Belgian Blacks between the shafts, their plumes and feathers bedraggled by the rain. Behind them were four Mercedes stretch limousines, their black cellulose gleaming under the raindrops.

'Miss Jenner. You and your companions in the first car,' said the director.

'Fine,' said Chas. 'It all looks perfect.'

The director almost fainted with relief. It had not been his idea to make the arrangements, even though he was due to make a big profit on the day. And he knew that if he made a mistake with this funeral he would live to regret it, and had been most careful to sort out the protocol. 'And there's a police escort waiting,' he added.

'Who organised that?' asked Chas, almost amused that the enemy would be there to assist one of their most wanted villains on his last journey, instead of escorting him to the local police station in handcuffs, as usually happened.

'Inspector Lewis from Barton Street,' he said. 'They've closed the roads.'

'Have they?' said Chas. 'How thoughtful of them.'

The mourners dispersed to the various cars, the horses pawed the ground, and pissed and shit as horses will. Resplendent in frock coat, top hat and with a huge black umbrella unfurled above his head, the funeral director led the procession out of the service area and on to the Walworth Road. The road itself had been closed by uniformed police 'black rat' outriders, causing huge traffic jams through Brixton, Camberwell, Kennington and Waterloo. As the cortege entered the street it was joined by two more Metropolitan Police outriders. The crowd roared, and there was a barrage of flashes bright enough to illuminate even that miserable day, which set the horses rearing and neighing.

As the official procession motored slowly up the Walworth Road, other motors joined it from almost every direction, until the cortege was almost a mile long. And behind them came the media. The hearse and every car present seemed to be submerged in flowers. The local florists had to have been rubbing their hands with glee at the profit they were making. Not since the last royal funeral had their shops been stripped of every bloom and display – and all at premium prices.

Slowly the procession ground towards the Elephant and Castle roundabout, the police outriders clearing the route as they approached, and then down the Old Kent Road towards St Martin's Church in Deptford and the cemetery beyond.

Both sides of the street were lined with sodden spectators. Coffee stalls and hamburger wagons were doing a roaring trade. At the Bricklayer's Arms, a pair of dwarves danced for silver. By the new Tesco's supermarket, a little further down the Old Kent Road, a chain swallower exhibited the vomit he had dredged up from his stomach for the edification of the crowd. A Jazz band outside a wine bar played New Orleans funeral marches. Every pub on the route was doing premium business. Pickpockets and bagsnatchers had a field day. A couple of prostitutes worked out of a Transit van, giving blow jobs on a pair of mattresses. All in all, a wonderful south London holiday atmosphere pervaded the soaking streets.

The church service itself was remarkably restrained. Chas had seen to that. And afterwards, the massive procession travelled on a further mile to the cemetery.

Through the pouring rain, the mourners watched John Jenner being deposited in the ground. News crews and press cameramen vied for a view, held back by uniformed police officers. They listened as the priest spoke comforting words from the Bible, before throwing clumps of dirt on top of the coffin, which had been lowered into the grave. They landed with damp thuds, as all around the graveside official mourners and gatecrashers trod the wet earth to mud, trampling on other graves as they craned for a look. But not all the people present cast their eyes in that direction. There were policemen spotting villains, villains eyeballing the coppers they recognised, and some coppers were looking at their off duty colleagues and wondering about their motives for being there.

After Martine dropped a white rose into the maw of the grave, she slumped against Chas, who shook his head sadly and helped her back to the Mercedes, through rain that almost blinded him.

Mark watched the burial from a distance, as he'd watched the cortege arrive at the church. He knew he wouldn't be welcome, Chas had spoken to him several times on the phone during the week and they'd met once. 'She still blames you,' the big man had said. 'I can't get it through her head that it could've happened any time.'

'But it didn't,' said Mark. 'It happened when he was pulled in for questioning about something I was responsible for.'

'He was involved too, don't forget,' said Chas. 'He put you up to it. If it hadn't been for him, none of this would've happened.'

Mark shrugged. 'So what?' he said.

Chas slid a parcel across the table in the quiet Fulham pub where they'd met. 'There's some cash in there for you,' he said. 'Twenty grand. And half the coke that Tubbs bought that day. John would've liked you to have something. Everything else goes to Martine, according to the will.'

'No,' said Mark. 'You'll need it.'

'He would've given it to you himself if he was here,' said Chas. 'He wanted you to have all the proceeds. And there's plenty left for her. You'd be surprised the bits and pieces of money he had stashed away. And then there's the house.'

'But what about you, Chas?'

'I'll be all right. She wants me to stay on. And John set up a nice little pension fund for me years ago. Who'd've thought it, eh? Gangsters with pension funds.'

They both smiled at the thought and Mark said, 'So this is it. You won't see me at the funeral, though I'll be around.'

'And then?'

'And then, who knows? I'll worry about that when the time comes.'

He left his old friend and stashed the money and drugs into the compartment in the Range Rover that had held the streetsweeper. There it lay next to Mark's other weapons. He spent another lonely night in another lonely hotel, this time in Penge. By then, the wound in his back was healing nicely. Martine must've done a better job than either of them had thought. He'd peeled back the bandage and the lips of the cut were clean and knitting together well. I bet she wishes she'd stabbed me herself now, he thought. But that's life.

And he knew he couldn't show his face at the funeral, even if he had been welcome. Too many of the mourners would have been plainclothes coppers. Instead, he stood under the shelter of a tree, collar up and a recently acquired trilby low over his eyes, as he watched Chas helped Martine from the lead car behind the hearse and support her into the church, and afterwards did the same at the rain-soaked cemetery. He watched as Jenner's black-draped coffin was lowered slowly into the ground and as the priest spoke words he couldn't hear. And he saw Martine throw a single white rose into the grave before going back to the car with Chas.

When everyone, apart from the gravediggers, had left, he walked down the path through the deluge and said his own final farewell to the man who had taken him into his home, all those years ago. By then he didn't care if a whole platoon of armed police arrived and took him in. It might even have been a relief.

But no one showed and, with just a raise of his hand, he turned away and back to his car.

He drove to Croydon, parked outside Linda's house, noticed that her four-wheel drive was sitting outside, and rang the front door bell.

Linda opened the door herself and her eyes widened when she saw who it was. 'What the hell are you doing here?' she asked. 'Don't you know how dangerous it is? Half the police in London are looking for you.'

'Only half. Well, you can't have everything. I came to see you.'

'Well, you've seen me. Now you can go.'

'Don't be like that, Linda,' he said.

'What do you mean "like that"? You run out on me and I don't hear from you for ten days, then my brother lets it slip that you're a wanted man, and now you just turn up as if nothing had happened. And looking like hell, I might add.'

'John died.'

'I know that. I read the papers. The funeral's today, isn't it?'

'It's just over. Listen, can I come in?'

'No,' she said, blocking the doorway with her body.

'Fair enough,' he said. 'I'll say what I came to say out here.'

'Which is?'

'I've got to leave the country. It's too hot for me here.'

She shrugged. 'That's what you always do when things get too hot for you, isn't it? Leave.'

'Yeah,' he agreed. 'But this time it's different.'

'How?'

'I want you to come with me.'

'Me?'

Another nod.

'What about the children?'

'Bring them.'

'You are joking.'

'No. We could be a family.'

'More like the authorities are looking for a man on his own, not one with a woman and two kids in tow.'

'That's unfair, Linda.'

'Nothing's unfair when it comes to you, Mark.'

'Listen, I know I've been a bastard, but I'm so…'

'Don't say sorry,' she interrupted. 'Just bloody don't. And your girlfriend phoned.'

'Who?'

'Who else? Martine, of course.'

'What the hell did she want?'

'To tell me you two had slept together.'

'And you believed her?'

'Why shouldn't I?'

'Because it's not true. I've never slept with her in my life.'

'Then why did she tell me you had?'

'Use your loaf, Linda. To split us up once and for all. She blames me for her father's death. She tried it on one night and I slung her out. You've heard about "a woman scorned"?'

'I've been that woman.'

'I know. But it's not true. What do I have to do to make you believe me?'

'We're past all that. I don't care anymore.'

'Are you sure?'

'I've never been more sure of anything in my life.'

'So you won't come?'

'Just leave all this?' She gestured back inside.

'A house in Croydon? When I met you that was the worst case scenario. You didn't want to end up like your parents, and now you have.'

'It's a bit different, Mark.'

'I don't see it.'

'Well, it is. And you just want me to leave everything and go abroad. Go where abroad, exactly?'

'Not Spain. Too many villains. Portugal maybe. South of France.'

'And what do we do for money?'

'I've got some. You must have loads. You could sell the house. It's worth a bloody fortune.'

'You're having a laugh, aren't you, Mark? You expect me sell everything to bankroll our life together?'

'Until I get myself straight.'

'Which means until you get involved in some other bloody villainy and end up going away.'

'I haven't gone away yet.'

'But you will. And I'll be left living in one room with two children.'

'I don't think it'll come down to one room, Linda,' he said. 'I think we can do better than that for ourselves.'

'We'll never know, because I'm not coming.'

'If you can't come now, you could follow me later,' he said with one last try.

'No, Mark. And if you don't go now I'm going to tell Sean you're here. He's up in his flat.'

He laughed then. 'Running to big brother, eh? Grassing me up. I don't think so. Not after all we've been to each other,' he said and shook his head. 'OK, Linda. Fair enough. But don't say I didn't ask this time.'

'I won't,' she said. 'Goodbye, Mark.'

'Goodbye,' he replied, turned on his heel and crunched across the wet drive and back into the Range Rover, not caring if Sean saw him or not. He sat for a moment, deep in thought. He'd only loved five women in his life and none of them were here for him now. His mum and Hazel were dead, Lan was God knows where, and Linda and Martine, for different reasons, didn't want to know him. That's the way it goes, he thought, switching on the engine, pointing the nose of Range Rover south towards the sea and what lay beyond. He put his foot down.

'But I'll be back,' he said aloud. 'Count on it.'

But if he could have seen through the walls into Linda's house – where she stood in the hallway, head bowed, one hand on the bannister rail for support – he would have seen the tears running unchecked down her face at the thought of losing him… again.

TWENTY-EIGHT

On the morning that Jimmy Hunter was released from Brixton Prison, there was no welcoming committee. No bells and whistles. No streamers, balloons and bunting hanging from the trees. Not even that old staple of a million films and TV shows, the best mate waiting in a flash car with a bottle of champagne, cigars, a change of clothes and two horny tarts up for anything. Jimmy didn't have a best mate. Or any mate, for that matter.

He walked down the long road from the prison gate to Brixton Hill in the early morning light. Under one arm was a brown paper parcel, and in his pocket, £27.86. He walked alone. Other prisoners had been released that sunny, spring morning, but he left them to it as they met with friends and loved ones. He was soon standing alone on the corner, watching the rush hour traffic moving towards central London.

And that traffic. It hadn't been like this the last time he'd driven through London as a free man. Even the buses had changed – apart from the occasional, ancient Routemaster. Oh yes, he remembered them all right, and the part the traditional London double-decker had played in his downfall. Now, most buses seemed to be big, smog-spewing driver-only vehicles with their doors shut tight. He waited for a break in the traffic, crossed over and cut through the back streets, away from the crowded main road. If truth be told, although he would never have admitted it, the busy thoroughfares scared him slightly, used as he was to being alone for most of the day in his cell. Being a local boy, he'd known those streets like the back of his hand, and he remembered them well, although they had changed too. Instead of the rooming houses, crumbling bedsits and drug dealer's cribs that were once there, they'd been smartened up. Gentrified,

371

was the word he recalled from countless newspaper articles he'd read whilst inside.

Jimmy had kept up. To do otherwise would have been to ossify, and he'd had no intention of doing that. So he'd spent as much time as possible in the library devouring the daily papers. Not the tabloids, but the broadsheets that he'd never had the time for before. He knew what had been happening in society whilst he'd been away, and that scared him too – though once again, he'd never own up to it. So he shook his head as he walked, puffing on a tailor-made cigarette bought with what seemed like a terrifyingly large chunk of his available cash from the first newsagent he'd come to.

Eventually he sat on the wall of a council estate and took stock. He'd served his sentence in full, but as a convicted murderer he was still on licence. Fat chance! He had with him the address of a hostel and the time of an appointment with a parole officer at an office in Streatham. Bugger that, he thought. He was in the wind and meant to stay there. He was free. He smiled, though he felt as if his face would crack, finished the cigarette down to the filter and tossed it into the gutter, along with the paper with the addresses, torn into tiny pieces.

I wonder if I could get nicked for littering? he thought and laughed out loud. So loud, in fact, that several passersby looked at him sideways.

He started to pick up his parcel, then stopped to think again. He looked around until he saw a skip outside a house, strode over and tossed his bundle inside. There was nothing of meaning or value to him in it. Just a reminder of twenty wasted years.

So Jimmy Hunter, alone now with just what he stood up in, was ready to take on the world. And the first thing he needed was a bloody good drink and somebody to share it with. And for that he'd need some cash and he knew exactly where to get it... or, at least, he hoped he did.

Even before that he needed a bite to eat. He'd forgone the delicacies of a prison breakfast before he was released, just taking a mug of dishwater tea. A couple of streets away he found a dingy café. At least greasies hadn't changed, he thought as he entered. He ordered a full English with double egg and a mug of tea and took a seat in a quiet corner.

The food tasted like ambrosia after what he'd been eating for two decades. He scoffed the lot, lit another cigarette and sat back satisfied. This is the life, he thought, and his stomach clenched more from regret at what he'd wasted than from the gourmet breakfast, which, once again, seemed to be ten times more expensive than he remembered.

He left the café and caught sight of himself in the window as he passed. The suit he was wearing, the same one that he'd bought for the trial, with its wide lapels and slight flare to the trousers, looked ridiculous compared with the sharp fashions the Brixton men were wearing that morning. It's gotta go, he thought. Got to get some new threads. With this thought in mind he caught a bus for the City where he hoped an old friend still had his business.

Gerry Goldstein, another old mod, wasn't so much a friend as an accomplice in various nefarious goings on before Jimmy had been captured for the last time. He ran a diamond import/export company in Hatton Garden and was as known for his early hours as much as he was for his expertise in the jewellery business. Not to mention other endeavours that netted him sums that neither his accountant nor the Inland Revenue were aware of.

Jimmy hopped from bus to bus to get to the centre of town. There was no rush and he wanted to get a taste of London as it now was. It was amazing what had changed and what had remained the same, and, as he sat on the top deck of each vehicle, he was stunned at some of the things he saw. Of course, he'd seen photographs of the way London had expanded upwards and outwards over the years, but no photo could do justice to the shiny new buildings that passed in front of his eyes as he made the journey.

The City in particular was like nothing he remembered. The new bars and restaurants, the way pubs had strange new names. And the birds. Christ, he thought, as he sat next to beautiful, fragrant young women on their way to work, they're gorgeous. In fact, several times he had to pull his jacket over his lap to hide the erection that had arrived unbidden.

Eventually he reached High Holborn and disembarked. The old Daily

Mirror Building had gone, and whatever had been opposite it had been replaced by a brand new skyscraper. The red brick of the Prudential building still stood at the side of Leather Lane and he turned into it and on towards Hatton Garden.

Goldstein's shop was one of the things that hadn't changed, and Jimmy smiled inwardly as he saw its familiar facade. I hope the fucker isn't brown bread, he thought as he approached. Inside a dim light burned, but there was a CLOSED sign on the glass door.

Jimmy rapped hard on the glass with his knuckles. Nothing. Then again and, from the twilight at the back of the shop, a rotund figure emerged. Jimmy peered in. Could this rather overweight gentleman be the same Gerry Goldstein who'd danced the night away to the sounds of Tamla Motown in clubs from Kensington to Kensal Rise all those years ago? But the sharp eyes that peered back were the same. The figure tapped his watch as if to say 'Too early, come back later', but Jimmy shook his head.

Impatiently the figure pointed at the sign showing the hours of business were from nine to three on that particular day of the week.

Jimmy shook his head again and the figure pointed again. This time to the entryphone next to the door. Jimmy nodded and pushed the button. The figure moved away and a moment later a voice that could have been anyone's emerged from the speaker. 'We're closed,' it said. 'Come back after nine.'

'Is that you, Gerry?' said Jimmy.

'Yes.'

'Christ, but you've changed.'

'Who's this?' demanded the voice, and even the poor reception couldn't disguise the suspicion in it.

'Jimmy Hunter. Remember me?'

The voice was silent for a long time before saying: 'Jimmy? I don't believe it.'

'Believe it. Now open up, mate, you've got something that belongs to me.'

374

Goldstein approached the door and Jimmy heard the sound of multiple locks and chains being undone before it swung inwards and Goldstein beckoned him in. 'Christ, Jimmy, I wouldn't have known you.'

'Or me you,' said Jimmy as the door closed behind him and the gloom deepened.

There were no handshakes or hugs. No questions about where he'd been or what he'd been doing. Gerry knew precisely where he'd been because he had been sitting in court at the Bailey when Jimmy had been sentenced. Jimmy had caught his eye before being taken down and a small nod had passed between the two of them.

But that had been twenty years before, and things and people changed. Not just the appearances of two men now firmly in middle age, but other things too. Loyalty, for instance. 'Why didn't you let me know you were coming out?' asked Goldstein.

'Couldn't you work it out for yourself?'

'I suppose so. But time flies, and…'

'And out of sight, out of mind. Right?' said Jimmy.

'I'm sorry, Jimmy,' said Goldstein. 'But we always said we'd have no communication. I just thought that as your time came to an end…'

'Have you still got it?' asked Jimmy. He didn't need small talk from Gerry, just what he was owed. 'What do you think?' Gerry replied. 'Come through, the kettle's on.'

They went through the shop into Gerry's office at the back, which itself seemed the same to Jimmy as the last time he'd dropped by. Only the computer and other electronic gadgetry on the desk beside the tiny, filthy barred window was new. Jimmy looked at the bars and didn't like what he saw. It reminded him too much of his recent accommodation. No more bars, he thought. Only those that serve booze. He smiled at the thought and Gerry asked, 'Something funny?'

'No. I'm just glad you're still here.'

'They've tried to move me a thousand times,' replied the jeweller. 'But I've got a firm lease.'

'I'm pleased to hear it. I've been moved a few times myself.'

'So I heard. How are you anyway?'

'Older, wiser, poorer. But then I hope you can help me with that.'

Goldstein smiled like an old granpappy about to produce a present for his favourite offspring. 'Maybe I can,' he said.

'I hope there's no maybe about it.'

'Of course not. But you understand I've had some expenses.'

Jimmy looked round the dingy office. 'Expenses. Like what, you old skinflint?'

'Careful now, Jimmy.'

'Don't careful me. Tell me what you've got.'

'Everything you left me and more. This is not some cheap film Jimmy, where I've had it off with your loot and you kill me. Besides, you're on candid camera.'

Jimmy looked up into the corner where a baleful red light, like Satan's eye, glowed.

'CCTV,' said Goldstein. 'A marvel of the modern age.'

'I've seen it before,' said Jimmy. 'They have them in prison you know.'

'Of course. But let's get down to business, shall we? Take a seat, Jimmy.'

Jimmy did as was suggested whilst Goldstein, whistling gently between his teeth, made tea and presented the cup, together with a plateful of digestive biscuits. 'I've eaten,' said Jimmy.

'Just politeness,' said Goldstein. 'It's rare I see anyone from the good old days.'

'Me neither,' said Jimmy. 'But I intend to rectify that soon.'

'And not make their lives any brighter, I'll be bound,' said Goldstein.

Jimmy gave him an evil grin and tasted his tea.

Once the formalities were over, Goldstein leant his arms on the desk and said: 'You left me a quantity of cash and precious stones, delivered by a third party who shall remain nameless. I paid that third party upon your instructions a certain sum of money.' He opened his desk drawer and for one moment Jimmy thought this indeed might be a bad film and Goldstein would pull out a revolver and shoot him through the heart. But all that was in the jeweller's hand was an old ledger. Goldstein opened the book and ran his finger down a page. 'Hmm,' he mused. 'At the time, after deductions the amount came to seven thousand, six hundred and twenty pounds plus change.'

'More like ten grand,' said Jimmy.

'Deductions, Jimmy. Expenses. Some of that money was – how can I put it? – rather warm. It needed to go through a good wash and brush up before being allowed to go out into the world.'

'Fair enough,' said Jimmy.

'Times were good for a while,' said Goldstein. 'Very good in fact. The Eighties. What a decade for making money. Yuppies loved diamonds. Just like they loved cocaine and fast cars. I put your money and the tom to work, Jimmy, and at my last calculation, your credit stands at fifteen grand dead. Double what you left me. Only property could have seen you in better stead.'

Jimmy suspected that the ten large he'd lodged with Goldstein would in fact now be worth nearer thirty thousand, but beggars couldn't be choosers, and at least the Jew hadn't ripped him off totally. 'So let's see it then,' he said.

'I don't have that much cash here,' said Goldstein. 'But I can let you have five on account and the rest in a couple of days. If only you'd got in touch…'

Of course he was lying. Jimmy knew that, but there were certain protocols to be observed, and this was one. Anyway, five grand would do to be going on with.

'Come on then, Gerry, cough it up.'

Goldstein went to the small safe in the corner and opened it. He hid the contents from Jimmy with his girth, but Jimmy and he both knew that if he wanted to, the prison-hardened man could've taken whatever was inside, left the jeweller for dead and taken the film out of the closed circuit video machine. But Jimmy wasn't about to be done for murder again. He'd learnt patience on the inside and could wait. Goldstein knew better than to blatantly cheat him. Jimmy Hunter would track him down and hurt him badly if he did. Besides, the jeweller, though greedy, wasn't a fool. With hardly any effort, he'd made a nice few quid out of Jimmy's stash for himself over the past twenty years, and frankly, he didn't need the aggro.

He slammed the safe door shut and turned, a pile of notes in his hand. He carefully counted these out on to the desk. 'Happy now?' he asked, returning to his seat.

'It'll do,' said Jimmy, putting the money into his inside pocket. 'I'll be back the day after tomorrow. Friday. You'll be here?'

'All day until I have to join my family for dinner.'

'Then I'll be in around noon.'

They made their farewells and Gerry Goldstein opened the front door. 'Just one thing, Jimmy,' he said,

'What?'

'You used to be so stylish. Can I recommend the tailor just down by Chancery Lane tube station? Not bespoke, but quite fashionable.'

'I was just about to ask you,' said Jimmy. 'I remember those tweed suits you used to wear.'

'Happy days,' said Goldstein as he closed the door behind Jimmy. 'Happy days indeed.'

Standing outside in the street, Jimmy knew he'd been done up like a kipper by Gerry. Clockwork variety. But he'd had no choice at the time. He'd left the bulk of his money with Marje for the family, but that was, like her, long gone. At least Gerry had had the decency to give him something back. But then, he must have known that he would have been a dead man if he hadn't.

When the door to Goldstein's shop was locked again, the jeweller went back to his office, picked up the phone and dialled a number he'd committed to memory. It was answered after half a dozen rings. 'He's on the out,' he said.

'I know. This morning. Has he been round?'

'Just left.'

'Good. Did you give him his money?'

'Some. He's coming back for the rest Friday.'

'Perfect.'

'I don't like it.'

'You'd like it even less if you'd come up empty. How did he look?'

'Older.'

'Aren't we all?'

'But not bad. Apart from the suit he was wearing.'

The man on the other end of the line ignored the comment.

'Did you get him on tape?' he asked.

'Yes.'

'You're doing well, Gerry.'

'If he finds out what I'm doing...'

'He won't. Now, apart from the cash you're holding, he's skint. And he's not about to go for retraining on a government scheme. He'll want work and you're just the man to find it for him.'

'Christ, but I'm taking a chance.'

'Not half the chance you're taking if you cross me. Just be cool and no one will ever know. Ring me again on Friday after he's been.'

'OK?'

'OK.'

'Good. We'll talk then. And keep that tape.' And the phone went dead in Goldstein's ear.

Jimmy went back to Holborn, and found the tailors that Gerry Goldstein had referred to. It was all off the peg stuff, but Jimmy was fortunate that he was a stock size and hadn't put on or lost much weight inside.

The assistant brought him a selection of suits to look at, and Jimmy was amazed when he put on the first jacket that it closely resembled the mod styles he'd worn back in the early 60s, being tight, high buttoned, narrow lapelled with a back vent. When he examined the clothes closely he saw that the material could be better and there was scrimping over the seams, but he needed clothes so he picked out three suits, one navy, one black and one dark grey, half a dozen shirts in various pastel shades, underwear, shoes and a cashmere overcoat that set him back over seven hundred quid.

He stripped naked in the changing room and dressed himself in new clothes from the skin outward, collected together what he'd left prison in and asked the assistant to bin it. Then he took his packages and found a coffee shop. Where to stay was the next dilemma. He fancied a few days on his own before he looked anyone up, and a hotel would be favourite. Somewhere where he could come and go as he pleased and eat and drink in his own time.

From his wanderings around London all those years ago, he remembered a grand Gothic pile in Russell Square. He wondered if it still existed or had been pulled down. It was close to Goldstein's, an easy stroll, which would be handy. When his coffee cup was drained, he went outside and hailed a cab. When he got to the square he was pleased to see that the hotel was still there. He went in and up to the desk. 'I'd like a room for a couple of nights,' he said.

'Luggage sir?' asked the desk clerk.

'It's at the station,' Jimmy improvised. 'I've just arrived in town.'

He saw the look on the clerk's face and held up the carrier bags from the tailor's, adding: 'I'll pay cash. In advance.' Not that he cared about what some jumped-up little shit behind a desk thought, but he didn't need the hassle.

'No problem, sir,' was the reply.

'I'd like something high up,' Jimmy said. 'With a balcony.' He couldn't bear the thought of not being able to breathe fresh air, if indeed the air around there was that fresh.

The clerk sold him a corner room with a balcony and a view of the square and a bellboy took his bags and showed him the way. The cost of the room for two nights was astronomical to Jimmy, but he paid up. As far as he was concerned, there was plenty more where that came from, and he intended to get hold of it quickly.

The room was a fair size, about six times as big as his cell. Once the boy had gone – regarding the new pound coin in his hand much as one might look at dog shit on the sole of one's shoe – Jimmy hung up his new clothes, opened the French doors and went outside.

The view was perfect as far as he was concerned and, armed with a beer from the minibar, he stood and looked out over London and breathed deeply. In fact he was surprised at how much the beer affected him. Twenty years without certainly does something to a man. Not like the piss poor prison brew he was used to.

The rest of the day he spent exploring the new world he'd been released into. And what a strange world it was. Even the newspapers and what TV he was allowed to watch during the prescribed hours hadn't prepared him for what he was to see for himself. Sex, it seemed, was the new currency. Everything was about bunk ups. And everyone was at it. Or at least that's what you gathered if you relied on the media.

So he decided he'd get some. Christ, he thought, twenty years without a woman. Nothing but wanking and the likes of Terry the Poof for relief. But his first night he spent in the hotel, alone with the TV and the contents of the bar. Of course, there was a pay-to-view porn channel. Several in fact. So, dick in hand and totally pissed after a meal in the hotel restaurant, he fell asleep between clean sheets on a comfortable mattress.

He dreamed about the old days and revenge. He'd pleaded guilty to murder at the time. It was the only logical choice. But it still miffed him mightily that he'd never discovered who'd grassed him and the boys up for that bank raid in Brixton. The entire gang had gone away for varying sentences – apart from Dave Nicholls, of course, who'd died at the scene from multiple injuries. His body had been driven off in the coroner's wagon, and without any relatives to pay for anything better, he'd been buried in Potter's Field at the public expense.

Once he was settled with some real dough, Jimmy intended to look them all up, one by one, and find out the truth. But not all his dreams were revengeful. Some were quite pleasant. He dreamed he was down at the Scene club in Ham Yard, at the back of Piccadilly, where the mods gathered all those years ago to get blocked and listen to their favourite music.

* * *

He thought back to one event in particular. It was the night that The

381

Animals played their first London gig. Must've been Christmas, 1963, long before he'd joined up with John Jenner. Jimmy was working then at an advertising agency in High Holborn. Not far, in fact, from where he was sleeping now, and he'd clocked the building as he passed in the cab. In those days, he was a young buck looking for excitement. Jimmy was a dedicated mod and, after work every Friday, he'd stroll down Kingsway to the ATV studios near the Aldwych and blag his way into where *Ready, Steady, Go!* was being transmitted live. *RSG!* was the scene maker's show, presented by some old sod, but with the help of some of the coolest of the London mods. Cathy McGowan was Jimmy's ideal bird, and one night he actually chatted her up in the bar afterwards. But she had bigger fish to fry. Pop stars were her meat and potatoes, so Jimmy had no chance. She wanted a bloke with loads of dough and a flash motor. That night Jimmy vowed that one day that would be him.

It wasn't McGowan he dreamt about that night, but the girl he'd met at The Animals gig. The Scene was a tiny basement room, the steps leading from the street were narrow and steep and at the bottom stood a huge bouncer. And it was always packed. Sometimes the queue went round Ham Yard twice. That night it was freezing and Jimmy was dressed only in a suit. He refused to wear an overcoat because it hid the beauty of his outfit. Three button, single breasted, silver tonic Mohair with a pale blue, giraffe collar, tab shirt and a navy knitted tie. Highly polished black Chelsea boots from Topper in Shaftesbury Avenue completed the ensemble and, although Jimmy was shivering as he waited to go in, he knew three things.

One, the French blues he'd necked with a coke in a café in Soho were kicking in; two, he was the smartest geezer in the queue; and three, once downstairs the steam would literally hang over the crowd as they danced, so hot and sweaty did the club get within an hour of opening.

He was on his own that night, although he was aware of most of the faces waiting to enter, and nodded to several. And when he eventually gained access, he made straight for one of the booths that lined one wall. He bought a bottle of Coke on the way and sat at the table and checked out the crowd.

Guy Stevens was in the record booth, playing a selection of American soul and rhythm and blues. Just the music Jimmy loved. Ray Charles, Bobby Parker, The Impressions. One after another the little seven-inch singles pounded their music over the sound system. It was getting hot. Excitement was in the air. The Animals were the primo group from Newcastle, with just one single under their belt, and their singer Eric Burdon was the closest thing Jimmy had heard to his American favourites. Fuck Mick Jagger. He was nowhere compared to Burdon, and Jimmy couldn't wait for the set to start.

Then he saw her. When she and her friend entered, for Jimmy it was love at first sight. She was small, slim, dressed in a little two-piece mohair suit of her own. Navy blue. Underneath was a pale blue jumper and she wore Anello granny shoes with the little strap across the top and tiny heels. They were navy blue also. Her hair was short and black, viciously backcombed, and her face was white, with panda black eyes and a hint of red lipstick. She's for me, thought Jimmy, but he played it cool. It wasn't in the moddy boy make up to run after birds. They were supposed to make the first move, and the geezer could pick and choose.

Jimmy lit a cigarette and did a slow move with his hips to the music. He knew he was king of The Scene that night. Ever since he'd entered, his gear had got several approving nods from blokes who were real faces. Yeah, Jimmy was cool that night, and a bird like that on his arm would complete the ensemble. Not that Jimmy was without female company when he wanted it. He'd had loads of birds after losing his virginity one night in a Butlin's chalet a couple of years previously; he'd been spending a week down in Southend with a couple of lads from the mail room at the ad agency. But Jimmy wouldn't be tied down. That was, until Marje came into the room, and all that went by the board.

She'd noticed him too, he could tell. Although the room was getting crowded and smoky, he'd seen her eyes flash as they passed over him. He put the half-finished Coke on a shelf and did some fancy footwork with a reverse spin as *Night Train* by James Brown and The Famous Flames started. The two girls slid through the crowd in his direction and Jimmy smiled to himself as Guy Stevens segued into a stormer from Marvin Gaye. Jimmy leant against the wall and when the girls were within a few feet he allowed the smile to encompass them. 'Hello,' the girl of his dreams said, or rather yelled above the Motown beat.

'Hello, yourself,' Jimmy yelled back. But coolly. Always cool, always self absorbed, that was Jimmy. But for the first time ever, he felt that maybe it was time to let someone else into his world. The conversation, if it could be called that with the music cranked up to brain-destroying volume, was short. She was Marjorie, her friend was Susan. Both lived in Stockwell and both worked for a huge magazine company based on the South Bank. They'd been to school together, were two years younger than Jimmy and lived at home.

Jimmy liked the fact that they were south London girls. He'd dated women from all over London, and in those days the late transport was few and far between, and taxis, except in an emergency, were priced right out of the question.

'You blocked?' asked Marjorie after a few minutes.

Jimmy nodded through eyes as big as saucers. That speed was really working, helped by the carbonation in the Coca Cola, and he could feel it running though his veins like hot oil. 'You?' he said, feeling his teeth grind.

Marje shook her head, and Jimmy reached into his pocket, surreptitiously removed the envelope that he'd been given in a pub in the Strand earlier that evening. Inside were seven French blues. Jimmy had bought ten for five shillings earlier. He carefully pulled out two and gave one each to Marje and Susie. 'Have one on me,' he said.

The girls dutifully swallowed them, washed down by a mouthful of Jimmy's Coke. 'Sweet,' said Jimmy, then broke all the rules by asking Marje to dance. The next tune was one of Jimmy's all time favourites. *You Can't Sit Down* by the Phil Upchurch Combo, a rare and pounding 45 that had come out a couple of years earlier. Marje nodded, Jimmy gave his Coke to Susie to hold, and steered Marje into the centre of the tiny dance floor. The music, the girl's perfume and the amphetamine were a heady mix and Jimmy made his best moves as Marje danced close by. They touched, but didn't hold each other. He admired her style and could tell by her smile that she admired his. His only thought was that things didn't get much better than this.

The Animals were on late. They'd already done one gig in the suburbs but Jimmy didn't care. He was up for the night. He'd swallowed another pill and felt ten foot tall. Marje told him she had to be in by twelve or there'd be a row at home, but Jimmy had got paid that afternoon and was still holding folding and figured a cab ride to Stockwell was going to be a worthwhile investment – especially as he was then still living with his mum in Brixton Hill, only half an hour's walk away. 'Don't worry,' he said. 'I'll get you home, Cinderella.'

'And Susie.'

'Not a problem.'

The Animals played a storming set that night, but Jimmy couldn't remember any of it, apart from the great boots they wore. They played their first single, and as the crowd roared its approval, Jimmy felt Marje's sweaty hand slide into his, and his chest swelled with pride.

That was the start of a relationship that lasted almost twenty years. Then he was banged up and she married another man.

* * *

When Jimmy awoke in the hotel bed to dawn's early light, there were tears in his eyes. He'd loved his wife and he hadn't been around when she'd died, which had hurt him badly though he'd never admitted it. And the kids too, who he hadn't seen for years. They were also on his list for a visit, but Christ knew what he'd find. That was, of course, if he could find them at all.

Later, washed, shaved and dressed in his dark grey suit, Jimmy went down to breakfast. He felt good dining off white linen with silver cutlery and went for the Full Monty again. Afterwards he found the bellboy, and this time slipped him a tenner. When he had his full attention he inquired after the chance of some female company, and the boy smiled and winked. Jimmy listened as the young lad reeled off a list of likely young ladies. 'I don't care,' he said. 'Just as long as they do the business.'

'All my birds do the business, don't worry about that.'

'Fair enough.'

'I reckon it's been a while since you had a woman.'

'You're a clever little fucker, ain't you? But don't get too clever for your own good.'

The boy ignored the implied threat. 'Been away?' he asked, and instead of giving him a cuff for his cheek, Jimmy nodded.

'A long time?'

'Too long.'

'Thought so. You're kind of pale.'

'I'll give you pale, arsehole. Don't get smart with me or you'll be sorry.'

'I'll get you sorted, don't worry,' said the boy, not missing a beat.

'But it'll cost ya.'

'I've got dough,' growled Jimmy.

'You could've fooled me. It's been a long time since anyone gave me a quid as a tip.'

'Don't worry, you're making up for it now,' said Jimmy.

'So when do you want this bird?' asked the boy.

'Tonight. Are you working?'

'Never stop,' said the boy. 'Got me old mum to keep.' Somehow the boy reminded Jimmy of himself at the same age. 'How long you want her for?'

'All night.'

'Two fifty plus my commish.'

'Fucking Ada,' said Jimmy.

'But the bird I've got in mind is worth it. A lovely girl. Natural blonde and doesn't give a monkeys what she does.'

'Sounds all right.'

'A gram of coke would help, of course,' said the boy.

'I bet. How much?'

'Fifty for the best, plus my commish.'

'How much are you making out of all this then?' asked Jimmy.

'Fifty nicker will cover my trouble.'

'On top of the tenner?'

'What tenner?'

Jimmy smiled again and counted out five more notes. 'Now you vanish on me and I'll find you, and your old mum won't recognise you.'

'Do I look like that sort of bloke?' asked the boy with such a degree of indignation that Jimmy laughed out loud.

'No,' he said. 'I trust you. Thousands wouldn't. I'm off out today but I want her in my room by seven thirty tonight. And a couple of bottles of champagne on ice. Right?'

'Right,' said the boy. 'I tell you what, I'll get the bubbly in from outside. Half the price of what you'd pay here.'

'Plus your commish,' said Jimmy.

'Bloody right.'

Jimmy hung around the area for the rest of the day. Just clocking events and trying not to think too much about what he was going to do once he returned to south London.

At seven thirty he was in his room, out on the balcony with a glass of cold white wine. A minute later, there was a knock on the door. He opened it to find a tall, good looking blonde in a trenchcoat waiting outside. 'Mr Hunter?' she asked.

'That's right,' he said. 'But call me Jimmy. Come in.'

She entered, bringing with her an aroma of something expensive. He breathed it in and enjoyed the fact that it was perfume meant to entice him and no one else. He helped her out of her coat and hung it up. Underneath, she was wearing a simple black dress and dark nylons, all the better to show off her spectacular, curvy figure and long legs. 'I'm Jane,' she said. 'And I'm all yours.'

'That's great,' said Jimmy, almost stammering. Christ, he was feeling nervous. Not like the great Jimmy Hunter at all. 'Drink?' he asked.

'Please. But first, if you're happy with what you see, can we get the horrid money part out of the way first. Then we can relax.'

Jimmy smiled. He was beginning to like Jane. 'Sure,' he said.

'Two fifty. Right?'

'Perfect.' He counted out the money from his fast shrinking supply and dropped it on the dresser. She picked it up – didn't count it again, he was glad to see – and popped it into her purse. Probably right next to the can of mace, he thought.

'How long does that last?' he asked.

'Until you come.'

'Is that all?'

She made a moue with her mouth.

'Suppose I want you to stay all night?'

'Then that's extra.'

'How much?'

'A oner.'

What the hell, thought Jimmy. You don't get out of jail every day of the week. Or in fact, of two decades. So with a grin he counted out five more twenty pound notes. 'There you go,' he said. She put it with the rest in her bag.

'Until the morning then, unless I wear you out first.' She smiled.

'You might do that,' he said. 'It's been a while.'

'You've been away?' she said.

Was it that obvious to everyone? he thought, but then, maybe the bell boy had given her the SP.

'Yes.'

'Well, don't worry, I'll break you back in gently. Now did you say something about a drink?'

'Champagne,' he said. True to his promise the boy had arranged for two bottles of bubbly and they nestled in a huge ice-filled silver bucket on the dresser.

'My favourite. Oh and I brought this.' She went back to her bag and brought out a small envelope. 'Terry gave it to me to give to you.'

Terry must be the boy, thought Jimmy as he cracked open the wrap and found a quantity of white powder. 'Do you?' he asked.

'Does the Pope wear a dress?'

'Yes,' replied Jimmy. 'But he doesn't fill it like you.'

'Compliments,' she said. 'I think we're going to get along just fine, Jimmy. You're a real gentleman.'

'I try to be.' He opened the champagne whilst she cut out four generous lines of coke on the coffee table with her credit card.

'After you,' she said. 'It's your beak.'

Jimmy hadn't tasted cocaine as good as that for years. The stuff inside had been cut to the quick, but this stuff was primo, as he discovered when he took a snort. 'Jesus Christ,' he said. 'That's good.'

Jane followed his example and snarfed up her two lines quicker than it takes to tell. 'Fabulous,' she said. 'Is there any music?'

Jimmy found an FM station on the radio that played cocktail Jazz and slid the volume control to low, then said: 'I thought we'd have some dinner, if you fancy it.'

'You're treating me like a queen, Jimmy,' she said. 'I'd love some, but we'd better lay off the coke or I'll lose my appetite. But not, of course, for sex. It's my favourite pastime.'

Jimmy grinned and gave her the room service menu.

They ordered steaks and salads each, with a bottle of red wine. And while they were waiting, they finished the first bottle of champagne. 'This is like a proper date,' said Jane, as she sipped her drink.

'Do you mind?'

'Not at all. It makes a nice change from some of my punters. They're coming in their pants before I'm in the room.'

'You learn patience where I've been,' said Jimmy.

'Well, I'm glad there's no rush,' said Jane.

'Waiting makes it more fun,' said Jimmy, and she agreed.

The food came about thirty minutes later and they ate at the table overlooking the square. The sun had set and the lights and music were low and Jimmy could almost forget the previous twenty years, in the company of a such beautiful young woman.

When the dishes were empty and the trolley pushed out into the corridor, Jimmy put out the DO NOT DISTURB sign and Jane cut out more cocaine. In the haze of drugs and alcohol Jimmy forgot his previous nervousness and couldn't wait to fuck her.

It was better than he'd ever expected. She slid out of her dress and was wearing hooker's underwear. Brief, black and shiny with suspenders holding up her nylons. It was a convict's wet dream, and she did anything he wanted, plus some things he'd never tried before, even though she insisted he wear a condom. The hours flew by, but eventually they both fell into an exhausted sleep. As they were screwing, Jane noticed the scars from the bullet wounds he'd sustained that fateful morning in Brixton. 'Looks like you've been in the wars, Jimmy,' she said.

'A bit.'

She touched the one on his stomach and he flinched. 'Don't be afraid,' she said. 'I won't hurt you,' and she kissed it gently.

It was a strange feeling for Jimmy. In all his time inside, no one but the doctors had touched those scars. 'I'm not afraid,' he replied. 'It's just bad memories.'

'Tell me about them sometime,' she said. 'But now, fuck me again.' Which he did.

Dawn was breaking when Jane shook him awake. 'Sorry, Jimmy, time to go,' she said. 'Unless you want to pay double.'

Jimmy shook his head. The night had been everything he'd wanted, but it was time for business again. 'You were great,' he said. 'Can we do it again sometime?'

'If you've got the money, I've got the time,' she said and gave him her card. 'Not everyone gets one of these,' she said. 'Only special customers.'

'Do you mind a bit of a journey?' he asked.

'Not in the least,' said Jane. 'Call me anytime.' And she kissed him, grabbed her coat and she was gone, leaving him in bed feeling as if he were twenty years old again.

That morning Jimmy bought a suitcase and packed it carefully with his clothes. It was time to start sorting out his life, and the first call was on Gerry Goldstein to get the rest of his cash. Jimmy settled his bill at the hotel and left his bag, ready to pick up later. It was a cool morning and he wore his new overcoat for the walk from Russell Square to Hatton Garden. Lights were on in Goldstein's shop and he rang the bell. When the disembodied voice answered, he identified himself and the door clicked open. Goldstein got up from his seat as Jimmy entered the office.

'James,' he said, feeling the cashmere. 'Nice nanny.'

'It'll do. Have you got my money?'

'Of course.' He pulled a thick envelope from his pocket and gave it to Jimmy. Jimmy sat and checked the notes inside. Ten grand to the penny. 'Good,' he said.

'What are your plans?' asked Goldstein after he'd taken his seat again.

'That could depend on you, Gerry,' replied Jimmy.

'How so?'

'You used to set up jobs. Is there anything happening?'

'With all due respect, Jimmy, aren't you a bit old to be going back into business?'

'Never you mind about that. Is there anything in the wind or what?'

'Jimmy,' said Goldstein settling back and making a steeple of his fingers. 'Times have changed. I'm sure you've noticed. Since the advent of this thing…' he touched the monitor of his computer, '…most blagging is done electronically. It's so much easier and harder to detect. Going over the pavement has gone out of fashion.'

'Don't lecture me, Gerry,' said Hunter. 'We did get newspapers in prison. All I want is to do a blag, get some cash and straighten my life out. I've got things to do, people to look up. But I need more than a miserable ten grand. Now I don't want to get heavy with you. At least you gave me some of my money back.'

Goldstein made conciliatory noises.

'Don't fuck with me, Gerry,' Jimmy Hunter went on. 'I know you ripped me off but I'll let that go for now. What I want you to do is keep your ear to the ground. I can still hold a gun, so when you hear of someone putting a firm together put my name forward. Otherwise…' Jimmy didn't finish the sentence but Gerry Goldstein got the message.

'OK, Jimmy, I'll see what I can do.'

'Fine. You've got a mobile phone?'

'Of course.'

'Give me the number and I'll keep in touch.'

'Very well, but I don't get around like I used to.'

'Then start again.'

'OK, Jimmy,' and Goldstein jotted a number on the back of one of his business cards.

Jimmy took it and carefully placed it in his pocket. Then he rose and left the shop, walked back to the hotel, picked up his case and hailed a cab outside. 'Brixton,' he told the cabbie. 'Just by the Town Hall.'

When Jimmy Hunter had gone, for the second time that week, Gerry Goldstein called the number he'd memorised. Once more it took half a dozen rings to be answered. 'He's been and gone,' said the jeweller. 'Took the rest of his dough.'

'And?'

'You were right. He's looking for work.'

'Terrific. You know what to do now, don't you?'

'Yes.'

'Then do it. I'll be around soon to look at the tapes you've made. Keep them safe.'

'I will.'

'Of course you will, Gerry. Now just get on with your life and everything will be fine.'

'I hope so.'

'Make sure of it.'

And without a farewell, the phone clicked off in Goldstein's ear.

TWENTY-NINE

Jimmy Hunter received a call on a new mobile he'd bought two days later. He'd only given the number to Gerry Goldstein.

He was drinking a pint in the pub on the corner of the street where he'd recently rented a flat. When the cab had dropped him off in Brixton, he'd found a backstreet accommodation agency run by a very attractive black woman, who'd fixed him up with a one-bedroom conversion over a carpet shop just behind Brixton Hill, close to the old windmill and with a view of the prison walls. That appealed to his sense of humour. Jimmy and the woman had got on well, especially once she'd felt the material of his cashmere overcoat when she'd hung it on the rack in her office. She'd driven him to the flat in her Ford Fiesta, and he'd moved in there and then. He'd paid the deposit, security fee and one month's rent in advance, in cash. Jimmy noticed that she'd also admired his money roll, and he wondered if maybe he should give her a ring and ask her out on a date. The amount he'd forked out would've probably bought the whole building when he was a boy.

The call came about noon. The day was stretched out before him like a new roll of off-white, harsh, prison-issue toilet paper. 'Hunter?' said a voice he didn't recognise.

'Who wants to know?'

'Don't be aggressive, Mr Hunter,' said the voice. 'I understand you're looking for work.'

'What kind of work?'

'And obtuse as well. Never mind, I'm sure we'll end up the best of friends.'

'Who are you?'

'Just call me Bob. Gerry Goldstein gave me your number.'

'Yeah?'

'Yes. He said we should meet.'

'Why?'

'There you go again. You've been in prison too long, Mr Hunter. You've got to learn to trust people.'

'Is that so?'

'Indeed it is. Now, it seems to me that you're far too old for the kind of work you want, but as it's you, we're prepared to make an exception...'

'Who's we?' interrupted Hunter.

'All in good time. As I was saying, I don't know if you are aware of the way things are. Times have changed. It's rough out here in the world these days, Mr Hunter. Maybe too rough for a gentleman of your advancing years.'

'I'll manage. I always have.'

'Fair enough. But I must show you the kind of people you're liable to get involved with.'

'Go on then.'

'Right. I'm off on a bit of a jaunt tonight. Do you fancy accompanying me?'

'What kind of jaunt?'

'Oh, don't let's spoil the surprise. Where are you?'

'South London.'

'A big place. Can you get to the Isle of Dogs?'

'Suppose so.'

'There's a pub in Sugar Street, just off Manchester Road. It's called The Sad And Lonely Hunter. You won't forget that name in a hurry, will you?'

'If you're taking the...'

'Don't, Mr Hunter. Don't let my attitude get in the way of profit, and I won't let yours. Be at the pub by ten tonight. We're all off to Essex for a jolly.'

'No joke.'

'Not at all.'

'How will I know you?'

'That's better. You won't need to. I'll know you. Or someone else will. You're quite famous, in your own way.'

Hunter was silent for a moment. 'All right,' he said. 'I'll be there.'

'And don't worry, transport will be arranged to get you home.'

Just as well, thought Jimmy as he killed the connection. He was without wheels and, by the state of the driving he'd noticed on his travels around London, he'd need a lot more practice before he wanted to get behind the wheel again.

He arrived early at the street where the pub was located. It had been a convoluted journey involving bus, tube, Docklands Light Railway and another bus. It was a bloody nuisance. If he'd known, he'd've invested in a cab, but by the time he got there it was too late to worry about things like that. And the new Docklands was a revelation. He used to come to the Island in the 60s when it was a working river and one attraction was the drag acts that played the boozers. Then the quaysides were busy, with cargo constantly being lifted on and off boats; now the cranes were only used as decoration or for building new offices and flats for the people who worked in the offices. He hated to admit it, but the man calling himself Bob on the phone had been right. Times had changed, and he felt like he'd been left behind.

The pub he was looking for was at the far end of Sugar Street, close by the river. A mist lay lightly on the water and turned the lights to puffs of fluorescence. As Jimmy watched, a pleasure boat appeared silently through the fog. It appeared to float above the river, fairy lights gleaming along the cabin and, for a moment Jimmy imagined it was the spirit of the doomed *Marchioness*, moving in and out with the tides, its crew of ghostly revellers still looking for justice after all this time. But then the wind direction changed and he heard *Dancing Queen* by Abba bouncing across its wake, and he knew that it was real. Jesus, he thought, what's wrong with me? He turned his attention back to the Sad And Lonely Hunter public house. It looked as if it had seen better days, with peeling paint and a neon sign in the window for a beer that had gone out of production years before. But outside was parked maybe a quarter of a million quid's worth, maybe more, of fancy four-wheel drive machines that, to judge from their sparkling paintwork, had never been further off road than Tesco's car park.

Jimmy stood in the shadows and lit a cigarette, hiding the light by turning his back, and surveyed the scene.

Another monster truck was just parking up and four boisterous, well heeled punters tumbled out and hit the bar.

Jimmy couldn't understand what was going on and felt a nag of disquiet. But he needed money and, as ten o'clock approached, he headed for the pub and pushed open the door marked 'Saloon Bar'.

A crash of music and voices greeted him as he entered. It was hot in the bar, an unseasonable open fire burned merrily, the stereo pumped out dance music at top volume. And it was packed. Heaving with a mostly male clientele, all looking like they could afford to drink in establishments far better than this. Jimmy stood silently in the doorway. He still wasn't used to crowds, or noise – this place was full of both – and he felt like turning around and leaving.

Suddenly, a man appeared in front of him. He was tall, well built, in an expensive, hip-length suede jacket, about forty, with green eyes and a goatee beard. 'Jimmy, isn't it?' he said above the racket.

Jimmy Hunter nodded. He felt like this was some kind of trap and he was the victim.

'Bob,' said the man, not shaking hands. 'We're in the corner. Come and join us. Drink?'

'A beer,' shouted Jimmy as he followed the man to the bar where a bottle of Beck's appeared as if by magic and was pressed into Jimmy's hand.

They walked to the table, where another man sat. Younger, shorter, stockier. And hard, like Bob was hard.

'Jimmy Hunter,' said Bob as they sat. 'Tony. Tony Green.'

The younger man nodded.

Jimmy looked round the room. It was stifling and he eased out of the new leather jacket he'd bought that afternoon in one of the new, trendy menswear shops that had sprung up in Brixton. Five ton it had cost him but it looked and felt the business.

'Don't worry,' said Bob. 'We'll be off soon.'

'Where are we going?' asked Jimmy. He didn't like the idea of just going off to Essex – he knew there were too many bodies buried there in unmarked graves and under motorway extensions. He'd also heard a whisper that, for an unspecified sum, the furnace door at the old Ford factory in Dagenham could be left open for a quick and clean cremation, no questions asked.

'Don't worry,' said Bob again. 'You won't come to any harm with us. You spoke to Gerry?'

Jimmy Hunter nodded. He'd been on the phone to the jeweller as soon as he'd spoken to Bob earlier. Goldstein had assured him that he was to be trusted, even if he was a little flaky in his approach.

'That's all right then. Chill out, Jimmy. Drink your beer. They're starting to leave.'

The pub was emptying and outside the sound of powerful motors being revved was easy to hear. 'We don't all go at once,' explained Bob. 'And we don't go in convoy. Everyone goes more or less a different way. We don't want to attract too much attention.'

'Where we going then?' asked Jimmy.

'Just wait,' said Bob. 'You won't be disappointed.'

Jimmy looked at Tony Green, who just raised his eyebrows.

'What about this job then?' said Jimmy. 'I'm boracic.' He wasn't, but with jackets costing a monkey, he soon would be.

'Not quite, according to Mr G,' said Bob. 'Although I don't blame you for keeping your light under a bushel. And don't worry, we're not after stealing your stash.'

'It would hardly be worth it,' said Jimmy and he took a suck on the bottle of beer.

'Tony,' said Bob.

Tony nodded, and Bob said, 'Come on then, Jimmy. Time to go.'

They left their drinks and went outside, where Bob opened up a big

Dodge Ram truck and they climbed aboard, Tony taking the driver's seat, Bob next to him, and Jimmy sitting in the back. Tony switched on the ignition and the dashboard lit up like a NASA control panel. The engine started with a distinctive V8 rumble and they moved away from the kerb. For such a workmanlike vehicle, the interior of the truck was pure luxury and Jimmy sank back into the leather upholstery as Bob switched on the music system and from all around him came the sound of vintage Rolling Stones.

They headed east, picking up the A13 at Poplar, then the A11, until they joined the A12 at Ilford and drove, in silence except for the music, towards the east coast. Although Bob had said they didn't want to attract attention, Tony never let the big truck drop below the speed limit, flashing his brights at anyone in the way and it seemed like no time at all before they hit the Colchester ring road and moved into wild and woolly Essex badlands. Bob saw Jimmy's discomfort as Tony put on the full beams to light the darkness outside. 'Nearly there, and nothing much happens until the witching hour.'

Jimmy watched as the hedges rushed by the sides of the truck, the roads turned to lanes and became progressively narrower until twigs scraped the paintwork. Suddenly they turned through high gates and stopped as a guard came out of his hut and shone a torch into the cab. He nodded them through and they headed up a drive that opened into a circle, inside of which sat a huge barn illuminated by spotlights. All the four by fours that had been parked up outside the pub, plus a selection of other luxury cars, were standing empty, and a trail of men plus a few women were heading towards the barn.

'What is it?' asked Jimmy. 'Cock fighting?'

'Better than that,' replied Bob.

'Dog fights, bare knuckle? What?'

'Or all of the above,' said Bob. 'You're getting very warm.'

They exited the truck and headed towards the barn. Inside its cavernous interior, rough bleachers had been built of untreated pine around a huge sawdust-covered ring, walled with more pine to the height of an average man's shoulders. The whole place smelled of rotten meat and disinfectant, cheap perfume and testosterone. A massive PA system had been set up and was thundering out a drum and bass anthem that set Jimmy's teeth on edge.

Jimmy had witnessed all of those scenes he'd mentioned. Cocks that fought to the death, dogs that did the same, and men, stripped to the waist who went at each other with bare fists until only one was left standing. But even he wasn't quite ready for what he about to see that evening.

'Somebody owes me money,' said Tony Green, and he vanished into the crowd of people waiting to take their seats and treating themselves to drinks from cans and hip flasks as they queued. Those already seated were snarfing up various powders that could have been speed or coke or smack or almost anything that would get them high.

'So, Jimmy,' said Bob, taking him to one side. 'These are the sort of people you'll be mixing with if you come in with us. The new rich. The new movers and shakers who'll do anything for pleasure. Scum, most of them with too much money and not enough brains. The geezers are morons and the women are whores. They make me want to fucking puke.'

Jimmy shrugged. 'I don't care as long as there's money to be made.'

'Oh, there's that,' said Bob. 'But at what price?'

There was obviously plenty of money inside the barn as bookmakers were screaming odds and punters were almost throwing cash at them in the excitement of what was about to happen.

Jimmy and Bob took seats up in the gods and, as the lights above the spectators dimmed, spotlights beamed into the ring, bleaching it almost white.

The music ground to a halt and a booming male voice introduced himself as the master of ceremonies for the evening, and wished everyone in the building the luck they deserved. At that, Bob cracked a bitter little smile.

'And now,' said the MC, 'for the first event of the night, let's all put our hands together for a visitor from up north where the nights are long and the skirts are short, an old favourite down here at the barn. The one and very only, Mr Clubb.'

A gap appeared in the wall around the ring as a door opened and a huge man, stripped to the waist wearing tights and wrestling boots entered the ring. Around his waist was a bodybuilder's belt which included a codpiece to cover his privates, and his arms were protected by thick leather tied with laces. Around his bald head was a tartan bandanna. The crowd roared its approval at his entrance and he bowed from the waist, then raised both fists like prize fighters used to do in old photos as if to say 'Come on, if you think you're hard enough'. What Jimmy had first taken for fat coating his torso, gleaming with oil, now appeared as thick slabs of muscle, and every visible inch of his hide seemed to be covered in tattoos and scars. He struck more poses and reminded Jimmy of prisoners he'd met inside: gym freaks gone mental on steroids.

The crowd settled down as the man swaggered around the ring, the spotlights making shadows dance all around him. Then a huge bull terrier appeared from out of the shadows, straining on its leash.

Christ thought Jimmy. Man versus dog. He'd heard about this kind of fighting in jail, but never thought he'd witness it first hand.

If Jimmy had thought the man was scarred, the dog was worse. Its head had been so badly cut that his skull was clearly visible through the short hairs on its scalp, its ears were mere shreds of gristle, its back and flanks had been so cut and ripped, stitched and stapled that it resembled some hound from hell. And if he was the owner of a doggie soul then that too would have been scarred, Jimmy thought, for the dog had obviously been driven into a permanent fury. He – by the size of the bollocks hanging low between his legs, it was obvious the dog was male – growled and spat at the crowd and at Clubb, and at his minder, and as far as Jimmy could tell, at himself. He was thirty odd pounds of pure hatred, ready to kill the first thing he could get hold of. But it never barked and Jimmy just knew that someone had operated on the dog's throat to prevent it doing so.

Jimmy felt a strange affinity with the brute. Around his neck was a thick leather collar, covered in spikes, which looked as if they had been sharpened to points; they sparkled under the lights, as if tipped with diamonds. His legs were protected by laced leather, rather like that on

Clubb's arms, and the same went for his docked tail – though whether it had been docked or bitten off in some previous battle Jimmy didn't know. But more frightening were the metal spurs attached to the back of its legs, and the huge silver fangs that somehow had been attached to its jaws. This was a genuinely scary sight, and even Jimmy, tough as he was, could hardly suppress a shudder.

The dog was pulling so hard on the choke chain that kept him in check, that his owner was almost pulled into the ring after him.

The voice of the MC continued: 'And tonight, Mr Clubb is taking on an old favourite of ours, the wonderful Bullseye from Colchester, killer of over twenty dogs. Give him a great big hand, or should it be a great big paw?'

Applause burst from every corner, the betting was getting more frenetic, and Bob was jiggling in his seat from excitement. Christ knew what chemicals he'd been ingesting whilst Jimmy wasn't looking.

'Right, ladies and gentlemen,' continued the MC. 'Tonight we are privileged to witness – by public demand – a battle to the death between man and beast. No holds barred. Let the contest commence.'

Bullseye's handler slipped the leash and the dog leapt forward, climbing up Clubb's torso, heading straight for his throat, using the spurs for grip, baring those terrible metal fangs and ripping flesh as he went.

It was almost over before it began, but Clubb punched the dog hard on the snout and the animal flew backwards, hit the wall, crashed to the ground in a spray of sawdust, rolled and came back at the man.

Clubb's body was doused in blood and sweat which only added to the odour inside the room as the dog bit into his thigh through his tights, ripped off a chunk of flesh and material, shook it from side to side, drops of blood spraying like rubies. Clubb winced with pain but managed a vicious kick to the dog's side with his good foot, before limping to the side of the ring.

The cheers turned to boos as the dog circled the man, keeping him pinned to the wall.

'Come on, you cunt!' screamed Bob. 'We came to see a fight not a fucking dance.'

401

Jimmy sat and watched as Clubb tore off his headband and wrapped it round his injured thigh. The dog, knowing the first blood was down to him, backed off slightly, growling even louder, pink foam pouring from his mouth.

Christ, thought Jimmy. Maybe the sodding dog will kill this geezer. And it almost happened like that. Bullseye, game animal that he was, leapt again, this time fastening his jaws on Mr Clubb's left breast, biting clean through his nipple. The man screamed, the crowd echoed his cries and the dog landed on all fours and swallowed the chunk of flesh whole. Clubb held on to his chest, his face a mask of pain and for a moment it did look like the fight was over and the dog the winner. But it was not to be. Clubb moved forward and Jimmy saw that from somewhere he'd produced a set of brass knuckledusters, which he slid on to his right hand. He wasn't the only one to see, the place erupted with noise and Jimmy couldn't work out if Clubb was breaking the 'Queensberry Rules' of man versus dog, or if the audience was giving him their backing.

The dog leapt again, but Clubb was too quick and landed a mighty roundhouse punch with the knuckles to its jaw, which dislocated with an audible crack. Clubb was on it in a second, grabbing it by one back leg, and using its own weight to swing it round and bounce it off the wall. Then he picked it up by its tail and collar and smashed it down, back first, over his uninjured knee. If the sound from Bullseye's jaw dislocating had been loud, the sound of its spine breaking silenced the crowd. The dog was bent almost in half across Chubb's thigh, shit flying from its anus and vomit shooting from its mouth, soaking the sawdust. And from its mouth too came a high-pitched scream that froze Jimmy's blood almost solid. Its bark might've been removed, but nothing could silence that death sound, the last noise it would ever make.

Clubb lifted the dog high above his head, faeces and puke dripping down on to his body, and threw it clear across the ring, where it lay twitching until it was still. But the spectacle wasn't over yet. The man advanced towards the terrier, picked him up and stuck his hand down its throat. With a great growl, he tore out the dog's lungs and walked around the ring, exhibiting them to anyone with the stomach to watch, blood and mucus comingling on the pale flesh. Finally, he dropped them at his feet and kicked the mess across the ground, before throwing Bullseye's body against the wall of the ring where the animal lay dead.

The crowd was going mad. People who'd backed Clubb were screaming for their winnings, and the bookies were screaming about the legality – or otherwise – of the brass knucks. Jimmy could see it all going off big style when the dog's minder, obviously miffed at his pet's demise, appeared, carrying a huge wooden stave he'd found somewhere. Clubb was so busy taking his victor's bows that he didn't see what was happening until the stave smashed him around the back of the head so hard that it split in two. Clubb went cross eyed and hit the ground, where he lay next to Bullseye. Its owner then took the hound in his arms ignoring the blood and filth that coated its hide and gently held it close. Jimmy couldn't believe his eyes. Then Bob grabbed him by the arm and shouted in his ear: 'Ain't love grand? He probably used to fuck old Bullseye up the arse. Come on, we've seen enough. There's someone wants to see you.'

'Who?' said Jimmy as Bob dragged him back towards the doors.

'Questions, always questions, Jimmy. Be patient.'

They climbed down from the bleachers and made their way to the front door of the barn. Bob indicated for Jimmy to take a paved track through a small copse until a huge house came into sight. 'Blimey,' said Jimmy. 'You're full of surprises. What's all this about?'

'Used to belong to some rock star,' explained Bob. 'Forgotten now. He overspent his drug budget and it passed into the hands of the present owner.'

'Who is?' asked Jimmy.

'You'll see,' said Bob, and they went up to the front door, and Bob tugged on an old-fashioned bellpull. It was answered by a heavyset young bloke in a black suit and white shirt. Judging by the bulge under his left arm, Jimmy figured he'd never been to butler's school, or else he'd have got a better tailor.

'Hello, Andy,' said Bob. 'We're expected.'

Andy nodded and allowed them in, walking in front of them to a huge set of double doors, which he knocked on and, after a slight pause, pulled open. Bob gestured for Jimmy to enter, which he did.

Jimmy stopped dead in his tracks. 'Blimey,' he said to the man sitting in a deep leather armchair. 'Danny Butler, is that really you?'

THIRTY

Jimmy couldn't believe his eyes. Bob left, closing the door behind him, leaving Jimmy alone with his host. Daniel Butler, the fixer for the aborted raid on the bank in Brixton over twenty years earlier, sat in an expansive leather armchair, his feet resting on a leather stool, an antique coffee table at his side, sitting on which was a balloon glass of brandy, a decanter, and an ashtray in which burned a huge cigar. He had a smile on his face as big as a half moon.

'Christ,' said Jimmy. 'Your man said it would be a surprise, but I didn't expect this.'

Although Butler had aged, put on weight and his hair had turned white, Jimmy would have known him anywhere. 'Danny, I don't believe this,' he said, still stunned.

'Believe it,' said Butler, pulling himself to his feet and extending a hand that twinkled with diamonds. 'Believe it.'

'What the hell is all this then?' asked Jimmy when he'd let go of Butler's mitt and his host had waved him to a matching chair, lifted the decanter and made a quizzical face.

Jimmy nodded a reply and Butler poured a large measure into a second glass. Jimmy took the glass, inhaled the fumes and smiled. He smiled again when he sipped the heady spirit. 'Good stuff,' he said.

'Nothing but the best for me and mine. The wages of sin, my old friend,' Butler replied.

'Not bad wages by the look of things,' said Jimmy. 'Better than the minimum anyway.'

'Quite right. And how are you?'

405

'I'm out. And I'm hungry.'

'Oh, Jimmy,' said Butler.

'Do you really want to get back into the life?'

'I was never out of the life. Remember? I've just done a score as category A.'

'It should never have happened,' said Butler. 'But I told you at the time it was risky taking on that bank. Remember? The out was always the weak part.'

'I remember. But we were grassed. I remember that too.'

'So you were.'

Jimmy's eyes narrowed. 'Do you know who?'

Butler smiled again. 'Of course,' he said.

'Who?'

'Does it matter, Jimmy? It was all a long time ago.'

'Like yesterday to me. My life stopped that morning.'

'So did a certain detective constable's.'

'He was a traitor. He turned on his own.'

'He didn't turn on John Jenner, although he knew enough to put him away for years.'

'And Jenner knew all about him too.'

'Thick as thieves, those two were.'

'You can say that again. So who was it, Danny? Who blew the whistle on us?' Jimmy pressed.

'Danny. It's been a long time since anyone's called me that. Nowadays it's Mr Butler or sir.'

'Tell me,' said Jimmy.

'What's the rush? You'll find out, for all the good it'll do you. Savour it. Treat it like that excellent brandy you're drinking.'

'I've been savouring it for over twenty years.'

'Brooding on it, more like.'

Jimmy shrugged agreement.

'Then a little longer won't hurt, will it?' Jimmy didn't reply. 'Now Gerry Goldstein's been putting it about that you want work,' said Butler.

'Need money more like. That shyster stitched me up.'

'That's not what he told me. He says he gave you a fair return on your investment.'

'Bollocks.'

'He could've said he'd lost the lot. Have you checked the stock market lately?'

'No. I cancelled my subscription to the *Financial Times* when I went inside. Forget Gerry. Tell me about the grass.'

'Just another traitor, Jimmy. He was up for something very serious, and put you lot in it.'

'But who?'

'Like I said, Jimmy, all in good time. Let's get down to business.'

Jimmy sighed, but knew there was no shifting Butler when he was being stubborn. All in good time is right, he thought. 'OK. What's the job?'

'Be patient, Jimmy. But I can tell you it's big. And it'll be soon. But at the moment it's on a need to know basis and…'

'… And I don't need to know?'

'Not at this moment. You've been away a long time. No one knows, including you, if you've still got the old…'

'Bottle,' said Jimmy.

'Precisely,' said Butler. 'I think you should test yourself first on something small.'

'Are you taking the piss, Danny?'

'When it comes down to business, I never take the piss, Jimmy, you should know that. Now how's the kids?'

* * *

Sean Pierce knew that Jimmy was out. He'd got the information even before Jimmy himself was made aware of his release date. And on the morning that Jimmy reappeared into the world, he'd been watching the front of Brixton Prison from a doorway in flats across the road. Sean had made it his business to know what Jimmy looked like after twenty years. Which was just as well, because he would never have recognised the middle-aged man who walked out of prison as the young father he remembered. He followed Jimmy as he hopped from bus to bus on his way to Holborn, too busy gawping at the sights to realise he was being tailed. And he'd stood outside Goldstein's as Jimmy had transacted some unknown business there, then he'd trailed him again to the tailor's shop and even managed to utter the immortal words 'Follow that cab' to a taxi driver after Jimmy had taken a cab to the hotel in Russell Square.

But then Sean was due at work and he had to return to south London, where a split shift and the eventual need to sleep prevented another visit to the hotel until Friday afternoon. By that time, Jimmy had already checked out. Even so, Sean knew his father wouldn't be far away and that he would turn up soon.

Sean was still living in the garage flat adjoining Linda's house. He could've moved out months before but somehow it seemed easier to just stay put, to become increasingly involved in the upbringing of his niece and nephew, and to offer babysitting services on his lonely nights off when they happened to coincide with the nanny's. But Linda rarely ventured out after dark any more and no one ever visited. And over the past few months, Sean had watched her become increasingly jumpy and nervous, lose weight and begin biting her nails again, just like she had when she was a young girl. He tried to ask her what was wrong, but every time he did, she turned on him, and he soon stopped. Women's problems, he surmised.

But just as she was without a man, he was without a woman. He'd received a good few offers from women he met at work, both in and out of 'the job'. But he hardly, if ever, took them up on it. The shadow of his father's release sat heavily on his shoulders and Sean didn't need any further complications in his life. He'd actually made a date with DI Sally Cooper, who he'd met at the murder scene at Loughborough Junction, but it hadn't really worked. Her rank, and the fact that she'd talked shop all evening, had put him off.

Luckily, Linda's moods didn't seem to influence the children, who were both of a sunny disposition. So he left well enough alone and hoped that she'd eventually come through whatever crisis she was suffering. But in her own time.

That Friday evening, after he'd lost contact with Jimmy Hunter, he knocked on the kitchen door at the back of the house and Linda let him in. The children were in bed, the nanny was off at some au pairs' gathering – where they moaned about the meanness of their employers and the behaviour of the children in their care – and Linda had been sitting alone at the kitchen table. Alone, that was, apart from a bottle of white wine, a single glass, a packet of cigarettes, a lighter and an ashtray.

He frowned when he saw the clutter. 'I didn't know you were smoking again,' he said.

'There's a lot of things you don't know about me,' she said, fetching another glass from the cupboard and pouring him one. He sat down, opposite her chair.

He waited for her to enlarge on the remark, but when nothing was forthcoming he said: 'There's one thing I do know.'

'What's that?'

'He's out and on the move.'

For a second there was a flash of something in her eyes. Something like interest. Something like the old Linda. 'Who?' she asked.

'Our father.' He didn't add 'who art in heaven'.

'Oh, him,' she said, the interest dying as suddenly as it had appeared.

'Who did you think I meant?' he asked.

'Forget it.'

'And he may try and look us up.'

'If he does I'll stick my finger in his eye,' she said and lit another cigarette.

* * *

'My kids,' said Jimmy in reply to Butler's question. 'I don't even know where they are. Whether they're alive or dead.'

'But I do,' said Daniel Butler. 'Both very much alive, I'm happy to report. Did you know you're a grandad?'

Jimmy's eyes widened. He'd often thought it was a possibility but hadn't dwelt on it. Despite the excitement Butler's words generated, he fought to remain calm. Butler had too much on him already and knew far too much about him as it was. 'No,' was all he said.

'Well, you are. A boy and a girl. Luke and Daisy.'

The news was almost too much for Jimmy on top of everything else that had happened recently. 'Christ. Where are they?'

'You're in south London, I believe,' said William.

Jimmy nodded.

'Then not far away.' He smiled an unkind smile. 'And your boy. Sean, isn't it? Did you know he was a copper?'

Jimmy couldn't believe his ears. 'Do what?' he almost shouted.

'Detective Sergeant,' said William. 'Doing well. Course, not with your name. That would never do. They don't even know who his real father is.'

'How do you know all this? And how's Linda?'

'Proud mother of two. Sean hasn't married. Not even got a girlfriend. No, don't worry Jimmy. He's not a shirtlifter. He just seems more interested in looking after his widowed sister and her little brood and moving up through the police service than in playing happy families in suburbia.'

'Widowed?' Jimmy couldn't take it all in. 'What happened?'

'Car crash a year or so ago. Left her with a tiny baby girl who never knew her daddy. Linda came out of it quite well though. Got a decent pay-off as I understand.'

'So how do you know all this?'

'It always pays to know things, Jimmy. Information is power, isn't that the expression? And as we're such old mates, I made it my business to keep an eye on them. A friendly eye, of course. I've never interfered. Just filed every drop of information away for future reference. And if you're with us, I'll be able to give you the full SP.'

'Thanks,' said Jimmy. 'Thanks a lot.'

'But before you rush off to your family's waiting bosom, we need to talk business.'

'Yeah.'

'Yes, I've got a little job for you, Jimmy. Interested?'

'What and how much?'

'I want you to kill some people.'

'Do what?'

'That's what you do isn't it, Jimmy? Kill people?'

'Not recently.'

'But once a killer, always a killer – that's what they say, isn't it?'

'Who says?'

'The elusive "they". But let's not get metaphysical. Will you do it or not?'

'Who is it?' asked Jimmy.

'They're here. At the entertainment. By the way, did you enjoy it?'

'I saw more claret when we invaded the nonces wing at Gartree and gave them a good seeing to.'

'I'm sure you did. But we digress. The target is a man named Smith. Rodney Smith.'

'And who is he?'

'Just another traitor, Jimmy. It doesn't matter who he is and what he's done. It only matters that he did it, and now he has to pay.'

'And who's the other?'

'His wife. A horrible little ginger slapper. She won't be missed.'

'Is she a traitor too?'

'She cohabits with one, but otherwise she's just a tart.'

'So why do I have to kill her?'

'Because she'll be with him. They're always together. In fact, it's a kindness to put her out of her misery. She'd only pine with him gone… Just one moment.' Butler stood up and went over to an antique, roll top desk, where he opened the centre drawer and took out a pair of thin, black leather gloves which he tossed to Jimmy. 'I hope they fit,' he said. 'Put them on.'

Jimmy did as he was told. The gloves were skin tight and he made a fist of each hand to ease them on. 'They'll do,' he said.

'Come here, please,' said Butler.

Once again Jimmy did his bidding. The drawer was empty except for a small automatic pistol with a fitted silencer, a set of car keys and a folded sheet of paper. 'The gun has been cleaned inside and out,' said Butler. 'No prints on it or on the ammunition. Likewise the keys. The car is outside and clean too. You take it away with you tonight.'

'I haven't driven in over twenty years!' protested Jimmy. 'And I don't have a licence.'

'So you'll be breaking the law. What a surprise. Just drive carefully, Jimmy, and you'll be fine.' Butler picked up the paper, unfolded it and handed it across. On it was an address and a car registration number. 'Learn these,' said the white-haired man, 'then give it back.'

Jimmy looked at the address – which was in New Addington near Croydon – committed it and the car number to memory, before handing the paper back to Butler who used a gold cigarette lighter to set it on fire, before dropping the burning remains into the cold fireplace and crushing them to fine ash. 'Bob will point them out to you, and their car. It's a Lincoln. Very rare over here. You can't miss it. This is what you do. Tomorrow is the bitch's birthday. Rodney has booked a table at the Ivy for dinner. They'll drive up. They should be finished by eleven and home some time after midnight. The house is large, with a two-car garage under remote control. They'll drive in and you'll be waiting. The place is alarmed to the hilt, but don't worry about that. You don't need to be inside. Just follow them through the garage doors and do the business. You'll be in and out in seconds. Then take your car and drive it to Sainsburys at Nine Elms. You know it?'

Jimmy shook his head.

'Then find it some time tomorrow before you go. Park the car there with the keys on the back offside tyre and it'll be collected. Vauxhall Bridge is just a few minutes away. Drop the gun in the river, then go home and have a good night's sleep. Simple.'

'I'm not a shooter,' said Jimmy.

'That's not what Billy Farrow would say – if he could.'

412

'That was a shotgun. This is a pistol.'

'Thanks for the lesson in ordnance, Jimmy, but I can tell the difference. You've used one of these before, haven't you? Some time during your illustrious career?'

'Twenty five years ago.'

'You'll manage. Otherwise, forget it. I'll say goodbye, get Bob to drop you where you want to go, and no hard feelings.'

'No,' said Jimmy, picking up the pistol. He dropped the magazine out of the butt, pulled back the slide to make sure the chamber was empty, checked the load in the clip and slapped it back home. 'I'll be fine.' Then he unscrewed the silencer, put it in the inside pocket of his jacket and the pistol into the right side pocket. He lifted up the keys and stuffed them into his trouser pocket. 'What's in it for me?'

'Rodney and his wife both wear very expensive watches. Rolexes covered in diamonds. They're worth maybe eighty, maybe ninety grand altogether. Stupid waste of money.' The irony of the fact that he was wearing a handful of rings with more diamonds that Jimmy had ever seen seemed to escape Daniel Butler. 'They're yours. There have been a number of robberies by so called 'Rolex raiders' over the last few years. Some of them sadly ended in tragedy. This will be one such. Personally, I'd dump them into a drain as far away as possible, but it's up to you. They'll be the hottest pieces of tom in London by noon the day after. Still, maybe Gerry Goldstein will take them off your hands. Rodney always carries a fat wallet full of cash. That's yours too, and his and hers credit cards. But once again the best bet is to lose them somewhere where they'll never be found.'

'So all I get is a bit of cash.'

'And my eternal gratitude, Jimmy. That's worth more than gold round here. And of course, I'll know you're up for the job I'm planning, and I'll let you know who grassed you up all those years ago. You'll get a result, Jimmy. And there's always the matter of Sean and Linda and your pretty little grandchildren...' The way he said it was almost a threat.

Jimmy knew he was buggered. Damned if he did, damned if he didn't. He shrugged. 'You're not setting me up here, are you?' he asked.

'Don't be silly, Jimmy. If you get captured it'll be your own stupid fault. There's no connection between you and them. Not that any dumb plod could work out anyway. You don't know them, they don't know you. Just do it.'

'OK, Dan,' said Jimmy. 'Let's have a gander at them then.'

Butler smiled, picked up the phone on the sideboard, pressed in a single number and whispered something into the handset. Within seconds, Bob opened the door, a big smile playing on his lips. 'Come on then, Jimmy,' he said. 'It's getting late.'

Butler took Jimmy's gloved hand in his own and shook it. 'It's been good seeing you again, Jimmy,' he said. 'And all being well, we'll meet again in a few days. Just do the business and everything in the garden will be lovely.'

'I'll do it,' said Jimmy, disentangling his hand and following Bob out of the house. They went back to the barn, where things seemed to have hotted up in their absence. Inside it was as steamy as a sauna, and they pushed their way to the front where Bob grabbed Jimmy's arm and said: 'Your two o'clock.' Jimmy glanced over and saw an immensely fat man in a suit sitting next to a small redhead who looked as if she was one visit to the plastic surgeon over the limit.

'Fatty?' said Jimmy.

'That's the boy,' replied Bob. 'I hope he's enjoying himself. It's his last time here, so I believe.'

Almost his last time anywhere, thought Jimmy, if I do it right. But he said nothing.

'Come on then,' said Bob. 'You've seen enough. Your car's outside.'

They left the barn and walked to the makeshift carpark where Bob showed Jimmy a huge black American car that looked something like an oversized Jaguar. It had the same number plates as he'd seen on the paper Butler had given him. Further into the shadows was an anonymous-looking, dark-coloured saloon was parked. 'This is yours,' said Bob.

'Untraceable. Even so, try not to get any parking tickets,' and left him alone with a cheerful wave.

Nervously, Jimmy climbed in behind the wheel. He found the ignition and turned on the engine; it responded immediately and ticked over smoothly. It took Jimmy a few minutes to find the light switch and he inspected the control panel, which seemed to have many more dials than the cars he used to drive. He just shrugged. It was automatic which was a help. Jimmy engaged reverse, eased out of the space and, changing to drive, headed for the gates. Once outside on the dark lanes he realised he didn't know where he was going, but trusted to luck and, after driving around aimlessly for twenty minutes or so, found a signpost to the A12; before he knew it, he was heading in the direction of London and quite enjoying the experience. The roads were deserted at that late hour which was a relief but, when he reached the suburbs, he was surprised at the amount of traffic. He cruised across the river at Southwark Bridge and was soon in Brixton, where he parked as close to his flat as he could and was in bed by four thirty.

He was awake again by ten and, after a brief toilet and a cup of tea, which was all he could stomach with the nerves he was feeling, he hopped in the car and drove until he found the supermarket at Nine Elms. Satisfied, he headed down to Croydon, little knowing that he had actually passed the street in which his family were now living.

New Addington had always been a strange mixture. On the one hand there were the mansions of the old and new rich, sitting right next to one of the largest and roughest council estates in Europe. The rich and poor coexisted uneasily, but somehow managed to get along without too much trouble.

Jimmy drove slowly past the target address a couple of times. It was a mock Tudor pile, with neatly mown lawns and flower beds filled with flowers terrified into military formations. There was a high wall round the property and iron gates topped with vicious spikes. The back of the property was accessed via a small service lane and that looked to be his best bet. Jimmy thought he'd better get himself some climbing boots before he attempted to get inside and went back to Brixton to do some shopping. He then spent the rest of the day in his flat, watching TV and waiting for night to fall.

By ten o'clock he was back in Addington, the car park in a pub forecourt two streets away from the Smith residence, and Jimmy was strolling down the lane that backed on to the property.

There was no one about, though Jimmy had seen a couple of people taking their dogs out for a late night constitutional on his way there. He wondered if the Smiths were pet lovers, but decided that, if they were, Danny Butler would have told him about it. Or maybe not. Just a little surprise to keep him on his toes? With a quick glance up and down the dark thoroughfare, he was up and over the wall, glad of the time he'd spent in the various prison gyms during his incarceration.

There was broken glass embedded in concrete on top of the wall, but it was old and dull and Jimmy avoided being cut. Dropping to the ground, he crouched for four or five minutes until he was sure no alarm had been raised. Eventually, he stood up and slunk across the back garden, through the shadows that made him almost invisible in his dark jacket and jeans.

He found the back of the garage and worked his way around. When he'd peered through the gates earlier, he'd seen powerful spotlights mounted at the front of the house, and remembering conversations he'd had with various burglars inside, he suspected they were fitted with motion switches, so he stayed close to the ground and behind them. He took the pistol out of one pocket and the silencer from another, and screwed them together. He worked the action, putting a bullet in the chamber and cocking the gun; he flicked off the safety catch and settled down for his long wait until the Smiths returned home. He just hoped that they hadn't gone on to a club or something after their meal.

Whatever, he thought. At least it wasn't raining.

THIRTY-ONE

Time dragged on for Jimmy as he waited. It was all quiet in New Addington that night, and not even a cat or a dog fox disturbed his vigil. His eyes grew accustomed to the half-light that night time had become, even in the outer suburbs, and he could clearly make out the orange glow in the sky that was London. He had plenty of time to think about the events that had led him to this particular place at this particular time, and he wondered how things could have been different. Under different circumstances, could he have been tucked up in bed at home, an honest man with a wife, children and grandchildren who were proud of him and wanted his love?

Deep down Jimmy knew that it was too late for all that. It was even too late for regrets about what might have been. Even so, his mind went back to pleasanter times when he and Marje, Linda and Sean had been together and happy.

* * *

The 70s had been Jimmy's decade. The kids were just babies then. Thanks to a slight problem with the law, Jimmy had spent most of the late 60s banged up in Wandsworth, leaving Marje to keep their home together in Kennington. No conjugal visits in those days, hence no patter of tiny feet. But Jimmy made up for it over the next ten years. He was part of the Jenner gang then, and it was during those ten years that John, Hazel, Billy Farrow, Chas and the rest really made their impact on south London. Business was booming, even though the streets were in a turmoil, what with strikes of public service workers, garbage piling up and bodies lying unburied in the mortuaries. But it was the perfect time

417

to be a villain. As inflation spiralled out of control, the Jenner gang calmly doubled their rates and watched the loot roll in. *The Sweeney* was the most popular show on TV, watched by coppers and villains alike, and pretty soon it was hard to work out which was which. Friday afternoons there was almost a queue of unmarked cars outside Jenner's office as, one by one, Old Bill on the payroll popped in for their brown envelopes bulging with cash. And Jimmy still loved the music and the fashions, though he'd be loathed to admit it now. Punk rock. That had been his favourite, even though he might've been a little old for it at the time. But not too old to appreciate the punk girls in their gothic makeup and ripped fishnet stockings. And then came the 80s... and it all fell apart.

* * *

As he waited for his quarry to return home, he heard a few cars coming and going, and each time he tightened his grip on the pistol, but they were all false alarms. Eventually – his cheap watch told him it was one oh six in the morning – the sound of a vehicle approaching was followed by the rumble of gates opening at the end of the drive. He knew then that he was in show business.

The car slowed as the security lights came on and Jimmy shielded his eyes against the sudden light. The garage door began to roll up smoothly and Jimmy felt himself tense.

The huge black car crept forward into the garage and Jimmy stood, his legs cracking. Too old, he thought.

As the garage door began its downward journey, Jimmy ducked beneath it then jumped up, gun at the ready. The Lincoln had stopped next to a Volkswagen Golf, probably Mrs Smith's personal transport. The driver and passenger doors of the big car opened in tandem and Rodney Smith and his missus stepped out on to the concrete floor.

Rodney was the first to notice Jimmy standing there. 'What the... ?' he said, and Jimmy raised the pistol. But looking at the pair of them standing there, Jimmy made the one mistake that's unforgivable in the assassin's code. He stopped to think about what he was doing and, as he did so, the gun began to tremble in his hand. He had come down with what is known as 'shooter's shake', and all he wanted to do was to drop the gun and do a runner. But the next thought that flashed through his mind was, 'They've both seen me up close, now I've got to do it.' He grabbed his right wrist with his left hand in an attempt to steady it, and pulled the trigger. The silenced gun made hardly a sound as the first bullet missed by a mile. 'Shit,' said Jimmy out loud and fired again. The second shot punched a hole in Rodney Smith's neck, and exited in a spray of blood and meat. Jimmy squeezed the trigger again and a round hit the fat man in the chest. Smith put his hand on the roof of his car, blood flowing from both wounds and tried to say one last word to his wife. But all that emerged was a bloody gurgle and he fell to the ground with a crash.

Then Jimmy turned the pistol on Mrs Smith. But his hesitation had given her time to open the evening bag she was carrying and pull out a small, nickel-plated, pearl-handled automatic pistol and point it at him. He couldn't believe his eyes as they both fired together. His bullet hit her between her breasts and hers skidded across the side of the Lincoln, spun up and went through the right sleeve of his new leather jacket, chopping two neat holes as it entered and exited, hitting the closed garage door behind him and ricocheting around the garage before whacking into the wall of the house.

Mrs Smith's body hit the floor.

Jimmy stood for a moment before lowering his gun. He listened hard. The noise from his silencer and her tiny-calibre gun had made hardly any sound, but as quiet as it was outside, he wondered if the noise had carried to the neighbouring houses. He listened again: nothing stirred. He went into action. He checked her body first. She was still alive, but barely, and he held his gloved hand over her mouth and nose until he heard a rattle from her throat and she was still. He prised the gun from her fingers. It was a tiny .25 Sterling and he pocketed it. Then he went to Rodney. He was dead too.

Jimmy pulled up Smith's jacket and shirt sleeve and, just as Butler had told him, he was wearing a solid gold Rolex so covered in diamonds it was almost impossible to read the time. Jimmy unclipped the clasp, pulled it off and stuck that in his pocket. Inside his jacket, Rodney carried a thick wallet that was stuffed with fifty pound notes and credit cards. The cash went into one pocket and the wallet and cards into another. Then he checked Mrs Smith again. She wore a ladies version of the same watch and Jimmy tugged it off and added it to his loot. Her bag contained a purse, this time with just a few smaller notes but several more cards. Jimmy took the lot. By this time he was dripping with sweat and still shaking with nerves, but there was still no sound coming from outside and he reckoned his luck was holding. He stood and took one last look around before hitting the red button by the door, which, as he surmised, opened the garage from the inside. The sound of the door opening seemed as loud as a small war to his ears and he ducked through again and stood for moment in the harsh light outside, before heading back the way he'd come.

He was over the wall in a moment, briefly checking that no one was in the lane, and he walked as slowly as he could back to the pub car park, where his car sat in solitary splendour in a dark corner.

Once inside, he controlled the shakes, started the motor and headed towards central London, making sure he kept to the speed limit and obeying every set of lights. This was not the time to receive a tug from some keen traffic patrol. The Sainsbury's at Nine Elms was open all night and there were several vehicles in the parking lot. Jimmy dropped off the car, left the keys as arranged, and walked towards Vauxhall. He went on to the bridge and stood looking down at the dark river below. Although there were plenty of cars around, there was very little pedestrian traffic at that late hour. After a minute's observation, he dropped the silenced .22, Rodney's wallet and credit cards and Mrs S's purse into the water. He thought about dumping her gun too, but there was always a chance he'd need some firepower, the kind of people he was mixing with, and decided to keep it, dangerous though it might be to do so. Then he turned in the direction of home and walked most of the way, before picking up a night bus that dropped him off outside Brixton tube.

Jimmy Hunter didn't sleep very well that night.

The second person to see the Smith's bodies was Elsie Thomas, their cleaner. She let herself in the side gate as usual on the first of her twice weekly mornings. Elsie was almost sixty and looked every minute of it. She was widowed and lived alone in a one-bedroom flat on the New Addington Estate. She hated it. She hated the kids and the blacks and the Pakis. She hated the single mums with their screaming offspring, their late-night parties, drug taking and loud music. And for the fact that they could get a free home for just opening their legs and letting some randy git impregnate them. She hated her husband for dying without life insurance, and her children for leaving her. Sometimes she could hardly recognise herself as the young Elsie Richardson as she was then, who'd wet her knickers for Paul McCartney when The Beatles came to Croydon in 1963. She didn't think much of her employers, either. He was a fat pig and she was a mutton dressed as lamb tart. All those diamonds she wore... But they paid her well enough, and Mrs Smith was always there for a cup of tea and a chat. And the work wasn't too onerous.

That morning, as Elsie trudged up the drive, she saw that the garage door was wide open, both cars was parked up and the light was burning inside. That wasn't right. By the time she got close, she could smell something that reminded her of bonfire night and something else that reminded her of bad drains. Then she heard a faint buzzing and saw a small swarm of flies around the bodies. She didn't get too close, she knew not to do that. Elsie fished out the mobile phone that her eldest son had bought her 'just in case' to ease his conscience as his visits became less frequent, and called 999. Then she took out a packet of cheap cigarettes and her lighter, and smoked one in the warm morning sun, waiting for the police to arrive.

The scene of crime officers found two dead bodies, identified as the owner occupiers of the house where they'd been found, two bullet holes in the male cadaver, one in the female. Two .22 calibre bullets were dug out of the wall behind the deceased, one which had passed through the throat of Mr Smith, one which had not. A .25 calibre bullet was

421

discovered in the wall next to it; and on the floor, four .22 bullet casings without fingerprints and one .25 casing with some smudges. The bodies had been disturbed after death, and Mrs Elsie Thomas, who had discovered the double murder, confirmed that certain items seemed to be missing. Later, at the post mortem, three bullets were removed from the bodies. All .22 calibre. First conclusion: The unfortunate Smiths had been murdered by two or more armed assailants – hence the different calibre bullets – after a robbery had gone wrong. It wasn't the first time this had happened in the suburbs of south London and it surely wouldn't be the last.

The murders were going to be high profile for a day or two, and the police assumed that the killers had come from the estate up the road. They made plans to raid the flats of a few likely suspects.

Jimmy Hunter received a call on his mobile at about eleven. He'd finally managed to get off to sleep just after eight and, when the ringing tone woke him, he thought he was back inside and that it was the call for slopping out and breakfast. When he realised where he was and remembered what had happened the previous night, he reached for the instrument and summoned up enough saliva in his mouth to answer.

'Yeah,' he grunted.

'Good morning, Jimmy,' said Daniel Butler. 'But not for some.'

'Do what?'

'I read the news today, oh boy,' sang Butler, obviously in a fine mood.

'I don't know… oh yeah,' said Jimmy, recalling a Beatles tune he'd sung himself once.

'You did well, apparently.'

'If you say so.'

'I think we should meet.'

'Hold on,' said Jimmy as he swung his legs out of bed and made for the kitchen tap. He stuck his mouth under it and sucked down the water. Refreshed, he said into the receiver: 'Say again.'

'I think we should meet. We have things to discuss.'

'Like?'

'Your family's whereabouts, who dropped you in it twenty years ago. And your future employment. You've fulfilled your part of our bargain, and I've never been one to renege on a promise.'

Jimmy was coming fully awake by then and all he could think of for the moment were the two dead bodies in New Addington. 'Yeah, Dan,' he said. 'Whatever.'

'Could you make lunch tomorrow? My treat.'

'Lunch. Bloody hell, it's been a long time since anyone but the prison service bought me lunch.'

'Well, it's high time that changed. I know a little Italian in Kensington. Quiet, discreet and they do a fine veal Parmesan. Interested?'

'Sure.'

Butler named the place and Jimmy scribbled it at the top of the back page of yesterday's paper. 'One o'clock,' said Butler.

'I'll be there.'

'And everything went well?'

'As well as can be expected.'

'No hitches?'

'One. But nothing I couldn't handle.'

'You'll have to tell me all about it tomorrow.'

'I will.'

'One o'clock then.'

'See you there.' And Jimmy killed the connection.

He stood in his chilly kitchen, his feet cold on the composition floor, and filled the kettle. Once it was set to boil, he went to the bathroom, made a fast toilet and, once dressed, put a tea bag, milk and sugar in a mug. He knew he'd not be able to face food just then, and drank his tea looking out of the front window at the street below, wondering how soon, if ever, the cops would come for him.

It wasn't a happy thought.

The discovery of the bodies was too late to make the morning papers, but was reported on the local radio and TV during the day and made a splash in *The Standard* that evening. Not much of a splash, but enough to

423

make second story on page three of the early editions. It was just such an edition that Linda Spiers was reading when Sean arrived home from work that evening. He'd called in to see how Linda was, before going up to his flat. It was the au pair's night off and Linda had given the children an early supper and bath, packing them off to bed, before digging out the inevitable wine bottle and ashtray.

'Bad business,' Sean said, tapping the paper before getting himself a glass. He figured that it was easier to join her than to make some comment that would just set her off.

'New Addington,' she said. 'Just round the corner. This place is getting worse. What happened? Do you know?'

'I heard a bit,' he replied, taking a sip. 'At first they thought it was just a robbery gone wrong, but forensic figured out that the woman had a gun.'

'How?'

'I shouldn't be talking about this. But apparently there were a few bullets in the walls and they worked out that one had been fired at the shooter. And bugger me if it wasn't the woman who did it.'

'How do they know?'

'Well, once they figured the paths of the bullets, they checked both bodies for gunpowder residue, and it was on her hands.'

'Gutsy girl.'

'Gangster's moll, more like. Those two were rotten.'

'You know a lot.'

'I make it my business to know what's going on where I live. Anyway, neither gun's been found, so it's possible that more shots were fired, and that our killer's got a bullet in him.'

'They say in the paper that some valuable jewellery was stolen.'

'Yeah. Perk of the job. Or maybe the killer wanted to put us off the scent.'

'I can still wear my Mickey Mouse watch without fear?'

Sean didn't find the comment amusing. 'I suppose,' he replied.

'So what do you want?'

'Just to see that you're OK.'

'And not passed out on the sofa, with a cigarette in my hand, setting fire to the furniture.'

'Don't, Linda.'

'Sorry, Sean.'

'I wish I knew what was wrong.'

'So do I,' she lied.

Jimmy spent that day and night at his flat. He was in no mood for company, haunted as he was by the sight of the two people he'd gunned down in cold blood. He watched the story on the box and tried to read between the lines as to what the cops were doing. He ate little, kept the little pistol he'd taken off Mrs Smith handy, and marvelled at the intricate gold and diamond work on the two watches he'd stolen. Eventually, he found a loose board in the corner of the bedroom floor, levered it up and hid the Rolexes there. It wouldn't take much of a search to find them, but he figured that if the police got as far as his flat, he was done for anyway.

The cash he'd taken from the Smiths totalled about six hundred quid, but his leather jacket was ruined by the bullet that had come close to hitting him in the arm, and he knew he'd never wear it again. He bundled it up and put it in a black garbage bag ready to dump as far away as possible. He'd liked that jacket and intended to get another. So, cash wise, he'd come out of the job with less than a ton. Not much for two deaths, he thought. But at least he was going to get a free lunch out of it. If there was such a thing.

The next day dawned fine and Jimmy took a bath, shaved closely and dressed in one of his new suits. He set off early for his appointment with Butler, walked to the tube and made just one change to get to Kensington High Street. He found the restaurant just after twelve and, being early, he went into a pub on the opposite corner for a livener and to scan the paper he'd bought at the station. The murders got hardly a mention, so much other evil was happening in the world. He mentally shrugged, lit a cigarette and sipped at his lager. The door to the pub was open to let in the spring air and, all in all, he reflected that things weren't going too badly.

Jimmy was finishing his second pint when he saw a Roller draw up outside the Italian, with Bob at the wheel. Dan Butler got out of the back, said something to his driver, who pulled away. Jimmy watched through the open door as Butler entered the restaurant, then gathered up his cigarettes and lighter, left the paper where it was and walked across the street.

Once he'd pushed his way through the glass door of the trattoria, Jimmy saw that Butler was being seated by a skinny bloke in a black suit and white shirt, at a table set for four at the rear of the restaurant. A waiter approached him and Jimmy pointed to Butler's table and said: 'I'm meeting a friend.'

Butler looked up as Jimmy approached. 'Punctual,' he said. 'That's good. I'm having a G&T. Join me?'

'Why not?' said Jimmy and Mr Skinny bowed and left them. Jimmy pulled back a chair and sat opposite Butler. 'Expecting company?' he asked.

'No,' replied the white-haired man. 'I always get a big table in here. I like the room.'

'Fair enough,' said Jimmy, taking out his cigarettes. 'Mind if I smoke?'

'Course not. That's a good thing about Italians. They don't care if you smoke and eat at the same time. Very civilised. Not like some places these days, where they bring out the fans if you light up.'

'I wouldn't know,' said Jimmy, putting flame to the tip of his cigarette. 'Like I said, I've been eating in for the last twenty years.'

'But not any more,' said Butler, lowering his voice, although the opera playing softly on the music system and their distance from the other occupied tables in the restaurant would've made it impossible for anyone to eavesdrop. 'You did well, Jimmy.'

'I didn't enjoy it. You never said that bitch would be armed. She almost shot me.'

Butler laughed, then noticed the skinny bloke returning with their drinks and touched his lips with one finger.

Once the glasses had been set in front of them, Skinny asked if they were ready to order, and Butler shook his head. 'I'll call you, Luigi,' he said. 'There's no rush.'

'Of course,' said Skinny and left them alone.

'Cheers,' said Butler raising his glass.

'Cheers,' said Jimmy.

'I'm sorry about that,' Butler continued. 'I didn't know she was carrying, otherwise I would've warned you.'

'What kind of fucking woman does that?'

'A dead one,' said Butler. 'My spies tell me the cops are baffled.'

'And they'd know?'

'That's what I pay them for.'

'Good. Now, what have you got to tell me?'

'Slow down, Jimmy,' said Butler. 'All in good time. Let's order. I told you about the veal, didn't I?'

'Yeah. But not for me. I did a lot of reading when I was away. Books, magazines, newspapers. Anything I could get my hands on. It helped to pass the time. I know how veal calves are raised. Reminds me too much of being banged up.' He opened the huge leather-bound menu. 'I'll have minestrone and a steak.'

'Please yourself.' Butler gestured for Skinny to come back, which he did, and took their order. Butler asked for a bottle of something Jimmy didn't recognise, but he let it go. He'd drink any old plonk. His taste buds had been destroyed by prison food.

When the waiter – or whatever he was – had left them, Jimmy lit another cigarette and took a pull of his gin. 'My children,' he said.

'Living in Croydon,' answered Butler. He took a piece of paper from inside his jacket and gave it to Jimmy. 'Linda and Sean's address.'

Jimmy shook his head. So simple, he thought. 'And they're well?'

'Apart from Linda being a widow and Sean being in the filth. Yes, they're fine.'

'How old are my grandchildren?'

Butler told him and Jimmy sighed. 'Just babies,' he said.

'What are you going to do?'

'I don't know. Do they know about me?'

'Of course they do. Why wouldn't they?'

'I don't know what Marje told them. The last time I saw them they weren't much more than babies themselves.'

'And then Marje divorced you.'

'That's right.'

'Didn't that piss you off?'

'For a bit. Then I realised she'd done the right thing.'

'You're very cool about it.'

'It was a long time ago, Dan. And you learn to be philosophical in the shovel. That, or go mad. She did what she thought was right for herself and for them. And she was right. She was always skint. Always just about managing to scrape together to raise the fare to see me. Those bastards made it difficult for her. Always shifting me round the country from one place to another. It broke my heart to see them. In a way, I was relieved when she gave me the elbow. But I'd love to see my kids one more time. And my grandchildren...'

'They're a gift from God.'

'What about you?'

'One son. He has three little ones. Two boys and a girl. He married a girl from Edinburgh he'd met at university. He does something in computers. They live in Bristol.'

'See much of them?'

'Yes. I make time for frequent visits.'

'Does the boy know what you do?'

'Not really. My wild years were over before he was born. And you know I never did time.'

'You were lucky.'

'I trusted the right people.'

'And talking of that, Dan,' said Jimmy, as the starters were being served. 'I think there's something else you were going to tell me.'

'Indeed I was,' said Butler as he spooned Parmesan over his soup. 'Remember Dave Nicholls?'

428

'Yeah, course.'

Butler pulled a wry face.

'Dave?' said Jimmy, his minestrone untouched. 'Never.'

'It's a fact.'

'You're kidding me.'

'I've never been more serious in my life.'

'And then he got run over. Fuck me. But why? He was a good lad. Staunch. And how do you know?'

'Why? Because he was up for another blag. Billy Farrow had him in for a chat. All on the quiet, you understand. No PACE in those days. Anyway, Dave spilled the lot. Put you in the frame and expected to get off with a slap on the wrist. The banks were offering big rewards for information in those days, if you remember. So he was looking to have a nice little nest egg waiting when he got home.'

'I don't believe it. Who told you all this?'

'An ex copper. Well, he wasn't ex then. He was there. Ironically, it was him nicked Jack Dewhurst that day. Remember?'

Jimmy didn't, but he nodded anyway.

'This copper became a mate of your old friend, John Jenner. He made a few quid helping some of us out over the years. Sharman, his name was. A bad fucker. He spilled it over a drink a bit later. Thought it was funny. Poetic justice he called it, getting hammered by a Transit after using one so many times blagging.'

'Fucking hilarious. I've been planning on finding the bastard who did it for the past twenty years, and he's brown bread all the time. Why didn't anyone ever tell me?'

'Thought someone would've,' said Butler. 'But you were out of the loop. Anyway, you don't have to worry about it now.'

Jimmy dipped his spoon into his soup. 'It's amazing what goes on,' he said around a mouthful.

'Isn't it.'

The meal continued peacefully. The food was good, the service was discreet. The restaurant was busy and noisy, but not noisy enough to intrude, just enough to ensure that the two men at the table for four retained their privacy.

Both passed on dessert and ordered coffee and brandy. When it arrived, Butler sat back and lit a cigar. 'So there's just one other thing,' he said.

'Yeah,' said Jimmy.

'Yeah,' said Butler. 'I promised you some work, didn't I?'

Jimmy nodded.

'And I'm a man of my word. Like I said, Jimmy, you did well the other night. Very well. Better than I expected, to be honest.'

Jimmy felt a light bulb come on over his head. 'You knew she was carrying, didn't you?' he said.

Butler smiled.

'Fuck you, Dan,' said Jimmy, but not loud enough to cause a commotion. 'Was it her?'

Butler cocked his head.

'It was, wasn't it? It wasn't him you wanted done, it was her.'

This time Butler smiled. 'Very astute of you,' he said.

'Why didn't you tell me?'

Butler shrugged. 'It was a test and you passed. No hard feelings, I hope.'

'She could've fucking killed me.'

'But she didn't. Are you interested in some work or not?'

Jimmy nodded.

'Right. No details now. That'll come later. But I'm putting a little firm together for a job. It's big, Jimmy. Very big. And I need men who are prepared to use violence. Maybe even kill. Are you one of those men?'

'You know I am. But what's in it for me?'

'A lot. I reckon the job could be worth well over twenty million.'

'*How much?*'

'You heard, Jimmy.'

'Christ.'

'But of course a million isn't what it used to be. Inflation, you know.'

'But even so. And my cut?'

430

'I reckon it's a seven-man job. I take thirty per cent off the top, leaving... what? Say twelve or thirteen mill, perhaps more. Even split amongst the seven of you. Work it out for yourself.'

'A lot,' said Jimmy.

'A new life, Jimmy. Somewhere far from here. How does that sound?'

'It sounds good.'

'So are you in?'

'Do you need to ask?'

'No. But from now on, Jimmy, if you're part of the team, you're in one hundred per cent.'

'No problem.'

'Good. Well, I'll pay up and be gone. I'll be in touch when I need you.'

'When's that likely to be?'

Butler smiled. 'All in good time, Jimmy. Now Bob's waiting for me. I've got business in town this afternoon.'

'I'll be going then.'

Butler nodded as he called for Skinny to bring the bill. 'You do that.'

Jimmy got to his feet. 'OK, Dan,' he said. 'I'll be seeing you.'

'You will.'

'And thanks for the lunch.'

Later that evening, a mobile phone rang somewhere in Europe.

'Hello.'

'It's me, Gerry,' said Gerry Goldstein.

'Yeah.'

'He's in.'

'Is he?'

'Yeah. He took the bait. Did a bit of business.'

'What kind of business?'

'You on the Internet?'

'I can be.'

'Check out yesterday's *London Evening Standard*. Page three. With reference to New Addington.'

'I'll do that.'

'So what next?'

'Break out the champagne. I'm coming home.'

THIRTY-TWO

Since John Jenner's death, things had not been so good at the house in Tulse Hill. Martine had quit her job to look after Jenner's money and property. In fact, there had been much more than he had admitted to Mark and Chas before he died. When Martine had gone through his papers, all sorts of investments in stocks and property had come to light. There were deeds to shops and houses in some of the more dilapidated parts of south London and Martine set about converting them into cash, which she then reinvested. Or at least she said she did. But to Chas it seemed she spent most of her time out clubbing it, often inviting new friends home to keep the party going far into the night and through to the next morning. He suspected she was seriously into drugs, but when he as much as hinted that that was the case, she flew into terrible rages.

Chas stayed on in his flat at the back of the house and Martine lived upstairs. But with John Jenner gone, the life seemed to have leeched out of the house and Chas knew it was only a matter of time before he went too. But where? He had no family or friends, and little money of his own. Just the pension John Jenner had set up for him, which wasn't performing too well. He'd dedicated his life to the family, and now he could only watch in dismay at what had happened to them.

One bright Tuesday in May, everything changed.

At around one in the afternoon, the telephone rang. Chas answered it in the kitchen. 'Hello.'

'Hello. Chas?'

'Yeah.'

'It's me.'

'Who?'

'Me.'

Chas suddenly recognised the voice. 'Mark?'

'No names. You never know who's listening.'

'Christ. Where have you been?'

'Around.'

'Where are you?'

'On a boat.'

'Where are you going?'

'I'm coming home.'

'Are you crazy? The police are still looking for you.'

'Are they?'

'Sure.'

'Too bad. How's Martine?'

'Not so good.'

'Does she still blame me?'

'Yes.'

'Listen. I don't want to talk for long. Can we meet?'

'Of course. Where and when?'

'You remember the pub we went to one night after driving around that estate?'

'Yeah.'

'Meet me there, day after tomorrow, at noon.'

'I'll be there.'

'And tell no one.'

'Course not.'

'See you then.'

'See you.'

And Mark hung up. Two days later, at precisely twelve o'clock, Chas entered the pub he and Mark had visited after looking for Beretta's flat. It was even more dingy than it had been that time, and just a few customers braved the gloom. The place smelled of cigarettes, badly cooked food and despair. Not exactly the place you'd ask for a chilled Vichy water with a slice of lemon. He looked around but recognised nobody. He went to the bar and ordered a pint of bitter then sat down at a table. In one corner sat a man with a deep tan; his head was shaved almost to the bone, and he wore a beard and dark glasses despite the semi-darkness of the bar. As Chas looked at him, the man rose and walked over. 'Don't you say hello to old friends?' he said, taking the chair opposite.

'Christ,' said Chas. 'Mark? Is that you?'

'Sure is,' said Mark Farrow, taking off his shades to reveal a pair of dark brown eyes.

'What have you done? I didn't recognise you. Your eyes... ?'

'Contacts,' replied Mark. 'Took me weeks to get used to them.'

'And the beard. You look older...'

'I feel bloody older,' said Mark, searching for a packet of cigarettes.

'Where have you been?'

'All over the place. Portugal mostly. Down by the sea. I rented a little place.'

'So what are you doing back here?'

'Jimmy Hunter's out.'

'Mark. You should forget about him.'

'I know. But I can't. He killed my father. If it hadn't been for that, my mother might still be alive. He fucked up my family. Then there was Linda. Him being who he was screwed that too. And I know... I probably would never have met her otherwise. But everywhere I go and everything I do leads back to that bastard. Remember that night in the scrap yard?'

'With Bobby Thomas?'

Mark nodded.

'How can I forget?'

'I did the right thing that night. But all I could think of as I killed Thomas was that I wished it was Hunter. And now he's on the out. Free and clear. Well, he won't be if I've got anything to do with it.'

'I understand, son.'

'Good. What are you doing?'

'What can I do? I'm a fat old man. I sit and watch TV, cook, and sit around as Martine falls apart.'

435

'Will you help me?'

'What can I do?'

'Come on, Chas. You were one of the best enforcers in the business. You aren't that old and fat that you've forgotten that.'

Chas shook his head. 'I miss him, Mark. John, I mean.'

'Course you do. So do I. And Hazel, and you and Martine. I miss you all. My life's shit, Chas. I'm a wanted man wherever I go. I've been lucky so far, but my luck's bound to run out sooner or later. But first I want that fucker dead.'

'So?'

'So he's webbed up with Danny Butler. Remember him?'

'Vicious bastard.'

'Butler's putting together a little firm to do some sort of robbery. It's all on the QT at the moment, but I've got someone on the inside. Someone who owes me.'

'And?'

'And my inside man tells me Butler put together that job in Brixton where my dad got killed. So he was as much a part of it as Hunter. I intend to fuck up their little scheme and fuck up Butler and Hunter into the bargain.'

'Christ, but you're taking a risk.'

Mark shrugged. 'So what? I've got nothing going for me. I'm tired, Chas. I don't care what happens to me now. Everything I touch turns to shit.'

Chas said nothing.

'So will you help?' asked the younger man.

'If I can.'

'Good. Got a mobile?'

Chas nodded again.

'Gimme the number.'

Chas did as he was asked and Mark drank up. 'I'm off now, but I'll be in touch.'

'Take care.'

'I will. I'm used to that. And remember, not a word to a soul.'

Chas nodded and watched as Mark walked out of bar. Christ, what memories had come flooding back at seeing that young man. Billy Farrow, Susan, Thomas, Hazel, John Jenner and all the boys they'd ganged up with. Nearly all gone now.

But mostly he thought of Hazel.

He'd never admitted to anyone how much he'd loved her. Really loved her, in a romantic way. Chas had never had much to do with women before he met her, and truth to tell, hardly anything after. It hurt him to admit that he was a one woman man, and that woman had fallen in love with and married his best friend, who was also his boss. Bit of a sickener, he thought as he sat in front of his glass in a dismal pub in Brixton. But that was the truth. The impossible dream. Like the song. Just like the song, in fact. To love, pure and chaste, from afar. What a mug. But the day she'd blown into his life, invited round for tea by his sister Pam, was the day he'd fallen in love for the first and, as it turned out, the only time.

* * *

The girls had been in school uniform. Blazers, white blouses with striped ties, gym slips and black stockings. But Pam and Hazel had adapted their uniforms to the latest fashions. The shirts were tight over their young breasts and their gym slips were so short that there was the occasional glimpse of white flesh above their stocking tops. Dressed like something out of a blue film, they were a dirty old man's dream. Or a dirty young one, for that matter. Pam's dark hair was tied in two pigtails, but Hazel's lush red mane cascaded down her back in Renaissance curls. The second Chas saw her, he was smitten, and when she smiled her crooked smile, he was hers for life.

That day Chas's mum gave the girls a bollocking for their appearance, obviously a regular thing, but they just giggled, and Hazel winked at Chas and he thought his luck was in. Hazel had appeared on the scene since Chas had done his time in borstal, and she was obviously fascinated that her mate's brother was a 'jailbird', as she called it. Chas would never have taken that from anyone else, but he would've crawled over broken glass to listen to her say it.

She was a regular visitor to the house and Chas somehow always managed to be around when she was there. Eventually he plucked up courage to ask her to go with him to the Bali Hai one evening for a drink. Of course, Pam had to come too, but Chas didn't care. Just to be in Hazel's company for an evening was like a dream come true.

But of course, his dreams were dashed when he saw the way she and John Jenner looked at each other that first time. He knew he'd witnessed two people falling in love.

It took Chas some time to stop resenting the pair of them and their obvious happiness. But, almost despite himself, he was happy for her. So to stay close and protect his one true love, he teamed up with Jenner, and soon found himself practically loving the man too. Not in that way, of course. But as a friend, and eventually as one of the family. And so he'd stayed. And now, another adopted member of Chas's family needed help. And help he would get.

Eventually Chas left the pub and drove home. For the first time since Jenner's death, he had a small smile on his face.

* * *

Meanwhile, Mark Farrow was making his plans. He sat in a room in a small hotel on the southern outskirts of London and called Gerry Goldstein on the phone. 'I'm back,' he said.

'I'm not sure if that's good news or bad.'

'Who for?'

'Pick a number.'

'So what's happening?'

'Not on the phone.'

'Fair enough. We need a reunion, Gerry.'

'It seems to be a time for reunions.'

'Doesn't it just.'

'Not here.'

'Fair enough. Where?' asked Mark.

'I'm doing a bit of selling down in Hastings tomorrow. How about there?'

'Seems OK. I used to like going to Hastings. Where and when?'

'I'll be done by noon. There's a pub in the old town. The Jenny Lind. We could meet there for a drink.'

'Twelve thirty suit you?'

'That's fine.'

'I might even buy you lunch, Gerry. For old time's sake.'

'I don't know if I'll have much of an appetite.'

'I will. The sea air always brings it out in me.'

'Fine. Whatever you say. I'll see you then.'

'You will.' And they both hung up.

Mark made the drive down to the coast in just under two hours. He didn't rush. He didn't want anyone looking too closely at the paperwork on the Ford Explorer he was driving. Or at his personal paperwork, which was in the name of Steve Sawyer. He'd picked them up in Gibraltar, a month or so previously. The man who'd sold him the job lot had guaranteed their authenticity, but Mark had heard similar stories before and stuck to the speed limit all the way.

He left the truck in a municipal car park and strolled through the warm spring air like a man without a trouble in the world. He found the pub just before twelve and ordered a small lager, sat at a table with a view of the street outside and lit a cigarette. The season was well under way, the town filling with holiday makers, and he didn't expect any trouble. Not from the cops, anyway. Gerry Goldstein might be a different matter.

At twelve thirty, on the dot, he saw the rotund jeweller puffing down the road towards the pub. Mark smiled. He wanted him off balance. Goldstein pushed through the door and stood inside, scoping the place.

'It's me, Gerry,' said Mark, getting up from his chair.

'Christ,' said Goldstein. 'What have you done to yourself?'

'Funny how everyone asks me that. A strict regime.'

'And your hair. A bit drastic, isn't it?'

'I thought shaved heads were all the rage. Want a drink?'

'Does a baby love the tit?'

'I'll take that for a yes. What'll you have?'

'A large brandy.'

'You driving, Gerry?'

'I'll worry about that, if you don't mind. I need one.'

Mark fetched him a drink and they sat together at the table.

'Successful morning?' asked Mark.

'So far.'

'Good. Let's hope it carries on that way. Cheers.'

'Cheers,' said Goldstein, sucking down half his drink. 'So what do you want this time?'

'I want to be in on the job that you and Butler are setting up.'

'Are you kidding me?'

'I don't kid any more.'

'With Hunter?'

'Why not?'

'Because of who you are.'

'He wouldn't know me from a hole in the ground.'

'He might guess.'

'Why?' asked Mark removing his sunglasses.

'Jesus,' said Goldstein. 'What happened to your eyes?'

'Just a couple of bits of plastic. Would you recognise me? You didn't when you walked in. And nor did Chas.'

'He knows you're here?'

'Of course.'

'And who else?'

'That's it. Chas won't talk. He's got the closest mouth in south London. It had to be that way, working for John.'

'And he knows what you're up to?'

'Some.'

'And how do I get you in?'

'Use your loaf, Gerry. You're famed for it.'

'I don't like it.'

'Think of the alternative. I know all about you, Gerry. I know the people you've stitched up. You know I do. And some of them are still around. Want me to make a few calls?'

'No,' said Goldstein, sweat breaking out on his face. 'That wouldn't be a wise move.'

'Not for you maybe, but for me....'

'OK, OK, I'll do what I can.'

'I think you'd better do more than that. I think you'd better row me in.'

'Oh, Christ. If Butler finds out...'

'Then don't let him.'

'And you know what Hunter did in New Addington?'

'You sure that was him?'

'It was him, all right. Butler used it as a test. An initiation, if you like. See if he still had the balls he used to have.'

'And he did.'

'He certainly bloody did. Lunatic. And it cost Butler nothing.'

'Dirty deeds done cheap.'

'If you like.'

'But what about the tom he nicked? I bet he tries to sell them on to you.'

'Those fucking watches. I wouldn't touch them with a barge pole. Well, not for a year or so anyway.'

'You're priceless, Gerry.'

Goldstein sat there fiddling with his glass as Mark smoked a cigarette.

'Fancy lunch?' Mark asked at length, stubbing the butt out in the ashtray. 'There's a little French restaurant over the road. Looks OK.'

'I'm not hungry. I'd better get back to town.'

'Please yourself.'

Goldstein drained his glass and got up to leave. 'I'll be in touch,' he said.

'The sooner the better, Gerry.'

'As soon as I've got something to say.'

'Fair enough. Now, you take it easy. I wouldn't want to lose you. And you've still got the tape of Hunter round your place?'

Goldstein nodded.

'I'll be round to see it soon. I want to know what he looks like these days.'

Goldstein said nothing, just nodded and walked out into the sunshine.

Mark sat in the pub for another few minutes, then finished his drink too and decided to try the restaurant anyway. He was used to eating alone.

On the other hand, Jimmy Hunter wasn't used to eating on his tod. He'd spent too many meal times in the company of anything from a dozen to a hundred other diners. But he was beginning to know what it was like. He was no chef and ate out two or three times a day. Not French cuisine very often, but Brixton and its environs now hosted scores of eateries. Everything from the McDonald's on the site where his last attempt at armed robbery had gone so badly wrong, right up to restaurants where he didn't really know which cutlery to use. In prison it had been easy. A plastic knife, fork and spoon had covered every culinary eventuality.

So the waiting began. Butler had told him he'd be contacted when he was needed, but meanwhile, time hung heavy.

He'd kept the piece of paper that Butler had given him with Linda and Sean's address on it. And the same day that Mark Farrow and Gerry Goldstein met in Hastings, he plucked up courage to take a train down to Croydon. For, although Jimmy was a hard man and had worried little about slaughtering the Smiths in New Addington, just the thought of seeing his son and daughter, now grown up, and the chance of getting a glimpse of his grandchildren, turned his bowels to water.

It was early afternoon when he stepped down from the train at East Croydon station. The weather was fine and Jimmy was wearing his replacement leather jacket and dark cotton trousers. He bought an early edition *Standard* from a vendor outside the station, and when he asked about the address, the man told him which bus to catch, and where to get off. Ironically, the bus's final destination was New Addington itself, which Jimmy took as an omen, but whether good or bad, he wasn't sure.

The journey took only a few minutes and Jimmy was the only passenger to alight at the stop. He looked round and saw that the road he was searching for was just opposite where he stood. He lit a cigarette with

442

trembling fingers, crossed the street and entered it. It was typical suburbia, tree lined and quiet in the afternoon sun. The houses were large and set back behind gated walls with paved or pebble-covered drives that cut through neat front gardens filled with spring flowers. The perfect place to bring up children safely, he supposed.

Jimmy contrasted it with the tiny house he'd bought in Stockwell, and where he'd lived with Marje and the kids before his last arrest. He walked on slowly until he came to the house he was searching for, with a four wheel drive truck parked by the front door. He knew better than to stop. There were plenty of lace curtains and blinds at the windows of the houses. He knew from bitter past experience that, in areas such as this, prying eyes were always on the lookout for suspicious characters. So he walked on until he came to the entrance to a small park, empty at that hour in school time, where he sat on a bench, lit another cigarette and looked at his paper without taking in a word written on it.

He knew he was mad to come. A waste of time. But he'd been drawn there as surely as if he'd been programmed. Which in a way he had been. He finished his cigarette, dogged it out with the toe of his boot and wearily stood up. Go home, he thought. Just go bloody home. So he retraced his footsteps, head down. He passed the house on the other side just as the front door opened and, Christ, it couldn't be… A woman, the spitting image of his late wife Marjorie came out, carrying an infant in her arms. Jimmy just couldn't believe his eyes and he stopped dead in his tracks, his heart beating like he was going for a coronary, and his legs – as cheap novelists always put it – turning to jelly. It was Marje, but it wasn't. It had to be Linda, and the little girl she was buckling into the child seat in the back of the motor had to be Daisy. His granddaughter.

Jimmy forced himself to cross the road slowly, his eyes devouring the sight. Once finished with Daisy, the woman climbed behind the wheel and started the engine. Jimmy kept going and she let him cross in front of her as she stopped the vehicle at the gates. She looked at him without recognition and he smiled and waved a thank you, and she smiled back, and Jimmy almost died with happiness.

Linda's truck moved into the street and stopped briefly at the end, before turning left and vanishing from Jimmy's sight. She must be going to pick the boy up from school, he thought, and he walked back to the main road, looking for the stop for his bus back to East Croydon, as oblivious to the Ford Explorer that followed Linda's car as the bearded driver of it was oblivious to him.

When he'd finished his lunch, Mark Farrow had decided to return to Wandsworth via Croydon. It wasn't much out of his way, and he had nothing else to do until Gerry Goldstein came back to him. He'd let his Ford drift through the town until it reached Linda's road. It was stupid, he knew, but when he saw her car in the drive he stopped around the corner, in sight of the house, and smoked a cigarette. I'll just wait a minute, he thought, as a middle-aged man in a leather jacket crossed the road in front of him. He could have ploughed him into the tarmac without scratching the paintwork, if only he'd known who it was.

The man approached Linda's house as she came out and Mark saw through eyes that teared up as he recognised her, that she was just as beautiful as he remembered, if slightly thinner. She put Daisy in the back of the vehicle and drove out, allowing the middle-aged man to walk slowly in front of her and acknowledge her with a wave before she drove off. Mark followed Linda, but knew it was pointless, and he peeled off before she got to Luke's school, and headed home.

Jimmy headed home too, his brain reeling. He couldn't settle, his apartment feeling as confined as any of the cells he'd lived in. So he decided we was going to to call up the tart, Jane, and see if she was up for a night out. The next day, just before noon, he called the number on the card she'd given him. She took a while to answer, and sounded disorientated when she did. 'Did I wake you?' he asked.

'What time is it?'

'Twelve.'

'Noon?'

'Yes.'

'Then you did.'

'Sorry.'

'No problem. Who am I speaking to?'

'Jimmy. From the Russell. Remember?'

'Jimmy. I thought you'd lost my number.'

'No. I've been busy.'

'Too busy for me?'

'Just trying to sort things out. You know how it is.'

'I do. So what can I do for you?'

'I wondered if you fancy going out?' he said.

'Not staying in?' She was waking up now and being coquettish. Jimmy liked that.

'Well, later on, you know…'

'I do.'

'So are you up for it?'

'Like a date?'

'Sort of.'

'But not a freebie.'

'Of course not.'

'When?'

'Tonight.'

'You are eager. Let me look in my book.'

She was gone for a moment. 'Well,' she said when she came back. 'I could manage to fit you in.' Then she laughed. 'If you know what I mean.'

'I know,' he replied.

'So what did you have in mind?'

'Dinner. Then maybe some music and back home.'

'Not my home.'

'I've got a place now.'

'Where?'

'Brixton.'

'I like Brixton.'

'Do you?'

'Yes. I used to live there myself.'

445

'Where do you live now?'

'Marble Arch.'

'Posh.'

'I've got a friend who helps out… But I shouldn't be telling you things like that.'

'Could you get to Brixton?' asked Jimmy. 'I'll spring for a cab.'

'I've got a car, Jimmy. Lots of girls drive these days.'

He laughed. 'You're a cheeky cow.'

'Aren't I just. But you love it.'

He had to admit he did. 'What's your favourite food?'

'I don't mind. As long as there's a tablecloth and they serve champagne. Just like last time. Remember?'

'How could I forget? Why do you think I called?'

'So where should we meet?'

'You know the Ritzy cinema?'

'Yes.'

'Outside at eight. I'll book a table somewhere. How much?'

'For the night. The same as last time. Is that a problem?'

'No.'

'So eight it is.'

And eight it was, as Jimmy stood outside the cinema close to the centre of Brixton, kitty corner from the damn McDonald's, and he watched as the punters shuffled in for the last shows of the evening. Then a shiny little dark-coloured car skidded round from the main road, he saw a blonde head inside and the driver tooted the horn. Jimmy smiled, feeling almost like a normal bloke meeting his bird for food and sex. Of course he had to pay, but at least he knew what he was getting at the end of the evening.

Jimmy walked around to the passenger door and climbed into the tiny front seat. Inside, the car smelled strongly of perfume. Jane grinned as she greeted him. 'Where to, Jimmy?' she asked.

'Acre Lane,' he replied. 'Tablecloths and champagne a speciality of the house.'

She leaned over and kissed him briefly on the cheek, before chucking the motor into gear and taking off with a screech of rubber. 'Got any drugs, Jimmy?' she asked as she joined the main road again.

'No. Sorry.'

'I thought everyone in Brixton was at it,' she said. 'Good job I have. I always come prepared. But it's extra, I'm afraid.'

'No problem.'

'You must be doing well.'

'Not too bad.'

'If you pay me before we go inside, I'll be like your girlfriend, won't I?'

'That's just what I was thinking.' Jimmy coughed up the dough, including an extra fifty for the glassine packet of coke that Jane had hidden behind the passenger seat sun visor. Jimmy tucked it away in his wallet, and she took his arm as they entered the latest high class restaurant to try its luck on the mean streets of south London. But not as mean as they used to be, thought Jimmy, as they sat down.

The meal cost him an arm and a leg, and included two bottles of bubbly at eighty notes a throw, but with Butler's heist on the horizon, Jimmy couldn't have cared less. 'Live for the day' had been his motto since he'd come out, and Jane looked to be worth every penny in her scarlet mini dress, cut low front and back and held up only by two spaghetti straps that proved to all and sundry that not only wasn't she wearing a bra, but that she didn't need one.

When they were on the cappuccino, brandy and cigarettes, Jane asked: 'Did you get a flat or a house?'

'A flat. Just a small one. And I rattle around in that.'

'Has it got a bedroom?'

'Of course.'

'Then we can rattle around together.'

'Sounds good to me.'

'I like you, Jimmy. I've always liked older men.'

'Shall I take that as a compliment?'

'If you want. I mean it. It's always nice when punters are human.'

447

'But still punters.'

'That's the way of the world. It's a hard life, Jimmy.'

'Is that a joke?'

'No. But it could be.' She was suddenly serious and leant over and placed her hand on his. 'Let's forget about the music, shall we? Do you want to go home?'

'Sure.' Jimmy signalled for the bill and paid in cash.

They went back to the car and he directed her to his street. She parked on a yellow line and said: 'I'll have to be off early. I don't want a ticket.'

'Don't worry about that. If the worst comes to the worst, I'll pay it.'

'Oh, Jimmy,' she said. 'I'm getting to like you more and more. You do spoil me. Now it's my turn to spoil you.'

They went inside. She asked for a moment to freshen up and Jimmy showed her the bathroom, whilst he went into the living room, put some music on the little stereo he'd bought, broke open a bottle of brandy and poured two decent-sized slugs into a pair of glasses.

When she joined him again, she'd taken off her dress and was wearing only black stockings, red suspenders and red silk knickers, so tiny as to be almost against the trades description act. Jimmy smiled when he saw her and felt himself start to harden. 'Where's that coke?' she said. 'I need something to get me in the mood for being really dirty. You deserve it.'

'I'm already in the mood,' said Jimmy, tossing the envelope on to the coffee table.

'Don't worry, I'll be with you soon. Then I'll be a real coke whore,' she replied.

'I thought you already were.'

'Cheeky.'

Jane found a credit card in her purse, wiped the table top with a tissue and poured out a good quarter gramme. 'It's good and rocky,' she said. 'I like that.' She cut it up fine, then pulled out four fat lines. She took a silver straw out of her bag and handed it to Jimmy. 'You first,' she said. 'But I hope it doesn't make you go soft.'

448

'With you around, impossible,' he replied, before snorting one line, then another.

'So many compliments,' said Jane. 'I know this is going to be a fun night.'

'And a long one, I hope,' said Jimmy.

'Trust me.'

The coke was primo gear and went straight to Jimmy's heads – both his big one and his little one – and he felt his cock swell even more in his pants. Jane started to undress him and he loved the feeling of her soft, smooth hands on his body. Finally she released him from his underpants. 'Nothing wrong with that,' she said, taking him in one hand and caressing his balls with the other. 'You're going grey down there, Jimmy,' she said. 'Very distinguished.'

'It looks like Stewart Granger,' he said.

'Who's that?' she asked, and he laughed at their age difference.

'I bet you don't know who Manfred Mann is either,' he said.

'Never heard of him.'

'He's a he and a band,' said Jimmy.

'News to me.' And she knelt in front of him and took his penis in her mouth. The warmth and wetness made him even harder and he leant his head back, opened his mouth and groaned with pleasure.

'Good?' she asked as she let him slip out, a thin line of saliva still joining them.

'Perfect.'

'I aim to please.'

'And you do.'

She went back to blowing him and he forced her head on to his prick until she gagged. She moaned too, as he began to pump into her mouth, but she wrenched her head back and said, in a voice thick with sex: 'No. Don't come. Not yet. It's too early. I want more coke.'

He let her go, and she strung out more lines and they both indulged and he could see that the crotch of her knickers was wet with lubrication. 'Are you enjoying yourself?' he asked.

'More than I should. This is business.'

'Forget it. I want to fuck you.'

She found her bag again and fished out a condom.

'No,' he complained.

'Oh yes,' said Jane. 'I know what you boys get up to in prison. It's a rule. No going bareback.'

'I'm clean.'

'So am I. And I intend to stay that way. I told you that last time. Don't worry. These are extra thin. You'll feel everything, just like the last time.'

She ripped off the foil packaging and expertly rolled the rubber up over his cock, then pushed him back on the bed and mounted him. 'I love being on top,' she said. 'Hope you don't mind.'

By this time Jimmy didn't care what position they were in as long as he could come and she rode him like a pony until he spurted into the condom.

'God, but that was good,' he said as she gently lifted herself off. 'But it's too early.'

'I'm not going anywhere,' she replied. 'Let's have another drink and I'll show you how I can make you hard again.'

Which she did by whispering dirty stories into his ear. Stories he loved to hear and he kissed her passionately and she responded in like style. 'You're a dirty bitch,' he said.

'And you're a very dirty man.'

'A dirty old man.'

'If you like.'

'I do. And you're very naughty.'

'So what do you want to do about it?'

'I think I should smack your arse.'

'Do you? Well, go on then,' and she lay across his lap, her pert bottom sticking up in the air.

'God,' he said. 'I don't think I've ever done this before.'

'There's always a first time,' she replied. 'Go on, daddy. Punish me.'

So he did. He raised his right hand and brought it down hard on her left cheek. 'Oww,' she cried. 'Ooh, that hurts.'

'But you love it.'

'No, I don't.'

'Yes you do,' he insisted and spanked her hard until both buttocks glowed pink.

She rolled off him and when she sat up she said: 'That really stings.'

'Come on,' he said. 'Let's do it again.'

'You're the boss,' she said. 'How do you want me? On my back or all fours?'

'I don't care.'

'So let's do both.'

And they did. Their sex going on half the night until Jimmy, at least, was exhausted. 'I can't keep up,' he said as a distant clock struck four. 'I need some sleep.'

'Do you, old man?' she said. 'Can't we just do it once more?'

'I don't think so.'

'Fair enough. But don't say I didn't offer.'

'I'll never say that.'

They climbed into the wreck of the bed and Jimmy was soon asleep. Jane lay next to him until she saw the beginning of the dawn, and then she too closed her eyes. Tomorrow is another day, she thought, looking at the man lying next to her.

Earlier that day, someone else had been looking at Jimmy. But this time on a tiny screen in the back of Gerry Goldstein's shop. Mark Farrow had telephoned first thing and caught the jeweller as he'd opened up. 'I need to see that tape,' he'd said.

'OK,' said Goldstein. 'I'm free this morning 'til twelve.'

'I'll be right over,' said Mark. He left his hotel and drove up to the city. Goldstein let him in and took him through to the back room, where he played the tapes showing Hunter's two visits to the shop. Of course, Gerry Goldstein being Gerry Goldstein, the CCTV he'd had installed years before was tired and old and the tapes had been used so many times, they were almost transparent. The small monochrome monitor wasn't exactly state of the art, either. Jimmy hadn't helped matters by keeping his face out of the frame most of the time. Whether this was deliberate, by

451

accidental or through instinct, Mark didn't know. But occasionally there was a clear shot of him. The first time, Mark frowned and said: 'I know that geezer. Where the hell…?'

Then it struck him. It was the man walking by Linda's house the previous afternoon. 'Well, I'll be fucked,' he said.

'What?' said Goldstein.

'He was there,' said Mark.

'Where?'

'Never mind,' said Mark. 'But I could've mullahed him, no problem.' He laughed. 'Bugger me,' he said. 'Talk about missing your chances. But I'll know the fucker next time.'

THIRTY-THREE

The next morning, Jane was awake, up and dressed by nine and shook Jimmy until he opened his eyes. 'Time to go time,' she said.

'What time is it?' he asked with a mouth gummy from booze and drugs.

'Nine.'

'Do you have to?'

'Sure do. The clock's running.'

'Can we do it again?'

'Any time, Jimmy. I enjoyed myself.'

'Me too.'

She leant down and kissed him on the cheek. 'You're all stubbly,' she said.

'That's life.'

'Call me,' she said as she went to the bedroom door. 'I'll find my own way out.'

'Hope your car's OK,' he said.

'You promised to pay the ticket if it isn't.'

'And I will.'

'So I'll see you?'

'You will,' he said, and she blew him a kiss and left. He heard the front door slam and he lay back on his pillow.

Outside, Jane rescued her car – which was ticketless – turned the stereo up as loud as it would go, and roared out of the street.

Further up the road from Jimmy's flat, a man sitting alone in a nondescript motor saw her leave and jotted down the number of her car in a little notebook he'd taken from his jacket pocket.

When Jimmy was totally awake, he washed, shaved and put on water for coffee. He checked his wallet and realised how much last night had cost him, and when he'd had his breakfast, he phoned Gerry Goldstein.

'How long before we go?' he asked once the jeweller had identified himself.

'You'll find out soon enough.'

'I need some cash.'

'And you'll get it. Relax.'

'Just as long as you haven't forgotten me.'

'How could I, Jimmy?'

'As soon as you know something, call me.'

'Of course I will. Trust me.'

'OK, Gerry. But I hate waiting.'

'It's out of my hands, you know that,' said Goldstein.

'I know. All right. I'm just getting impatient. It's been a long time.'

'Soon, I'm sure.'

'Right. Speak to you later.'

'Later, Jimmy,' replied Goldstein, and they both hung up.

Goldstein sat and wondered just how he'd got himself into such a mess. What with Jimmy on one side, and Mark Farrow on the other, he felt he was stuck between a rock and a hard place. And that wasn't even taking Butler and his mob into consideration. If it was ever discovered that he was playing both sides against the middle… well, he knew it wouldn't be a good time to start getting interested in TV serials.

And it could have been so different, he thought, if only he hadn't got himself in a mess over money.

* * *

Gerry had been a Stamford Hill moddy boy in the early 60s and had met John Jenner and his little firm at clubs and concerts all over London. Gerry had been a loner, famous for always wearing tweed suits whatever the weather, and Jenner had approached him one night in Klooks Kleek, a little club over a pub in West Hampstead. 'Tasty suit,' he'd said. 'Where'd you get it made?'

454

'Sam Arkus,' said Gerry, proud that Jenner had noticed that the suit was bespoke.

'Good tailor. Got any gear?'

Gerry shook his head.

'Want some?'

'What you got?'

'French blues. Interested?'

'Yeah.'

Jenner had sold him a few pills and Gerry joined him and his boys on the dance floor, where they'd made their best moves to the sound of some loser band trying to be the next big thing and failing miserably.

Afterwards they'd cabbed it down to Soho and spent the rest of the night at some club or other where they served soft drinks over the counter and scotch under it. Gerry was working for his father in Hatton Garden, learning the jewellery trade, including the more lucrative area of fencing stolen goods, which was where good old Dad made his real money. Gerry and John had often met over the intervening years and Gerry had made lots of cash from the Jenner gang. But he was greedy. As his bank balances expanded in line with his stomach, he married a nice Jewish girl called Rebecca and had three daughters who spent as prolifically as their mother. But business wasn't always that good and he began taking more and more chances in order to support their extravagant lifestyle.

It was a risky business, but so was denying his family their cars and furs, designer dresses and anything else their greedy little hearts desired. Gerry had to skate closer and closer to the edge to make up the shortfall in his finances until, one day, a certain lawless individual whose name doesn't matter – but the very mention of it in certain areas of London could still empty pubs and clubs and have mothers cover their children's ears for fear they would be corrupted – arrived in Gerry's life, bearing certain items that were so warm, he almost had to wear asbestos gloves to touch them. Gerry thought then that he could see a way out of his troubles.

This individual was well aware that what he had obtained could not easily be turned into cash money, so he came up with the idea that Gerry would supply him with ten percent of the insurance value up front, then he'd approach the insurance company that held the policy on the items and obtain the going reward – something like fifty per cent of said value. Then they could split the money to the tune of sixty/forty, the lion's share going to the individual in question, with hopefully, no questions actually being asked.

It took a lot of nerve, as the police weren't happy that robberies were taking place under their noses in the first place, never mind that the villains and the insurance companies were then colluding to hand out what were essentially tax-free lump sums to villains. And, as the deals required that the police not be informed until after the event, there was no real fear of capture for the perpetrators. In response, the busies were getting busy, recruiting a network of informants only too pleased to put names in the frame and sit back and collect their own little bit of tax-free bunce.

So, when Gerry made a meet with a claims adjuster concerning the bag of tomfoolery the certain individual had happened upon on his nefarious way around London, someone put the boot in good and proper and Gerry got carted away to the nearest nick, cautioned and bailed with the assistance of his notorious and expensive brief.

Things didn't look too bright for Mr Goldstein, because when the individual discovered that his bag of swag was resting at Her Majesty's pleasure, he told Gerry in no uncertain terms that, unless the story had a happy ending, *his* particular story would not. In particular, he said, the Thames was very cold and deep and that no matter how artfully they were coiffed and dressed, Jewish women didn't float. Especially if their pretty little feet were encased in concrete.

So Gerry went to his old friend John Jenner in the hope that he might remonstrate with the individual, both having a certain history in crime together, but John knew from day one that it was a no go situation. Then Mark Farrow came up with a plan. He was a daring young man and the nick in question had long had the nickname of 'the sieve' for the very good reason that it was famous for losing evidence. One dark night, Mark and Eddie Dawes - dressed as police constables - dragged Tubbs into the station, demanding that they take care of their prisoner until transport

456

could be arranged. The custody sergeant made the trio welcome until Tubbs pulled out a pistol and stuck it into his ear, forcing him to show them where the evidence locker was. By the time they'd had it on their toes, not only was the evidence on Regina v Goldstein missing, but also a good kilo of pure cocaine.

The jewellery was returned to the individual who later employed another go between to sell it back to the insurance company, with no arrests being made at that time.

So Gerry Goldstein lived to fight another day and the women in his life had no idea how close they had come to a watery grave. Of course, Gerry was most grateful to Mark, who told him that one day he could return the favour. But Gerry didn't have an inkling of what that might entail until Mark let him know that the only way he could wipe the slate clean was to give him Jimmy Hunter on a plate.

And there was the rub.

Gerry wasn't the only one obsessed with Jimmy Hunter that day. DS Sean Pierce also had him on his mind. After he'd lost contact with his father at the Russell Hotel, Sean failed to find hide nor hair of him. He wasn't to know that Jimmy had a flat just a couple of miles from where he sat in the CID office at Streatham Police Station, biting the end of his pencil and looking through the window at the building site opposite. Sean had the feeling that his old man wouldn't be down the Job Centre looking for honest work that spring morning, and he wondered when he'd pop back up on the police radar. When rather than if. And then how would Sean be able to keep their relationship secret?

Meanwhile, on the other side of London, preparations were being made towards the very job that Jimmy had hassled Gerry over that same morning. Daniel Butler had discovered an old printing works on one of his reconnoitering missions through east London. The building was dilapidated and leaked water, but it was ideal for Butler's needs, being around the size of a football field and hidden away behind high, gated walls. The printers had gone out of business years before, when new technology had overtaken them. All around were new developments of flats, but somehow that particular brownfield site had been forgotten. Using one of his shell companies, with registered offices in the Isle of Man, Butler approached the owners with an offer of a short term rental with an option to buy. They, a City bank who had purchased great swathes of the East End with the intention of sitting on them until the boom and bust property market sorted itself out, agreed. To them it was a small part of a much larger portfolio. To Daniel Butler it was part of a master plan. To the local citizenry it was just more fucking yuppies on the make.

One Monday morning in late spring, a couple of heavy-looking lads in dungarees and big boots moved into the premises. They cleaned up the toilets and made the office inside liveable. They weren't going to be around for too long, but it helped to be able to make a cup of tea and have somewhere comfortable to drink it. There were rats in the building, so they brought in air pistols and spent many happy hours picking the little bleeders off.

A week later, a truck arrived, complete with another couple of men who set about getting it ready for its big day.

It was a ten-wheeled Volvo semi-tractor of the type seen every day pulling trailers up and down the motorways of Europe. Bringing in tools and materials, the four began converting this commonplace vehicle into an urban tank that would throw open the doors of a building that, within a few weeks, would contain a king's, queen's, indeed, a whole royal family's ransom.

First of all, they took all the glass out of the windows of the Volvo. The last thing anyone needed when they came smashing through metal gates and doors was a faceful of safety glass. They fitted racing harnesses to the triple seats in the cab, plus anti-roll bars and a huge rollover bar. If, by bad luck, the motor did take a tumble, it would be good to know that the roof wasn't going to crush the occupants.

They beefed up the already massive suspension and welded girders all around the body. At the back they strapped full cement bags between the twin axles and wet them, then let them dry until they became solid. Not only would that hold down the rear wheels, it would also add weight to help the truck smash through solid steel. The job took a week. When it was ready, they raced the Volvo from one end of the huge building to the other and back again. Once they were satisfied that the driver had a feel for the vehicle, they tarpaulined it up and left it behind heavily secured doors.

Butler was forever popping in and out, checking on progress and generally getting in everyone's way, but the mechanics usually just ignored him and got on with their business. This included servicing and spraying a stolen seven-seater Chevrolet Suburban, the other vehicle to be used on the heist, plus making sure that another pair of cars, to be parked up on the escape route, were in equally tip top condition.

THIRTY-FOUR

As the work continued at the old printers, Butler decided it was finally time to unveil his complete plan of attack to everyone involved. Phone calls were made and Gerry Goldstein called Jimmy late one night on his mobile. 'It's on,' he whispered.

'When?'

'You'll find out. You remember that bloke Bob you met?'

'How could I forget?'

'He's going to give you a call, let you know what's what.'

What was what was that Bob was to pick Jimmy up at his flat the following Sunday night and drive him up to Essex for a meet. 'You know where I live?' said Jimmy, not best pleased.

'Course we do. Who do you think you are, James Bond? You're not hard to find,' said Bob.

Soon time to move on, thought Jimmy, as he put down the phone. As soon as I've got some decent dough. Spain would be nice, he decided, and maybe Jane would like a holiday in the sun too. Maybe a permanent one. He could see them living together in a villa on the Costa del Sol with a load of his old mates for company – when they needed company, that is.

Sunday night rolled round and, at about ten, there was a knock on Jimmy's door. He took the pistol he'd liberated from Mrs Smith to the door with him. Though the spyhole he saw the man with the goatee standing outside.

Jimmy slid the pistol down the back of his trousers and opened the door.

'Hello Jimmy,' said Bob. 'How's it going?'

'Not too bad.'

'That's what I like to hear. You fit?'

Jimmy nodded.

'Let's go then.'

Jimmy shut the door and followed Bob to a waiting Audi saloon. Jimmy was still a little miffed that Butler & co knew where he lived, but he managed to stay cordial during the ride, which wasn't difficult as they probably only exchanged half a dozen words the whole journey. The meeting was to take place at Daniel Butler's house, and they drove through the big iron gates – past the guard in his hut who gave them a wave – as the digital clock on the dashboard of the Audi read midnight. Bob parked up on the turnaround in front of the house, next to an assortment of cars, ranging from the mundane to high-end luxury. 'Some people are doing well,' said Jimmy as they climbed out of the Audi. He lit up, the smoke from his cigarette hanging in the misty air.

'We'll all be doing well if this works out,' said Bob, leading the way to the front door, which stood ajar.

Bob led Jimmy to the vast old ballroom of the house, where a row of mismatched chairs had been laid out. Butler was standing in front of them, and beside him hung two blackboards, pinned with what looked like maps or blueprints or both, covered over with plain paper. At one side of the room, on a long table, was a huge chrome coffee dispenser, together with milk, sugar, cups, saucers, and bottled water and glasses.

A group of hard-looking men were scattered around the room and when Bob and Jimmy entered, Jimmy recognised Tony Green from the pub on the Isle of Dogs. The others were strangers. When Butler saw them enter, he clapped his hands and said: 'Right, gentlemen, we're all here. Please take your seats.'

Jimmy and some of the others helped themselves to coffee, and they all sat down, their chairs scraping on the polished wood floor.

A small man with the face of a boxer sat next to Jimmy and offered him a cigarette. Jimmy took it with a light, and the little man said: 'Don't I know you?'

Jimmy looked again and shrugged. 'Dunno,' he said.

'Walton, weren't it?' said the little man. 'E Block.'

'Could have been,' said Jimmy.

'My name's Toby Lee,' said the little man. 'And on the big day, I'm driving one of the motors.'

'Fair enough,' said Jimmy. 'Pleased to meet you.' Although he wasn't particularly. He was there for the job. Do it, collect his cut and vanish. He hadn't come all this way to make new friends.

'And you are?'

'I'm Jimmy.'

'Nice to see you, Jimmy,' said the little man.

Butler clapped his hands again. 'Right,' he said. 'This is the first time we've all been together. Some of you know each other. Some don't. But you all know me. And I don't piss about. You can use your real names here or not, as you please. I couldn't care less. All I do care about is that we succeed in the venture I'm just about to describe to you.'

Butler turned towards the first blackboard and peeled back the plain paper, revealing a large scale map of east London.

Butler took a laser pointer from his pocket and switched it on. He directed the beam at the map; the red dot picked out the Isle of Dogs and moved right. 'This is Docklands,' he said, 'as you're all probably aware.' The dot moved past the old Royal Docks. 'In particular, Silvertown. Not a particularly salubrious area, but trying hard. The City Airport's close by, a university, shopping centres, and new developments of apartments. There are also several industrial estates, and this one, close to the Woolwich ferry, is where we'll be heading on bank holiday Monday, two weeks from tomorrow.'

There was a rumble of comment.

'This is going to be dangerous, gentlemen,' he continued. 'Because where we're going will be guarded by armed men, who will do their very best to see that we don't succeed. That's why all of you will be armed too, and some of you will – I repeat, will – have to use those guns. Now, you've all had this explained before and I will only say it once: there's no backing out. You're in now and you will remain in. That's a fact, and I can't emphasise it enough. There's only one way out for you now. Feet first.'

Jimmy knew Butler meant it, and when he looked around the room, he knew the other men realised it too.

'This is a seven-man job,' Butler went on. 'Seven on the ground, that is, plus support staff. They have been preparing the vehicles you will use for the job and for the getaway afterwards.'

Jimmy shook his head. Plans. Too many plans and too many people. And where there were people there were big mouths ready to boast about the job. And others prepared to sell out the whole deal for their thirty pieces of silver or to save their own skins. Jimmy knew that, only too well. But it was the only game in town for him and he knew it. Maybe his last chance to put something away for an old age that was creeping up fast. So that was that. No point in worrying. He just had to do his best and hope for the same.

'Right,' said Butler. 'Let me get down to specifics.'

'Where we're going is a depository for precious stones.' Butler pulled the paper covering the second blackboard to reveal a photograph of a concrete building that resembled nothing so much as an oversized pill box. There was one main door of truck height, with windows that were tiny and heavily barred. 'That's why the stakes are so high,' Butler went on. 'Inside the main vault of this anonymous-looking building in east London, fortunes come and go. On bank holiday Monday there will be a minimum of twenty-five million pounds' worth of uncut diamonds in the building. Possibly more. With your help, I intend to take them. We have a buyer who will pay cash at the rate of fifty per cent of their market value. Fifty pence in the pound. Fifty cents on the dollar. I think we can walk out of this with over twelve million quid. I know this because, as you may have guessed, I have someone on the inside. This information is kosher.'

Butler paused, triggering off another rumble of whispering.

'And I guarantee each of you here tonight with a minimum of one million in cash,' said Butler with a big smile. 'At the very least. Very possibly more...'

'And how much for him?' whispered Lee.

'I heard that, Toby,' said Butler. 'And it's a good question. I take a third off the top. In exchange I know the where and when, organise the crew, pay them their wages, supply transport and ordnance and provide a safe getaway. Don't you think that's fair?'

'Fair enough, Mr Butler,' said Lee. 'I weren't complaining. Just wondering.'

'And so you should. The rest of you, it's a straight split, including my inside man… or woman. Don't worry. There'll be more bunce than you can spend for a very long time. Even you Toby, with your bad habits.'

More laughter.

'No probs, Mr Butler,' said Lee. 'Nuff said.'

'Right,' said Butler. 'It's a simple job. Two vehicles. One, a truck to batter down the front gates and hit the main doors. Two up. Tony driving, Bob with him. Then another car containing the rest of you, Toby driving that one. The stones will be being sorted and graded and the vault will be open. There are two guards inside, armed with automatic weapons. They have to be taken out. You load the diamonds into the boot of the number two car, leave the truck and get out fast. There are alarms, panic buttons through to the local police station and CCTV on site. The alarms won't be switched on during working hours, but the panic buttons will be available. And the local nick, believe it or not, only opens nine to five during weekdays, and closes for lunch. I think it's a disgrace, the cuts in public services…' There was laughter at that.

'And on bank holidays there's only a skeleton crew on duty in the area. But there will be crime cars floating about, so it's a quick in and out. If you see any police vehicles, put them out of action. You've got the firepower. Use it. There will be two more cars waiting at a designated spot. Transfer the stones to Bob's motor and he'll bring them to me. Tony with him. The rest of you will be dropped off as and when from the second car and Toby will lose the motor. Bob's motor will also be lost after the stones are in my possession. The money will be available within forty-eight hours, and the split will take place here as soon as possible afterwards. Any questions?'

No one spoke.

'Fair enough,' said Butler. 'We'll meet again soon. This time it'll be where the vehicles are being stored. Feel free to study the maps and blueprints. I want you to introduce yourselves to anyone you don't know. You're going to have to trust each other with your lives. Some of you may not survive. That's a fact. Deal with it.' And with that, Daniel Butler turned and left the room.

Bob gestured for Jimmy to join him, and they joined the others. 'Jimmy, meet Ronnie, Les and Paul,' said Bob. 'Tony and Toby you've met. Tony's going to drive the truck we'll use to get inside. I'm riding shotgun with him. Toby's driving the other car with Jimmy and the rest of you. It's simple. But what Mr Butler said was right. There'll be armed men on the plot who're prepared to shoot to kill. You've got to be ready too. Any problems with that?'

No one spoke.

'Fine. Now all of you but Jimmy know what ordnance you're using. Jimmy, come with me and find something you'll be happy with. The rest of you can go. Now, you ain't got wheels have you, Jimmy?' It wasn't a question. 'Toby, you going back to London?'

Toby nodded.

'Hang around for a bit, will you? I've got to stay here. Can you give Jimmy a lift?'

'No problem,' said Toby. 'A pleasure.'

'Right,' said Bob. 'The gun room's down here.'

They left the others and Bob led Jimmy along several corridors, before they came to a blank door which Bob opened with two keys. 'Can't be too careful,' he said as he switched on the lights.

Fluorescent tubes stuttered into life and Jimmy walked through to be confronted by a row of glass-fronted cabinets bulging with guns. 'Christ,' he said. 'What's this? Woolwich Arsenal?'

Bob grinned. 'Mr Butler likes to have some firepower on hand. What do you fancy?'

Jimmy walked along the row of cabinets, inspecting the contents.

There were H&K MP5s, Kalashnikov AK 47s, Skorpion Model 61s, Beretta Model 12s, Mac 10s and all sorts of other automatic weapons, plus rifles and shotguns and enough revolvers and semi-automatic pistols to equip a terrorist army.

Jimmy went for a Remington pump-action shotgun with a short barrel and a six-shot capacity. 'Don't know machine guns,' he said. 'This'll do me.'

'Used one before?' asked Bob.

'Oh yeah,' said Jimmy, not elaborating. He'd killed Billy Farrow with something similar. He'd used one before all right.

'Take a handgun too,' said Bob.

Jimmy already had one tucked down his strides but didn't let on. Instead he helped himself to a Browning nine.

'Want to give them a go?' asked Bob.

'Do what?'

'There's a range downstairs. Come on.'

Taking the two guns, Jimmy followed Bob out of the room, which he locked behind him, and through another door which led down a flight of stairs. 'Got big cellars these old houses,' said Bob as they descended. 'Useful for wine and all sorts.' They came to another door, which Bob opened before hitting a light switch. Inside was a full size shooting range.

'Fully soundproofed,' said. Bob 'You could let off an H-bomb in here and no one would be any the wiser.' A touch to another switch and an extractor fan sprang into life. 'No expense spared,' he added.

At the side of the range was a long table piled with boxes of ammunition. 'Help yourself.' said Bob. 'There's goggles and muffs in the drawer underneath.' Jimmy grabbed a handful of double ought shotgun cartridges and loaded six into the Remington, then carefully placed it on the table, the barrel pointing at the wall, the safety on. He then took out the Browning's magazine and broke open a fresh box of fifty 9mm rounds. He loaded the clip with thirteen bullets and slapped it into the butt of the gun to make sure it was firmly in place. He pulled back the slide to put a round into the chamber, set the safety, found a set of yellow shooting glasses and ear muffs and put them on. He picked up the shotgun and approached the range, setting the Browning on the shelf in front of him, barrel pointed away again, and squinted down the length of the room.

There was a cardboard target set at twenty metres, with a picture of a grim-looking soldier, weapon cocked and steel helmet firmly on his head. Jimmy let go with the Remington and the target blew up in a cloud of cardboard dust. It only took three shots to completely destroy the target and Jimmy stopped shooting. Bob operated the pulley that brought what was left of the paper soldier up close, so that Jimmy could check his work and replace it with a fresh one. It was barely recognisable, ripped and torn apart as it was. He clipped on a new target, and the wires hummed as it was sent back to ten metres. 'Handgun,' shouted Bob, and Jimmy picked up the Browning, clicked off the safety catch, took a stance and fired. The gun kicked hard in his hands and the bullets chopped holes in the target around the heart and the head. When the gun was empty and the action blown back, he put it on the shelf and stepped back.

Bob took off his muffs, joined Jimmy and said, 'Fair shooting. You'll do. But what happens when someone shoots back?'

'I'll do what's necessary,' replied Jimmy. 'Don't worry about me.'

'Ain't you a bit old for this lark?' asked Bob.

'You're as old as you feel,' said Jimmy. 'And with these beauties, I feel about fourteen.'

'Fair enough.'

Jimmy reloaded and practised with the guns until the range, even with its extractors on full blast was full of smoke and the stink of used gunpowder overpowering.

'That's enough,' said Bob. 'You'd better get off. Leave those guns. I'll get them cleaned for you. You can pick them up on the day.'

'Cheers,' said Jimmy, who'd never cleaned a gun in his life, just used them and slung them.

The two men went back upstairs. Toby Lee was sitting in the ballroom, waiting with a cup of tea and a cigarette. 'There you are,' he said. 'I was about to give up.'

'Sorry,' said Bob. 'Jimmy was getting used to his weapons.'

'S'all right,' said Lee. 'Racing doesn't start 'til this afternoon.'

'Toby likes a flutter,' explained Bob.

'Too right,' said Lee. 'It's a curse. If I'd saved all my all money all my life, I'd be living in clover now.'

'But think of all the fun you'd've missed,' said Bob.

'And all the porridge I wouldn't've eaten.'

Bob took leave of them at the front door. 'Later,' he said. 'I'll be in touch.'

'See you,' said Lee.

Jimmy gave a half salute and he and Lee watched him walk back into the house.

'Not a bad bloke,' said Toby. 'Ex-army.'

'Thought so,' said Jimmy.

'Saw a lot of action in Northern Ireland and in the Gulf, first time around.'

'Good man to have on our side.'

'I bloody hope so. This one could get hairy.'

'Oh, well,' said Jimmy. 'Better than signing on.'

Lee grinned. 'It was Walton, wasn't it?' said the little wheel-man.

Jimmy grinned back. 'I was there.'

'Thought so. Category A, right?'

'If you say so.'

'I knew it. I was doing time for a little tickle in Acton. Jewellers. Those were the days.'

'Sure were,' said Jimmy. Despite himself, he was beginning to warm to the little man. Old school, he thought. Just like me.

He and Lee went out into the early morning air. It was just beginning to get light. A faint line of gold painted the eastern horizon as Toby led him to a three-litre Capri, with a powerbulge on the long red bonnet. 'This is mine,' he said. 'Great motor.'

They climbed inside, strapped themselves in and Toby Lee started the engine, which caught with a roar. He grinned, slipped it into gear, gunned the motor and set off in a shower of gravel. They shot down the drive and through the gates that had opened in front of them, turned right with a squeak from the tyres and roared down the lane. Jimmy held on to the grab handle and he saw Lee grin as he worked through the gears, pushing the car too fast over the narrow strip of tarmac. 'Don't worry,' he yelled above the engine noise. 'I've never had an accident yet.'

There's always a first time, thought Jimmy.

THIRTY-FIVE

So everything was falling into place. Summer was coming and for everyone involved in the robbery, things were going well. But that was about to change.

Mark phoned Gerry Goldstein on a fine, bright morning. The trees were in full bloom and the birds were singing, but his mood was anything but spring-like.

'So?' he said.

'So?' replied Gerry, his hand sweating on the receiver.

'So, how's it all going?'

'Well.'

'Got a date yet?'

Gerry hesitated. 'Come on,' said Mark. 'Spit it out.'

'Bank holiday Monday.'

'That's only a week away. Why didn't you tell me?'

'I just did.'

'But why didn't you tell me before?'

'I just found out. Honestly, Mark.'

Gerry Goldstein to honesty was like George Bush to world peace, but Mark didn't push it. Instead he said: 'I need an in.'

'To what?'

'To the job,' said Mark slowly, not believing the way the jeweller was jerking him around. 'Come on, Gerry. Don't fuck with me, or things could get nasty.'

'But how can I get you in?'

'That's the whole point of me being here, Gerry,' said Mark.

'You're in on this and I need to be too.'

'I've told you all I know.'

'In a pig's ear. Christ, there must be some way of getting me on the inside.'

'Only if someone drops out.'

'So someone will have to drop out, won't they?'

'I hate it when you talk like that, Mark.'

'You're too squeamish, Gerry. John always said you were.'

'It's just my way. I abhor violence.'

'Especially when it's directed against you, eh?' said Mark, leaving the rest unsaid. 'We need a meet,' he added after a moment.

'What, again?'

'Have I got BO? Is that the problem?'

'I just don't want to be seen with you.'

'Tough. Shall I come to the shop?'

'No. You never know who's about. Once was enough. I'll come to you.'

'All right. There's a nice little boozer on Anerley Hill. The Spread Eagle. You can't miss it. It's next to the station. I'll be there tonight at seven.'

'I don't know about tonight... Rachel will have dinner ready.'

'Tell her something's come up. What are you, under the cosh? Just be there.' And he hung up.

Gerry phoned his wife and made up some story about a special customer wanting to see him out of business hours, but in fact she didn't seem that worried. Lately, she didn't seem to care whether he was around or or not. As long as the credit card bills were paid promptly every month, his presence seemed more and more irrelevant. He wondered if she was having an affair. He wondered if he really cared. He decided he didn't, much.

He closed the shop early and drove his BMW down through the jams of rush hour south London, found Anerley with some difficulty, and parked up by the Spread Eagle just after seven. Mark was waiting in the lounge bar with the evening paper and a pint of lager. 'You look stressed, Gerry,' he said. 'Have a drink.'

'Brandy,' replied Goldstein as he looked around the bar. It was half full

472

of unhappy commuters just off their trains, who couldn't face the rest of their journeys home without a drink. He knew how they felt.

He sat at Mark's table and idly glanced through the *Standard*. It was full of the usual stories about how London was falling apart, and he pushed it aside. Mark came back with two more drinks and got straight to the point. 'I want to know the plan.'

'Jesus,' said Gerry.

'I thought you lot crucified him.'

'They'll bloody crucify me if they ever found out I'd talked about it. And what about my profit? It was going to be my pension.'

'Put some money into Abbey Life,' said Mark. 'Look, Gerry. This job is fucked whatever way you look at it. I'm going to make sure of that. Jimmy Hunter isn't going to retire rich. He's going to retire permanently.'

'Then why don't you just kill him? You've done it before, haven't you, killed people?'

'Yes, I've done it before. But that's too easy. This is my swan song, Gerry. I intend to take him and Butler down with me.'

'But why?'

'Because I can. Now tell me.'

So Gerry Goldstein did. The whole plan. He knew what Mark was capable of, and he had never been a particularly brave man. And as he told the story, he saw his future dissolve in front of him. He was too old, too tired for the life he'd been living. It was a young man's way, and his youth had gone.

'I get it,' said Mark, when Gerry finished. 'Simple really. Tell me about the drivers.' And Gerry did that too.

'I don't fancy driving that truck,' said Mark, when he'd finished. 'I want to be with Hunter. What about the bloke driving the car?'

'Toby Lee. He's one hundred per cent.'

'So what would happen if he disappeared?'

'They'd have to replace him.'

'So, I'll make him disappear. Simple. Like you said, I've done it before.'

For all the villains he'd known in his life, Gerry still found it hard that Mark could talk so casually about killing someone, especially in the lounge bar of a quiet public house in Anerley.

'So where do I find him?' asked Mark.

'He lives down Hammersmith way,' said Goldstein.

'Big place, Hammersmith.'

'On that council estate by the river. He drinks in a pub called The Drover's Arms, on the towpath.'

'Regular?'

'As clockwork. Drives this souped-up Ford Capri. Bright red. Loves it. Never goes anywhere without it.'

'Easy to find then. What's he look like?'

'Little. Flyweight, he was for a bit, but he didn't like getting hit, so he took to crime.'

'And he's a good wheelman.'

'The best.'

'Married?'

'No.'

'So he won't be missed.'

'No. Only by Butler and the rest.'

'So they'll need another driver sharpish, if this one goes missing. The job just being a week or so away.'

'Of course.'

'I'll have to meet Mr Lee, the driver, then.'

'If you say so.'

'I do.'

'And then?'

'And then I'm afraid, the driver comes to the end of the road. Sad, but true.'

'This is getting out of hand.'

'No, Gerry. I've got it all sorted.'

Mark drove to Hammersmith the next afternoon. The Drover's Arms was on the riverbank, close to Hammersmith Bridge. It was one of those boozers that couldn't make up its mind if it was an old fashioned local or an up market eaterie. There was a pool table and Sky Sports in the public bar and seared tuna in the restaurant tacked on to the side. Mark parked his car on a meter a few yards up the road and checked out the pub's tiny car park. There was an old but beautifully maintained red Ford Capri in one corner.

He pushed through the door to the saloon bar and ordered a pint of lager. Across the counter, he saw a little man with a broken nose in the public side. He was wearing a leather jacket and had a pint glass and a sandwich in front of him, one eye on the racing pages of the *Standard*, the other on the TV.

Mark grinned, lit a cigarette, sipped his drink and made for the other bar. He found a stool one away from the little man, who'd looked up at his entrance, then returned to the racing form.

'Got anything good?' asked Mark.

Toby Lee looked up again, then around to see who Mark was talking to.

'The geegees,' said Mark, gesturing at the paper.

'No,' said Lee. 'Hopeless.'

'Just like me then.'

'Donkeys. That's all I fucking back lately.'

'I know the feeling,' said Mark. 'It's a mug's game.'

'Yeah. But the sport of kings.' Lee tossed the paper on to the bar, adding: 'And you need to be a king to afford it.'

'Bit skint?' said Mark.

'Up and down, you know.'

'Only too well. What's your game then?'

'This and that,' said Lee.

Mark drained his glass and called to the barmaid for a refill. 'Want one?' he said to Lee.

'Why not? I ain't going nowhere.'

Mark ordered another lager and a pint of bitter for Lee. When the drinks arrived, they saluted each other. 'Cheers,' said Lee.

'Cheers mate. That your motor outside?'

Lee suddenly looked suspicious. 'What motor?'

'The classic Capri.'

'What makes you think that?' said Lee, taking a cigarette from the packet in front of him, but not offering one to Mark.

'Because I'm looking for a man who drives one.'

'Is that so?'

'Yeah,' said Mark, lighting a cigarette of his own and squinting though the smoke. 'I heard that this particular man could handle himself behind the wheel.'

'Where did you hear that?'

'Around and about.'

'Are you Old Bill?'

Mark laughed out loud. 'Fuck me, hardly,' he said. 'Now that is funny.'

'Why's that?'

'Because me and the filth aren't exactly mates. Old Bill, me? I'll have to remember that.'

'So what are you looking for a driver for?'

'A little job.'

'No, mate,' said Lee. 'I'm booked.'

'Just a few hours' work. Nothing too strenuous. It's worth a grand.'

'I don't know you.'

'My name's Steve, Steve Sawyer. And you must be Toby Lee.'

'Might be,' said Lee.

'Come on, mate,' said Mark, moving closer and dropping his voice. 'Don't be shy. Your reputation precedes you.'

'Is that right?' Despite himself, he was flattered. Toby Lee didn't have much to boast about in his life, except for his driving, of which he was, quite rightly, inordinately proud.

'That's right.'

Toby nodded and smiled.

'So Toby, you interested?' asked Mark.

'Who told you about me?'

476

This was going to be the difficult part for Mark. He knew the little bloke would be suspicious about working for a stranger. 'Gerry Goldstein,' he said. He took out his mobile and put it on the bar in front of Lee. 'Give him a ring.'

Gerry hadn't been overjoyed when Mark told him that he intended to use him as a reference. 'Why me?' he'd asked.

'Don't be silly, Gerry,' Mark had replied.

'He knows you.'

'He might tell Butler.'

'Why would he? He'll be on an easy grand or whatever.'

'I don't like it.'

'Then learn to like it,' said Mark. 'You're a fucking traitor, Gerry. And you know what Butler thinks of traitors. And what he does about them. Lee will phone you, and you'll tell him I'm golden, or else I'll find a way to grass you up.'

Goldstein had given Mark a look that told him he'd better watch his back. Goldstein was scared of him. What he might do. And so he should be. But Goldstein had friends, nasty friends, and Mark could tell he was getting close to the end of his tether. Fuck his luck, he thought. Just a little while more and it probably won't matter.

Lee tapped in the numbers and waited for the pickup. 'Gerry,' he said, 'got a bloke here named Sawyer.' Pause. 'Wants me to do a bit.' Another pause. Mark saw Lee's look. 'So he's all right? OK, fine,' he said. Lee broke the connection and handed the phone back. 'Fifteen hundred,' he said. 'Half in advance.'

'Don't you want to know what you've got to do?'

'You said a few hours. That's it. You piss me about and I'll make sure you don't do it twice.'

Hard man, thought Mark. Let's see how hard he is when I've finished with him. But he said nothing, just smiled and said: 'Let's take a walk by the river.'

It was a fine afternoon, couples were strolling hand in hand, even though it was midweek. The river was calm and swans sailed by, like galleons in full sail. Pretty, thought Mark, but underneath, those webbed feet are going nineteen to the dozen. Just like life. They found a bench and sat down, watching a small child tearing off hunks of bread and throwing them to the birds. More like, at them, thought Mark as one lump of crust caught a swan in the eye.

'So,' said Lee. 'Where's the dough and what's the job?'

Mark reached into his jacket, took out an envelope containing a thousand pounds in fifties, counted out fifteen, and handed them over. 'I want you to collect a car and deliver it,' he said. 'Simple.'

'What's in the car?'

'None of your business.'

'Fair enough,' said Lee. 'Where and when?'

'Tomorrow night,' said Mark, taking a set of keys out of his pocket and handing them to Lee. 'A black Beemer seven in the carpark of the Ibis hotel at Heathrow. Know it?'

'I'll find it.'

'Fair enough. Registration S411 YEV. Take it to the underground carpark at the East London Uni, at Beckton. Know that?'

'I'll find it.'

'Good. It's Saturday so it'll be open but empty. Leave the car there and take a walk. The rest of your money will be in the glove compartment.'

'That's all?'

'That's all.'

'Seems like a lot for a run across London.'

'Better than bus driver's wages, that's for sure.'

'Why don't you do it?'

'I'll be doing something else. Now this ain't a quiz show. Do you want the job or not? If not, gimme the cash and the keys back and I'll find someone who does.'

Lee though for a minute and nodded. 'I'll do it.'

'Get the motor to the carpark by ten. Don't be too early and don't be late. OK?'

'OK.'

'OK, Toby. And try Lancaster Gate in the three-thirty at Thirsk tomorrow. You might double your money.' And with that, Mark got up and left.

Dev had supplied the stolen BMW, two sets of keys and a new set of plates, and Chas had driven it over to Heathrow. He'd left it in the hotel car park, with an envelope in the glove box containing another fifteen fifties, then caught the tube home. It was good for him to have something useful to do for a change – and this wasn't his only job that weekend. Just like old times.

At seven the next night, Mark picked Chas up in his Ford Explorer, and they drove over to east London. They were early, but they didn't want to miss Lee's arrival. Mark had scoped out several locations before he'd settled on the Uni, but he'd found that the campus carpark was the only one open that could be counted on to be dead on a Saturday night. He parked the truck close to the entrance, its tinted windows hiding the two occupants from view, and they waited.

'I miss John, you know,' said Chas.

'Course you do.'

'It's a bit dull without him.'

'I bet. And Hazel too, yeah?'

'For sure.'

'It must've been great, the three of you in the old days.'

'Are you kidding?'

'Tell me about him and Hazel.'

'Like what?'

'Like what they were like back then.'

'Back then. The old days. You make me feel like Methuselah.'

'You know what I mean. Come on, we've got time.'

'That's what we always thought. Loads of time. But time flies. There was one day…'

'Yeah?'

'Yeah. They were bad you know, the pair of them. Very bad. We all were. But John… He was the worst. And she didn't help. Not at first. She calmed down when they got married and Martine came along. No, not calmed down. Just... Christ, I don't know. She just managed it better.'

'So what happened?'

'When?'

'That one day you were talking about.'

'Oh yeah. It was summer, 1967. Great summer that was. The real summer of love. 'Cept we didn't love much, not our little firm. Only each other. Real hippy days, but John always hated hippies. Anyway, we found out that there was this bunch of public school boys doing a roaring drug trade up in Notting Hill. That was when it was a real dump. Not that's it's any better now, just property values are higher. Being from down south, I don't know. We never felt right over in west London. Streatham, Brixton, Clapham, Battersea, that was our manor. Chelsea for clothes and the West End for nights out. But I always felt that Notting Hill, Shepherd's Bush, round there was like alien territory. But anyway, these kids had a great big house in one of the squares up there. I forget which one now. Belonged to one of their dads. He was something big in the admiralty, of all things, and he let his kid live in this house. Massive it was. One of those like in *Performance*. You've seen that movie?'

Mark nodded.

'Good film. Realistic, if you know what I mean. White the house was, with a bloody great set of steps at the front, and white pillars on either side of the door. Christ knows what it would be worth these days, but then they were mostly split into bedsits for students and lowpaid workers and spades and all. Anyway, we heard these fuckers were doing good business. They ran some kind of underground newspaper and the dope paid the bills that Daddy didn't. But what got under John's skin was that they were posh fuckers pretending to be the lads, if you know what I mean. Pissed John right off.

'Anyway, how you got the gear was to phone up, tell 'em that so-and-so had told you the SP and pop round with the readies. Not before two in the afternoon though. These people liked to sleep late. And that fucked John off too. Always was an early riser, John was. The get in was

480

easy. No steel doors like nowadays. These kids thought they were golden. Hardly ever even locked the door. Mugs. So we got the phone number and Hazel says she'll go in first, sweeten 'em up, if you like. But she really only did it to wind John up, if you ask me. You should've seen her. Fuckin' 'ell. Did she look the business that day? Like I told you, it was summer. Hot, sticky. And she turns up in this little flowery dress that's so short it hardly covers her arse. And you can see right though it. No bra and just a little pair of white bikini pants. The rest of us didn't know where to look. Oh, I forgot. There was me and Martin, who used to be called the Goon, in the motor too. Some great big thing. A Zephyr I think, we'd got off Dev. Always had to have a big motor we did, even if it burnt a bit of oil. So the four of us shoot off to Notting Hill in the car, but it's still a bit early, so we go to a pub and start getting tanked up. Hazel loved a drink, remember?'

Mark nodded again.

'Christ, she couldn't have been more than eighteen that summer. They'd've called her a "wild child" in the 80s, but then she was just a mad bird. So, like I said, she volunteers to go in first and John ain't happy about that at all. But he stays calm. Or at least as calm as he ever was, back then. I mean, when you knew him, he'd quietened down too, so's you can imagine what he was like before. Fucking mental when he got on one. So she goes to a phone box and does the business, comes back and everything's hunky dory. "Cool," she says. "They're holding. Give me half an hour," and off she flounces, wiggling her bottom and I can see John seething, but he doesn't say anything. So we're in the pub and John keeps looking at his watch, and after twenty minutes, he says "Fuck this," and goes to the phone too. Now the plan is, he phones, goes in, susses out the situation and thirty minutes later I phone up too and go in with Martin and we take them down. Rip off what we can and split. Sweet as. But of course, as you know, plans can go wrong.'

Mark nodded once more. He knew better than most.

'John comes back to the pub and gives me the thumbs up and so I get me and Martin another drink and John goes off. So now I don't know what's happening, but I managed to put it together later from what him and Hazel tell me.

'He goes up to the house where the paint's all peeling off the front and there's garbage strewn about outside. Now you've got to remember that him and Hazel are living together in this little flat in Streatham at the time. We've made some dough but it always seemed to vanish, so we're not loaded like maybe ten or fifteen years later, when we hit the big time. We're just monkeys really. A bit of dealing, some protection, nicking motors. We were young, Mark, and we wanted to have a good time. But this flat they've got, fair play to 'em. They kept it nice. Buying bits and pieces here and there, and Hazel always was house proud, nutty bird or no nutty bird. But this place is a tip. For all their money and education they treat it like shit. Dirty old furniture, posters and bits of hangings on the walls. No carpet, just painted floorboards, and apparently this don't make John's mood no better. And there's some crap Indian music on the stereo, Ravi Wanker or whatever. And what makes it even worse, is, when he steams in, Hazel's sitting on some hippie's lap with his tongue in her ear. Now they were always doing that. Copping off with someone just to make the other jealous. It was like a game, but woe betide anyone who got involved because they both had quick tempers and a predilection for violence. Good word that, "predilection". Got it in a crossword years ago.'

Mark smiled. He loved these stories. He looked through the tinted glass of the truck and watched the sun go down over west London. Notting Hill, he thought. What he wouldn't have given to be there that summer of love afternoon with John Jenner and Hazel in full flow.

'Now, like I said,' Chas went on. 'These fuckers were posh. All got the accents, know what I mean? And when John turns up, the bloke whose dad owns the house decides to call John "Cockney Boy". Bad mistake. Fellah starts putting on the old mockney. Thinks he's a bit of a comedian apparently. Telling John he'd been to Hackney and Dalston which of course cuts no ice as, being from south of the river, John couldn't care less. But he swallows all the old bollocks, because what he's really interested in is what these cunts are holding and how he's going to part them from it. So he makes enquiries, and these fuckers turn out to be the real deal. They've got LSD, hash, coke, smack, grass, uppers, downers, the whole nine yards. And plenty of it. It's like Boots the bleedin' chemist in that gaff, and of course, being connected – the right hon this and the right hon that – they think they're magic, like I said. Above the law. Which they probably were. But not our law.

'So this geezer, the comic – little fat cunt with Lennon glasses and some kind of fucking Afro hairstyle – starts showing off. Mug, like I said. He don't know John from Adam. Just, like, "Joe sent me", on the dog and you're in. I think they learnt their lesson that day. So the geezer shows John the kit in a big trunk and John shows him a big wad of cash and everyone's getting on amazing. 'Specially this cunt with Hazel on his knee. Good looking boy he was too, 'cos you've got to remember, I turn up later and see the lot of them. Not as good looking as John, mind. He looked really well that day. Long, black hair. This big white shirt tucked into real tight jeans. John wouldn't wear flares, said they was only for hippies. And big biker boots. Looked like a fuckin' pirate, he did. And he's got a Colt .45 automatic that he bought off some black GI down the Flamingo under his shirt, and a huge hunting knife, with a blade as big as a butcher's cleaver, down his right boot. This knife, I tell you what, it scared the shit out of me. One side of the blade was like a saw, the other was sharp, and it had a wicked point. Anyway, apparently Hazel's wriggling about in this bloke's lap and John's shaking like a leaf with anger. The Afro bloke notices and makes some remark and John tells him he's got to get well, which makes some other fucker pull out a wrap of smack and the works and they start fixing up. Hot spoon, the whole bit. See, there was loads of people there. Like I told you, this place is massive, and there's hippies in every room, like rats in a nest.

'Anyway, John's waiting for me to make my call and he has to watch Hazel showing out, and eventually he can't stand any more and says "Pull your dress down love, I can see what you had for breakfast."

'"I haven't had my breakfast," she pipes back, and this bloody hippie

483

she's crawling all over says: "No? Well you can eat my sausage any time you like."

'Which just makes things worse, and about then it starts to go pear-shaped. But before John can do anything, I make my phone call which sort of cools the situation off a bit, but not for long. Anyway, Afro answers, I give the code and he invites me up. I say I've got someone with me. And the geezer says, "The more the merrier." Twat. Well I'm round there in less time than it takes to tell, with old Martin. Me, I'm dressed up to the nines too. Granny Takes A Trip jacket. Pinstripe flares. Nice shirt. But poor old Martin. He never could get anything to fit, being the size he was. So he looks like a great big schoolboy in grey flannels and an old denim shirt he'd found somewhere. So of course these fucking hippies start taking the rise. And them always on about peace and love and all that shit. Pisstaking fuckers. And some other bird's arrived on the scene too.

Probably got woken up with all the excitement. Tasty she was too. Black hair, all done in them curls like in the old photos. She wearing this white dress and nothing underneath, You can see her bush when she walked. Black as ink.'

'A natural brunette,' said Mark.

'Something like that. Blimey, Mark, it was like Sodom and Gomorrah in there, what with this bloke with a needle in his arm and half-naked birds everywhere. Anyway, this other bird susses out that John's holding folding and fancies her chances. So she goes up and whispers something in his ear which none of the rest of us can hear, but you didn't have to have a great imagination to work it out. She was up for a shag with Johnny and no mistake. Well, Hazel can dish it out but she's not too happy about getting it back, so she gets off this geezer's lap and walks right up to the bird and smacks her one on the nose. Breaks it. You could hear the crack clear to the Bayswater road, I reckon. And so suddenly there's snot and claret all over the white dress and Hazel says: 'Leave him alone, bitch. He's mine.'

Course this causes a commotion as the hippies don't know what the fuck's going on. John decides it's time to take charge of the situation and pulls out the Colt. Well, there's another little geezer in the room all curled up in the corner like the Dormouse in *Alice In Wonderland*. Little fair-haired bloke. Poofy. Know what I mean? Like he doesn't know what he is, a boy or a girl. But fuck me if he doesn't sit up and he's got a gun too. But it ain't real. This kid's been akip and thinks we're playing games. Cowboys and Indians or something. Must've been trippin'. You can tell this gun's a fake a mile off. A little kid's toy shooter. Cap gun. But John isn't amused at all. It's just one mistake after another they're making. Compounding their felonies, if you know what I mean. So John walks over to this kid, grabs the toy and slams him right in the gob with it. More claret, and I reckon that bloke will've been a regular customer at his dentist ever since, as he's spitting teeth all over the floor.

'That's when the shit really hit the fan. Afro literally pisses himself. Oh yes. He's wearing these faded denims and suddenly there's a big stain in the crotch. Fucking little prick. So I grabs him by this bunch of hair and puts him on the floor and John turns to the hippie who had his tongue in Hazel's ear and he points the Colt at him. "What was that about a sausage?" he says and this geezer just about turns green. Anyway, I can see big trouble coming and, not wanting to leave any dead bodies about, I says to John, "Where's the gear?" and he tells me and I get Martin to grab hold of it and then to John, "Let's go then. We've got the loot," or something like that. And so he sort of hesitates and takes the knife out of his boot and puts it right by the hippie's eye and says, "You mess about with my bird again and I'll stick this right through your brain, understand?" And the hippie nods and John says, "I think an apology's in order," and of course, this geezer does as he's told and I'm going: "Come on, mate, let's split," because of all these fucking people about. John tugs the phone out of the wall and lobs it through the window, but unfortunately it's not open so there's breaking glass and all sorts going on and John, well, he just laughs and fires a couple of rounds into the ceiling just for badness. Hazel grabs the other tart by the hair and tells her she's lucky to still have any, as the last bird who tried it on with John, she shaved her head and she might just be back with an open razor. Martin's still standing there with this great big box that weighs a ton, and we split out the door and all into the motor and away. Just another day in the life, if you know what I mean.'

'Fantastic,' said Mark.

'Poor old Martin, he saved my life a few years later. He died for me and I was always a bit narky with him. You just never know, do you?'

'No, you don't,' said Mark, and then he saw a black BMW come cruising down the street. 'Well, look who's here,' he said.

As the car passed them, Mark jumped out of the Explorer and loped after it. Despite the warm, dry evening, he was wearing a light mackintosh, and gloves. In the mac pocket was a large, shapeless hat and his shades, which he put on as he went, plus a Glock .45 automatic loaded with hollow points and fitted with a short, home-made silencer that was probably only good for a couple of shots. But a couple of shots was all Mark intended using it for. He walked across the tarmac as Lee left the BMW. 'Hey, Toby,' he shouted as he went.

'What you doing here?' asked Lee.

'Change of plan,' said Mark.

'What?'

He took out the pistol and pointed it at Lee's head.

'What the fuck's the matter?' said Lee.

'Back to the car,' said Mark.

'What? What's going on?' but he did as he was told.

Mark used the spare keyfob to crack the boot. 'Inside.'

'You're having a laugh, aincha?'

'It's not funny, Toby.'

'I don't get it.'

'Wrong place, wrong time,' said Mark. 'It's nothing personal.'

'I'm not...' said Lee, and Mark smacked him with the silencer. A red weal appeared, dripping blood, and Lee went down against the side of the car.

'In the fucking boot,' said Mark.

That time Lee crawled into the space illuminated by a tiny bulb.

'Sorry, mate,' said Mark and fired twice, the explosions making puffing sounds like an asthmatic on his last legs. The bullets hit Lee in the head and chest and he was dead before Mark slammed the boot lid. He collected the two cartridge cases from the concrete floor and dropped them into his pocket, unscrewed the silencer and put that in too, to be disposed of later. He got behind the wheel, started the engine, and drove out of the carpark and followed Chas, driving the Ford to a cement depot in Newham. Chas had the key to the front gate and they parked up close to a conveyor belt that led up to one of the massive cement mixers. Chas broke the lock on the conveyor belt's motor and started the machine, sounding like a 747 taking off.

Mark opened the boot of the BMW and they pulled Lee's body out and manhandled it on to the belt. Mark went through his pockets, which were empty, apart from the envelope containing the seven hundred and fifty quid Chas had left in the glove compartment and another three grand, rolled up tight. 'I told him Lancaster Gate would win,' said Mark, slipping the cash into his pocket.

With a crunch of gears, Chas manipulated the levers that started the belt moving, and Lee's body was transported fifty feet into the air, before dropping into the cement mixer with a plop. Chas turned off the belt and they left. The Beemer ended up at Leamouth in flames and Mark dropped Chas off in Tulse Hill before heading back to his hotel.

Mark phoned Gerry again the next day. 'Looks like there's a vacancy,' he said.

'Oh Christ.'

'I want the job.'

'This is insane.'

'When will Lee be missed?' asked Mark.

'There's a meet the day after tomorrow at Butler's place. We'll all be there.'

'Perfect. So your job is to put me up as the new driver.'

'They don't know you.'

'But you do.'

'If they find out…'

'Then put yourself as far away as possible, Gerry. Take the family on holiday. I hear Florida's nice this time of year. But don't think about crossing me. Because I swear, if you do, I'll come back from the grave to get you. Or someone will. I've got friends. And anyway, you're in too deep to change your mind now.'

'I know that.'

'Then keep it in mind. I saved your life once before, Gerry. You and your women. Now you belong to me.'

Gerry's stomach turned at the thought, but all he said was, 'OK, Mark, but you're taking one hell of a risk.'

'I know. But I never was one for the quiet life.'

Gerry Goldstein almost vomited before going into the meeting. Lee was immediately noticeable by his absence. 'Someone find him,' said Butler. 'And get the little git in here. It's too close to the big day for anyone to start playing silly buggers.' But of course, he was nowhere to be found. His car was neatly parked outside his flat, and no one at the Drover's Arms or the local betting shop had seen him since Saturday when he'd had a result on the horses. 'Won a bundle,' said the betting shop manager. 'Maybe he's gone on holiday.' Someone entered his flat without disturbing the dust. It was empty, and what food there was in the fridge was beginning to spoil. That was it. Lee had vanished and a replacement was needed.

'I know someone,' offered Gerry Goldstein. 'A red hot driver.'

'Who?' asked Butler.

'A kid called Steve. Just back from the Continent and looking for work.'

'I don't know him.'

'He's good.'

'Shit. That fucker Lee. Wins some money on a horse and vanishes. Typical. I never should've rowed him in in the first place. Gamblers. They're worse than junkies for doing a runner when you need them most. All right, Gerry. I'll take him on your say so. Make a meet between this Steve bloke and Bob. If Bob says he's OK, then we'll go with him.'

The meeting was arranged in an empty car park deep in the bowels of the city of London, close to Goldstein's shop. Bob turned up with a Jaguar XJ. He tossed the keys to Mark and said, 'Impress me.'

Mark got in behind the wheel and demonstrated every driving trick that Dev and Chas had taught him. He threw the powerful motor from one end of the concrete floor to the other, tyres screaming and smoking, as Bob held on to the passenger grab handle with white knuckled fingers. Mark demonstrated one-eighties and three-sixties, hand-brake turns, doughnuts, the lot. Ending up by using one of the ramps to flip the car up on to two wheels and do a perfectly balanced circle of the garage with Bob's head only a foot or so above the floor, before dropping it back with a bang. 'What do you reckon?' he asked when Bob had regained his cool.

'Where did you learn all that?' asked the ex-soldier.

'Here and there.'

'Gerry tells us you've done this sort of thing before.'

'Once or twice.'

'Don't give much away do you?'

'This and that.'

'All right, Steve. You're on. You'd better come in for a briefing tomorrow.' And he told Mark where and when.

And so Mark Farrow joined the team as the wheelman on the second motor.

That night, Gerry Goldstein sat alone in the study of his detached house in Golders Green with only a bottle of Remy Martin for company. Rachel was in bed in the room where she slept alone, watching *ER* on TV, and their daughters were out spending his dough clubbing. Rachel's hair was in curlers and she'd covered her face with the latest miracle cream to keep it youthful. She'd already been cut and tucked three times in a private hospital in Kensington, which had set Gerry back the profit on his most recent foray into a life of crime. It just wasn't fair. And now Mark Farrow was intent on screwing up a most lucrative little earner. He could go to Daniel Butler and confess all. But where would that lead? Mark had made it very clear that if Gerry blew the whistle, things would get very unpleasant indeed.

Gerry poured another drink, slopping just a little on to the polished top of his desk. He looked at the drops pooled on the wood and contemplated a life without all the comforts he took for granted. Fuck them, he thought. Fuck Rachel and the girls, and fuck Danny Butler and Jimmy Hunter and fuck Mark Farrow. Fuck them all. I'll show them. And he opened the top desk drawer and took out a small revolver. He checked the load of six tiny bullets, pushed the cylinder home and cocked the hammer. Alone in his study, he drained his glass, then opened his mouth, inserted the barrel of the gun and pulled the trigger.

Upstairs in her bedroom, Rachel Goldstein heard the shot, but only faintly. And as County Hospital in Chicago was under siege by gang-bangers looking to put one of their own out of his misery, with that handsome young Croatian doctor being held hostage in one of the emergency rooms, she assumed it was one of many gunshots on the soundtrack and ignored it.

No one missed Gerry until the next morning.

THIRTY-SIX

Mark Farrow waited until the Thursday before the bank holiday to put the next part of his plan into action. He wanted enough time for Sean Pierce to organise a police operation, but not enough time to check too deeply who was involved.

He rang Streatham Police Station mid-morning from a callbox in Crystal Palace, and got put through to the CID office. A woman answered, 'CID, DC Webb speaking.'

'Is Sean Pierce there please?' asked Mark.

'Yeah. Who's speaking?'

'Steve Sawyer. He doesn't know me.'

'Concerning?'

'I've got something for him.'

The phone went down with a bang, he heard voices and then it was picked up again. 'DS Pierce,' said Sean.

'Sean Pierce?'

'That's right.'

'I've got some information for you.'

'What sort of information?'

'Important information.'

'About?'

'Not on the phone.'

'Do I know you? Sawyer, is it?'

'I told the DC you don't.'

'So, why are you talking to me?'

'I heard you were a decent copper,' replied Mark. 'Someone I could trust.'

491

'Who are you?'

'Like I said, someone with information.'

'If you're not going to tell me—'

'Don't blow it, Sean,' interrupted Mark. 'This could be the making of you.'

'Oh yeah?' But Mark could tell he was interested.

'Yeah. We need to meet.'

'I'm a busy man.'

'We're all busy, Sean. I could always take this elsewhere.'

There was a pause. 'OK, where and when?'

'No time like the present. How about in an hour. Do you know the Beehive pub in Streatham?'

'Course I do.'

'Eleven thirty.'

'All right. How will I know you?'

'I'll know you.' And Mark hung up.

He was already at the pub when Sean entered. Mark was wearing his shades and gloves. It was an old trick for a copper to pick up a drinker's glass and check his prints for identity. But the last thing Mark wanted was for Sean to know who he was. Although he'd never been convicted, Mark's prints were on file, and he assumed lodged somewhere in the Police National Computer. Maybe, maybe not, but he wasn't about to risk it. And only God knew what he'd find if he checked on the Continent.

Sean looked round the almost empty bar and Mark raised one hand. The young policeman came over and stood by Mark's table. 'Sawyer?' he said.

'That's me.'

'Right, I'm here. What's this all about?'

'It's all about you making inspector,' replied Mark. 'And this will take a while. Sit down. Drink?'

'I'll get my own,' said Sean who went to the bar and ordered an orange juice.

When he'd returned and sitting in front of Mark, he said: 'I don't have long. What is it you've got to tell me?'

'There's going to be a robbery soon. A big one.'

'Yeah, sure.'

'Take my word.'

'And how do you know?'

Mark lit a cigarette and saw Sean's look of thinly veiled disgust. Pious fucker, he thought. 'Because I'm part of it.'

'And you want to blow the whistle.'

'S'right.'

'Why?'

'Personal reasons.'

'Why me?'

'Sorry.'

'Why tell me? Are you sure I don't know you?' He studied Mark's face carefully.

This was the moment Mark was dreading. All those years ago when Mark and Linda had been having their illicit relationship, he had mostly managed to avoid her family. No one but Linda had known who he was, and, more importantly, who his father had been. Even so, there had been times when Sean had spotted them together. It was inevitable. But after all this time he couldn't possibly remember. Could he?

Mark took off his glasses and looked Sean in the face. 'I don't think so,' he said. He looked him straight in the eye with his contacts in place and saw no sign of recognition.

'OK,' said Sean. 'So, why me? I'm just a DS.'

'I told you why,' said Mark. 'I heard you were something rare. An honest cop.'

'Where did you hear that?'

'Around.'

'OK. So you've got information about a big robbery, or so you say.'

'Why should I lie?' asked Mark.

'There's a million reasons. Maybe I've put a friend of yours away and you're winding me up. Trying to make me look a fool. Or maybe this is a gag on behalf of the boys at the station.'

'Or maybe it's true,' interrupted Mark. 'Christ. I'm giving you this on a plate and you think it's a wind-up.'

'It wouldn't be the first time.'

'Shit,' said Mark. He could hardly believe this. Here he was with the information of the year and the dozy fucker wouldn't believe him. 'Have you ever heard of Daniel Butler?'

'Danny Butler?'

'That's right.'

'He's retired. Gone to live in Essex.'

'Retired fuck,' said Mark. 'He's the architect. He's got a bunch of heavy duty villains in to do the job.'

'Where?'

At last, thought Mark. 'Docklands,' he replied.

'When?'

'Bank holiday Monday.'

'Next Monday?'

Top of the class, thought Mark. 'Next Monday,' he echoed.

'And you know the full story?'

'Sure.'

'Would you be prepared to meet a more senior officer?' Mark shook his head.

'No,' he said. 'I'm taking a big enough risk meeting you alone. These fuckers are serious. They're armed with automatic weapons and they're prepared to use them.'

'And what's your part in all this?'

'I'm just a driver.'

'And the reason you're here is personal? You want someone banged up?'

'Something like that.' In a fucking coffin, thought Mark.

'Who's the person you're out to get? Do we know him?'

'Oh yes.'

'Name?'

Mark shook his head again. 'Don't worry, you'll know when the time comes.'

494

'And a reward?'

'It'd come in handy, but I don't really care. But I want to get away. I don't intend to do any time.'

'I can't guarantee that.'

'You're going to have to. I'll give you the full details and it's your job to make sure I don't get my collar felt.'

'I'll have to talk to my superiors.'

'Go on then. Don't let me stop you.'

'All right. But first tell me what you know.'

So Mark did. Most, but not all. No mention of Jimmy Hunter, of course. That was Mark's little secret. But he did tell Sean that Daniel Butler had an inside man or woman on the plot. 'No one must know that you know,' he concluded. 'Otherwise they'll call the party off.'

'That makes it very difficult,' said Sean.

'I never said it was going to be easy,' said Mark. 'But if you pull this off, what's the betting on some promotion?'

Sean considered. 'If you're lying...'

'Why would I bother?'

'It'll be a big operation.'

'It's a big job. Armed guards, twenty-five million in stones.'

'And all just on your say so...'

Mark blew air out of his mouth in frustration. Didn't this dickhead know good intelligence when he heard it? 'Listen,' he said. 'Check out an old printing works in Canning Town.' He gave Sean the address. 'See what's going on there. But be careful. There's blokes around with guns who wouldn't be pleased to see you. I mean it. One less copper to them would be a bonus.'

Sean looked at him long and hard. 'OK, I'll do that. But there's not much time, if what you say is true. And if you're having me on...'

'Do you think I'm having you on? This is bloody serious. One word that I've spoken to you about it and I'm dead.'

'You must hate this man very much.'

Mark cocked his head.

'The man you want banged up,' said Sean.

'Believe it.'

'What did he do?'

Mark smiled. 'That's for me to know.'

'Fair enough. How can I get in touch?'

'You can't. I'll call you later.' He got up then and made as to leave. 'There's no one outside waiting to follow me is there?' he asked.

It was Sean's turn to shake his head. 'No,' he said.

'OK, I believe you.' But even so, when he left the pub, he took a very circuitous route back to his hotel, even though he was eventually convinced he wasn't being followed.

He phoned the nick again late that afternoon and Sean was waiting for his call. 'All right,' he said. 'I've been up to Canning Town. There's something happening there for sure. I've got a provisional go ahead. But I'll need to know more. Can we meet again?'

'Sure. But just you. And don't be clever. I can spot a tail a mile off.'

'Fair enough.'

They arranged to meet at a car park in Crystal Palace and Mark walked the short distance from his hotel. Sean was waiting in his Mondeo. Mark got in and said: 'Drive.'

They talked as they went. Mark turned the rearview mirror so that he could see the road behind and, just as he thought, two cars joined them. But he said nothing. It was just what he expected.

'I'm going to take a look-see tomorrow at the depository,' said Sean.

'Well, be cool.'

'I will. My guv'nors have spoken to the bosses there. They're having kittens. I'm going in as public health.'

One of the cars following turned off, but then another appeared and the first car overtook them and vanished into the traffic. Mark knew that three or four cars was the minimum for a good tail. 'You disappoint me, Sean,' he said.

'What?'

'You know we've got company. That's no way to build up trust.'

'Don't know what you're talking about.'

'Course you don't. But I hope you're better at finding some way for me to get out,' Mark said as he set the mirror straight.

'Don't worry, I will. Tell me more about the numbers and weapons.'

'Seven are going in. Like I told you, armed with automatic and semi-automatic weapons.'

'Any names?'

'First names only. And some are using fakes. I don't know who the fuck they are. I'm just a driver, don't forget. Low man in the pecking order. I do what I'm told and that's that.'

'How'd you get the job?'

Mark smiled without mirth. 'Someone dropped out,' he replied.

'What's your share?'

'An even split after the top men take their cut.'

'Is that the problem?'

'No, I keep telling you. It's not money I'm interested in. There's someone there I want to see go down for a long time.'

'Well, you must know his name.'

'Course.'

'So tell me, and I'll make sure.'

'That's not part of the deal.'

'Dark horse, aincha?'

The dusk was gathering in the early summer evening and Sean saw Mark nod his head in the light from the street lamps that were popping on one after another on the main Camberwell road. 'OK,' said Sean. 'But how can I make sure we get him?'

'Oh, you'll get him all right. I'll make sure of that.'

'Are you going to be armed?'

'What do you think?'

'You'll have to lose your weapon.'

'I don't care. I don't intend to use it,' Mark lied.

'Right. I've written my mobile number down. Use that from now on.'

'I don't want to meet you again,' said Mark.

'Maybe just once more, over the weekend.'

'Maybe. But it's risky.'

'A favour for a favour.'

'OK, Sean, but make it brief.'

'Do you have a mobile number?'

'Yes. But I'm not giving it to you. I'll be in touch.'

'Where do you want to be dropped off?'

'Anywhere here will do,' said Mark. He had nothing to do, and didn't want to make it easy for whoever was following them to get on his tail. When Sean stopped the car, Mark jumped out, ducked into a side road, went to the end, stopped and lit a cigarette. A young couple, man and woman entered the street too, and he waited until they were close and walked back towards them. He saw just a slight look of alarm from the bloke and he smiled and passed them, went back to the main road and joined the queue for a bus that was just stopping. He chucked the driver a pound coin and saw the couple on the corner, the woman talking into a mobile phone or radio. The bus pulled away and Mark immediately rang the bell for the next stop, jumped off and walked into a pub on the corner. He ordered a lager and watched the door. The only person to enter in the next fifteen minutes was a grey-haired man with a grey-haired dog. Mark finished his drink and went outside. It was twilight by then and he pulled up his collar and walked down the road until he came to a minicab office with a couple of old bangers parked outside. A bubble driver was only too pleased to run him up to Crystal Palace, and Mark got him to drop him off round the corner from the hotel. Even so, he still didn't go straight back but took another circuitous route until he was sure he was clean, and then went in and had a drink at the bar before going to bed.

The next day he went to see Linda.

He knew it was a crazy thing to do, but he couldn't help himself.

It was a fine, warm morning and, once again, he parked up outside her house and watched Sean leave for work. It was suicide if Sean saw and recognised him, but, like a junkie dying for the next fix, Mark just couldn't stay away.

As school time approached, the nanny came out with Luke and took him off in the car. Mark smoked a cigarette, and just as he was about to walk over and knock on the front door, it opened and Linda came out with Daisy. The little girl was in some sort of child chair in one hand, and Linda carried a wicker basket containing gardening tools in the other. Linda was dressed in khakis and a T-shirt and she sat her daughter in the shade of the privet, pulled on a pair of canvas gloves, knelt and started digging in one of the flower beds. Mark ditched his cigarette, got out of his car and walked across the road. He stood by the front gate and looked at the two females enjoying the morning air. 'Watch out for worms,' he said. 'I believe they eat little girls.'

Both looked up, one non-comprehending and the other with a frown. 'I beg your pardon,' said Linda. 'Were you talking to me?'

'Yes, Linda, that's right,' said Mark.

She did a classic double take when he called her by name, and suddenly recognition filled her eyes. 'Mark? Is that you?'

'You always say that?'

'God, you look old.'

'Thanks. But then, I feel old.'

'What are you doing here?'

'Chatting up a pair of good looking birds.'

'Be serious. Are the police after you?'

'Always. You know that.'

'If Sean saw you...'

He already has, thought Mark, but said: 'I watched him go off on his mission to keep the streets safe for decent members of society.'

She looked up and down the road as if fleets of black marias were about to arrive. 'You'd better come in,' she said.

'What about nanny?' asked Mark.

'She's going up to London, after she's dropped Luke off. Shopping. She won't be back 'til lunchtime.'

'I could use a coffee.'

'Come on, then, though I don't know why I...'

'Because,' said Mark and opened the gate and walked in.

Linda discarded her gloves into the tool basket and grabbed Daisy. Mark followed her into the kitchen, where she transferred the infant into a high chair. Daisy chewed on a rusk and gave Mark pensive looks.

'So what's all this about?' asked Linda after she'd put the kettle on.

'I couldn't stay away.'

'That's why I've heard nothing from you for months.'

'You didn't want to know. I gave you first refusal and you refused.'

'That didn't mean I couldn't've been convinced.'

'I had to go.'

'Always the same old Mark. Always on the run.'

'I had no choice.'

'So you left.'

'You wanted me to go.'

'No, I didn't.'

'Well, you did a fair impression of someone who did.'

'You just turned up out of the blue. I hadn't seen you since that night at the flat where you left me all dressed up and nowhere to go.'

He smiled just a little at her choice of words. 'I told you I was sorry.'

'Mark, you've been apologising to me since we met.'

'I know. Some relationships are like that, I suppose.'

'Relationship. What relationship? We never had one except for a little while at the start. Then when you told me who you were...'

'Who you were, more like.'

'And who was I?'

'You know.'

'No. Tell me.'

'The daughter of the man who murdered my father.'

'That was never my fault and you know it.'

He didn't reply, and the silence stretched to near breaking point.

Eventually, he said: 'I wouldn't be here if you'd come with me that day. We'd be somewhere warm together. You, me, Luke and Daisy.'

'Happy families again, is it, Mark?'

'Something like that.'

'Because you never had one?'

'I did. John and his.'

'But not yours, Mark.'

'Is that wrong?'

'No. But just to turn up like that and demand I leave everything. Everyone I know, everything I own.'

'Would it have been so hard?'

She turned away before he could see the tears that sprang to her eyes. 'If only you'd waited,' she said.

'What?'

'If only you'd waited. Like you did that day at school in the rain. Remember?'

'I'll never forget that day. You sent your friend with a note.'

'I know. Most of the bloody school was looking out at you sitting there getting soaked.'

'It was wet.'

'So, why didn't you wait the last time?'

'I was being pursued by half the police in England. Your brother's a cop. You said you'd call him. I had to go.'

'I would've come. If only you'd persevered.'

'Don't say that, Linda. Don't make me regret something else.'

'I don't think you know the meaning of the word.'

'Of course I do. I've had more regrets than most.'

'Don't start singing *My Way*, for Christ's sake. I couldn't take it.'

He smiled again.

'I promise I won't do that.'

'So, where did you go?'

'Like I said, somewhere warm. Portugal. I found a little place where I could see the sea, and there was a bar and restaurant within a few minutes walk. It was good. Comfortable. You'd've loved it, and the kids....'

'They'd've loved it too, I know.'

'And we could've stayed there the rest of out lives and forgotten all

501

about this.' His gesture took in London, England, everything. 'We could've been happy.'

'And now we can't?'

'I don't know.'

'Where are you living?'

'Out of a suitcase. I've been staying in hotels. Moving around. You know.'

'No, I don't. Have you seen Chas?'

'Briefly.'

'And how's Martine?'

He had wondered how long it would be before she came into the conversation. 'She's fine, as far as I know,' he said. 'I haven't seen her. She still blames me for John's death.'

'But I bet she'd have you in a minute.'

He dismissed Martine with another derisory wave of his hand. 'She's nothing to me.'

'Then she should be. Her family took you in.'

'I know that.'

'Then show some bloody respect. Well, you have. You went to bed with her.'

'I did not.'

'She says you did.'

'She's a liar. She'd do anything to split us up.'

'She doesn't need to. You can do all that for yourself.'

'Thanks.' Although he knew it was true.

'So, what are we going to do?'

'That's up to you.'

'I find it very hard to like you these days, Mark, let alone love you.' But she was lying. She knew it, he knew it, even Daisy knew it, smiling a very cynical smile for someone so young. Or it could've been wind.

'I still love you,' said Mark.

'And what does loving me mean? Picking me up and dropping me whenever you feel like it. Taking me and my family away from everything

502

we know and dragging us from one hiding place to another until we don't know who we are anymore. And what happens when Luke and Daisy grow up? What kind of people would they be? Expats. Strangers from their own country, not knowing who they are.'

'I can't make life perfect, Linda. I've tried that and it doesn't work.'

'When have you ever tried to make my life perfect?'

'There's no answer to that, if you don't know.'

'I don't, Mark. I've spent the last months since you went away again, trying to work it out, but I've come up empty.'

'Is there anyone else?'

'No. There's never been anyone else. I've told you that a hundred times. Even when I was married I still cared more for you than for my husband.'

'I'm sorry about that, Linda, I really am,' said Mark.

'I know,' she said. 'I know you are.' She looked at him sitting there, bearded, in his sunglasses, with his cropped hair streaked with grey, his face lined like a man years older than he really was, and her heart melted in her chest, just like in the romances she'd read as a girl. Just like it always had since that first day in the Wimpy bar in Croydon. 'So why don't we do it?' she asked.

'Do what?'

'Piss off out of here.'

'Are you serious?'

'Of course I am.'

'I don't understand. Me going, and Martine, and every bloody thing.'

'I love you.'

'I love you too.'

'So, let's do it. Let's go. Let's find this Shangri-La you're always telling me about.'

'You're kidding me.'

'I've never been more serious in my life.'

'And Luke and Daisy?'

'They'll come with us. It'll do them good to see something of the world.'

'But their schooling?'

'We'll find somewhere, Mark. Have you got cold feet all of a sudden?'

He thought about the weekend, and what was going to happen. 'No,' he said. 'Not at all. I just can't believe you'd change your mind like that.'

'A woman's prerogative, I believe.'

His brain was running full tilt. 'Oh, Linda, why are you doing this to me?'

'Because I can.'

'I know.'

'Well, let's go then.'

'When?'

'Today.'

'No, Linda, not today,' he said. 'You'll need to sort things out.'

'What things?'

'All sorts of things. The house, for instance.'

'Sean's living here. He can look after it. And put it on the market. It's worth a good half million now.'

'And what then?'

'We'll live on the money. I get an income too. If we're careful we can last for years on that and my investments. You'll never need to work again. If you can call what you do work. You'll be safe. I'll be safe. We'll all be safe.'

'It all sounds very nice…'

'I hear a "but" coming.'

'No,' he said. 'No buts. We'll do it. We'll leave on Monday.'

'Why so long?'

'I have things to organise too. Pack up over the weekend. We'll drive to the Continent. We'll take your truck. My one's a bit warm, if you know what I mean.'

'I think I do,' said Linda.

'OK. I do need a couple of days, I suppose.'

'Course you do.' There was an awkward silence until Linda said, 'I think it's time for Daisy to take a nap.'

'Do you?'

'Don't you? We've got hours until anyone comes back.'

'Do you mean what I think you mean?' asked Mark.

Linda nodded. 'I've never done it with anyone with a beard.'

'It's the best offer I've had all day.'

'I should hope so too. Come on, Daisy, time for a little lie down. For all of us,' she added. Mark smiled and followed them upstairs.

Afterwards, they lay together in Linda's bed, the door open so that she could hear Daisy in the next room. They needn't have worried, the child slept like the baby she was. 'That was good,' said Mark, feeling content for the first time in a long time. 'It's been a while.'

'How long?'

'Nosy.'

'No, how long?'

'Since the last time with you.'

'Liar.'

'I swear.'

'What about those Portuguese senoritas, or whatever you call them? Did none of them catch your eye?'

'Lots of them caught my eye, but most of them threw it back. What about you?'

'Same here. I'm an honorary virgin.'

'Not any more.'

'That's true. Can we really make it happen, Mark?'

'I hope so.' Suddenly, it all came flooding back. Hunter, Butler, Sean, the job, and he felt the same old heaviness descend upon him. 'Oh, Linda, I really hope so.'

They discussed the time and place to meet on Monday afternoon. They decided on the street where Linda's old school had been, opposite the park where they'd first met, at four o'clock.

'So what do we do about tickets and all that?' asked Linda.

'I'll worry about that. We can get tickets at the ferry. Just bring your passports.'

'It will be good to have someone else in charge, for a change. I'm tired. So tired. You won't let me down, will you?'

'No,' he said.

'Promise?'

'Promise.'

'Can I see you over the weekend?'

'I don't see why not. If you can get away. I've got one or two things to sort out, and I might have to go out of town for a bit. But otherwise, I'll be around. But not a word to Sean, mind.'

'Of course not.'

'You've got to carry on as normal.'

'That's the last thing I've been recently – normal. Come downstairs, I need a cigarette.'

'Still smoking?'

''Fraid so.'

'My fault.'

'If you like. Sean hates it.'

'I know,' he said, remembering her brother's look in the pub when he'd lit up.

'How do you know?'

'What?'

'That Sean hates smoking.'

He realised he'd made a blunder and hastily said: 'I dunno. You must've said something about it some time.'

'Yeah, I suppose I must.' She jumped out of bed and pulled on a silky dressing gown quickly, but not quickly enough that Mark didn't see the curves, angles and secret places of her body and begin to get aroused again. 'Christ, it has been a long time,' he said. 'I fancy another.'

'Down, boy, I've got to check on Daisy. And I really need a smoke. There'll be plenty of time for that later. Won't there?'

'You bet your life.'

Or mine, he thought. She left the room and Mark got out of bed and dressed, before going down to the kitchen where Linda was sitting at the table smoking. 'Want one?' she asked. He took a Silk Cut from her packet and lit it with her lighter.

'Listen, I'm going to go. Like I said, things to do. Can I call you?'

'Sure.'

'Same number?'

'Of course.'

He nodded.

'Do you remember it?'

'That's one number I'll never forget. If I give you my mobile, can you remember that?' She nodded and he reeled off the number and she repeated it. 'Great,' he said. 'What are you going to tell the kids?'

'That we're going on holiday. Not that Daisy will know what I'm talking about. I'll tell Luke on Monday. It's a bank holiday and school's off, and I've let Greta have a few days off too, so we'll be on our own.'

'Great. I'd better go now, but I'll be in touch.'

'Make sure you are.'

He leant over and kissed her, smelling smoke and perfume and sex and he smiled. 'Love you,' he said.

'I love you too.'

Then he left.

Later that afternoon, he phoned Sean on his mobile.

'It's on,' said the policeman.

'So it should be.'

'You'd better be right about this.'

'How many more times?'

'OK, OK.'

'So the stones will be there?'

'That's right. I need to see you. I've got your way out.'

'Tell me on the phone.'

'No. Face to face.'

'When?'

'Tomorrow night. I'll pick you up in the same place as last time.'

'OK. But listen. No more tails. It makes me nervous.'

'All right. I'm sorry about that, but my guv'nor insisted. I told him I thought you were too fly to fall for it.'

'Nice work, Sean. Lull me into a false sense of security. But I mean it. I'm too old to be looking over my shoulder all the time.'

'You've got my word.'

'And your word is your bond.'

'Yes.' With a copper's word and half a quid I could get a packet of wine gums, thought Mark, but said nothing. 'What time?'

'Same as last time.'

'I'll be there.'

Later that evening, he was in his hotel room and his mobile rang. It was Linda. 'Hello sweetheart,' he said.

'Hello yourself. How are you?'

'All the better for seeing you.'

'Just seeing me?'

'And the rest.'

'I've been singing to myself all day. Daisy's looking at me like I'm mad.'

'That's what a real man will do for you.'

'Still as conceited as ever.'

'And for good reason, wouldn't you say?'

'No comment.'

'I'll make you comment when I get hold of you again.'

'How about tomorrow night?'

'Tomorrow?'

'It's the only time I can get Greta to babysit. She's off on Sunday.'

'I can't. I've got to make a meet.'

'Can't you change it?'

'I don't know. I'll try.'

'Try your best.'

'Course I will.'

But Sean was adamant. It had to be Saturday evening. The rest of his weekend he was busy sorting out the operation. 'Sorry,' he said. 'Got a date?'

'Something like that.'

'Break it.'

'I'll get back to you.'

He phoned Linda and gave her the bad news, and he heard the same old disappointment in her voice when he did. 'Don't worry,' he said. 'Monday'll be here sooner than you think.'

'Just don't let me down,' she said.

'I'll be there. Four o'clock on the dot.'

'You'd better be.'

He phoned Sean back and and simply said: 'It's me. I'll be there.'

And he was, and either Sean had kept his word or else the tail was much better. Even so, Mark made Sean drive him to Stockwell tube station, where they pushed through the barriers, ran down to the platform, caught the first train that came in, got off at Victoria, and took the first south bound train back. As far as Mark could see, no one followed them. 'You are careful,' said Sean when they got off at Pimlico and went into the nearest pub.

'It's kept me alive,' said Mark. 'You can get a cab back to your car.'

'And you?'

'I'll manage.'

'Still got a date?'

'No. You screwed that up good and proper.'

'Sorry. Now listen. There's a back door at the depository leading into a car park. The car park is walled, but there's another door leading on to some waste ground. That door will be open and I'll be waiting outside with a car. You take the car, drive away and dump it somewhere. I don't care where. That's your out. Clear?'

Mark smiled. 'Sounds good to me. But we could've done all this on the phone.'

'I wanted to see you again,' said Sean. 'You remind me of someone, but I can't think who. Are you sure we haven't met before?'

'Maybe in a previous life.'

'Maybe.' Sean shook his head. 'I just can't place it,' he said.

'Never mind,' said Mark, who'd gone cold at Sean's words. 'Perhaps it'll come to you.' But I hope not, he thought.

'Perhaps,' said Sean.

'So, see you Monday,' said Mark.

'I'll be there.'

'You'd better.' And with that, he left his drink and walked out of the pub. Arsehole, he thought. And for the last time – at least Mark hoped it was the last time – he ducked and dived a circuitous route back to his hotel.

The die was cast, and all he had to do was get out of it alive, meet up with Linda and everything would be fine.

The next morning, Sean Pierce went in to see his boss. 'I met him last night,' he said.

'And everything's going ahead,' said Mobray.

'That's right.'

'Good.'

'What about the people at the depository?'

'What about them?'

'Will they be ready?'

'For what?'

'For the operation. Will the armed guards be stood down?'

'How can they be? We know they've got someone on the inside.'

'Yes, but they're armed.'

'So are we.'

'And so are the gang. Surely they'll be told on Monday.'

Mobray shook his head. 'We've spoken to the chairman of the board. He's prepared to let the raid go on.'

'But he won't be there.'

'Of course not.'

'You mean you're just going to let seven men armed with automatic weapons break in and not warn anyone inside?'

'If we do our job, no one will get hurt.'

'Sir. This was my operation.'

'*My* operation, Pierce? This is not a private war. It's *our* operation. In

510

fact it's a Serious Crimes operation out of our ground, and you're lucky to still have anything to do with it.'

'But—'

'No buts. You go there on Monday and get your man away. Let Serious Crimes and SO19 do the rest. Understood?'

'Understood, sir,' said Sean. But afterwards, standing in the corridor outside Mobray's office, he felt the cold hand of dread clasp at his gut.

Mark had only one more job to do before the robbery. He called Chas up and checked that he and Martine would be home on Sunday lunchtime. 'Yeah,' said Chas. 'But don't make it early. Her highness likes to sleep late. She'll be out clubbing 'til all hours Saturday night.'

'No problem. Mind if I drop by? I'd like to see you both.'

'No problem with me,' replied Chas. 'You're always welcome here as far as I'm concerned. I wouldn't be so sure about her, though.'

'I'll take my chances.'

Two o'clock Sunday afternoon, and the streets of Tulse Hill were deadly quiet as Mark parked the Explorer outside the gates of John Jenner's old house. He pressed the buzzer by the gate and looked up and down the familiar street as he waited for an answer. 'Yeah?' It was Chas. 'It's me,' he said, and with a grunt and groan the gates began to swing open. Chas opened the front door and the two men hugged. It was an embrace that encapsulated years. 'Is she up?' asked Mark.

'I heard some movement. Come into the kitchen, have a drink.'

'A beer would be good.' Mark followed Chas downstairs and through to the back.

He sat at the kitchen table and Chas pulled two bottles of Beck's from the chiller and popped the tops. He handed one to Mark and they touched the bottles together. 'Cheers,' said Chas.

'Cheers,' Mark echoed.

'What a cosy scene,' said Martine's voice from the doorway, and the two men looked around.

'Hello, Martine,' said Mark. 'Late one, was it?'

'What are you doing here?' she demanded. She was fresh from bed, wearing a silky housecoat and, for a moment, it could have been Hazel standing in the doorway. Except for the expression on her face. Hazel had never looked that sour in her life.

'Just come to say goodbye,' said Mark.

'Going away again?'

'Obviously.'

'You needn't have bothered. Why did you let him in, Chas?'

'This used to be his home.'

'Not any more. Not since Daddy died.'

'Still think it was my fault?' asked Mark.

'Yes.'

'I'm sorry about that. You know I loved the man.'

'For what he did for you, you mean.'

'No. Him. Him and Hazel. You and Chas. You were my family.'

'"Were" is right.'

'I'm sorry you feel like that.'

'What other way is there to feel?'

'Do you want a cuppa, Martine?' Chas interrupted.

'Always a cuppa, eh, Chas?' she replied. 'The answer to all our problems.'

'Don't have a go at him, Martine,' said Mark. 'This was my idea.'

'Fine.' Martine flounced over to the sink and filled a glass with water from the tap. 'So where are you going?'

'Dunno,' replied Mark. 'Somewhere far away. Somewhere warm and safe.'

She fixed him with a gimlet gaze. 'All on your own?' Mark didn't reply. 'You're not taking that bitch with you, are you?' she said. Mark still remained silent. 'You are.'

'You still can't bear it, can you?' said Mark. 'That I'd choose her over you.'

The glass left her hand and smashed against the wall behind Mark's head. 'You bastard,' she said. 'And I thought I'd fixed you.'

'What?' said Mark.

'Nothing.'

'No. Not nothing. Fixed me, how?'

'Forget it.' And she made for the door.

'No,' said Chas, blocking her exit. 'I want to know too. Fixed him how?'

Martine said nothing.

Suddenly it dawned on Mark. 'It was you, wasn't it?' he said to Martine. 'It was you who told Old Bill.'

'I don't know what you mean.'

'That day down in Basingstoke when I nearly got captured. The cops knew I was going to be there. Then they came around here. Someone grassed us up. It was you.' Martine swallowed hard, but still said nothing. 'I can't believe it,' said Mark. 'You turned snout on your own father just to get at me. And you've blamed me all the time. But you put him in the frame. If it wasn't for you he'd never have been arrested that day and ended up in hospital.'

Martine started to sob quietly.

'Christ,' said Chas.

'Yes, I did it,' she shouted. 'You came back here like a conquering hero and Daddy fell for it like he always did.'

'He asked me back,' said Mark.

'So what are you going to do about it?' said Martine. 'Kill me?'

Mark shook his head and stood up. 'No,' he replied. 'Oh yeah, I could kill you, Martine, and maybe I should. Or ruin your face, but you look too much like Hazel. It would be like hurting her. No. I reckon doing nothing is best. Your punishment is living with yourself.' He turned to Chas. 'Sorry about all this, mate. I didn't have a clue, honest. I'd better go.'

The two men picked their way through the broken glass on the floor back upstairs to the front door. 'Shit,' said Chas. 'I had no idea. She more or less killed John.'

'Yeah,' said Mark. 'What are you going to do now?'

'Christ knows. I can't stay here. I should've gone months ago.'

'Where?'

'Who knows. I'll find something. Maybe I'll look you up. Somewhere warm and safe, you said. Sounds about right to me.'

513

'Do it, mate. I'll let you know where I am, one way or another.'
'I'd like that.'
They hugged again, and Mark left the house for the last time.
And he didn't look back once.

THIRTY-SEVEN

Bank holiday Monday dawned fair. An unusual enough event for it to feature heavily in the local news bulletins that morning. 'Couldn't be better,' said Daniel Butler as the men gathered at the old print works. 'Perfect.'

There were a dozen men inside the building altogether, including the clean up crew whose job it was to make sure that nothing was left behind for the cops to find.

Mark packed his bags and checked out of the hotel after breakfast, then he drove to Croydon with his things in the Explorer, which he left in the public car park next to East Croydon station. Then he caught a train up to London Bridge and took a taxi on to east London. He got the cabbie to drop him off about half a mile from the printing works and walked the rest of the way. The sky was high and blue, criss-crossed with vapour trails, the sun was hot on his head and what tiny breeze there was whipped dust devils across the dirty tarmac of the road. The only sound was the tattoo his boot heels beat on the pavement.

He was wearing jeans and a leather jacket over a grey T-shirt. Just a bloke taking a morning stroll, maybe to pick up a paper or a pint of milk, or to find a pub with early doors. The night before he'd looked in the bathroom mirror and considered shaving off his beard, but that would have made things too complicated, so he compromised by trimming it down to a thick stubble. It felt strange under his fingers, but there'd be time later, if there was a later, to worry about things like that. And now his almost-shaven hair was beginning to grow out, he began to recognise himself as himself again after so long. He'd left the contact lenses off, keeping them in their case in his pocket, and the deep blue of his eyes

515

was disguised behind his mirrored shades. His eyes felt strange without the constriction of the fine plastic. Free. As if he'd got his own personality back after hiding who he really was. Which of course he had. He wanted to face Sean and Jimmy Hunter wearing his own face. His father's face. The last face Jimmy would ever see on this earth. At least, that was the plan.

From his stash of weapons, he'd chosen a Glock 19 with the safety on the trigger, and a fifteen-round magazine. It nestled in a sheepskin-lined leather shoulder holster under his jacket, together with a fully loaded spare clip. As backup, he slid a Colt Commando .38 calibre revolver down into his boot.

The last thing he'd done before going to bed the night before was to phone Linda and confirm their meeting that Monday afternoon. Mark knew that it would be all over one way or another by then. He told her not to worry, that everything would be fine, and that he loved her. He told her to sleep well and that by the same time tomorrow they'd be well on their way to a new life. She told him she loved him too, and when they'd hung up, he hoped that everything he'd said would come true. He'd considered not showing up at the print works. To simply forget the whole thing and let the gang go in without him. But so much time and effort had already gone into screwing Butler and Hunter that he felt he had to go through with it.

He was still thinking about Linda as he crossed the deserted industrial estate, everyone who worked there, it seemed, taking advantage of the extra day on their weekend. And the only movement he saw as he walked the empty streets was an old tabby cat, washing its paws in the shade, its yellow, almond-shaped eyes following him as he went. 'Here, kitty,' he said as he passed. The cat ignored him, trying instead to prise something out from between its claws. 'Sod you then,' said Mark.

The old works loomed ahead, looking as empty as the buildings around it, but Mark knew that that was only an illusion. He walked through the open gates and across the concrete yard, overgrown with weeds whose crushed stems were the only hint that anything was going on inside.

Mark knocked on the Judas gate next to the metal roller door aware, not for the first time, of the irony of the name. An armed man opened it and beckoned him inside. 'Cheers,' said Mark, and wondered if the man would live to see the evening. If, in fact, any of them would.

Inside was a hive of industry. He walked over to Bob and they shook hands. 'All ready?' Bob asked.

'As I'll ever be,' replied Mark.

'Need a weapon?'

'I brought my own.'

'Show.'

Mark slipped the Glock from its hiding place, reversed the gun in his hand and passed it to Bob who nodded his approval. 'Nice weapon,' he said. 'Traceable?'

'Only to a robbery of a gun shop in Switzerland, five years ago.'

'Fair enough,' said Bob, returning the gun to Mark who stashed it away, before going to lean against the Chevrolet Suburban, that it was his job to drive, and watch the last-minute preparations as he smoked a cigarette. There was food and drink laid out on tables in one corner, next to a couple of old sofas the blokes who'd fixed up the Volvo had brought in, and two portable toilets had been set up in another. Jimmy Hunter walked over, carrying his shotgun over his shoulder, and Mark forced a smile on to his face. 'Morning,' he said.

Hunter just grunted.

'Been here long?' asked Mark.

'Too fucking long,' replied Hunter.

'That's the breaks.'

'Sure,' said Hunter and turned away.

Mark shrugged, left his perch and wandered the concrete floor. He didn't want to talk to Hunter. Time enough for you later, he thought. He didn't know anyone well enough to strike up a conversation, so he just sat down on one of the old sofas and made himself as comfortable as he could. He looked at the food, but he had no appetite, so he left it. He could feel the tension start to build up inside and his stomach grumbled. This was it, there was no going back now.

The morning passed slowly. The rest of the gang armed themselves and they all got ready for the off. Handheld portable two-way radios were issued to both vehicles and every man was given a black wool balaclava in order to hide his face. CCTV covered the inside and outside of the target building, and no one was that keen to get their face on to *Crimewatch UK*.

At precisely twelve-thirty, Daniel Butler clapped his hands for attention and climbed on to the running board of the Volvo tractor. 'Right,' he yelled. 'This is it. Let's get started.'

Mark went back to the Chevrolet, where Jimmy Hunter was already sitting in the front passenger seat, his balaclava on his head like a black cap, and the short Remington shotgun across his lap. Mark slid in behind the wheel and fired up the engine, which ticked over nicely. 'Belt,' he said, and Hunter grunted again but did up his seatbelt. They were joined by Ronnie, Les and Paul who jumped into the back as he watched Tony Green and Bob climb up into the cab of the Volvo. It looked like something out of a Mad Max movie. 'Jesus,' he said. 'If any coppers spot that, I reckon they'll make them produce their documents.'

'Bob'll produce something,' said Les from the back. 'And it won't be fucking documents.'

'You don't see many Old Bill round here,' said Paul.

'Only when you don't want them,' said Hunter.

'It's a bank holiday, man,' said Paul. 'They'll all be in the pub.'

The Volvo turned tightly in front of them, and Mark followed it. The roller door opened, filling the building with sunshine, and both vehicles went outside, through the open gates and headed for Silvertown, just down the road from where Mark had met John Jenner, all those months before. Mark wondered if it was an omen. And if so, whether it was good or bad.

The two trucks sped through the deserted streets of an east London on holiday. The traffic was light, and they were in position under the railway bridge, beside the depository, within a few minutes. Mark looked at his watch. They were ten minutes early. When he saw Bob get down from the Volvo, he switched off the Chevrolet's engine. The five men decamped from the Chevy, and those who smoked, lit up. It was quiet and deserted where they were, the only sound being the burble of exhaust from the Volvo's tall stacks. The guns Mark was carrying weighed heavily and he could see the slight tremble in his fingers as he held the cigarette. 'Nervous?' asked Hunter.

'Oh yes. Always. You?'

Hunter shrugged. 'Not too bad,' he replied.

Bob walked over and said, 'You all ready?'

The five men all made sounds of affirmation in reply. It was too late now to be anything else.

Bob squinted down at his watch. 'Come on, then, look smart,' and the smokers dropped their cigarettes and everyone got back into their vehicles. Mark looked away from Jimmy so that the older man wouldn't be able to see his eyes, removed his sunglasses, rolled the balaclava over his face, and put his shades back on. He knew it looked ridiculous, like something out of an old Invisible Man movie, but he didn't care. Immediately sweat broke out on his face and the wool of the material started to itch. Jimmy rolled his balaclava down too, and the two-way radio burst into life.

Bob's voice said: 'Go, go, go!'

The heist was on.

The two vehicles moved off together, gathering speed, and Mark turned and grinned at Jimmy, though through his mask, the smile was invisible. 'This is it, then,' he shouted, and Jimmy racked a shell into the breech of his shotgun. Mark could hear the bolts of automatic weapons being set to fire from the others in the back seats.

As the vehicles left the main road and turned on to the industrial estate, all seemed quite and empty. Mark wondered where the cops were hiding.

The Volvo hit its stride as it approached the front gates of the depository, Tony Green accelerating smoothly through the gears, and Mark saw the uniformed guard at the gate peering through the glass front and reaching for his phone. 'Fuck it,' he shouted. 'He's sussed us.' The Volvo smashed into the gate, which stretched like elastic, then tore free from its hinges and flew up over the top of the truck and hit the road, narrowly missing the bonnet of the Chevy. The guard was desperately pressing buttons on his phone when Green swung his wheel hard and dropped down a gear, the back of the truck swinging round, its tyres screaming and leaving black tracks across the concrete and smashing the gatehouse clean off its foundations, sending it and the guard tumbling across the ground in a shower of broken glass. 'Fantastic,' yelled Mark as he skidded the Chevy to a halt and Jimmy leapt from his seat and fired three rounds into the wreckage.

Jimmy ran back and leapt through the open passenger door, reloading on the hoof, and Mark sped away.

The Volvo hit the main doors of the depository and Mark saw them burst open and the truck vanish inside. He followed, broadsiding the Chevrolet to a halt, and Jimmy dived out, with the others following quickly behind.

Inside the depository was chaos. Workers sat at benches covered with black velvet upon which sat a fortune in precious stones, glittering under the fluorescent lights. The Volvo flew across the concrete floor sending men leaping out of the way. One moved too slowly and was crushed under its giant tyres, his body bursting like a blood blister.

Two armed guards were stationed on a mezzanine floor and Mark saw their amazed looks as they fumbled with the safeties of their Heckler & Koch submachine guns, as the Volvo skidded to a halt half in and half out of the open vault door. One man, not in uniform, made for the switch to shut it but was cut down by a hail of fire from Bob's H&K, which he fired from inside his cab. The gang was inside but not yet in control. Ronnie, Les and Paul began to fire upwards at the guards and both were cut down before they had a chance to return fire.

And then, over the tops of the warehouses from the direction of the river, came the roar of a helicopter engine, and a police chopper rose up. Mark realised that his plan was coming good and that the most tricky part of the day was yet to come.

Armed police appeared as if by magic from every direction, dressed in dark blue boiler suits, padded with body armour, their heads encased in tight helmets, their eyes hidden by tinted goggles and gas masks covering the bottom of their faces. They lobbed tear gas grenades and the building filled with acrid smoke. The cops were screaming and shouting for everyone to drop their weapons and get down on the ground, robbers and guards both. But no one paid any heed. Jimmy calmly raised the shotgun and fired, and a copper went down, blood spurting from his legs. Jimmy knew better than to aim for the body, and Mark couldn't help but grin.

His nervousness gone, Mark pulled the Glock from under his jacket and started firing. He was as calm as if he were on a shooting range as he picked his targets. He stayed close to Jimmy and yelled above the noise of the chopper, the motors and the sound of gunfire and men screaming: 'Jesus Christ man, we've been screwed.'

Everyone was shooting by then, coppers at robbers, guards at robbers, and the robbers at anything that moved in uniform. The muzzle sounds magnified inside the confines of the building, the bullets fizzing through the air and ricocheting off the walls. But Mark somehow knew that it wasn't his time. Not yet. It might be his day to die, but his work wasn't over yet. Mark kept shooting until the Glock's mechanism blew back empty. Next to him, Les took a round in the chest and fell on his back, the AK-47 he was carrying hitting the deck. Mark didn't have time to reload the Glock so he stuck the gun back in its holster and picked up Les's weapon. It was set for full auto and Mark fired off a burst, not caring who or what he hit.

Behind the building, away from the action, Sean stood by his car and watched the whole thing go off from a distance. He was dressed in old jeans and a leather jacket. In the boot of his car was a Kevlar flak jacket. The vest was hot and uncomfortable, especially on a day like this, and he always felt like a fool wearing one. But rules were rules and Sean believed in keeping them, so he reluctantly he took off his leather, put on the vest and pulled his jacket back over it. He watched the Volvo truck blowing the gates, the guard hut and the main door to hell and gone, the helicopter arriving and armed police entering the warehouse. Then the shooting had started and he knew this was going to be a big one. His informant had been right, and now he wanted his reward, and it irked Sean to be the one to give it to him. But these were the breaks, so he just stood, watched, and waited for Steve Sawyer to make it over to him.

Inside, as the firefight grew hotter and the gas more dense, Mark knelt beside the Chevrolet and fired at the doorway and saw a cop hit the ground. He grabbed Jimmy. 'This is fucked,' he said. 'Let's get out of here.'

Jimmy nodded, and they left the shield of the vehicle and legged it across the floor towards the offices at the back of the building. There were bodies everywhere: robbers, guards and coppers too. Mark and Jimmy raced through the open-plan offices, jumping over desks and dividers, heading for the rear. 'What about the others?' gasped Jimmy as they dropped behind a filing cabinet for a breather.

'Fuck 'em. Let them take care of themselves,' said Mark.

'How the fuck did the filth know?' said Jimmy.

'It's fucking obvious. Someone grassed.'

'I'd like to know who.'

'Me too,' said Mark. 'But there's no time for that now. Are you coming?'

'Just show me the way.'

That's exactly what I wanted you to say, thought Mark and he shoved Jimmy down a corridor, yelling that there should be a back door close by, and there it was, just like Sean had told him, like he'd seen on the building plans he'd so carefully studied at Butler's briefing. A metal-covered door right at the back of the building. Sean had said it would be open, but Mark didn't want Jimmy to know that, so he emptied the Kalashnikov into it before pulling it open. He dropped the empty gun and shouted at Jimmy, 'Come on, man, let's get gone.'

Jimmy took one last, longing look back in the direction of the precious stones, then shrugged and followed Mark.

There was no one outside in the parking area, and they dashed through the rows of vehicles towards the gate. This was where Sean said he would be waiting.

Mark spotted it. He hit it with his shoulder and it flew open. 'How... ?' said Jimmy.

'Just lucky.'

The pair of them dived through the door to where Sean was waiting next to his unmarked Mondeo, Mark's getaway car. He was holding a pistol in his right hand and his police radio in his left. Jimmy skidded to a halt and raised his shotgun.

Sean looked shocked at the sight of two masked men instead of the one he expected. He brought up his gun, too. 'What's going on?' he shouted.

'Surprise,' said Mark. 'It's OK, it's me, Steve.'

'Who's this, then?' said Sean, his gun on Jimmy.

'Don't you recognise him?' said Mark. 'No, of course you don't. Jimmy, take that stupid mask off and meet your son.'

'Jimmy?' said Sean.' Not Jimmy...'

'Hunter,' said Mark. 'The one and only.'

Jimmy ripped off the balaclava and looked back at Mark. 'What the fuck's going on? Who's this? What about my son?'

'Don't you recognise him? Christ, are you thick or what? He looks just like you, Jimmy. It's your son, Sean.'

Jimmy peered at Sean as the sound of gunfire continued on the other side of the high wall.

'Sean?' he said.

'Yeah,' said Mark. 'Your son. Who's also Old Bill. It's a reunion, Jimmy. Aren't you going to say hello?'

Jimmy stood mystified, his shotgun hanging from one hand. 'But what's he doing here?'

'I told him we'd be here.'

'You did…?'

'That's right, Jimmy. I grassed us up.'

'Why?'

'Because I wanted you to meet your son. And because you killed my father,' said Mark, and he took off his glasses and balaclava and showed Jimmy his stubbled face and his blue eyes. The exact same colour blue eyes that had looked at Jimmy from Billy Farrow's face seconds before Jimmy had killed him. 'Do you know me now, Jimmy?' said Mark. 'Don't you know who I am, either?'

'Farrow?' said Jimmy, his face full of confusion. 'Billy? It can't be you'

'No, it ain't. I'm Mark,' said Mark. 'My dad was Billy. I'm Mark. You killed Billy Farrow and left me and my mum to live alone.'

'I don't get it.'

'Then you're more stupid than you look, Jimmy.'

'But the job…'

'Fuck the job. I only took the job to get next to you. I fixed your mate Toby Lee so they'd hire me.'

'And you did all this to get me?'

'That's right. And Butler, too. He was the architect on that bank job when you killed my dad. I owed you both.'

'But how did you find me?'

'It wasn't hard. I've got good at it over the years.'

'What do you mean?'

'I found Sean, didn't I? And Linda, too.'

'What are you on about?'

'Your daughter. Linda. Remember her? I know you do, because I saw you once outside her house. Yeah. I didn't know who you were then. Christ but I wish I had. I'd've run you down like a dog.'

'Have you hurt her? Linda?'

'Yeah. But not how you mean. We fell in love and I dumped her.'

Jimmy couldn't believe his ears. 'You did what?'

'I fell for her. We were going to be married, but something happened.'

'What?'

'My mum killed herself. After you killed Billy she took to the booze and got mixed up with a right bastard. He fucked her up good and proper and one night she slashed her wrists and I found her lying in a bath full of blood. Then I killed the fucker who was responsible. At least one of them. You're the other. I've been waiting for you to get out ever since. You brought out the killer in me, Jimmy. You and him. And that's what I've been doing ever since. Killing people. And now it's your turn.' And he reached inside his boot for the .38 concealed there and raised it and aimed it at Jimmy Hunter's heart.

'No,' said Sean, pointing his pistol at Mark. 'No. I'm arresting you both.'

'We had a deal,' said Mark.

'I had a deal with Steve. You're not him. So I'm arresting the two of you for armed robbery. Other charges may follow.' He began to read them their rights.

'You've got some balls, I'll give you that,' said Mark.

'No,' said Jimmy, pointing his shotgun in Sean's direction. 'I'm not going back inside. Not for you or anyone else. Son or no son.'

So there they stood, as the gunfight diminished inside the building behind them. Mark pointing his gun at Jimmy, Jimmy pointing his gun at Mark, and Sean moving the barrel of his gun between them both, not sure who was the most dangerous. 'Put your guns down, both of you,' he said.

'Fuck off,' said Mark. 'Take your best shot, Sean.'

But the tableau was disturbed as two armed coppers ran through the door behind them. 'Armed police,' they shouted in unison. 'Put down your weapons.'

'I'm job,' shouted Sean, 'Don't shoot.'

'Put down your weapons,' screamed one of the men his arm bleeding from a bullet. 'Now.'

Jimmy fired once at the cops who returned fire, their bullets thudding into his chest and knocking him off his feet. 'That's my father,' screamed Sean, and without thinking fired too, his bullet going through the right-hand lens of the wounded marksman's goggles and blowing the back of his skull into his helmet. As he fell, dead before he hit the ground, the second copper fired at Sean, blowing holes in his leather. The bullets meant for his chest were absorbed by the flak jacket and he was knocked back against the body of the Mondeo, sending his radio flying from his hand and out of sight.

Mark pulled the trigger of his revolver, aiming at the legs of the second copper. The bullets blew meat from his thighs and he folded up like a concertina. As he fell his finger pulled the trigger one last time and the bullet his Sean in the groin beneath the Kevlar protection and he screamed in pain. Mark turned and looked at Sean, as he leant against the boot of the car, blood pulsing from his wounds and darkening the denim of his jeans. Calmly he walked over to Jimmy Hunter, prone on the ground, his eyes staring at the sky. Mark felt for a pulse but found none. 'Dead,' he said without emotion. 'Good bloody riddance. I'm just sorry it wasn't me who did it,' and he leant over Jimmy's body and closed his eyes with the palms of his hands.

'Ambulance,' wheezed Sean. 'I need an ambulance.'

'I'll take you,' said Mark, and pushed him into the back of his car. But before he could get behind the wheel, the copper he'd shot in the legs came back into the game, pulled his semi-automatic pistol from its holster and fired. The bullet hit Mark low in the back and he cried out, 'Bastard!' as he fell into the driver's seat.

The keys were in the ignition and he switched on the engine, chucked the car into gear and took off in a cloud of dirt, dust and stones as the policeman fired again and the side window of the Mondeo imploded, the bullet ending up somewhere in the roof lining. Mark slammed his foot on to the accelerator and the car went temporarily out of control, fishtailed and almost spun until he dragged it back on to the straight. He bounced it across the wasteland and on to the main road, wrenched it hard around, geared up, put his foot down and headed in the direction of the City Airport. Sean was moaning behind him, and suddenly a police car appeared in his rear view mirror, lights flashing and two-tone siren screaming. 'Shit,' said Mark, and accelerated harder, only for another to come from the opposite direction and turn to block the road ahead. Mark twitched the wheel and the Mondeo mounted the pavement, demolished a road sign and scraped along a brick wall in a cloud of sparks.

'You'll never get away,' said Sean through gritted teeth from the back.

'Don't you fucking believe it,' said Mark, and the Mondeo clipped the bumper of the approaching police car and it tipped over on to its side and smacked into the one behind. 'It's just like snooker,' he said. 'You've got to get your angles right.'

'You're hit,' said Sean.

'Too fucking right. There goes my plans for tonight.'

'Which were?'

'Running off with your sister and her kids. Going to find somewhere warm and live there, happily ever after.'

'You were what?'

'Save your breath, Sean. It's fucked now. Me and Linda were always fucked up.'

'Are you going to the hospital?' wheezed Sean.

'No,' said Mark. 'I reckon you and me should have a talk.'

'Bollocks to talking, I need help,' said Sean, taking out his mobile. His hands were sticky with blood and felt weak and clumsy, and the phone slipped from him grasp. Mark slowed the car, picked it up from the floor and tossed it out of the window on his side, under the path of a white van.

'Sorry,' he said. 'Battery's flat.'

At the airport roundabout, Mark headed away from London towards Beckton and the North Circular until he saw a piece of derelict land next to a small park. He skidded across two lanes of traffic, bounced hard over the kerb and swung through a gap in the fence that fronted the site. The car sped across the ground, leaving a trail of dust until it slewed to a halt in the shadow of an electricity pylon whose wires hissed in the heat of the early afternoon. The dust slowly settled on the car's paintwork like a dry drizzle as Mark switched off the motor.

As the engine noise died, Sean poked his pistol through the gap between the two front seats towards Mark. His body was a mass of pain below his waist and, although he know his wounds were possibly fatal, his mind was still clear. He'd shot another police officer, found and lost his father, been shot, and had been played by the man who betrayed his sister, all in a few minutes. And now this.

'We need to get to a hospital,' he said, through lips white with strain.

Mark knew they were both in deep trouble. The blood from the bullet wound in his back had pooled on the driver's seat and the scent of it was sharp in his nostrils. 'No hospital for us, mate,' he said. 'No point. I don't think that either of us is going to get out of this alive.'

'Take us,' said Sean, cocking his pistol, 'now.'

Mark laughed out loud but the sound was too much like a death rattle for him to really appreciate the joke. 'What you going to do, mate?' he asked. 'Shoot me, then drag yourself round and drive? Look at the state of you, you can't even move.' He looked into the rear of the car at Sean's blood-soaked clothes. Using the back of his seat as a rest, he pointed his gun at him, grimacing with pain at the effort of the movement.

Sean said nothing.

'Can you?' pressed Mark. 'You're buggered, mate, and so am I. But that's nothing new is it, for either of us?'

Sean knew it was the truth but wouldn't admit it. 'Hospital now,' he said, 'or I'll kill you, I bloody will.'

'They call this a "Mexican standoff" - did you know that, Sean?' asked Mark. 'I saw it in an old cowboy film one afternoon on TV. Black and white. Funny the things you remember.'

'You should do something better with your time. Apart from robbing and killing innocent people, if you know what I mean.'

'Hark at Mr Perfect. Talking of robbing and killing, how about your dad? How about yourself? You killed one of your own back there, son. It's all up for you now, whatever happens. They don't like coppers in prison, so I've heard. It's all shit in the chocolate pudding or ground-up light bulbs in your tea. Or maybe it's the other way round.' He laughed again.

Sean was silent.

'Got no answer, have you?'

Sean wouldn't meet his gaze.

'Ever heard of a place called London Necropolis?' asked Mark after a moment.

Sean shook his head. 'What the fuck are you talking about?'

'It was a station at Waterloo.' Mark saw the look in Sean's eyes. 'Honest. No time for lies now, mate. A railway station for trains full of dead bodies, run by the London Necropolis Company. On their way to Woking. A place called Brookwood Cemetery. Biggest in the world, it was supposed to be. Enough room for every stiff in London. That was the plan. If it was still going, we'd all end up there. All of us. Your dad, my dad. You, me and Uncle Tom Cobley and all. But it never happened. The company went skint. Then it got bombed in the last war. The station did. But you can still see the entrance if you know where to look: 121 Westminster Bridge Road. Bloody yuppies' bar now. I'd like to see some of them yuppies on the way to the cemetery.' He laughed and started a fit of coughing. 'Funny, isn't it, mate? What you find out from books.'

'From the prison library?' said Sean.

'Never done time, son,' said Mark. 'I was always off the radar. Real gangsters never go inside. Only fucking stupid losers who come out, write a book and make more than they ever did from blagging. Not fair, is it? Funny really. Know what else is funny?' He didn't wait for an answer. 'I'll tell you. All the people who've died in the history of the world since time began and nobody knows what it's like to die. Not really. Seeing the white light, out of body experiences, I reckon that's all cobblers. What do you think?'

Sean didn't answer, but Mark wasn't really expecting a reply.

'Bloody strange,' he went on. 'But not to worry, you and me are going to find out soon.'

'Not if I can help it. Not me anyway.'

'Save it, Sean,' said Mark. 'You're a dead man walking. Or at least sitting down.'

Sean said nothing, but deep down he knew that Mark was right.

'Mind if I smoke?' asked Mark. 'I know you don't approve. But one thing's sure, neither of us is going to kick off from lung cancer. At least there's that.'

Sean didn't reply, so, with an effort, Mark pulled the pack from his pocket. The cigarette he extracted had bloody fingerprints on it, and he lit it with his Zippo, and the simple effort caused him so much pain he almost cried. Smoke drifted through the empty window frame and vanished.

'So what now, then?' said Sean.

'We sit here,' said Mark. 'Have a chat.'

'I've nothing to say to you.'

'Nothing? I don't believe you. There must be something, for Christ's sake. I mean, we have a past. I thought for sure you'd recognise me that day in the Beehive. Steve. I ask you.'

'I should've,' said Sean. 'But it's been a long time, and you looked so different. The beard and the glasses. And your eyes.'

'Good job you didn't,' said Mark. 'Or I'd've never got a result.'

'Call this a result?' said Sean.

'Could've been worse. Could've been a lot worse... Or maybe not.'

'You're bloody crazy,' said Sean.

'All the things we've got in common,' Mark continued, as if Sean hadn't spoken. 'Never a talk. But if we're ever going to do it, now's the time, before it's too late.'

From far away they both heard the scream of a police siren, but it faded away on the hot afternoon air.

'No help there, then,' said Mark. 'Too fast for that lot.'

'They'll be here.'

'Not until we're beyond help,' said Mark. 'But then we've always been that, haven't we, Sean, my boy?'

'Says you.'

'Says me.'

'So you've been seeing Linda,' said Sean after a moment.

'Yeah. Never could leave her alone. I came back before. Last winter. Uncle John wanted my help.'

'John Jenner.'

'Yeah,' said Mark, pausing to take a breath. 'I'm glad I got to see him before he died. I was there the day you and your sidekick called at his house about that thing in Basingstoke.'

'That was you.'

'Yeah. Your grass was right. It was funny, John and Chas both knew who you were. What your dad did.'

'They never said.'

'They wouldn't, would they? Then I found Linda again, and we... Well. You know. But then I had to go away. I hurt her again.'

'I wondered what was up with her.'

'I was never very good for her.'

'You can say that again.'

'We had some good times, though.'

'Did you?'

'Sure.'

'I wish you'd never met her,' said Sean.

'Would've been for the best, probably. But I wanted to see you both, after what Jimmy did.'

'So everything was all about my father.'

'Yeah. In the first place. Then circumstances sort of took over.'

'Why didn't you just leave me?' asked Sean. 'Just now. Why bother with all this?'

'Like your dad left mine? No mate. No such luck. All our lives we've been heading for this, and I didn't want to spoil it.'

'You are mad.'

'No. Just a bit annoyed.'

'Is that why?'

'Why what?'

'You know.'

'What?' said Mark. 'Come on, say it, mate.'

'Why you went after Linda?'

'No. Don't you bloody understand? I loved her the minute I saw her.'

'But you never treated her right,' said Sean.

'We didn't have much of a chance, if you think about it.'

'You can say that again.'

'Still, it's over now. Or it soon will be.'

'It'll never be over,' said Sean, 'Until you and me are both dead.'

'That's exactly what I mean,' said Mark. 'Exactly.' He leaned back in his seat and groaned at the pain in his back. 'Exactly,' he said again as the hot sun beat down on the car.

Sean was the first to pass out. His wound was still pumping blood. 'Please, Mark,' he begged. 'For pity's sake, get us out of here.'

'Pity,' said Mark. 'I've noticed there's not much pity around these days. Anyway, we'll be gone soon enough. To a better place perhaps. What do you think?'

There was no reply.

'Sean,' said Mark. 'Sean. Can you hear me?' But all was quiet from the back of the car.

Mark pulled himself out of his seat and into the back of the car to join Sean. He felt for a pulse but it was so faint as to be almost nothing. 'Brothers,' he said. 'Like fucking brothers we were. Sorry mate, you deserved better. We all did.' He gathered him in his arms as their life's blood mixed.

* * *

A small boy on a bike saw the two men in the car with its window blown out, and pedalled home fast. His mother, who had stopped believing his wild tales years before, was eventually dragged from her terraced house in the modern close not far from the wasteland, uttering dire threats about what would happen if he was lying. When she saw the two bodies on the back seat, glued together with their own blood, flies already feasting on them, she ran home and called the police.

Within minutes, armed units had surrounded the Mondeo. After no response to several shouted warnings, the ranking inspector authorised the troops to move in. Six blue-clad coppers gingerly made their way across the waste ground to the car where they found the two men huddled together in the back.

'You'd better get some medical help here, fast,' said the first policeman on the scene. 'They're alive, but it doesn't look good.'

The inspector called for the air ambulance from the London Hospital. 'Get here now,' he ordered, 'I want them alive.'

Fifteen minutes later, woken by the relentless whirring of the helicopter's blades, Mark's eyes fluttered open. As he slowly focused on the shape beside him, he finally recognised Sean. He was perfectly still. Mark opened his mouth and tried to speak, but was unable to make a sound. He felt as cold and heavy as a stone. The weight of his eyelids was too much and, as they slowly closed, the darkness enveloped him.

* * *

Linda was at the rendezvous half an hour early. Her old school was deserted because of the holiday. The back of her truck was packed with suitcases. Mark had said he would be travelling light, so she'd only left a little room for his bits. She couldn't believe what she'd had to pack for Luke and Daisy. There wasn't much of her own stuff, she figured she could shop when they'd arrived at their new home. Inside her handbag were their passports and five thousand pounds in cash, her credit cards and cheque book. She'd left a note on Sean's flat door telling him she would be away for a while and that they'd be in touch soon. There was no mention of Mark.

Daisy was strapped into the child seat, fast asleep with a little white sun hat down low over her eyes. Luke was playing with some handheld video game and bouncing about under the constraint of his seat belt. She parked in the shade of the trees at the edge of the park where, all those years ago, Mark had waited for her in the pouring rain, and wound down her window to let in some air. The stereo played something from the 80s and she got out to smoke a cigarette away from the children. Neither of them seemed to notice. The afternoon was still and close and, away from the truck's climate control, she had to pull her blouse away from her back to allow some air to reach her skin. Nothing was moving in the suburban street, except for a big black crow that froze when it saw Linda, then flapped its wings and took off, leaving her alone with her Silk Cut. She walked up to the school gates and gazed up the drive, remembering... remembering everything. The good and the bad times both.

When the appointed hour arrived, she scanned the street for Mark's car but, of course, it didn't appear.

She stayed there for an hour, pacing the street and smoking, but there was still no sign of him. 'Damn him,' she whispered to herself, as she added another filtertip to the ones flattened in the gutter around her feet. 'Damn him to hell.' She tried his mobile but it was switched off. She didn't leave a message.

As the shadows started to lengthen and Luke complained that he wanted to go to the toilet, she finally climbed back into the truck and switched on the engine. 'Are we going on holiday, Mummy?' the boy asked as she slowly drove away, still hoping that Mark would miraculously appear and smile the smile she loved and take her gently in his arms and promise her that everything was all right and that they were together forever this time.

'I don't think so, darling,' Linda replied, as she tried to see through the tears that filled her eyes. 'We'll go another day.'

And with that, she pointed the car in the direction of home.